RIDGE

DAY ONE

Book One of the Ridge Series

Shawn P. B. Robinson

BrainSwell Publishing
Ingersoll, Ontario

ISBN 978-1-989296-39-4

BrainSwell Publishing
Ingersoll, ON

Dedication and Thanks

To Liam, who helped me to work through some of the problems and challenges for the book before I wrote it and who was the first one to read the book, after it was written.

To Juanita, who somehow manages to still get excited every time I talk about my books.

To Ezra who lets me talk about my books and loves to hear about them.

To Rob who encourages me with my writing.

To Deb. You are a fantastic editor. Thanks for being picky but in a gracious and kind way! You have a gift!

This book is a work of fiction.
Characters and places and such are fictional.
While there are some matters that are somewhat
allegorical in nature, this book is fiction.
Accept it.

Preface

The idea for Ridge hit me in 2017. I was looking at some free eBooks, and the cover of a book grabbed my attention. I can't tell you what book I was looking at, but I believe it was an indie book.

It had a picture on the front cover of some kind of cliff or something (yah... I know how vague that is, but, well... my memory isn't all it's cracked up to be). When I saw the picture, something in me said, "Ridge!", and the story started to come to me about a nation that is built on a Ridge.

I then spent the next sixteen months or so developing the idea and talking it over with my son, Liam. We chatted through various plot issues and ideas, and he helped me work out a lot of problems and create some new stuff.

I started to write the actual book in the fall of 2018. It took me a while to get it done, but I finally finished, printed a very rough copy of the book to give to my son (so he could be my Alpha Reader), and away we went!

I hope you enjoy Ridge, for the story continues to captivate my heart!

Shawn P. B. Robinson

CHECK OUT THESE BOOKS BY
Shawn P. B. Robinson

Adult Fiction (Sci-fi & Fantasy)

The Ridge Series (3 books)
ADA: An Anthology of Short Stories

YA Fiction (Fantasy)

The Sevordine Chronicles (5 Books)

Books for Younger Readers

Annalynn the Canadian Spy Series (6 Books)
Jerry the Squirrel (4 Books)
Arestana Series (3 Books)
Activity Books (2 Books)

www.shawnpbrobinson.com/books

Table of Contents

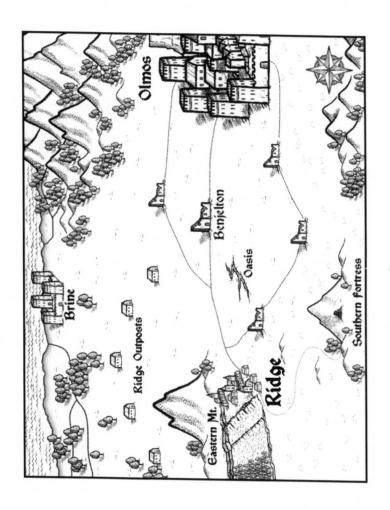

PROLOGUE

The Beasts hit the wall and began to scramble up the side.

Soldiers rushed along, giving orders to those under their command. The young General stood near the edge of the wall, watching every move and every reaction. General Hamel had never seen the Beasts move with such anger or purpose before.

He had always hated the battles with the creatures. It was nothing more than a slaughter. His soldiers fired their rifles from the top of the wall, and Beast after Beast fell as they ran through the open area that his people called the Valley Floor.

The Beasts were tall, nearly one and a half times the height of an average human. They walked and ran upright on their two legs and used their arms and hands to throw spears, hold shields and climb. The fur-covered creatures were stronger than any animal Hamel had ever seen and far more vicious.

"What if they make it past your defenses, Hamel?" Pulanomos asked. He had come as the new Ambassador from Olmos less than a year before, but it was his first visit to the wall during a battle.

"I don't know, Pulanomos," Hamel replied and offered his friend a broad grin.

"You don't know?" Pulanomos began to back away along with his young assistant. The boy, Churoi, was not much more than eleven years old. He faithfully stood by his master, but the terror on his face was far greater than that of the Ambassador.

"Nope. No idea!" Hamel replied. He turned to a Lieutenant standing by. She was perhaps nineteen but was proving herself to be a capable officer. He sent her along the wall with orders to the Captain for a new deployment.

Hamel watched Pulanomos out of the corner of his eye and fought down another grin that threatened to creep up his face. "What's on your mind, my friend?"

Pulanomos stepped up beside Hamel. The two men were both twenty-three years old. Each man was new to his respective position, but it was far from Hamel's first battle. The Ambassador held Hamel's arm as if his presence could keep him safe.

"Hamel, please," Pulanomos began. "I know this is common for you, but I have never been on the wall during an attack by these creatures. Please, tell me what happens if they enter the city."

Hamel laughed and passed out some more orders to two young Lieutenants waiting nearby. "Pulanomos, we have never had such a thing happen before. We have always held them back. If they were to make it through, our soldiers would fight them on the walls. If we fall to the Beasts, we have six battalions stationed at the second wall. Do not worry about the people in the city."

Pulanomos nodded his head. The fear in his eyes had not lessened.

"Oh, I'm sorry, Ambassador," Hamel replied, doing his best to provoke his friend. "You aren't concerned about the people in the city, are you? It is *your* life you are worried about. My dear wife and child back in the city are not a concern to you? I thought you had grown fond of them over this last year."

Pulanomos's face turned red, and he stepped away. "I'm not a soldier, Hamel! You know that. This is not something I am used to. Our nation is a peaceful nation. It has been many centuries since we have experienced war."

Hamel smiled. "I'm just teasing you, Pulanomos. I know you…"

Hamel stopped mid-sentence and leaned over the wall to get a better view of the Battle. He watched the Beasts closely and grabbed the arm of a young Lieutenant standing by. "Quick, send two full battalions to the southern end of the wall. Do not hesitate. RUN!"

The Lieutenant rushed to the Captain and passed on the orders. Within less than a minute, the signals were sent, and soldiers on horseback rode along the inside of the wall to the southern section. Hamel gripped the stones which formed the top of the wall as he watched the battle.

"What's happening, Hamel?" Pulanomos asked. His voice betrayed panic.

Hamel took a glance at his friend and the young Churoi. He grieved for the boy. They stood on the Valley Wall, one of the two barriers between the people and the Beasts. It was no place for a child during a battle—especially an Olmosite, unaccustomed to the Beast threat.

"The Beasts are acting strange," Hamel replied. "I think they are about to attack the southern edge of the Valley Wall in just a minute or two."

"How do you know?" Pulanomos asked.

"I don't. But look how the attack is focused here in the center of the valley. Notice as well that all the Beasts traveling along the southern end of this attack are veering slightly to the south as if their eyes are drifting more in that direction. I think they expect something to happen in that direction. I suspect this attack is a diversion."

"Do you really think the Beasts are that intelligent?" Pulanomos asked in shock.

As if in answer to his question, hundreds of Beasts rushed out of the forest to the south on the Valley Floor. Hamel stepped up onto his platform to give himself the height he needed to see the southern end of the wall. He felt relief flood over him as the soldiers were reinforced. He had caught their diversion just in time."

An hour later, the battle was over. The Beasts remained on the Valley Floor but not to attack. They always carried off their dead. The Soldiers of the Ridge gave them the time they needed.

When the last of the Beasts had disappeared into the trees, Hamel went to go speak with his officers and hear their reports. Movement at the edge of the forest caught his eye, and five Beasts stepped into view. A young Corporal blew the trumpet, and the soldiers prepared for another assault.

"Hold your fire!" Hamel called. Word of his orders spread down the wall, and the men and women held steady.

"What's happening?" Pulanomos asked.

"I'm not sure, Pulanomos. I've never seen the Beasts act this way. This is new. I'm going to have to ask you to be quiet, my friend. I will need to be alert for this new threat."

The five Beasts loped forward. Each one carried something small. While Hamel did not think there was cause for concern, he could not imagine what might be contained in the bundles.

The Beasts stopped ten paces from the wall. They were large creatures, solidly built and not something Hamel wished to face without a rifle.

All five Beasts threw the items in their arms against the wall and let out a loud, mournful cry. Hamel heard a similar cry emerge from the forest. He suspected thousands of Beasts had joined the cry. The Beasts turned and raced back to the forest, wailing the entire way. Hamel could hear the sound of the Beasts among the trees grow quieter as they disappeared deep into the forest.

The battle was over, but Hamel needed to find out what lay below. Whatever the Beasts had thrown against the wall caused them a great deal of grief. In addition to their grief, the Beasts had fought that day with an intensity unlike anything he had seen since he had joined the army.

While he did not know what had happened, he was confident this new development was not a good thing. He feared their defense against the Beasts had taken a turn for the worse.

CHAPTER 1

THE DAY BEGINS

21 years later.

A flash of fire shone on the buildings in the dark night, and screams echoed across the city. Hamel ran as hard as he could, but he could not find his way through the streets. He turned left, then right, but he never reached them. Maybe he could save them. Maybe they would be okay. Maybe if he could get there, they would survive. Maybe…

Hamel jumped out of bed. His fists were clenched so tight, his nails dug into the palms of his hands. His body was drenched with sweat, but his breathing was controlled, and his eyes alert. He was ready to attack. He was ready to kill.

Hamel scanned the room for movement. A shadow moved across the wall, and he nearly attacked but stopped as he realized it was light from a passerby on the street.

The rage burned inside as strong as it had most mornings for the last ten years.

He unclenched his fists and calmed his mind. The nightmare had not been as bad this time. He had not seen her face amongst the flames. That was a relief. He had not heard the cries of his children, either. In all the pain and all the loss,

1

it was the thought of his children crying out for him, their Patir, to rescue them that caused the most agony.

He could not protect them or their Matir. He had lost them all. He had lost his chance to raise his children and be with his Lillel.

Hamel collapsed in a familiar position on the floor, and the tears flowed freely. The first eight years after the accident, he had somehow managed to stand strong, but the last ten had been too much. Only his adopted daughters knew how bad it was for him.

Hamel pulled himself off the floor and straightened his back. He closed his eyes and took a deep breath. When he opened his eyes, he stepped before the mirror. He set his jaw and stared deep into the eyes of his reflection.

Hamel steeled himself to face the day. It was an important day.

"I am not without family. I do not face the world alone. I must continue. There is work to be done."

Hamel relaxed his body and let the truth of Lertel's words sink in. He could not afford to give up. It was time to move.

The sun had not yet risen. It rarely had when his nightmares forced him awake. He enjoyed the early morning. Few people were up before the sun, and it gave him the chance to exercise.

He opened the door to his home and stepped outside. The air was warm, and the breeze felt cool on his face. It was going to be a beautiful day.

Hamel's morning run through the city took him along a familiar route. The streets ran up and down the uneven ground and made for excellent exercise.

Few civilians ran through the Ridge Capital. He knew some in the small villages a short distance outside the city ran, but it was not considered necessary. Only the military needed to push themselves physically. The rest of the people were already young and healthy. Hamel was the exception.

Patir Hamel saluted two soldiers standing watch at the end of their shift. They stood alert and ready. They always

2

did. He often wondered if they were as alert as they were because they knew he regularly ran through their area at the end of their watch.

He remembered his own nights on watch in the city. He had always tried to be alert, but he had never stood so straight and so sharp when the sun came up.

The number of people on the street began to grow. The sellers were out, and the farmers were heading to the fields. It was time to end his morning run and return before people slowed him down.

As he ran up one of the hills toward his home, a young Matir with her child waved him down. "Honored Patir, will you bless my child?"

Hamel smiled to himself. There were few joys greater than blessing a child. As a man of his position and age, he was often afforded the privilege. He came to a stop beside the young woman and placed his hand on the child's head. "What is the child's name?"

"I have named him Hamel, after you," she said, her face beaming with pride.

Hamel smiled. "I am honored." He examined the child for a moment. He appeared to be around four years old and had a mischievous look in his eye. "May you, young Hamel, grow to be strong, faithful, and kind."

He removed his hand from the child's head and placed his hand briefly on the woman's head. "May you pour your heart and soul into this child, and may he leave a legacy equal to your own."

The woman bowed her head slightly to offer her gratitude, and Hamel ran on. He had to grit his teeth and focus to make it home. The little boy was about the same age his daughter had been. If he recalled correctly, it had been just the day before the crash that he had met an Honored Matir and asked her to bless his own little girl and young, infant son. He could remember how honored he felt to have that same blessing placed upon his children and then to have her own hand of blessing on his forehead.

3

He could not remember the Honored Matir's name, but *he* could see her face in his mind. Her hands shook, and *her* voice wavered. The Dusk had fallen upon her, and she *had* been near the end.

It was a great honor to be blessed by her. There were *few* memories so precious to him as that day.

He often reflected on that day. As a man who had escaped the Dusk.

Before he reached home, he was stopped by a young Lieutenant seeking advice in dealing with those under her command and a young man seeking counsel on a large business transaction to take place later that day. It was difficult to stop mid-run to offer wise counsel, but it was his duty and privilege as an Honored Patir among the people.

When he arrived home, the sun was fully up. It had indeed turned out to be a beautiful day, although he expected the midday heat would be intense.

Hamel arrived at the gate to his house and waited as Markel opened it. The fourteen-year-old boy had been a guard to Hamel for nearly three years. He was a strong, confident young man. Markel would do well in life.

Hamel made his way into the small yard behind his home and spent an hour and a half completing his exercises and routines. The walls stood high around his property. There was no concern for security, but he loved the privacy.

As he began his routines, Markel joined him. They rarely spoke during such times. Markel was much like Hamel, focused on the task before him.

Although Markel was dwarfed next to Hamel's height and bulk, he consistently proved himself a capable fighter. Hamel had trained few soldiers with as much potential as the young man.

Hamel called a halt to their training once he felt he had pushed the boy enough. Markel stood panting and dripping with sweat. He looked quite relieved that their training had come to an end for the morning.

In the house, the two washed up, and Markel set to making breakfast. When they sat down, they took a moment to ask for a blessing for their food and their time together.

Markel had his own quarters in the guardhouse by the gate, but he often joined Hamel for meals. Since Mariel, Hamel's youngest daughter, was regularly away with responsibilities of the Council, Hamel found it comforting to have a friend nearby.

For a few minutes, the young man ate in silence. He often did before he asked a difficult question. "May I ask you a question, Honored Patir?"

Hamel smiled and set down his knife and fork. It had become a daily ritual. "Markel, how many times must I tell you that while we are in my home, you must call me Hamel."

"I think you will have to tell me yet again, Honored Patir," Markel replied, a hint of a smile creeping up at the corners of his mouth.

Hamel understood. It was dishonoring to speak to someone of his rank with anything less than reverence. To speak with too much familiarity could be misinterpreted as contempt. While he did not wish to see Markel dishonored, it was difficult to have no one around for whom he could just be "Hamel." He wished the young man could see him as less of an Honored Patir and more of a friend. Besides, in one's own home, formality was often set aside.

"What is your question, Markel?" Hamel asked.

Markel bowed slightly in reverence to his friend and mentor before asking, "Will you be meeting Mariel today?"

"You know I will, Markel," Hamel replied. His stomach tensed, and his appetite disappeared. He knew where the events of that day would lead, and he did not wish to follow the path he knew he must.

"I suspect she will ask you again for your blessing," Markel said, not meeting Hamel's eyes.

"Yes." Hamel did not enjoy the conversation, but he would endure as he knew his friend well enough to know Markel's heart was heavy with concern.

"Will you give it? Will you give your blessing to her?"

Hamel raised his eyes to find Markel's eyes locked on him. He decided to be difficult. "May I ask your intentions with such a question? Is it because you have an eye for her?"

Markel's face turned red, and he dropped his fork on the table. Mariel was a beautiful young woman. There were few young men who were not enamored with her. Her beauty, however, was far exceeded by her course in life. There was little doubt she would be an Honored Matir in time. A woman of such intellect, grace, beauty, and obvious influence was an honor simply to know, let alone to marry.

"Honored Patir, you know I do not have my eye on her. She is far more than a lowly guard could even consider. I am also too young for her. I have not received the education a woman such as she deserves. I am not intelligent enough for her. And she has eyes for Captain Cuttel. She is also…"

"Markel," Hamel said with both hands in the air, "I am teasing you. I will disagree with you about your intelligence, and I don't believe your position as a guard is too low for her. I would be honored to give you a blessing for marriage to a daughter, but you are right in saying you are too young for her and that she has eyes only for Cuttel. I am simply trying to distract you from the question you asked. I do not wish to answer."

Hamel lowered his eyes. He poked the food on his plate with his fork and moved a few pieces of egg around in a circle. He had no appetite left, but he also knew his body would need the energy. It would be a difficult day. He took another large bite and began to chew.

"Honored Patir, will you give your blessing?" Markel asked again.

Hamel frowned and raised his eyes back up to the young man. "No."

Markel nodded, but the expression on his face indicated he was not satisfied. "I do not wish to speak out of turn, Honored Patir, but you know she is of marrying age. She is twenty and not for much longer. She does not wish anyone else. To add to this…" Markel stopped and looked as though he recognized how far he had crossed the line.

"Go on, Markel. You are my friend. I will overlook this and many more insults." It was not proper to remind an honored one of tradition, but Hamel had long since stopped caring about his pride around the young boy.

"This is the third time she will have asked for your blessing. If you refuse today, she will have full cause to take the issue to the Council. They will side with her as there is no clear reason for your refusal. Your honor will not be enough to force them to declare Mariel to be in the wrong. They will give her their blessing, and you will lose everything."

Hamel examined Markel. The young man's hands shook, and a tear had formed in his eye. He was a good friend. He was strong, faithful, and kind. He was also loyal and would risk his own honor to protect the honor of another. Hamel had always known Markel would be a great man one day. At fourteen, he was already showing the wisdom and courage of a man twice his age.

"Markel, thank you for your kind words," Hamel said. Markel's shoulders relaxed, and the young man let out the breath he was holding. Hamel added, "I am prepared for what I must do."

"Honored Patir, I don't understand why you won't give your blessing to her."

Hamel shoved the last of the food in his mouth and stood up. It was time to go. He would not be late for his meeting. He finished the food in his mouth and set his eyes on Markel. He didn't want to be firm with his young friend, but he did not want to continue the discussion. "Markel, I will not give her my blessing today to marry that man. She will only marry him if the Council overrides me."

With that, he turned and walked away from the table. He knew Markel would feel shame for pushing Hamel so far, but he could not allow his resolve to waver. There was too much at stake.

It was time.

CHAPTER 2

THE DAY TURNS SOUR

Hamel made his way out of the house and let himself through the gate. To have a guard to open and close the gate was far from necessary. It was merely a privilege of the honored.

While he often took the quiet paths to the town center, that day he chose the main route. It would take him through the upper residential areas and by the market. He would be noticed by many, and he would be stopped repeatedly by those seeking blessing or advice. He typically preferred to avoid such attention, but today was not a day to hide. It was a day to stand firm.

The first to ask his blessing was a young boy seeking an apprenticeship with a baker. Hamel learned the boy's name was Zemmel, and he was ten years old. From the pain in the young boy's eyes, Hamel suspected the Dusk had just taken his parents. He blessed the boy and was about to walk on, but stopped. He reached down and placed his hand on the boy's shoulder. He would not be able to ease the grief the young boy felt after the loss of his parents, but he could at least guarantee the success of the boy's request.

He led Zemmel through the streets to the bakeries. No one stopped him. A hand on the shoulder was a sign of blessing and a matter of great honor. The boy pointed the way

8

to the place of his hopeful apprenticeship, and the two walked in through the front door.

As they entered, the entire shop grew silent. Hamel was always recognized. Few had the lines on their faces that his extra years had given him. Even if he were not recognized, the crest on his shirt revealed him to be an Honored Patir.

The baker stepped forward and bowed in reverence to Hamel. "Honored Patir, I did not know you were blessing this young boy's apprenticeship. It was foolish of me not to accept such a worthy young man immediately. Please accept my apologies."

"All is forgiven, my worthy baker. I have come not to rebuke, but to meet the man who wishes to train such an honorable young man as Zemmel," Hamel said and bowed lower than had the baker.

Hamel had to hold back a grin as the baker giggled with glee. His ample belly shook as he laughed. Hamel's words had honored the man greatly.

Before the baker could respond, Hamel turned to the door. He had to reach the City Center. It was not far from the bakery, but he would never make it there without interruptions.

When he finally arrived at the City Center after countless blessings and much advice offered, he sat down on a bench by himself. He would have peace while he waited. It was inappropriate to ask for a blessing while someone rested. He smiled as he soaked in the morning sun.

After a few minutes, someone caught his eye. He watched as a tall, thin, beautiful young woman walked down a side street and entered the large open area. She paused briefly at a small stand to purchase a flower and placed it in her light brown hair, just behind her ear.

Hamel chuckled to himself. She had always loved putting flowers in her hair. When she had first come to him, she had been only eight. She had been so traumatized. The Dusk had taken her Matir, and her Patir had fallen in battle. Few children transitioned smoothly to their new homes, but Mariel had found it harder than most.

9

He had taken two months away from the military to help her through her time. When she had begun to stand strong and he could see what kind of a child she was, he had been shocked at her intellect.

He had not thought it possible to adopt such a wonderful young woman. He considered her to be one of his greatest honors, and she continued to be his greatest joy. Hamel was smiling like a fool.

Hamel's thoughts drifted to why he was there, and his face fell. It broke his heart to have to do what he was about to do, but there was no choice. He would carry out his plans, regardless of the cost. His daughter would pay a price. He only hoped he would have the strength, and that it would all be worth it in the end.

He quickly forced a smile as their eyes met, and she made her way across the small grassy park. He stood to his feet and waited for his daughter.

When she was two steps away, she stopped and bowed her head so slightly. "Hello, my Patir."

It always thrilled him to hear those words. Anyone could call a man "Patir" or a woman "Matir." It was a sign of respect and honor given to another. His own title of Honored Patir was even greater. It was a term so full of honor, but so full of distance.

Only family, however, could call him, "my Patir." It was a sacred gift. To hear Mariel call him "my Patir" reminded him that he was not alone.

"Hello, my daughter," Hamel replied.

Once the formalities were out of the way, she came in and wrapped him in a hug. To act with too much enthusiasm or joy in public was the way of fools, but when it involved a parent and child, one could laugh and hug all they wanted in any situation or circumstance. There was no shame in family.

She let go and stepped back. Hamel knew the question needed to be asked, and he knew he must face it.

It was the third time she would ask for his blessing on her marriage. The question needed to be asked in public, and it required a clear answer. On that day, there was no room for anything but clarity.

"My Patir, you know why I have asked to meet you," Mariel said, her voice shaking just slightly.

"Yes, Mariel, I know."

"I would like to formally ask you to give me your blessing to marry Captain Eafti Cuttel."

People gathered around. It was one thing for the People of the Ridge to ask for a blessing on their marriage, but to see an Honored Patir give his blessing to his own daughter was an honor. The people formed a circle around Hamel and Mariel, and the crowd grew.

Hamel opened his mouth to answer, but Mariel spoke again. Her voice had regained its typical confidence, and she spoke loud enough for all those gathered to hear. "This is the third and final time I may ask you for your blessing on my marriage. You have refused me your blessing the first two times, as is your right to give and as is my honor to receive."

Hamel dreaded what was to come, but was proud of her for speaking with confidence and such conviction. One day, she would be a great Honored Matir on the Council, and she would lead the nation well.

"Speak, my daughter. Ask your question."

"I am nearly at the end of my marriage year. If I do not marry before the month end, I will not marry. I do not wish to marry anyone else. I wish only Cuttel. I, Rezin Mariel, ask you this third time for your blessing to marry Captain Eafti Cuttel."

Hamel paused for a moment and calmed his heart. He did not want any emotion to show in his response. When he spoke, he also spoke with enough volume for all to hear. "I will not give you my blessing, Mariel."

A gasp went up among the crowd of people. To refuse a request to marry three times required a solid reason. It would be cruel and dishonoring to refuse a marriage blessing without cause.

"May I ask you why?" Mariel responded. It was not proper to ask when the first or second requests were brought forward. Only on the third could a reason be required.

Hamel took a deep breath and spoke the words that had tormented him for so long. "Because I know this young man. He is an officer under me, and I see what he is like. We have fought constantly over trivial matters. Everything is a battle to him, and his decisions, choices, and actions declare him to be a man without honor. If this is the kind of officer he is, then he will be that and more as a husband. A man such as that will not love you. He will not care for you. He will not protect you or your children. He will not stand by you. You will be alone."

Mariel clenched her fists, and Hamel could see her knuckles turn white. He had not seen her angry for many years. She was a woman of such control.

Mariel paused before she continued the tradition. "If you will not give me your blessing, I will be forced to take this to the Council. If they find your reasons unworthy, they will require that I reject you as Patir. They will override your decision."

The emotion appeared too much for Mariel, and tears streamed down her cheeks. If she pursued the matter, as he knew she would, it would lead only to pain and dishonor.

He forced himself to laugh loud enough for the entire crowd to hear and settled his face into a foolish grin. Not only was he willing to take it to the Council, he would force it in that direction. A price needed to be paid, and Mariel would, unfortunately, pay her part.

"You would not dare," Hamel began, speaking loud enough that even those in the back of the crowd would have no difficulty in hearing his words. "I am your Patir. You are my child. I am tied to you and you to me. We are one. We are honored family. Nothing can change that. Would you rather be as Cuttel? Parentless? He may appear free, but he is left to face the world alone. He lives as one full of selfishness and rebellion!"

12

The faces on the people in the crowd revealed the horror they felt. Honor was about to be lost. When it was lost by those of such high status, it was a painful experience for all. By refusing to heed her Patir's denial, Mariel was losing all her honor in one single moment. But all those standing by knew if she took the matter to the Council, she would regain her honor, but the Honored Patir Rezin Hamel would be shamed and declared a man without honor. To refuse a request for marriage on the basis of opinion alone was not the road a man of honor walked. No good path lay ahead.

Those with young children grabbed them and pulled them away. They would not want their young ones to see such a public display of shame. Hamel could hear their voices as they told their children that no good could come from such a disagreement.

Hamel felt the anger he had built inside boil. He had been stoking that fire. It was a necessary evil if his plans were to play out. It was time to let it out and pave the way for what was to come. "You would truly take this matter to the Council, Mariel?" he asked, letting the rage be heard in his voice. "Would you stand before the Honored Matir Karotel and bring your case before her? You think she has the wisdom to decide such a matter?"

Hamel did not look around, but he knew the few who remained were beyond shocked. If refusing his daughter such a request was shameful, it was nothing compared to publicly criticizing the Honored Matir or Patir of the People of the Ridge. He knew those who still stood by would wish to flee, yet they were aware they were witnesses. As much as the people wanted to run, it was their duty to remain.

It was time to let it all out. He stepped forward, and Mariel nearly tripped as she stepped back. Hamel was a large man. His height and his build, along with his obvious anger, was enough to bring even a seasoned soldier to question his or her safety. No one would think he would harm his daughter, but to threaten with his movement was nearly as dishonorable. He yelled, "For the last five years, Karotel has proven herself to be the fool!"

13

Mariel stepped back again. Hamel did not think it was because of his anger. He was a large man, and he had a reputation for being a fearless warrior. His training had taken him far beyond any other soldier, and no one had dared challenge him in years. He knew he struck fear in people, both by his size and his reputation. But he also knew Mariel had never feared him.

He wondered, in that brief moment, if she had stepped back in shock. No one was to speak the Honored Matir's given name publicly without her title. She was an Honored Matir. She was worthy of the respect of her title.

It was time to lay it all out for Mariel and for all those standing by. "You want to take your case to Karotel, but she is the very one who has acted without honor. She has been building houses along the edge of the city for the past five years. She has emptied the treasury and used our soldiers as carpenters, leaving our Valley Wall and our northern borders weakly defended. For what? To build houses along the edge of the wilderness? There are whole sections of the city full of empty homes. Is that not enough? Must she build more? We do not have enough people to fill the homes we have! Is that the kind of woman you want to take your case before? She has all but abandoned our closest allies, and every decision she makes declares a drive for power!" He raised his voice to a scream as he bellowed again, "Karotel is a fool!"

Mariel's eyes remained focused on the ground by her feet. Her mouth fell open, but she closed it again as if she could not find the words to speak. The young lady reached up and pulled the flower out of her hair. She stared at it in her hands and turned it over and over. The tears streamed down her face, but she wiped none of them away.

The flower she held was a beautiful rose. He was reminded again of her love for flowers and how beautiful they looked in her hair. The memory now only brought grief.

"I will take this to the Council," Mariel said quietly, but loud enough that those standing closest could make out her words. "Will you be there?"

It was time to calm his words and speak once again as an Honored Patir. He was risking the loss of all his honor, but for the moment he still had some. "When is the next meeting?"

"Tomorrow evening," Mariel replied.

"I will be there, as I am able," Hamel said with a calm and steady voice.

Mariel paused for another moment, her gaze locked on the flower. She had not met his eyes since he had first called Karotel a fool.

It was time for Mariel to go, but she was too honorable to simply turn her back on her Patir, even after all he had done. "May I leave, my Pa..." she choked on the name and paused while she took a breath.

"You normally keep a flower in your hair, my daughter," Hamel said with kindness in his voice.

"This flower brings me no joy anymore," Mariel replied. She took a deep breath, and he could see it took all her discipline not to weep. "May I leave, my Patir?"

"Yes, my daughter," Hamel replied quietly.

Mariel took one final look at the rose and dropped it where she stood. She turned and, without another word, walked away with her head low.

He watched her go as the crowd, knowing they would be permitted to leave, turned away. He could see her shoulders shake as she walked. She was weeping. The time until the meeting would not pass quickly for her.

But it was only the beginning of what was to come. There would be more tears and more loss before he was finished.

CHAPTER 3

THE DAY TURNS TO THE WALL

Hamel knew the time until the Council meeting would pass slowly.

Word of the disagreement between him and his daughter would spread throughout the People of the Ridge and even into Olmos. The Olmosite Ambassador would send word to his people quickly. It was not every day that an Honored Patir of Hamel's rank found himself in such a shameful situation.

Hamel was already a mystery to most people. At forty-four years of age, he had lived nearly ten years longer than the oldest living person in recorded history. No one knew why. The doctors were baffled as to how he had avoided the Dusk. His day should have ended years ago—yet he remained.

The rage inside him built again. It built every time his thoughts drifted to his past. He felt so alone. He felt like a man out of sync with his time. He knew he should be dead, but death had eluded him.

He often wished he had been in the accident with his family. He might have been able to save them, but if not, he may have died alongside them. At times, death seemed a welcome release. Only his surviving adopted children and faithfulness to his people kept him going.

He looked around and saw he was near Command. He had an office there as the highest ranking General in the army.

There were people around, but no one approached him. He knew word of his argument with Mariel would have already spread, and most would be unsure if they could ask for his blessing. It was uncommon for a man of his status to be engaged in such a scandal. His blessing would still stand and still be respected, but it would take the people a little while to come to grips with what had happened. The dishonor would afford him a short reprieve from the duties of his position.

He repeated the words in his head. "I am not without family. I do not face the world alone. I must continue. There is work to be done."

Hamel clenched his fists and closed his eyes, going over the words once again. As he finished, his wife's face appeared in his mind, and he quickly opened his eyes to dispel the image. He would not do well at that moment to dwell on the pain of the past.

His thoughts were interrupted by a blast of a horn. It was the signal they were under attack at the Valley Wall. It was a common enough occurrence, yet those who stood around tensed up, and some even rushed away. Hamel suspected they were heading home.

He decided to go to the wall and at least observe the battle. It would take his mind off matters.

There were many roads leading down into the valley. The one he used was primarily reserved for soldiers moving to and from the Valley Wall. Every few minutes, he stepped aside to let soldiers pass as they rushed to their posts.

As he stepped down onto the Valley Floor, he reflected yet again on the problem with the Beasts. The attacks had increased in frequency over the last two decades. It was still unclear what the Beasts were after, but it was obvious they were enraged with the People of the Ridge.

He entered a large stable built of solid stone and waited for the stable boy to bring him his horse. There was always a horse saddled and ready for him, in case he wished to go to the Valley Wall. The soldiers ran, but it would be considered improper for a General to run into battle on foot, unless the circumstances demanded such action. A General needed to get to the battle quickly.

The horn had not blown a second time, indicating the battle had not yet begun. The Beasts always gathered in ranks before their attack. The creatures occasionally took upward of two to three hours to organize themselves. Once, Hamel recalled waiting two days for them to gather. If that were the case this time, he would miss the Council Meeting.

He smiled to himself at that thought. It would show even greater disrespect for the Honored Matir than he had already shown. Such a thing might even serve his purposes.

The protected area of the Valley Floor itself was beautiful. It was mid-summer, and the crops grew tall. It would be a good harvest. The land between the city and the Valley Wall was some of the most fertile soil anywhere in the world. The current year's harvest would provide more than enough for their entire nation as well as some to export to Olmos. No one should starve that year.

When he reached the Valley Wall on the far side of the farms, he tied off his horse. The steps leading to the top were called the Two Hundred Faithful. Two hundred stone steps leading to the top of the largest structure in all of Ridge Nation—a wall to protect them from the Beasts.

Before climbing the steps, he entered a door at the base of the wall. A young Lieutenant was in charge of the ground troops that day, and she appeared nervous.

"General, welcome to the battlefield," she said loud enough for her voice to carry across to many of the soldiers. "It is an honor to have you among us. Do you wish to assume command of the ground troops today?"

It was proper for an officer to relinquish his or her command to a General, but it would never be proper for a General to take command of any position other than to lead the entire battle. A leader of his experience and reputation would be wasted in any position other than as commander of all the troops.

"You honor me, Lieutenant, but I would never assume command from a person of your skill and leadership," Hamel replied.

She smiled her gratitude, although Hamel could see she was not as honored as she would have been on any other day. He realized word had spread even to the wall of his conversation with Mariel. He was not surprised it had happened so quickly.

"May I return to my command, General?" the Lieutenant asked.

"Yes, please. Lead us to victory," Hamel said. He took one more look to fulfill the need for the General to inspect the troops and walked out.

He began to climb the Two Hundred Faithful. He stopped again at the mid-wall defense and, yet again, was offered command. He refused and after a quick inspection, continued up the steps.

At the top, he was met by the soldiers guarding the stairs. Each man saluted and bowed their heads in respect, but neither one made eye contact with him. Not only had word spread, but his honor had been shaken.

Hamel scanned the soldiers for the Captain. He would be well engaged in the responsibilities of command and would not be able to speak with Hamel for a time. Hamel took the opportunity to look out over the wall to evaluate the situation.

The Valley of the Beasts lay stretched out before him. The land immediately on the other side of the Valley Wall was open and clear of trees. It was in that area that the battle would be fought. On the far side of the battleground was the tree line, and the forest of the Beasts continued on into the distance. The forest itself was walled off by a cliff face on the sides, surrounding the entire area.

No one ventured into the Forest of the Beasts and lived to tell of their experience. It had long been declared illegal to do such a thing, and all who did were declared traitors to the People of the Ridge. Their presence in the Forest of the Beasts enraged the monsters.

On that day, the Beasts had rallied themselves quickly. They were out in full force. It would be a bloody battle.

The Beasts were at the tree line, nearly four hundred paces from the wall. The open area between the wall and the forest was trampled and well-worn from previous attacks.

Hamel always grieved each and every battle. It felt to be such a terrible waste. Not one Beast had made it over the wall during an attack in all the years since the wall had been built, yet they still came. They would rush upon the wall, growling and snarling and do their best to climb up and over. They could find a foothold or handhold on the slightest crack or crevice and climb almost as quickly as they could run across the ground.

The ground troops would shoot through slits in the base of the wall. The Beasts who made it past the rifles would climb, and the mid-wall defense troops would use spears and rifles to slay any Beast attempting to make their way past. The soldiers on top of the wall would fire both at those approaching the wall and at any Beasts which made it past the mid-wall defense.

It was a simple strategy overall. The challenge was to make sure the troops were stationed at the right places. The Beasts would swarm in different locations. Troops needed to run from one section of the wall to another at a word from the one in charge.

Hamel looked again for the Wall Commander and spotted the Captain on duty. It was Cuttel. It would not be long before another confrontation took place.

One of the Lieutenants leaned in and said something to the Captain, and Cuttel looked back at Hamel. He did not compose his face quickly enough to hide the look of disdain, but regained his honor immediately as he formed a respectful, but focused expression.

He approached Hamel and saluted. "General, welcome to the battlefield." It was obvious his voice was lacking all respect due to Hamel's position, yet he maintained tradition. "It is an honor to have you among us. Do you wish to assume command of the defense today?"

"You honor me, Captain, but I wish to observe your tactics and strategies. I will remain silent but vigilant." Hamel felt he had been particularly creative in his insult. From the expression on Captain Cuttel's face, the insinuation was not lost on him.

The Captain saluted again and bowed just enough to maintain tradition before he turned back to his troops. Hamel watched carefully. The man was a competent leader. He maintained the discipline of his troops and had a gift for strategy and foresight for where the Beasts would attack next.

It had been years since the young man had apprenticed under Hamel, and, despite what he had said to Mariel, Cuttel was a quality officer. There was hope for the People of the Ridge with Cuttel in charge of defense, but competence was not what the young man needed to win Hamel's blessing to marry his daughter.

The defense of the city went as planned, but Hamel grieved yet again at the loss of life. He never understood why the Beasts attacked at all, let alone with greater intensity and frequency over the previous twenty years. Cuttel performed his duties well, and the Beasts retreated.

When the last of the Beasts disappeared into the forest, Hamel closed his eyes and fought down the revulsion. He always dreaded what came at the end. Hamel, as a General on the wall, could not be seen turning away from the battlefield due to such a thing as a weak stomach, but he did not wish to watch.

It had happened at the end of every battle for the last twenty years or more. Once they lost, the Beasts would retreat back to the tree line. A few would then return, only to throw the lifeless bodies of six or seven of their infants against the walls. There would always be one or two that would be thrown wrapped in the uniform of a Ridge soldier.

He watched as the Beasts threw seven bodies against the wall. It was a revolting sight each and every time.

Once they had finished their bizarre ritual, they, along with the surviving Beasts in the forest, let out a terrible, deep sound. It was a cross between a scream and a roar. Hamel had always felt it was a mournful sound. He suspected they either grieved the loss of the battle or the death of their children.

The battle was done. The Beasts never attacked twice at one time. Once the battle was finished, it was finished.

Captain Cuttel sent a soldier down the steps with orders to the Lieutenant to secure the battlefield. He then approached Hamel. "General, with your permission, I am going to leave the wall and examine the battlefield."

"You have my permission, Captain," Hamel replied. "I will join you today."

The lack of encouragement or any form of congratulations for leading well would not be lost on Cuttel or on the soldiers present. Hamel was well equipped to grant honor or to withhold it. With Cuttel, it was always withheld.

The two, along with Cuttel's personal guard, made their way down the steps with Hamel in the lead. The phrase, "examine the battlefield" had come to refer to the abhorrent task of removing the Ridge uniforms from the bodies of the infant Beasts.

When they reached the Valley Floor, they found the gate leading out to the field open. The Lieutenant was standing by the wall, examining a body. Hamel and Cuttel approached and saw it was a Beastchild wrapped in a Ridge uniform. It looked as though it had been strangled. Hamel hated to see such a thing, even among his enemies. There was no honor in killing a child. There was no honor among the Beasts.

Cuttel, as Wall Commander, was responsible for retrieving the uniform. It had belonged to one of his soldiers.

The Captain pulled the uniform off the Beastchild and held it up for examination. He looked at the name stitched on the front and announced, "This belonged to Lieutenant Effel. She was assigned to the ground troops."

Cuttel turned to the Lieutenant who had been leading the ground troops during the battle. Her face had lost all its color. "Lieutenant, where is Effel?" His use of Effel's name without the title sent a clear statement among the troops.

The Lieutenant hung her head in shame. "I don't know, sir," she said with a shaky voice. "Lieutenant Effel... I mean, Effel did not report for duty this morning. I was assigned in her place."

"Lieutenant, take thirty soldiers and go immediately to Effel's home. If she is there, bring her to me in chains. If she is not there, you are ordered to take an additional seventy soldiers and do a thorough search of the city, including the lower sections. I wish for a full report by noon tomorrow."

The Captain's eyes landed on Hamel. For a brief second, Hamel thought he saw tiredness in Cuttel's eyes, but the Captain quickly regained his composure. He said, "General, thank you for the honor of your presence today. The battle is complete. It appears as though another one of our soldiers has betrayed the People of the Ridge by entering the land of the Beasts. I will see that this matter is resolved to the best of my ability."

"Well done, Captain," Hamel said. It was proper to commend an officer on a successful battle before leaving, but Cuttel would receive no more.

"General, may I speak freely to you about a personal matter?" the Captain asked. His expression suggested he was employing all his discipline to keep a respectful expression on his face.

Hamel did not want to have the discussion. He assumed it would be on the topic of Mariel, and he was still upset after his conversation with her.

He decided he would not give any honor to the young Captain. Instead, he simply said, "No," and walked away.

The soldiers were all too well disciplined to gasp or react in their shock, but he knew they would be horrified. It would be hard for them to work through the dishonor placed upon their Captain. Hamel had not only declared his disdain for Cuttel's leadership on the wall but to declare him unworthy of simple conversation was an insult worthy of challenge.

Hamel smiled to himself. No one had challenged him in years. He was far too skilled a soldier, and he was far too honored for most to feel they could challenge him. Since he had somehow lived so long, avoiding the Dusk, many even thought he might have some secret power. He didn't encourage the rumor, but he had never denied it either. Captain Cuttel would not challenge him that day.

He walked through the gate and out into the fields. It would be a long walk back. A General or any officer was not to ride a horse back to the city after a battle at the wall. The troops could return any way they wished, but the officers could not rush. The soldiers were the victors on the day of battle.

As he walked along the road, the farmers began to return to their fields. They always left and stood behind the Inner Wall at the city boundary during an attack. It was an extra layer of protection against a savage enemy.

The fields always offered him such peace but reminded him of his wife. Lillel had grown up as a farmer's daughter. When her parents had reached their Dusk, she was adopted by other farmers. It had been a quiet life.

He stopped at a large oak tree near a spring and sat down on a boulder. The spring in that area helped to water the fields and with the shade of the tree, was the perfect place to stop and rest.

The field to the north of the spring was planted, and he nodded to the young man returning to care for the crops. It had been Lillel's family field. The young man was probably related to Lillel somehow, but Hamel had outlived her only sister. Even her sister's children would be nearing their Dusk.

The young man knelt to weed around some of what appeared to be vines. Hamel had never learned how to recognize the different crops. His focus had always been on military and political matters. The boy could easily be Lillel's great-nephew, and as he worked, Hamel realized he was kneeling right about where Lillel had been standing when Hamel had first noticed her.

He remembered the day clearly. It had been just after a battle. Hamel had apprenticed under his adopted mother, General Rezin Mathel. He had been given some time to relax before his training had resumed, and he had chosen that spot under the tree. He was forever grateful for that choice and for the relationship that had grown out of his meeting with Lillel. Only a few years after that day, he had wed Lillel and begun their few precious years together.

He made his way back into the city. The day was nearly finished. There would be few left who had not heard of his argument with Mariel.

His heart went out to her. He longed to make things right, but he would not. He could not give his blessing to her and Cuttel.

His thoughts were interrupted by a young man and woman. They stood before him with hesitation written across their faces. He could tell from their ages and their lack of rings, but also how close they stood together that they were about to be wed. They were in a difficult position. They were standing before an Honored Patir and would like his blessing, but he had dishonored himself. His dishonor was not formal, so his blessing was still a privilege to receive, but he could be formally dishonored at the next Council. It would be difficult for them to know the proper course of action.

He decided to make it easy for them. "Are you asking for my blessing?"

Both the young man and woman relaxed, and a smile grew on each of their faces. The young man stepped forward and asked, "Honored Patir, will you bless our marriage?"

"When is your marriage to take place?" he asked.

"Tomorrow morning, at dawn," the man replied.

Dawn was when all marriages took place. A wedding symbolized new beginnings. Such an event would need to be celebrated with the start of a new day.

Hamel raised his voice and said, "May your marriage be a light to others and an example of God's true love for us.

May your children be strong and lead lives of honor for all the People of the Ridge."

The two thanked him and bowed their heads slightly in gratitude and respect. While he remained in a place of dishonor, it would be difficult for people to know how to respond to him, but that act of blessing would help many work through the matter.

Word of his blessing over the young couple spread, and before long, many others found him and asked for his blessing. No one mentioned Mariel. They would leave the matter with the Council.

He arrived at his house and thanked Markel for opening the gate. Hamel did not like company most evenings, so the young man said his goodnight and locked the gate.

Hamel knew he should not spend his evenings wallowing in old memories. It did not serve him well, but there was a certain amount of pleasure found in grief.

He sat on his couch and opened a drawer. Inside was a doll that had belonged to his daughter. She would have turned twenty-two in three days' time and would be a couple years older than Mariel. No one lived long enough to watch their children grow into adults. It seemed so wrong that the only man who could live long enough to see his children marry and even his children's children had lost his family at such a young age.

He had given her such a pretty name, too: Keptel. He found his heart breaking with the memory of her and reveled in the pain.

Hamel pulled out a small stick from the drawer. It had belonged to his son. Lillel had named their son Draggel. The little guy had found the stick just lying on the ground in the yard and would not go anywhere without it. He seemed to think it was all he needed. No toys held his interest. Just the little stick.

Draggel would have been nearly twenty. He might even have been considering a young lady for marriage.

Hamel smiled at the thought of what might have been but then felt his heart crumble inside. It did not matter. None of it mattered. They were all gone.

He felt the rage build inside him once again. It was such a senseless accident. It truly could not be blamed on anyone. The fire was no one's fault. The young oil merchant whose wagon had lost a wheel... the wheel driving into a horse and breaking its leg... the night watchman on horseback who had fallen, his torch landing on the spilled oil...

It was an accident. A strange, horrible accident, but an accident just the same.

He blamed no one. No one but himself for not being there with them.

Hamel placed the doll and the stick back in the drawer and decided it was time to get some sleep. He stood to his feet and recited the words. "I am not without family. I do not face the world alone. I must continue. There is work to be done."

CHAPTER 4

THE DAY'S FINAL PEACE

His run the next day was typical of every day. The people had accepted the fact that Hamel had dishonored himself but was not yet formally dishonored. As soon as the sun had crested the horizon and people began to walk the streets, the requests for blessings and advice began.

The only difference he found was in the soldiers on watch. The first two soldiers he came across were leaning on their rifles. With the next soldiers, one sat on the ground, picking at his nails while the second appeared sound asleep on his feet. No one stood at attention as he ran by.

Hamel held his tongue. There was no benefit in establishing his authority with them. He would let the dishonor stand. Cuttel was a young officer, but on track to be a General one day. Hamel had dishonored one of their own for no perceivable reason. As much as he didn't appreciate the lack of respect, he understood.

At his house, after the run, Markel joined him in his morning training and exercise. The young man was a solid fighter and would make a good soldier one day. As they sparred, he never once met Hamel's eyes.

An hour later, Markel poked at his breakfast with his fork. The young man had held his tongue since Hamel had returned from his run and only spoken if asked a direct question.

Hamel did not care to avoid the issue that morning, "Out with it, Markel. Say what you must."

"Honored Patir…" Markel began.

Hamel decided to forgo his usual invitation for Markel to call him "Hamel" while in his home. The atmosphere felt as though there was no room for humor. He waited while Markel gathered his courage.

"I have heard a report of your conversation with Mariel. I have heard that you publicly criticized the Honored Matir. I do not wish to believe it. Is it all true?"

"I suspect so, Markel. I refused Mariel's request for my blessing, and I called Karotel a fool."

Markel dropped his fork. Hamel wasn't sure if it was because the reports were true or because he referred to Karotel without her title.

"May I ask you a direct question, Honored Patir?" Markel asked.

"Certainly," Hamel said with a great deal of enthusiasm and a smile on his face. "Anything you wish, my friend. But I do not guarantee an answer, nor do I guarantee that if I do answer, you will like what you hear."

Markel did not hesitate. "You have proven yourself to be one of the greatest men in history. There is no one I have read about who has your list of accomplishments, who has received as much honor, who has acted with such integrity," Markel began.

"You flatter me, Markel," Hamel replied. "What is your question?"

"Over the years, I have seen your disrespect for the Council grow. I have heard you speak more and more against them and their decisions. While it has never come to the point that you have called a member of the Council a fool, it has bothered me greatly. Yesterday, you said and did things you cannot take back. I do not see how you can recover your honor. Why would you do this?"

Hamel smiled. It felt good to smile, although he did not feel he had much to smile about. "Young Markel, I am sorry to say that this is a question I will not answer. I will, however, say this. When I meet with the Council later today, I will not humble myself. I will not seek my honor. I will take my stand against them. I will bring this matter to a head, and time will prove who among us has honor."

Markel's hands shook, and he placed them under the table. Hamel could only suspect that the young man feared Hamel's sanity was in question. He grieved the pain he was causing in young Markel's life, but he would not deviate from his course.

It was time to act for Markel's benefit. "This morning is the end of your employment for me, Markel."

Markel's eyes filled with pain, and his chin quivered. Hamel knew Markel would do anything for him and would even stand beside him in the Council, bearing Hamel's shame. It was time to send him away.

"You will pack up your things after you are finished eating, and you will report to Captain Cuttel. You will tell him that I am assigning you as his aide," Hamel ordered.

"But…" Markel began before closing his mouth. He paused for a moment and then nodded his head. He was too honorable a young man to question Hamel's orders. "Yes, Honored Patir."

Hamel laughed. "Finish your sentence, Markel. Don't say 'But…' and then not tell me what you are concerned about. Speak!"

"Honored Patir, Captain Cuttel despises you. If I go to him as his aide, assigned to him by you, he will suspect I am a spy sent to him to report on all his actions. He will despise me, and I will never have a chance to be a man of honor."

"I understand your fear, Markel. I will say this: you have your honor already. You will not lose what you already have. You also have your orders. See to them."

Markel stood and collected the empty dishes. Though he had been dismissed, he cleaned the dishes and asked permission to go his way. Before he left, he thanked Hamel for the time in his service.

Hamel sat on the couch. His heart was heavy with the pain of the months and years leading up to that moment. But none of what he had done compared to the events of the last day. He had crushed Mariel. He had dishonored Cuttel. He had spoken against Karotel. He had assigned Markel a task that would terrify the young man. That night, he would challenge the Council, and whatever the result, nothing would remain the same from that day forward.

CHAPTER 5

THE DAY OF DISGRACE

Hamel remained in his home the entire day to avoid contact with others. He did not wish to see anyone or speak to anyone. No one called on him at home.

Mid-way through the morning, he heard the horn blast, giving warning of an attack at the Valley Wall. The attacks came often enough those days.

Hamel grabbed his cloak to head to the wall, but placed it back on the hook by the door. Too many years serving in the Armies of the Ridge had conditioned him to act when the threat was near.

His stomach tensed as he considered the ongoing threat of the Beasts. Whatever it was that drove those Beasts to attack needed to be addressed. The Council had refused to allow the Generals to lead their forces into the forests of the valley, which left the Armies of the Ridge with no other option than to continue their strategy of maintaining a solid defense.

Hamel had agreed with their decision, although he had led the charge against the Council's refusal. He believed the threat was outside the valley. The Beasts were merely creatures. They acted on instinct. He did not think that the problem with the Beasts lay amongst the trees. He had long suspected it lay elsewhere.

He pushed the threat of the attack out of his mind and settled his thoughts. The day wore on, and he busied himself around his house.

Hours later, Hamel watched the sun move toward the horizon as he ate his evening meal. He loved the summer months. The heat, the sun, and the green vegetation made him feel at peace. He would need to enjoy what peace he could.

He pulled his Council robes over his head and adjusted them until they sat just right on his shoulders. Anyone could wear whatever they wished to a Council meeting, but he would attend that night's meeting in full robes. He would stand with honor. Before he left, he examined himself in the mirror. He had always felt humbled by the privilege of wearing the robes. His eyes lingered on the crest, declaring his position as Honored Patir. It featured prominently on his chest. He did not think that crest would remain his for much longer.

He had not left much time to get to the Council Chambers, but it was improper for someone to stop an Honored Patir on the way to a Council meeting. He would have just enough time to arrive a few minutes after the Council began. All the Council would be there, and he would be able to make an entrance.

The walk to the Council meeting was quiet for the most part. No one disturbed him, and he was grateful for the peace. The air was calm, and the sound of children playing in the streets helped to ease the stress. He suspected that walk would be the last peace he would have for a long time. He took the time to enjoy the cool of the evening, the sounds of the birds, and the bustle of the people.

As he approached the steps leading into the Council Chambers, he heard the blast of the horn yet again. Rarely did a day pass when the Beasts did not attack twice. He ignored the matter. A different battle lay before him.

As he stepped into the Outer Council Chambers, he found he had timed his arrival perfectly. The session had just begun. He took a deep breath and smiled. He was about to act in a shameful and disturbing manner, but he felt as if he were embarking on an adventure. He was about to undertake a journey no one in recorded history had ever traveled—at least willingly.

He swung open the doors to the Inner Council Chambers just as the Honored Matir Rezin Karotel announced the agenda for the meeting. Hamel had always despised agendas and did not miss the days when he would have to walk the Council through all the points listed on the record.

As he stepped inside, the room grew silent. He quickly scanned the faces of each of the members. It appeared as though some of the twelve Council Patirs and Matirs had assumed he would not come. Karotel rose to her feet, and the other Council members followed her example.

Karotel was a tiny woman. She was short enough that she was often mistaken for a child. But despite her small frame, no one questioned her ability to lead. She was considered by all, Hamel included, to be one of the most intelligent people who had ever lived among the People of the Ridge. Even in the midst of their greatest conflicts, Hamel had never questioned her intellect.

Sitting one level down from Karotel and the Council members were the Council aides. There were twelve in all, and each one would be expected to rise to the position of Council member in time. Seated in the place of honor among the aides was Mariel. She faced Hamel, but he could see her eyes were fixed on a spot on the wall just above his head.

On each side of the door stood an officer. On his left, Hamel turned to see Captain Cuttel. The Captain saluted and said, "General, welcome to the Council." He turned to the right and received a similar response from Major Ornel.

Hamel nodded in reply to each of the men. Even in that moment, Cuttel followed tradition.

Typically, there were no soldiers present at a Council meeting. Only in circumstances requiring a military presence was a soldier assigned. For that evening's meeting, a Council member was acting out of order. The Captain would have been assigned to the Council in response to the need to confront Hamel. The Council meeting was not expected to go well that night. Hamel knew as well that the choice of Cuttel specifically was intentional.

Major Ornel, however, was unexpected. The man was a solid, committed, respected officer. His honor and dedication were without question. Hamel had known Cuttel would be there, but not the Major. He wondered if Ornel had specifically requested the opportunity to stand in witness. It would not matter, however. His higher rank would mean nothing as the Council would defer to Captain Cuttel and would treat Major Ornel as though he were not even present.

"Honored Patir Rezin Hamel," Karotel began. "The Council welcomes you and declares that they are honored to have you in our midst. Will you be taking your place of honor this evening?"

"I will, Karotel," Hamel replied.

The Council gasped. Hamel's position allowed him a certain amount of freedom to speak as he wished. But to publicly call an Honored Matir by her given name without her title in the Council Chambers was an insult beyond what even a man of his position could afford. The Honored Matir would be well within her right to have Hamel arrested and dragged from the Council Chambers.

He made his way to his seat and sat down. He took a quick glance at Cuttel whose eyes were fixed on the Honored Matir. His stance suggested he was ready to move on an order from her to arrest Hamel.

Instead, she simply asked, "Will the Honored Patir be exercising his right to lead the Council this evening?"

Hamel had held Karotel's position before his retirement. All Honored Matirs and Patirs were required to retire, in a manner of speaking, at age thirty-two, just before the onset of the Dusk, but they all retained their full position, authority, and freedom. It was expected the Dusk would take them before long, and their authority would naturally end. Unlike all before him, the Dusk had not taken Hamel. He had continued on as Honored Patir of the Council through the leadership of two of his successors. Karotel had never led without having to offer him the leadership each day he arrived.

"No, Honored Matir," Hamel replied. "I will not lead the Council this evening." He decided to use her title so as not to push the matter of honor too far, just yet. She had ignored the insult once, and he had made his point.

Honored Matir Karotel took her seat, followed by all the Council members, then Mariel as first of the aides, followed by the rest of the aides. Only Captain Cuttel and Major Ornel remained on their feet. Although Cuttel stood as sentry for the Council, all knew he was there for another reason.

The meeting progressed as all meetings did. They worked through all the mundane matters of state, as well as responded to a few complaints from the people. Since Cuttel was present, they did not read the military report but asked him to give a verbal report of the state of the army and defense of the Valley Wall.

Hamel stayed silent for the entire meeting, even refusing to vote on any matter. He was determined to declare his disdain for the Council in any way he could.

At one point, he glanced toward the door to find Cuttel's eyes on him. The man's expression was deeply respectful. He did not betray the emotion that Hamel knew must be raging within.

Hamel set his jaw and clenched his fists. The man would not marry his daughter by his blessing. It was a steep price the young man would pay, just as Mariel would have to pay as well, but Hamel would have his way. He had walked the road of public honor for too long. It was time to walk another road.

He let his eyes continue to drift around the room and was deep in a daydream when he heard his name. The address pulled him back to the moment. Mariel stood before the Council and was stating her case.

It was time.

Since he was the object of discussion, he left his seat and made his way down to the Council Chamber floor.

Mariel took the time to explain that she had requested three times that her Patir give his blessing on her marriage. He noticed she described the third event in detail, yet left out any insult to the Honored Matir. She was humble and kind, even in her pain. When she finished, she sat down.

Karotel paused for a moment, then stood. "This is a troubling report about the most Honored Member of our nation, Honored Patir Rezin Hamel. It is to the Council's dishonor to receive this report without hearing from the Honored Patir himself and, if necessary, hearing from witnesses. It is also rumored that the Honored Patir spoke shamefully about the Honored Matir. Once we are finished examining the issue of Honored Aide Rezin Mariel, we will examine the issue of Honored Patir Rezin Hamel's rumored words."

Everyone turned to Hamel. There was no tradition stating who was to speak and when, but his position afforded him the courtesy to respond to every comment.

"I do not wish to drag this matter out," Hamel began. He would not spend the night hashing through the matter. He did plan on sleeping before his run the next day. "It is all true. There is no need for witnesses. I refused Mariel's request for my blessing on her marriage without giving any reason but my own declared disdain for her potential husband. It was the third request, and she is fully within her right to take this matter to the Council. As for the rumored words, I will tell you plainly what I said. I called Honored Matir Karotel a fool."

The Council did not gasp or react in any way. They knew the accusation was true. He could see the disappointment on their faces, but there was no surprise. He noticed one of the older Matirs wiped a tear from her eye. Hamel had mentored her on her way to the Council and even brought her name forward for consideration. The disappointment on her face cut deeply into Hamel's heart.

The matter, however, could not be let go. He had already spoken Karotel's name without her title. He had acted without honor, and he knew to confirm the accusation about his insult to her would simply make the process easier.

The room sat in silence for at least a minute. No one made any move to speak until Hamel spoke again. In a loud voice, he called out, "Karotel has been leading the nation poorly. She has not strengthened our relations with our main ally, the people of Olmos. She has limited the Armies of the Ridge rather than support and encourage the military as we defend this great city. She has emptied our treasuries with her endeavor to build homes all along the edge of the city at the wilderness. We have hundreds of empty homes in the city. Anyone can request a home if they need one. Yet she still builds more." Hamel's voice grew louder as he railed against the Honored Matir. "Not only that, she has used the military itself to build the homes. Our soldiers must be stationed to defend the city, not work as carpenters! I said it yesterday publicly, and I declare it now; Karotel is a fool."

Hamel decided to finish off his speech with a large grin. He had acted against the Council. It was time for them to see how far he would take the matter, and it was time to see how far they would go to respond to his challenge.

Karotel, still on her feet, stood with her hands clenched. Her knuckles turned white, and she ground her teeth.

With a shake in her voice, she declared, "I will temporarily ignore the accusations against myself and this Council while we deal with the matter at hand regarding your blessing on Rezin Mariel's marriage. If that matter can be dealt with amicably, then we will address the second matter. If not, I suspect responding to the insult to this Council will not be necessary." She turned her eyes to Mariel and nodded her head.

Hamel smiled again. He had spoken publicly against the Honored Matir, yet she was both an excellent politician and a woman of honor. She did not let her emotion or pain affect her decisions or commitment.

Mariel rose to her feet while Karotel took her seat. The young woman faced Hamel and declared loud enough for all to hear, "My Patir, I wish to marry Captain Eafti Cuttel. Since he does not have a Matir, the Captain has received the blessing of the Honored Matir in order to wed. I, however, still need the blessing of my Patir. I believe Captain Cuttel to be an honorable man and…" Mariel's eyes dropped to the floor, and her voice lost all its strength. When she finished her request, she spoke in just above a whisper, and her voice shook. "I humbly request that you give your blessing for me to marry."

The Council room was silent as each Council member waited for Hamel's response. He knew he should respond with flowery, formal language, but he would not give anything to the Council. Instead, he simply said, "No."

The tension in the room increased, but Hamel stood confident. It was time to see how it would all play out.

He could hear Captain Cuttel shuffle in his place by the door. Mariel was still on her feet, but tears flowed freely again. As she cried, she continued to face him. She was a strong young lady.

The Honored Matir rose to her feet. He knew she would have to choose her words carefully. She would need to challenge Hamel, but he was still the Honored Patir of the nation. She would never challenge him publicly, at least while his honor remained.

The Honored Matir spoke using his full title. "Honored Patir Rezin Hamel, do you have a justified reason for refusing this request?"

"Because Cuttel shows himself to be a worthless young man," Hamel declared. "He makes decisions that suggest he is only seeking power. He has been raised parentless. He may appear free, but he is left to face the world alone. As the great poet Yellel wrote, a child without direction is a child who is full of selfishness and rebellion."

Karotel's eyes landed on the papers in front of her, and her fingers played across the pages. Hamel suspected she was not looking at anything in particular, but rather collecting her thoughts.

When she spoke, her voice was calm and controlled. "Do you not have a solid, objective reason for refusing her request, Honored Patir? We cannot accept generalities or opinions."

"That reason is solid enough, and I stand on it," Hamel replied. His lack of effort in providing specifics declared disdain for the people seated before him.

The Honored Matir nodded her head to declare her acceptance of his reason, and the other Council members followed suit. The matter would need to be escalated if it were to go any further.

Mariel spoke again, but this time, she looked to the Honored Matir. "I humbly request that the Council override my Patir's refusal to allow me to marry Captain Cuttel."

Mariel risked much. If the Council refused to give her what she wanted, she would be dishonored as one who could not trust the wisdom of her elders. She stood confident, but Hamel could see her face was flushed, and the tears continued to flow. He knew the tears were not for her, but for what she was about to do.

Hamel turned from Mariel to the Honored Matir. Karotel's face was serious, but he knew her well enough to see she was pleased. He knew this was exactly what she wanted. The political situation was about to change.

Karotel turned to Hamel and, with a show of great deference, offered him one more chance to change his mind. Hamel was shocked. Such a thing showed great wisdom and even greater honor. It was not required that she allow for a change of mind. The fact that she did such a thing declared that she valued his honor. If he accepted, he would retain some of his honor, but never again achieve such a position as he had held until that day. If he refused and they overrode his parental right, he would be disgraced.

"I will not change my mind, Karotel," Hamel declared. "You have declared yourself to be the fool. I will not relent. Not to you. Not to this Council. Not to anyone." Such a statement would make it easy on the Council to do what he knew they had already decided to do.

Karotel took a deep breath and said, "Then I propose the Council overrides the required blessing of Mariel's Patir and grant Honored Aide Rezin Mariel a Council blessing on her marriage to Captain Eafti Cuttel. All in favor?"

The Council members hesitated, but Hamel had left them no choice. They each raised their hands one at a time. It was unanimous. Mariel's blessing only needed to be received, and Hamel was about to be disgraced. There would be no need to deal with his speaking against the Honored Matir. The disgrace of refusing a proper request of his adopted daughter for no solid reason was greater than the insult to the Honored Matir.

"It is decided, then," Karotel said. "Mariel, you have received the Council's blessing, and it will be considered as proper as your Patir's blessing. You will be wed one week from today, if you so choose to finalize the receiving of this blessing. The Council offers you its congratulations." Karotel smiled at the young Mariel.

Mariel thanked the Honored Matir and turned back to Hamel. The matter was not yet complete.

Karotel then turned to Hamel and declared, "The Council has decided to overrule your decision. However, the blessing of your daughter will not be finalized unless tradition is fulfilled."

Hamel smiled. "Now we will see which one of us truly rules this Council, Karotel."

The entire Council, Karotel included, gasped. Hamel's motives were on the table. It was time to see where the allegiance stood.

Karotel stood silent for a moment. She appeared to be struggling to collect her thoughts, and her face flushed red. "You are… we…" she began but stopped as she stared blankly at the table before her.

Hamel nearly smiled. He enjoyed the fact that he could still surprise even Karotel.

She closed her eyes for a moment and took a deep breath before she continued. "The Council is now faced with the question of whether or not to finalize the decision. We will now act on the matter and determine if the Honored Patir Rezin Hamel will remain an Honored Patir and maintain his authority to offer the blessing or refuse it. The Council must stand and declare their position."

One by one, the Council members stood and turned their backs on Hamel. He watched as Matirs and Patirs he had mentored and led for many years chose to turn away. His mouth dropped open as each of the eleven regular Council members turned. There was only one member of the Council left: Karotel.

When it came time for Karotel to turn, she did not hesitate. Mariel, however, stood with her feet rooted to the ground. At that moment, everything rested on his youngest daughter.

Hamel smiled and spoke loudly, "You do not have quite the control you thought you did, Karotel. Your actions against me are worthless if my daughter does not approve. You are finished, Karotel."

He then looked back into the eyes of Mariel and saw not only tears but resolve. He felt his face flush, and his fingers and lips go numb. He vision blurred, and he stumbled backward at the sight.

Mariel spoke in a whisper, only loud enough for Hamel to hear, "Please, my Patir. Please change your decision. Give me my blessing. Give me my Patir's kiss. Do not make me do this." Mariel wept.

Hamel nearly gave in. He wanted to give her his blessing, but he would not. The decision had been made, and he would stand by it. He whispered back, "I am tied to you and you to me. Nothing can change that. Do what you must, my child."

His heart thumped loudly in his chest, and his own tears began to flow as she turned her back. She announced loudly, "I reject you, my Patir. I love you, but I reject you. You are no longer my Patir, and I am no longer your daughter."

The words dropped Hamel to his knees. He felt the room spin and feared for a moment that he would lose consciousness. He had known the moment would come and had planned for it, but he had not been fully prepared. The rejection was too much. He wanted to crawl away and hide.

He was pulled back by Karotel's voice. She had turned back to face him. It was time for his disgrace to be completed. Her voice shook as she spoke. "Honored Patir Rezin Hamel, you are not only rejected by your daughter, but you are declared by the Council to no longer be a Patir. You have lost your daughter. You have lost all your children. The only family you had left are now no longer yours. I hereby revoke not only your title of Honored Patir but your honored name of Rezin. You are now merely Hamel, a man without honor."

Hamel shook at the words. Most formalities were designed to speak honor into a situation, but his circumstances were beyond such a point. The words were designed to hurt.

The moment for honor, deference, and respect had passed. He was a disgrace to the people. Karotel's hands balled into fists, and she screamed, "Stand on your feet, Hamel!" There was to be no more kindness for him. "You will pay the Council the honor of their position!"

He rose to his feet. He would at least hold his dignity. He did not wipe his tears away. They were evidence of the pain he felt. He would not hide it.

Karotel turned to Cuttel. "Captain, there is a disgraced man in our midst who is wearing the crest of an Honored Patir. It brings shame to every Son and Daughter of the Ridge to allow such a thing. Please remove the crest."

Hamel turned to the Captain as he approached. It was one thing to dishonor himself, but it was immoral for a disgraced man to pretend he was a man of position within the Council Chambers.

Cuttel had a grin on his face, and he appeared quite pleased with the situation. Hamel's disgrace not only freed Karotel from living in Hamel's shadow, but Cuttel no longer had to worry about his General. Hamel's rank had not been taken away, but without his honor, his position was not much more than a formality. For Cuttel, there was more opportunity for advancement. The fact that he could wed Mariel was an added bonus.

Hamel thought he'd take another opportunity to show his disdain for the young Captain. "Stand straight, soldier! You walk like a child afraid of the wind!" It was immature to speak to him as though he was a new recruit, but it felt good to act in a childish way in such a serious moment.

Hamel's head was spinning before he knew it, and he found himself on the ground. The Captain had struck him in the side of the head.

"Stand on your feet in the presence of your betters, Hamel!" the Captain yelled.

Hamel obeyed and held his tongue. It would all be over soon.

Captain Cuttel reached up and grabbed the crest on Hamel's uniform. He yanked it violently, and the entire crest came off, along with a large section of his shirt. A few of his medals awarded over the years fell to the floor. Hamel's eyes drifted across each one, and he was struck by how worthless they had become.

"Your disgrace is complete, Hamel," Karotel said quietly, and Hamel turned to face the Honored Matir. Her hands were on the table before her, and her eyes were closed. While she appeared to be doing her best to keep her face neutral, Hamel could still sense the overwhelming grief she felt. He knew her too well. She was capable of hiding a great deal of emotion from many, but not from Hamel. He could see it all.

She continued in her quiet voice but raised her head and made eye contact with Hamel. "You are no longer welcome in the Council Chambers. Leave now on your own two feet, or the Captain will drag you out."

"I'll leave, Honored Matir," Hamel said. Without his honored position, he could not speak her name without her title.

He turned to the door and hung his head. He could feel the eyes of each member of the room on him and wondered what Mariel's expression might be. He dared not look. He did not feel he had it in him to see more of her tears.

When he reached the door, Major Ornel opened it for him, but Captain Cuttel stood in the way and would not move. Hamel walked around him, careful not to touch the officer and risk offending a man of his position. As he passed Major Ornel, the man's face expressed shock and horror. He nodded to Hamel out of respect, and Hamel returned a half-hearted grin.

Once out in the fresh air of the evening, the full impact of what had happened hit him, and he collapsed on the steps of the Council Chambers. He had been a man of honor since his youth. He had been made a General in the Armies of the Ridge at age twenty-three and named the Honored Patir, head of the Council within the same year. Hamel had been the first ever to reach the rank of General before the age of twenty-six and the first to be named both the Honored Patir of the Council and a General of the Armies of the People of the Ridge.

Now he was disgraced and worse than a common thief.

He pulled himself to his feet and descended the steps. It would be a long walk back to his house. It might take until the next day before word of his disgrace traveled to all parts of the city, but word would doubtless reach all people.

Hamel moved on at a fast walk along the road which led his house. As he moved through the streets, he wrapped his arms around himself to hide the ripped shirt and pulled his hood up over his head.

When he reached his house, he found the rooms empty and dark. Markel had cleared himself out of the guardhouse, and there was no sign he had ever been there. He knew Markel would be okay. Cuttel was a Captain in the Armies of the Ridge. He would recognize the wisdom and intellect of the young man despite the circumstances.

Hamel made his way to his bed. He would not indulge in his nightly grief or his walk through his memories. His life

45

had changed that night, and everything would be different for him moving forward. Grief was no longer an option.

He crawled into bed, and despite the disgrace, the shame, and the events of the months leading up to that point, he was at peace.

Everything had gone according to plan. The cost had been high, but he was free to go where no man of honor went.

He recited the words once again. "I am not without family. I do not face the world alone. I must continue. There is work to be done."

In moments, Hamel was sound asleep.

CHAPTER 6

THE DAY IS DIFFERENT

His nightmares were worse than usual. He awoke once again to his own screams.

Hamel sat on the edge of his small bed, his body covered in sweat. He slowed his breathing and calmed his heart.

He rubbed his hand and examined the new hole in his wall, just next to where his head had been on the pillow. He often woke up ready for a fight but never before had he thrown a punch while asleep.

His knuckles had two or three small cuts on them, but no bones were broken. He would need to be in good condition for the coming weeks. Life would not be the same moving forward.

Hamel stepped out of his house for his morning run. He decided he would not run as far that morning in the hopes that he could return home before many people were out.

He made his way down a hill near his house and along one of the main streets running through his area of the city. No one was on the streets, except for the occasional soldier. Most eyed him warily, and no one saluted him. Word had spread. He was no longer an Honored Patir. He was no longer even a Patir. Even his honored name, Rezin, given to him by his Matir, had been taken from him.

As he rounded one of the last corners, he came across two soldiers. They were both sons of men who had served under him years ago, and their adopted Patirs had each served honorably. The two soldiers, however, were of a different sort than their Patirs.

They stepped into the street and held up their hands for him to come to a halt. Their faces bore expressions of disgust and disdain.

He took a second to evaluate his options. He knew the confrontation would turn violent. He had learned to read the look in men's eyes long ago, and those two men were seeking a reason to strike him.

Hamel considered his own reputation. Since he had been disgraced and was now an outcast living among the people, his word would carry less weight than would the word of a soldier. They could not, however, kill him without a formal investigation, and he knew the judges would be fair on the matter. Murder was never tolerated and carried with it the penalty of death.

He also considered the part of his reputation which had not been lost. He was known to be a well-trained and well-disciplined soldier. No one had stood up to him in any form of strategy or combat in over twenty years. They were likely seeking not only to take out their disdain for him in a violent manner, but they were also seeking to prove themselves able to overpower the great Hamel. The confrontation was a matter of pride.

Hamel realized out of all the Soldiers of the Ridge, he would not expect any one of them to challenge him in such a way—aside from those two men. He knew of them. They had always been men of questionable honor. It was no coincidence that they were stationed there on that morning on his regular route. Cuttel was involved. The man did not miss an opportunity.

Hamel knew he could overpower both men without difficulty. He did not, however, wish to hurt them. If he did, he could be accused of attacking two soldiers and, considering the events of the previous evening, few judges would look further than the soldiers' own testimony.

Hamel had only one choice. He would let them attack, but he would not let them strike him in a way that would leave him defenseless. He would take bruises, but not debilitation.

"Good morning to you, Soldiers of the Ridge," Hamel said in the most respectful way he could, bowing to them far lower than he had bowed in many years.

"What did you say to us?" the soldier on the left yelled. "You dare speak to us with such disrespect?"

Hamel rolled his eyes. He had hoped they would at least put some effort into finding offense.

The first soldier struck him on the side of the head, and Hamel let himself hit the ground. The man had struck him in the same spot Captain Cuttel had hit him the night before. It hurt far more than he had expected it to.

He pulled himself to his feet and stepped close to the second soldier. He could see the man's knife was on his right side. The soldier was left-handed, and Hamel hoped to avoid getting hit in the same spot again.

He was pleased to find the man granted him his silent wish and hit him on the right side of his face. Since there was no bruise there, it did not hurt as much. He had been hit enough times over the years that he knew how to take a punch.

He let himself fall to the ground again in the hopes the men would feel satisfied that they had overpowered him. He began to pull himself to his feet the second time when he saw the first soldier reach for his rifle.

Rifles and sidearms were rarely used outside of battle. It was considered in poor taste to use such a weapon in a one-on-one confrontation. A soldier's strength was not decided by whether or not he or she could pull a trigger.

The fact that the man reached for it was odd, to say the least. Hamel knew the man would not shoot him. His intention would never be to murder a General. He would, however, be willing to use it as a stick with which to strike.

He could not allow himself to be hit with a rifle. A solid weapon could break bones or even break a back. He had to end the confrontation.

The soldier swung the rifle. Hamel jumped to his feet and, before the man knew what had happened, he knocked the rifle to the ground. He then grabbed each man by the collar, shoved them back against the wall, and pulled each of their knives from their sheaths.

The soldiers' mouths dropped open, and neither one moved. Their expressions suggested they had not expected to be pinned against the wall with their own blades held to their throats. Neither one looked angry. Their faces bore an expression of resignation as if they understood that Hamel had merely allowed them their victory. They had just crossed the line.

Hamel paused as the distant sound of a horn echoed across the city. The Beasts were active early that morning. The faces of each of the men betrayed their fear, not only of Hamel, but of what might come if any one of the attacks at the Valley Wall ended with the breach of the defenses. He felt his heart soften toward the two men as he recognized their concern.

"Listen very carefully," Hamel began, pulling himself back from his thoughts of the Beasts. "I have let each of you strike me, so you will have your chance to declare that you knocked Hamel to the ground. I will not, however, allow you to harm me in any way. Your weapons will not be used on me. Do you understand?"

The second soldier was the first to respond. He said, "Yes, General, we understand." The first soldier nodded his head in agreement.

"Perfect!" Hamel said with a big smile on his face. "Now that we understand each other, I will take my leave."

He tossed one blade away, grabbed each man's rifle in turn, tossed them as well, and returned to the street. He tossed the remaining knife aside and resumed his run.

Hamel smiled. The one soldier had called him "General." Though he maintained his rank, no General served over the army without honor. In the midst of the loss, that one word was good to hear.

He arrived home and went into his backyard to train. He trained hard, but only for half an hour before he stepped into his house for breakfast.

He enjoyed the quiet. While he missed Markel, it was nice to have some time simply to himself. He suspected he would have a lot of time alone in the weeks to come.

When he had finished breakfast and cleaned up for the day, he found some food, collected a small amount of money, and filled a waterskin. He then put on a cloak and stood before a mirror.

"I am not without family. I do not face the world alone. I must continue. There is work to be done."

The words felt empty. It was not as though the words were without meaning. The pain was so great, the words no longer felt as if they carried much weight in his mind.

There was work to be done. That was what mattered at the moment. He was no longer an Honored Patir. He was no longer a man with respect. He was no longer trusted. He was nothing in the eyes of the people. It was time to walk a different path.

There was work to be done.

CHAPTER 7

THE DAY LEADS DOWN

Hamel closed the front gate behind him and turned east, then north. His hood was up and fell just enough over his face to disguise him from everyone but his closest friends.

He moved down the road where he had run into the two soldiers just a short while before. The shift had changed, and two new soldiers stood at attention, watching carefully for any threats to the nation and any danger to its people.

His mind drifted back to the two men who had challenged him. He smiled at the memory. Somehow the whole situation seemed funny.

The road to the lower sections of the city was much like all the other roads: up and down. It continued like that for three miles through the city before it made a steep decline. The lower sections were filled with all those without honor as Hamel was now. Everyone from thieves to murderers lived and worked out of the lower sections.

Hamel had not been in that area for many years. When he was seventeen and apprenticing under his adopted Matir, Rezin Mathel, she had taken him down there one day to show him parts of the city he had not even known existed. She hoped that he would find a way to address what she had called the "pain" of the area. He had not understood at the time what she was talking about, but then came to realize how much the people of the lower sections were hurting. When he had become Honored Patir, he had invested much time in addressing some of the violence and despair that existed in the lower sections, but there was much more to be done.

On that first visit, many years before, he had been appalled by what he had seen. His Matir had introduced him to a man who had been disgraced. He and Mathel had spoken with the man at length. While his Matir had shown compassion and interest, Hamel had been disgusted by what he saw.

Many years had passed since that day, and he no longer felt such arrogance. In addition to the change in his heart, his own circumstances had become similar to that man. He wished for a few more minutes to speak with him, but the Dusk would have taken him decades before.

The point where the lower sections began was a very abrupt change from the upper sections. While in the upper section, buildings were well cared for—even the empty ones. The buildings in the lower sections were not. The walls were cracked, and some roofs had holes in them.

The people he saw on the streets did not walk in peace but moved warily with each step. Few of the men, women or children were without marks on their bodies, either from sickness or injury.

Now and then he would pass a man or a woman screaming out in fear or anger. The older ones, some appearing as old as thirty-three or even thirty-four, those who were well set upon by the Dusk, were lying on the side of the road. They called out for loved ones to either help them or yelled at people who were no longer there. No one came to their aid.

The cloak he had chosen to wear was far from clean or in good repair. He had selected that cloak because of its age and poor condition and had even added some rips and dirt in preparation for his journey. He wished to pass unknown and unrecognized for at least part of the day.

On one level, he knew he would be well accepted and even celebrated by some in the lower regions after his disgrace. Others, however, would see him as an enemy. He did not want to have to navigate either for the time being.

He wanted to familiarize himself with the area. While he had been down in the lower sections many times as an Honored Patir or in his role as General, it was a bit of a maze to most people. He had studied old maps of the area to understand the layout of that area of the city, but even so, much had changed since the maps had been drawn. Entire blocks of buildings had come down while streets and walkways had been closed off with new buildings. Where there had been a garden, there might be a market. Where there had been a fountain, there might be a series of poorly built homes.

The man he was looking for was named Eddel. Eddel fancied himself a man of great honor and had titled himself, Patir Eddel. The thought of calling such a man "Patir" turned Hamel's stomach, but the situation required him to overcome his bias.

Hamel wandered the streets for most of the morning. Three times he found himself the victim of an attempted robbery. Two of the times, the men who attempted to steal from Hamel regretted their action immediately. On the third time, it was a young child, and Hamel had let him go.

He wandered throughout the day and into the evening. When it came time to sleep, he did not make his way home again. He found an inn of sorts and paid for a room. He had never spent the night in such a place before. The smell alone was enough to drive him away, but he remained.

When he entered his rented room, there was already a man sleeping in the bed. The man did not wake while Hamel carried him into the hallway and set him gently in a corner.

The furniture in the room was old, broken, and scratched, but it served his purpose well. He used some of it to secure the room for the night and, once he felt the door was well barricaded, he used the blankets, a pillow, and a broken lamp to create the shape of his body on the bed. When he was finished, he looked on with satisfaction on the shape of a sleeping "Hamel."

He was a stranger in the area, and a stranger could mean money. He could take no chances. He settled in a corner just to the right of the door, dozing off behind a broken wardrobe.

When the three men came in, they did not hesitate. The door smashed open, and the furniture fell out of the way. Two men fired three shots each into the man-shaped pile before the third approached the bed and pulled back the covers.

Hamel did not like to kill, but he suspected the three men would not let the matter go if he merely incapacitated them. He also needed to get the attention of Patir Eddel sooner rather than later.

Hamel stepped from behind the wardrobe and drove the man nearest him headfirst into the stone wall. The second man fell to Hamel's knife and the third to his own sidearm, once Hamel had disarmed the man.

As he left the three bodies behind, he made sure not one lay in a position that suggested they had died peacefully. A message needed to be sent.

Hamel stepped into the street and breathed in the early morning air. It would be another beautiful day.

He set off down the street as the sun began to rise. He had packed enough food for a day and a half—enough to carry him through the mid-day meal. He did not care to find food in the lower sections until he better understood the situation. Poison was a lot more difficult to deal with than three untrained men he could face in battle.

CHAPTER 8

THE DAY OF CUTTEL

Once Hamel had explored the lower sections well enough that he felt he understood a portion of the layout, he finished the last of his food and wandered into an open-air market he had discovered the day before. He chose a table to approach, one selling rusted armor, discarded swords, and knives. As he examined what appeared to be a well-made, but poorly maintained, ancient dagger with a cracked handle, he reached up to scratch his head, and his hood fell back onto his shoulders.

He grabbed the hood and pulled it back up over his head, but in that short time, the merchant at the table recognized him. The man quickly whispered something to a little boy sitting on a stool against a wall, and the boy ran off into an alley.

He scanned the people present in the market area. Gossip spread quickly in the lower sections, just as it did in the upper sections of the city. He could see people glance his way. They tried to appear as though they were busy with other matters, but all attention had landed on him.

No one had ever fallen from the height of Honored Patir, former Head of the Council, and General of the Armies of the Ridge. Due to the honor of his former status, the depth of his shame would be that much greater. He was not sure what the people of the lower regions would think of him.

Eddel, on the other hand, was a different story. He knew he could be useful to Eddel, and Eddel could be useful to him. But he would need to be careful.

A commotion on the other side of the market pulled Hamel from his thoughts. People had begun to run and hide, and some merchants were packing up their wares in a panic. At first, he wondered what could have caused such a change, but then he remembered seeing the same reaction to himself as a General on his visits through the area.

Soldiers were approaching.

Around the corner came eight Soldiers of the Ridge and a servant with his head hung low. The young man trailing behind the soldiers was poor Markel. Hamel felt a twinge of guilt when he saw his friend, but he knew it was the best place for the boy to be.

The man at the front of the eight soldiers was the Captain himself. He stood on the edge of the market and turned his head around as if he were scanning the area. A man Hamel did not recognize stepped up beside Cuttel and pointed at Hamel. The Captain dropped a coin in the man's hands, and the man disappeared around the corner.

Hamel smiled and pulled back his hood. He hollered across the street, "So, Captain, I see you have been looking for me. Have you come to apologize?"

Cuttel ignored the taunt. "Hamel!" he shouted, declaring to all how far Hamel had fallen.

"Yup. That's me, Cuttel! How have you been, young man?"

Cuttel smiled. "I did not come to apologize," Cuttel announced. "I only came to see if you were settling in well, and if so," the young Captain smirked, "to see if I could change that."

The Captain's head turned, and he scanned the faces of the men and women present in the market. He stopped when he spotted a man standing in the shadows. Cuttel nodded to him, and the man waved at two others. The three approached the Captain.

The Captain paid the men what appeared to be a significant amount of money. Hamel did not think the men had been hired to leave bruises or teach him a lesson. The men intended to end Hamel's legacy.

Hamel's eyes turned to Markel. The young man stood ready. His feet were shoulder width apart, his knees bent just slightly, and his fists clenched. The boy was ready to fight on a word from Hamel. Hamel gave a slight shake of the head. Markel would follow Hamel's orders to stay with the Captain, even at the expense of Hamel's life.

"I wish you the best, Hamel, son of Rezin Mathel. I hope you enjoy your time with my friends." With that final word along with a laugh from his soldiers, the Captain turned and left the market.

Hamel turned his attention back to the three men. The two who followed the man Cuttel had paid were not a concern. Their walk was confident but revealed a lack of the military training that set soldiers apart. Each man had an angry, unkind look on his face, but angry men were often easier to overcome in a fight. The one who concerned Hamel was the leader.

Hamel had always been a tall man. He had also trained harder than any other soldier he had ever met, and that effort had only increased since his retirement ten years before. The training and years of experience had left him a solid threat to anyone who challenged him.

The thug Cuttel had hired, however, was also tall and had a disturbing amount of muscle. The man walked as if the muscle itself was getting in his way. Hamel wondered if his own bulk made him look so awkward.

The man's walk also suggested he had been trained as a soldier. The confident way he eyed Hamel caused the former Honored Patir to suspect the thug had also received the same elite training Hamel had received.

He examined the hired thug's face and searched his memory. The man had indeed served under him a year or two before. If he remembered correctly, the man had been discharged for violent and uncontrollable behavior. He thought his name had been Gatrel.

Gatrel was the threat.

Hamel positioned himself against the wall of a large building. He would not run, but he would not be surrounded either.

Hamel's military mind kicked into gear, and he put together his strategy. It was simple and would guarantee he had a decent chance. The two "extras," as he deemed them, would only be a threat if they were able to take part in his fight with Gatrel. Hamel would have to dispose of them before he would stand a chance. Gatrel was younger and perhaps faster than Hamel, but not as well trained or disciplined. If Hamel could face him alone, he might live to meet Eddel.

The two extras would not expect him to attack first, nor would they expect to be his first target. They would assume Hamel would focus on Gatrel, and they stepped off to each side.

Hamel kept his eyes on the large former soldier. Intimidation was always part of a battle.

His mind drifted to the rest of the people in the market Square, and he smiled. The men, women, and children in the market all acted as though nothing was out of the ordinary, yet they all watched Hamel. Some knelt on the ground as though they were tying their shoes but never managed to finish. Others picked items off tables and turned them in their hands, eyes fixed firmly on the four men about to fight. Some merchants even stood with their hands outstretched as though they were waiting to receive money from customers, but neither they nor their customers moved to finish the transactions.

Hamel reviewed his strategy in his mind. He would go for the throats of each of the two extras. If he moved quickly, he could incapacitate them and then find his way around behind Gatrel. A glint of steel near Gatrel's hands revealed not only was Gatrel right-handed, but Hamel would need to deal with the knife early on. Hamel saw similar weapons emerge with each of the other two extras.

The three men stepped within reach, and Hamel put his plan into action. He had always been adept at reading people and knowing how they would react given certain stimuli. He had trained himself well to lay out a plan and execute it perfectly without hesitation.

Hamel feinted to the left, and the extra on his right charged. Hamel disarmed him, killed him quickly, then tossed his body onto Gatrel. While Gatrel struggled under the weight of his fallen comrade, Hamel killed the man on the left, then drove his knife into Gatrel's right arm. A man in shock was never a threat.

Seconds later, it was all over.

Hamel scanned his eyes over the market area to confirm there were no other men ready to attack. He stood alone, and he could see in the eyes of the people milling around the market, pretending they had not noticed a fight, that he had earned a certain level of respect. He had lost his honor among the upper sections of the city, but honor would be found in the lower sections, albeit along a different path.

Cuttel's little stunt might have been just what Hamel needed to find his way into Eddel's trust.

CHAPTER 9

THE DAY TURNS CRIMINAL

Hamel made his way through the market and turned down a side street. In his study of the maps of the lower regions, along with his journey through the area over the last day, he thought he would find several open streets. He wanted to move. He hoped he could give the impression he did not want to be found, even though that was exactly what he wanted.

It did not take long. As he moved through the lower sections, Hamel glanced behind him now and then to see if anyone had followed him. No one stood out at first, but in time, he recognized a man he had seen in the market while he had faced off against Cuttel's men.

Hamel turned right down a side street, then into an alley. Coming out into a new street, he turned right again and doubled back to the same street where he had noticed the man. The man continued to walk ten paces behind him the entire way.

It was time to take matters to the next level. Eddel would be interested in Hamel, but perhaps not convinced Hamel would be a good man to bring into the fold.

He found his way to a table where a man was selling what appeared to be broiled rat meat. Hamel was not hungry enough to eat rat but wanted a place where he could pause to let the man following him get a little closer. When the man was only two or three paces away, Hamel turned and faced him.

The man jumped but managed to regain his composure and pretend he was just out for a stroll. When he tried to pass Hamel, the former Honored Patir grabbed the man and twisted his arm behind his back.

The man cried out in pain, and Hamel noticed two other men in the street tense up. There were three men following him.

"Why are you following me?" Hamel asked in his most cheerful voice. "I understand that I am quite entertaining to watch, and it must be thrilling to see a man who has lost as much honor as I have wander the streets in despair, but I don't particularly like being followed."

The man groaned and said, "I'm not following you. I'm…" but his words were cut off by a cry of pain as Hamel twisted the man's arm violently.

"Do you think I haven't noticed you behind me? Do you think I can't see there are two other men with you?" Hamel asked in the same happy, cheerful voice. He had learned many years ago that an unexpected tone of voice was a perfect interrogation tool.

The man relaxed, and Hamel could see the corner of his lips creep upward. "If you see the other men with me, you know that I could call them to come to my aid," the man said with a chuckle in his voice. "Maybe you should let go, and we'll let you walk away with only a few bruises."

Hamel laughed and said loudly enough for the other two men to hear. "Wonderful! I would relish another opportunity to stretch my muscles a little bit and apply some of that old military training you hear so much about these days." He then leaned in and said in his most sinister and threatening voice, "Were you not in the market an hour ago? If you were, you would know that you would be dead before

62

your friends arrived. You would also know that they would likely die as well. Now, you have two choices. You can either tell me who sent you to follow me or not."

"What if I don't?" the man asked. His voice betrayed curiosity, but also fear.

Hamel paused. He had thought the threat was obvious, but perhaps the man did not know what he was capable of. "If you don't, I'll break your arm and move on to the next man." For added effect, he twisted just a bit harder.

The man groaned again in pain and said, "Patir Eddel sent me. He's curious about you."

Hamel pretended to be surprised. "Patir Eddel? I've heard of him. Why would he be curious about me?"

"I don't know! I just go where the Patir tells me," the man replied.

"What's your name?" Hamel asked.

The man hesitated for a moment, but then replied, "Armel."

Hamel was inclined to think Armel was telling the truth, at least about Patir Eddel. He had to be careful. He needed to prove he was dangerous and therefore useful to Eddel, but at the same time, to harm one of Eddel's men on the street would be foolish and could alienate him from the criminal. It could even turn him into a target. Hamel knew he could stand against anyone Eddel sent against him, but he could only defend against what he saw coming. A bullet or a knife in a crowd could put a quick end to his plans.

He let Armel go and gave him a little push away. Eddel's thug turned and rubbed his shoulder while he looked at Hamel with both fear and disdain.

Hamel tossed a money purse to the man. While he had been holding him, he had slipped his hand into Armel's pocket and pulled out the man's purse. It was something his Matir had taught him about intimidation. "It is helpful when dealing with men of fear to surprise them with the unexpected," she had told him. "Do something they don't expect, but act like what you did was exactly what you always do. It will leave them thinking you are far more dangerous than they had once thought."

He did not typically slip people's money out of their pocket, but it had the desired effect. The man caught the purse and the fear, mixed with confusion, was written all over his face.

Hamel then declared, "Let Patir Eddel know I'm willing to meet with him."

The man nodded his head and left without saying another word. Armel waved to the other two men, and they followed him out of sight.

Hamel turned back toward the marketplace. He knew he shouldn't, but deep down inside, he was enjoying himself. He smiled and decided to head back home. He had accomplished what he had intended. The next day he expected to meet Eddel, but before that meeting, he wanted to clean up and find some food.

He moved on down the street as another horn blast sounded. The Beasts were attacking yet again, and it reminded him of the urgency of his plan.

CHAPTER 10

THE DAY FINDS EDDEL

The next morning, Hamel awoke at his usual time. He decided not to go for a run, but to spend the extra time in exercise and training in the yard behind his house. There was privacy within his walls. He could push himself to maintain his strength and be prepared for what lay ahead.

He assumed "Patir" Eddel was either looking for him or frustrated that he had returned home for the night. He expected the man would be anxious to meet him but unwilling to come to the upper sections of the city. Once Hamel knew Eddel wanted to meet, he was content to let the criminal wait.

Hamel cleaned up and had a full breakfast. He wasn't sure it would be safe to eat or drink anything in Eddel's presence or from the lower sections, so he packed some food and water. Many would not think twice about using poison to rid the world of the former Honored Patir. It was difficult to protect himself against that kind of thing, other than not to eat anything. He would eat his own food until he felt he could trust Eddel.

His full pack was well hidden under his cloak. He had enough to get him through at least two days, maybe more if he rationed. He also made sure he carried only enough money to get him through that time.

He thought his house would be safe. The area was well patrolled and, while there were few left who held any respect for Hamel, the soldiers would not tolerate thieves—even if they were targeting Hamel's home.

He packed up, secured a dagger to his side, and left for the lower sections. The coming days would be a new experience for him. He had never lived among thieves, murderers, and assassins.

Hamel made his way down toward the market area where he had run into Cuttel and his thugs. His mind thought through his upcoming meeting with Eddel, but he did not have enough information to lay out a definite plan. He did not even know what the man looked like, his age, or the extent of his influence.

Hamel went over the full name, "Patir Eddel," in his mind. He needed to grow accustomed to using the honorific for the man. The man was anything but worthy of such a title, but Hamel had no choice but to earn the man's trust and insert himself into a favored position with the man if he were to accomplish his plans.

Hamel entered the market before mid-morning and made his way to a table. The tall, thin merchant was selling bags made from what appeared to be old clothing. The material was worn and ripped in many places and covered with patches. As he looked through the bags, he found many had patches sewn on top of patches.

He had never quite come to grips with why there was so much poverty in the lower sections. There were plenty of empty homes for the taking in the upper sections. There was always work available. The army was always looking to take anyone who was hard working and dedicated.

Hamel's thoughts were interrupted by the sight of two men making their way toward him. He kept his head down but watched them out of the corner of his eye. As they walked through the market area, people stepped to the side and gave them plenty of space. They were his escort.

"Beautiful day today," Hamel said loudly before he turned his head to look at the men. From the expressions on their faces, Hamel suspected neither man was ready to engage in friendly conversation… or capable of such an action.

The man on the left hesitated before announcing, "The Patir would like to speak with you. Follow us."

"Yes, it is a beautiful day. Thank you for noticing," Hamel replied loudly. He wasn't entirely sure why he would try to provoke the men, but he did feel civility and tradition were both noble practices, and if they would not respond, he would.

The man looked at him with confusion in his eyes and said, "No, I didn't ask you if it was a nice day. I said the Patir would like to speak with you."

Hamel recognized a man well-endowed with muscle, but poorly equipped with intelligence. He decided not to bother wasting his time with activities such as conversation. There were simpler, easier activities in which the man would be ready to engage.

"Lead the way, young man," Hamel said.

Each man turned and walked off through the market. As they traveled through street after street, they made their way deeper into the lower sections. The Ridge Capital had once been home to many thousands more inhabitants than currently lived in the city and, as such, there was more space than the people could use. It also meant there was plenty of room for criminals, such as Eddel, to annex areas for their own purposes.

As they moved through the city, Hamel's stomach lurched as the horn blast sounded yet again. It was not often the Beasts attacked so early in the day. No one in the streets seemed to notice or care that an attack was about to take place, but it made Hamel want to tell the men to hurry up. He knew it would make little difference for that day, but he longed to find the answers he sought.

The frequency of attacks had increased over the years and months to the point where any attack could result in the breach of their walls. Hamel had often envisioned hundreds of Beasts rushing through the streets. The death toll would be…

He pushed the thought of a failed defense out of his mind. The matter had to be dealt with, regardless of the cost, and it would be, but he had to take one step at a time.

The way to Eddel's headquarters led them into an alley that ran between two buildings. The two structures were built so close together, the men had to walk single-file. Not far above his head hung a cloth that ran the entire distance of the alley. It gave the feeling that they were moving through a dark, dangerous area. At the far end, their way was blocked by a curtain. The man in front reached out and parted the cloth.

The two men stepped through the opening, and Hamel followed. What he saw on the other side shocked him.

Most of the lower sections were dirty and the streets full of garbage. The smell was atrocious, and no one wore anything other than rags or dirty clothes. The area he stepped into, however, was entirely different.

The area was vast. Hamel figured four or five buildings may have been torn down to make room for such a large courtyard. Most of the area was covered in a beautiful lawn. There were benches for sitting or the odd fountain here or there. The walls around the area were made up of buildings, but they looked to be in pristine condition. The people in the area, aside from the two men who had led Hamel there, were well dressed and clean.

He had walked into a world inside a world. There was nothing about Eddel's domain that resembled the other areas in the lower sections in any way. It was very much like some of the parks in the upper sections.

The only difference Hamel could see was in the eyes of the people. They smiled, yet did not appear happy. They stood as though they were relaxed, yet their posture was clearly a pretense. Even the children played as though they lived in constant fear. They played on the grass, but their eyes never settled. They continually looked around as if they feared some imminent threat.

Hamel wondered briefly if they were afraid because he had arrived. His reputation before his disgrace was as a man of focus, strength, and courage. If they considered that alongside his new, growing reputation as a man of defiance and brutality, they might fear he could be a real threat to them.

He did not, however, suspect he was the cause of their fear. There was something else that weighed on their hearts. He decided to be even more careful with Patir Eddel.

"This way!" one of the men called out. The other man had not yet spoken a word. He did not give the impression that speaking was his thing.

"Lead the way," Hamel declared. He put a bit of authority into his voice for those who watched.

The men complied and led through the middle of the courtyard. Hamel noticed the children scurry out of the way, while the adults found other places to stand.

Half-way through the courtyard, Hamel looked into the eyes of a young boy. The boy could not have been more than six or seven, but his cheeks were sunken, and his eyes were filled with terror. Across his face were bruises and cuts, some fresh, some old.

He sat on his Matir's knees, and she stroked his hair; her vacant eyes set on some point not in the courtyard. They were the only two who did not run from the presence of the two men, but Hamel suspected it was not because of courage. The young woman's mind was elsewhere.

The boy's eyes met Hamel's, and the former Honored Patir came to a stop. The abuse the boy had suffered was unthinkable. Hamel had never faced such a thing before and struggled to believe it could be true. He started to come up with other reasons why the boy was as bruised as he was, but as a soldier, he knew the look of someone who had received a beating.

His Matir's skin was pale, and her eyes lifeless. Her compassion shown to her son in the stroking of his hair was a testament to her love for her child, but there was no hope for the Matir and son in that place.

"Move!" one of the men hollered.

Hamel turned his head and scowled at the man. Worse things were going on in the lower sections than he had thought. He promised himself he would not forget the boy or his mother. While he could not address the situation that day, he would return when his plan had run its course.

The men walked through an ornately carved door into a small room which led only to another door. Standing on either side of the inner doorway were two new men. They appeared as friendly and talkative as his current escort, both of whom had taken up positions behind him. The men demanded Hamel pull back his hood.

He obliged, and the two men in front stood still, their eyes examining Hamel's face. One of the men growled, "You cannot carry any weapons into your meeting with the Patir. I'll need to search you."

Hamel had already suspected such a thing would happen. As he had walked with the first two men, he had evaluated their skills, training, and strength. He did not suspect either one had any military training, nor were they prepared to use their brain in a fight.

"I am carrying a dagger. I will keep it with me when I go into this meeting. This is non-negotiable," Hamel declared.

Confusion played across the faces of the two men in front, and he could hear the two men behind shift on their feet. He wasn't sure if their confusion was because he had refused their demand, or if they struggled to understand the word, "non-negotiable." He decided to wait it out.

After another ten seconds or so, the man at the door announced, "Kill him."

Hamel had decided not to use his dagger. He didn't think Patir Eddel would appreciate losing four men. He did, however, want to impress Eddel. If they were to work together, he wanted a healthy respect.

He took three of the men down in seconds and knocked the fourth back against the door. Hitting the door was intentional. He wanted anyone on the other side to know there was a fight going on. He grabbed the man as he was recovering and twisted him around. The room was small, and it was difficult to move with three bodies strewn on the floor.

He scanned the door in front of him and saw that it did not appear solid, so he ran the man as hard as he could

70

into the door in the hopes of smashing it open. He felt that throwing a man through the door would be a fantastic way to make an entrance.

The man bounced off the door and fell to the ground unconscious. Hamel nearly groaned in disappointment. He had imagined walking through the splintered remains of the door, brushing off a few small pieces of wood as he stepped over the body of the unconscious guard.

He accepted the fact that he would have to settle for "underwhelming" instead. He decided to knock before he opened the door. If he could not go for overwhelming, he might as well add a bit of fun to the situation. "Hello!" he hollered out in a cheerful voice before turning the handle.

The door opened into the room, and he did his best to pretend that he wasn't worried at all about what lay on the other side. He stepped into the room and brushed off his cloak from any dust or dirt that might have collected on it.

The room was large and contained ten people—six men and four women. The man he suspected was Eddel was sitting on a couch, against the far wall. The other five men appeared to be in the room because of their talent for building muscle. Each of the five stood with rifles aimed at Hamel.

None of the men scared Hamel. There wasn't much hope of getting past the rifles. The men stood only two paces away. It would be difficult for them to miss. He did not, however, think Eddel wanted him dead.

The women, however, turned his stomach. A quick glance at them told him something was terribly wrong. Not one raised their eyes from the floor, and each of the four appeared to be less "woman" and more "property." Hamel had never seen such a thing before, but the image was clear.

The situation he had witnessed with the people in the courtyard began to make sense. They were not free.

He gathered his thoughts and said with a big smile on his face, "Hello there! I apologize for the condition of the four men in the entrance. They had forgotten their manners, but I took care of it." He paused for a few seconds and then said as he glanced around at the men with rifles, "I'm looking to meet the Patir named Eddel."

The five men remained motionless while the man on the couch and the four women sat in silence. Finally, the man Hamel suspected of being Eddel spoke up. His voice was quiet and raspy as he commanded, "Lower your weapons and get the good Hamel a chair. I'd like to speak to him."

The men relaxed and slung the rifles over their shoulders. They retrieved a chair from the side of the room, and Hamel sat down opposite Eddel.

"Everyone leave the room. I'd like to have a conversation with my guest," Eddel said.

All the men hesitated. Hamel couldn't see any of them as they were all behind him but suspected they were glancing back at the four men groaning on the floor in the entranceway.

"Hamel," Eddel began, "are you going to harm me?"

Hamel paused for a moment. He had four reasons why he wanted to kill Eddel. Each reason had walked out of the room a moment before with her eyes on the floor. He reminded himself of the urgency of his mission and said, "No, Patir Eddel, not today."

The criminal smiled and said to the men standing behind Hamel, "You see? I'll be fine. A man such as Hamel will not lie. It would be dishonoring to do so, and he will not quickly choose that path. Oh, and remove those four men and close the entrance to this room. I don't enjoy listening to them groan as they wake up."

Hamel waited while the men removed the four unconscious guards, closed the door, and exited. As he sat, he examined the man sitting on the couch before him. Eddel was not entirely what he had expected.

Eddel was old. He was very old. From the nearly complete lack of hair, the white, ashy skin, and the sunken cheeks, it was clear that Eddel was well along in his Dusk. His hands shook, and his voice had grown raspy. Those two symptoms always came near the end. The last sign that the Dusk was about to take a man or woman was their breathing grew ragged and they slipped in and out of lucidity. He estimated the man was well into his thirty-fourth year.

"I suppose you are curious as to why I would want to meet you, Hamel," Eddel began, interrupting Hamel's thoughts.

Hamel smiled. He had not needed to wait long. "It has crossed my mind, Patir."

Eddel's lips curled upward, and he slowly said, "I'm surprised to hear you call me Patir. That's three times now you have used my title. People of the upper sections do not believe such a title can be awarded to a man like myself."

"It is true, Patir Eddel," Hamel said, "but as you can see, I am no longer a man of the upper sections of the city."

"You still live up there," Eddel replied.

"Yes. It is a useful indulgence," Hamel said.

"Indeed it would be," Eddel replied. He appeared to choose his words carefully. "I asked you here for several reasons, actually. Perhaps some of them you can guess."

Hamel kept silent at first but could see Eddel was waiting for him to speak. To make a guess at that point could give too much away. Instead, he said, "Perhaps, but I'm here more to learn than anything."

"Yes," Eddel replied. "You are certainly an Honored Patir through and through."

Hamel felt shame wash over him. Eddel's words were a reminder of all he had lost, and all he had gone through. He hoped the sacrifice and risk was worth it. He responded with a simple nod of his head.

"I'll lay it all out for you," Eddel said. "Here's what I want. You have certain skills and talents that I believe I can make use of, and there is information you might have that I want."

"Is that so?" Hamel replied.

Eddel's eyes bore into Hamel as though he were trying to read the older man's expression. "Yes, it is so. Your skills, for example, are impressive. First, most of the men I have working for me are nothing more than muscle. They're strong and intimidating, but they're stupid. You know as well as I do that their lack of intelligence is part of what allowed you to take out the first three men and then nearly throw the fourth man through the door. That would have been quite the entrance, by the way," Eddel explained.

Hamel grimaced. He still felt a little disappointed that it had not worked. He hadn't realized Eddel had figured out Hamel was trying to make a dramatic entrance. He found his respect for the man increased, but only a little.

Eddel continued, "So, I need someone of your intelligence who can help my men think a little more soundly. I need my organization to be more strategic in our approach to what we are doing."

Hamel slowly nodded his head. There were limits to what he would offer to Eddel. He would also only go so far in helping the man when it came to the security of the nation and the safety of people, but it would be worth it if Eddel had what he was after.

There was one problem, however. The man was well along in his Dusk. From what Hamel could see, he was only a few months at the most from the end. If Eddel was after money and power, he would not be able to use either.

He hesitated before raising the issue of Eddel's Dusk. Such a topic was sensitive unless the person experiencing the Dusk brought it up.

Eddel smiled and said, "Let me take a guess, Hamel. You are considering the fact that I am nearing the end. The Dusk is upon me, and my setting is near. You are wondering why I would seek money and power when I will not live to enjoy it. Am I right?"

Hamel smiled a genuine smile. He appreciated a man who was forthright and intelligent. If circumstances had been different, he thought he and Eddel could have been friends.

Eddel reminded Hamel of Pulanomos. His Olmosite friend was long dead, but the memory was still strong. His heart yearned for those days.

"That's exactly what I was thinking," Hamel replied. "I did not want to be rude and raise the matter myself. So, tell me, why would you be interested in power and money when you are at your end?"

"That's where you come in, Hamel," Eddel said with a big smile on his face.

Hamel's mind raced through the possibilities of what Eddel could mean. He could not imagine what he might have to offer Eddel in such a situation. "I don't understand how I might help in that area," Hamel said.

"Well, Hamel, my physicians tell me that I'm not going to make it more than a couple months at most. I've lived thirty-four years, which is more than many people get. The average is thirty-three years and eleven months. Did you know that?"

"I did, Patir Eddel." It was common knowledge.

"So, everyone dies at thirty-three or thirty-four," Eddel continued. "Everyone, that is, except you."

Hamel braced himself. He was certain they were alone, but that did not mean Eddel wasn't armed. As far as he could tell, there were two possibilities: Eddel wanted to know if Hamel could tell him how he survived, or Eddel wanted his physicians to experiment on Hamel to see if they could find out why he survived when everyone else died.

Hamel decided to address both matters right away. He raised his hand as if to stop Eddel and said, "I wish I could tell you how to avoid the Dusk. When we first realized the Dusk had missed me, I had doctors and researchers lining up to experiment on me. They spent years interviewing me, testing my blood, paying attention to the food I ate and more. Eventually, they grew bored with the research as they found nothing to explain it."

"So, you have no idea," Eddel rasped. His face filled with disappointment.

"No, no idea. After all the research, the only thing we walked away with was a hypothesis."

"What might that have been?" Eddel asked, leaning forward.

"We had always assumed that we only lived thirty-three or thirty-four years. We believed that was how long life lasted. The common belief was that our bodies came to a point where they were done living, and the Dusk came upon us. Like the sun, there is a time of dawn and a time of dusk, just before the setting."

"Yes, I know all that," Eddel said. He leaned forward a little more. "What was the hypothesis?"

"One of the researchers suggested that our life spans were not thirty-three or thirty-four years, but either much longer or perhaps even limitless. He suggested the reason we die is not that we are at the end of our lives, but because the Dusk comes upon us. It would then suggest that the Dusk is not merely a natural occurrence but a sickness," Hamel said.

"Interesting," Eddel said and leaned back on his couch. "Interesting. So, if it is a sickness, then the sickness could potentially be cured. Then, all of us might live on as you have."

"Yes, that is the hypothesis, but that is all it is. They then turned their attention to the Dusk to see if they could find why it came upon people. They examined me to see why I might be immune to a disease so common." Hamel paused for effect and let his eyes drift to the floor. "Even so, it is just a hypothesis. It was just a guess."

"Yes, I suppose it was," Eddel said as he leaned back on the couch. "But if one were to have such a cure, they could watch their children grow up. They could rise to a position of great power and influence in Ridge Nation and continue to lead and influence for many, many years."

Hamel didn't think it had been necessary to mention his children or to draw attention to the fact that Hamel had been disgraced and lost his position of power and influence. The pain of the Council Meeting just a few short days before was still fresh on his mind. He assumed, however, that Eddel was either seeking a reaction or trying to hurt. He decided it would be best to give Eddel what he wanted.

"It is true I have benefited in terms of my influence. But to live on without one's wife and children is a fate too cruel for anyone, Patir," Hamel replied.

"Yes, and you have even lost your adopted son and daughters as well. I do not think either of your daughters will have anything to do with you again," Eddel said.

Hamel lowered his eyes and let a tear roll down his cheek. The tear was both necessary for the moment and real.

"Interesting…" Eddel said.

"What is interesting, Patir?" Hamel asked.

Eddel smiled and said, "You were one of the most honored and revered men in history, yet you still call me Patir. Not only that, I point out some of the most painful and deeply hurtful experiences and losses of your life, and you do not attack. You hold both your tongue and your fists."

"Of course, Patir Eddel," Hamel began. "I have been disgraced and declared to be a man without honor, but that does not mean I am a man without honor. I will act as befits a man of honor."

"So, you expect to return to your former role?" Eddel asked.

"One day. One way or another, I will once again be Honored Patir Rezin Hamel," Hamel promised. "But for now, I am content to be a man of honor on the inside while I bide my time."

Eddel nodded. He took a deep breath and fell into a coughing fit. Once he had recovered, he spoke again in his raspy voice. "Hamel, it seems to me that having a man of your skill, experience, and insight on hand would be advantageous. Will you work for me?" Eddel asked.

Hamel could see Eddel did not expect any answer other than yes. He suspected the man would not let him walk out of the room alive if Hamel did not agree. "I will work with you."

"Will you commit to serve me and my successors your entire life?" Eddel asked.

Hamel quickly thought through his options. He could not commit to serving Eddel or his successors forever. There were limits to what he would be open to doing. In addition to that, once he regained his position as Honored Patir, he would not be in debt to a criminal. He decided to take his chances.

"No," Hamel replied. "I will serve alongside you for as long as it is beneficial to both of us."

Eddel laughed. "If you had agreed, I would have had my men kill you. I would know you were lying to me in a promise, and I would never be able to trust you." Eddel coughed and then said, "Welcome to our organization, Hamel. Perhaps if we cannot stave off the Dusk, you will be running this enterprise in a few months."

"Perhaps," Hamel said as the two men shook hands.

CHAPTER 11

THE DAY TO LEARN

Hamel spent the following week settling in and becoming an essential member of Patir Eddel's organization. He found the thugs and various employees avoided him or grumbled under their breath for the first few days. He even had four confrontations, each of which contributed to a new level of respect for him by Eddel's "employees." Most of the men wavered between distrust for him and amusement with the idea of a disgraced Honored Patir serving a criminal.

Eddel, however, gave the men the impression of complete trust in Hamel's abilities and loyalty. Hamel had the freedom to move about the lower sections and go anywhere he wished. Word spread that he was Eddel's replacement and by the end of the week, everyone gave him a wide berth.

Eddel did not, however, trust Hamel with everything. Such reservation was expected. He would have thought Eddel a fool to trust him without question. Listening to the man dance around certain topics or change the subject if the conversation delved too deeply into the organization's strengths, weaknesses, and ongoing activities gave Hamel confidence that he was only being used.

Hamel did not mind being used by Eddel. There were lines Hamel would not cross. Eddel's reservations helped to remind Hamel that they were both seeking a benefit from the relationship and each keeping their own secrets. They were using one another.

Eddel had assigned thirty men to Hamel's instruction. Hamel was to teach them to fight as a Ridge Elite soldier. He was also assigned three men to teach them war strategy and how to defend the Valley Wall.

It wasn't long before Hamel could see Eddel sought to take over the Council, the military, and the entire upper sections of the city. Hamel would not contribute to such treason, but he had no fear of such a thing coming to pass.

The men assigned to him for both training and strategy were far from capable. He knew he could pour into most of them for weeks, months, or even years, and they would never reach the level of even young Markel. Hamel was also very selective on what he taught them. They learned enough to think they were gaining the skills needed to control the Ridge Nation, but Hamel's training ensured they would never succeed.

After three days in Eddel's organization, the man turned his attention to learning how he might infiltrate the Council and rob the treasuries. Hamel gave his all to create the impression that he was on board, but not only would he never betray the Council in such a way, but he knew it was foolish to try.

Eddel wanted news of shady dealings, improper actions or betrayals regarding the Council members. Hamel, unfortunately, could give nothing to Eddel in that area. The Council members received and maintained their roles on the Council based on their honor. To have shady dealings or to be engaged in criminal activities would not only disqualify them for their roles, but it was also such an appalling thought that no member of the Council would do such a thing. Hamel knew each member of the Council better than most people, but he knew of not even the hint of crookedness. As a result, Hamel could give nothing to Eddel that he could use to extort the Council.

In regards to the treasuries, Hamel could be of more service. He knew the layout, locks, guard rotations, and everything there was to know about the security in place. Hamel had actually set the security plan in motion himself. He had spent a year fine-tuning the guard rotation, number of guards, security system, and more. Even if the alarm was taken down, there were still more than enough guards. Even if the guards were incapacitated, the locks would keep out thieves. If a thief managed to disable the alarm, remove the guards, and even unlock the doors, the guard rotation would kick in before the thief had time to get out of the treasury.

Hamel could not give Eddel a foolproof way to get inside and out of the treasury with the gold, but he could give all sorts of information. He was intrigued at how creative Eddel was in coming up with plans to enter and exit the treasury, but he also could see not one idea would work.

Two things bothered Hamel about Eddel's operation, in addition to the fact that it was all illegal. First, Eddel ran a one-man organization. Even though he was months from the end, he still ruled every aspect of all that was done within his reach.

The second thing that continued to bother Hamel was the matter of the women and children. The women outside in the streets and markets operated as women. The children outside in the streets and markets ran and played as children ran and played. The women and children within Eddel's compound walked and moved as though they were lifeless. They were property, owned by Eddel or whatever man they were attached to.

Hamel knew he could do nothing for them at that time, but he also knew he would address the problem once he was reestablished as an Honored Patir. He had known conditions were poor in the lower sections and had worked hard to address them, but until he experienced Eddel's operation, he had not known why the pain continued.

Deep inside, he wished he had been disgraced years ago. The thought that this had been going on all that time left him struggling to sleep at night.

His mind went to the young boy and his mother he saw the day he had first entered Eddel's compound. He vowed to himself that he would return for them and others.

Once he had been welcomed into Eddel's midst, he felt he had a certain amount of protection. He slowly began to eat and drink the food he was offered and was pleased that he did not keel over and die. Instead, he found the food strange and unusual. It was as if the people of the lower regions had their own unique delicacies. He enjoyed the flavors and found himself looking forward to meals that consisted of what Eddel described as normal, regular, everyday food.

Hamel had also learned that Eddel was far more influential than he had once thought. He learned that many men and women in the lower sections ran organizations dedicated to criminal activities. They ranged from everything from simple food distribution at a high price to slave trade. Hamel committed the names of the slave traders to memory but was shocked to find that each and every one of the criminal leaders in the lower sections reported directly to Eddel. He existed as a king among the people.

On the eighth day with Eddel's people, Hamel sat with the self-proclaimed Patir after the evening meal. They often sat after a meal and spoke. Eddel was always fascinated with Hamel's experience and with hearing about life in the upper sections of the city. Hamel had even begun to grow fond of Eddel, to a point.

On that particular evening, their conversation drifted to the topic of the city's security. Eddel had danced around the topic every time Hamel had brought it up, but that evening, he had no such reservations.

"Tell me, Hamel, about the Beasts."

Hamel was surprised. He had thought Eddel knew a lot about them. "What would you like to know?"

82

"Anything. Everything. I'd like to know it all. I really know very little about them. The defense of the city is maintained by the army. It is maintained quite well, by the way, thanks to you, I suspect."

"I have certainly invested a great deal of time and effort into the defense of the city. The Beasts have grown more aggressive over the last twenty years or so. We have had to be well prepared."

Eddel nodded his head and asked, "Why do you think they have become more aggressive?"

Hamel was intrigued by the question. He did not know if Eddel was asking because he was curious or fishing for information. "We don't know, but we are convinced it is because they are angry at us."

"Angry? At us?" Eddel laughed a raspy laugh and broke into a coughing fit. "How can they be angry at us? They are Beasts!"

"It is true. They do appear to be just animals, but they have a certain intelligence," Hamel replied.

"What do you mean? What would make you think they have intelligence?"

Hamel tried his best to read Eddel's expression. He wasn't sure how much the self-proclaimed Patir was holding back or pretending. He decided to play along for the moment. "I've watched them for many years. I've defended the wall. I've even fought them down on the Valley Floor. Once, a few years ago, two Beasts showed up in the city. We still have no idea how they got in. I lost thirteen soldiers that day. Two Beasts took down thirteen trained soldiers!"

"So, they are vicious and strong and capable warriors, but what makes you think they are intelligent?" Eddel asked again.

"I have watched their strategy," Hamel began. "They have tried to fool us time and time again as they have attacked. The Wall Commander must watch the Beasts closely, or the Beasts will overrun the defenses. I have seen them protect their injured as well. I once watched a Beast drag an injured Beast back to safety, using its own body as a shield to protect its fallen comrade. Only those with compassion act in such a way. I have watched them work together to protect one another in the attack to give themselves an advantage. I have watched as they have built themselves shields in an attempt to protect themselves from our weapons. I have even watched them discard the shields as they realized they were not useful. They may not be as intelligent as we are, but they are intelligent."

"You respect them," Eddel said.

"Respect? No, certainly not," Hamel replied. "I recognize their intelligence, but I hold no respect for them. I have nothing but contempt for the Beasts."

"Why is that?" Eddel asked.

"It is because of the way they treat their young. You can always know the character of a society by the way they treat their vulnerable," Hamel explained. "Are you aware of what they do with their children?"

"I had heard that they toss their young at the wall at the end of a battle," Eddel said. He did not appear bothered by the concept, nor had he picked up on Hamel's insinuation.

"Yes. It is a disgusting practice. It began about the time that the attacks increased twenty years ago or more. They wrap the bodies of their young in Ridge uniforms and toss the bodies against the walls. We have found that the young are already dead by the time that…"

"Wait," Eddel interrupted. "Did you say that the bodies are wrapped in Ridge uniforms?"

Hamel watched Eddel closely. He saw no deception in the man's eyes. "Yes, that is what I said. You did not know that?"

"I knew nothing of that!" Eddel said and laughed as though the concept was both funny and intriguing. "I knew that the Beasts tossed their young at the wall. Such a concept has never bothered me. But the uniforms… the uniforms… if they are wrapping their young in Ridge uniforms, that means they are somehow collecting the uniforms." Eddel's eyes drifted to the ceiling. He appeared deep in thought.

Hamel nodded. It was obvious the Beasts had access to the uniforms. It was a topic that had bothered Hamel and many others. The question was where they were getting them from.

"You have no idea how they are getting their hands on our uniforms?" Eddel asked.

Hamel noted it was the first time Eddel had referred to himself in any way as part of the People of the Ridge. He had always spoken in terms of those in the upper sections being a separate people than those in the lower sections. To speak in terms of "our" was a significant comment. "No," Hamel replied, "we have no idea. A soldier will go missing, and their uniform will show up wrapped around the body of a Beastchild."

"And the soldiers... what do you know of them?"

"We know a lot about them, Patir Eddel," Hamel replied. "They have friends and family. We can interview those who knew the missing soldier. We can ask around as to why they would do such a thing, but we never come to any solid conclusions. There seems to be no motive for the soldiers to go to the Beasts. I even once had a man very close to me disappear. A day later, we found his uniform in the field after the attack. It was covered in blood and wrapped around the body of a Beastchild."

"Yes, I remember that. What was his name?" Eddel asked.

"Eatal Lemmel. He was a Colonel who served under me. He would likely have ended up as a General within a month or two. He was highly intelligent and extremely honorable." Hamel's eyes fixed on the floor. He fought hard to maintain a neutral expression and to hold back the tears. It had been nearly four years.

"Yes, that's right. It's coming back to me," Eddel replied. "If I recall, Lemmel had been far more than a friend to you, Hamel. Come now, we are partners. Do not hold back from me. Lemmel was your wife's adopted son. Do you think I do not know what goes on in this city, Hamel?" Eddel leaned forward. Hamel looked up and saw compassion in the man's eyes.

Hamel nodded, and the tears began to flow. "Yes, it's true. He was my wife's adopted son. He was my son."

"I am sorry you had to endure such a betrayal, Hamel," Eddel said quietly. "No man should have to lose a child." Eddel leaned back and took a deep breath. "So, these Soldiers of the Ridge appear to be going over to the Beasts. Perhaps they are stirring them up and getting themselves killed in the process. The Beasts then turn their attention on Ridge and attack."

"Yes," Hamel replied. "That is what we believe is happening."

Eddel's face turned red. He clenched his thin fists and ground his teeth. As he spoke, he began to spit. Hamel had not seen the man angry before. The topic was a matter of great emotion for Eddel.

"These soldiers are betraying us," Eddel said, his raspy voice growing quite loud. "They are turning on Ridge. They are turning on all the People of the Ridge. If the Beasts get past the Valley Wall and defeat the army, they will not stop at the upper sections. They will make their way down here and wipe out all that is Ridge Nation. Those soldiers are traitors!"

Hamel continued to search for signs of deceit in Eddel's eyes. His new "friend" appeared sincere in his anger.

"What could cause soldiers to betray their own people?" Eddel spat as he continued. "What could cause them to turn on the people they love and bring down the wrath of the Beasts? If the soldiers could be found out… if the soldiers who are instigating this could be caught… they could be executed as a sign of the foolishness and wickedness of such betrayal!"

Hamel nearly shook his head in wonder. He had thought Eddel to be a man entirely without honor. His treatment of certain people and participation and involvement in so many criminal activities was disgraceful, but he had a drive for loyalty to the nation overall.

"Patir Eddel, have you ever explored why those soldiers would do such a thing?" Hamel asked.

Eddel sat with a scowl on his face, and Hamel could see him clenching and unclenching his fists repeatedly. His breathing was heavy and ragged. The man said, "I looked into it six or seven years ago. I wanted to find the source of the betrayals and bring them here to the lower sections. I had plans for them."

"Did you learn anything?" Hamel asked, leaning forward. He paid close attention to every movement Eddel made as he answered.

"Nothing. We paid off whomever we could. We extorted information at just about every level short of the Council itself. We could identify no traitors. We couldn't find any signs of betrayal until we heard the report that a soldier had been identified as a traitor," Eddel said. He stared at his feet on the floor and smiled, "We even tried to get answers out of you."

Hamel sat back and considered Eddel's statement. He thought back to all the times someone had tried to extort information out of him, blackmail him, or threaten him. There had been so many times and so many people who had paid the price of challenging the honor of a Patir.

"I don't know if I remember that," Hamel said. He was curious. He wondered how many times Eddel had been behind one of the blackmailers.

Eddel laughed out loud at the question. His eyes settled on Hamel, and he said, "They were sent to threaten your daughter and her family. She had just been married for a few years, and they were expecting their second child."

Hamel did remember the incident. He also remembered where he had been when they approached him. It had been night, and he had been visiting the Wall Commander to see how the watch was going. He had thrown two of the men over the wall and the third he had incapacitated. When the man awoke, he was in a prison cell, and Hamel was preparing to question him.

"I remember the men. I remember how quickly after I began the interrogation that the man keeled over and died," Hamel said.

"Yes, one of the soldiers we owned at the time poisoned him before he could be convinced to give you any information," Eddel said.

Hamel made a mental note to find out how many of his soldiers had been compromised. When he returned to his position as Honored Patir, he would launch a deep and thorough investigation.

He had assumed all his soldiers were reliable and trustworthy. He had thought they were men and women of honor. It did, however, make sense. Some were sneaking into the Valley Floor and enraging the Beasts. A person of honor would not do such a thing.

"Once I take over the Council," Eddel said, "all that will change."

"What will change?" Hamel asked. He was pleased to finally hear Eddel state his goals.

"I will put an end to the matter of betrayals. No soldier will betray our people to the Beasts. I will hunt them down and root out the traitors much more aggressively than has been done in the past."

Hamel forced himself to maintain a serious expression. He did not think his attempts to address the matter could be described as anything other than "aggressive." Besides, Eddel would have far too much on his hands if he attempted to take over the Council and the military.

Hamel's thoughts were interrupted by Eddel's raspy cough. "Enough of that. The topic of the traitors and the Beasts makes me angry, and it makes me cough more than I can handle. It is time to retire for the evening. Tomorrow, I wish to begin finalizing our plans to clean out the treasury. We will meet tomorrow at first light."

The man rose to his feet with Hamel's help and walked toward his apartments, deep inside the compound. Hamel watched him go and reflected on the contradiction in

Eddel. He was a man who was cruel and vicious toward the women and children in his compound. Hamel bristled at the dishonor of such a thing. Yet, at the same time, Eddel valued loyalty to Ridge Nation. Loyalty to Ridge was a deeply honorable quality. He was both a disgrace and a man of commendable loyalty.

Hamel shook his head and turned toward the apartments Eddel had given him. It did not matter what honor the self-proclaimed Patir showed in one area. His cruelty to children could not be overlooked. It would be better for the nation to fall from disloyalty than for the vulnerable to be treated as slaves.

None of those issues could be addressed that day, however. Eddel did not have the answers that Hamel needed. It was time to move on and search elsewhere.

Hamel's loyalty to Eddel had come to an end.

CHAPTER 12

THE DAY OF LOSS

Hamel kept to the shadows as he made his way through the lower sections. On his way out of Eddel's compound, he had decided not to slip out a window or sneak out a side door. Despite how close they had grown in the short time Hamel was with Eddel, he suspected the man had kept a watch on him day and night. He knew if he did anything suspicious, he would not see the bullet coming. He had, instead, walked out the front door, past the guards, and through the courtyard.

Hamel smiled to himself. While his new life was far from ideal, he found humor in the darkest moments.

As he had reached the entrance to the courtyard, heading out into the streets and alleys, the guards had eyed him suspiciously. He often found the best way to remove suspicion was to act with authority. The one in charge was rarely suspected of flight. He had approached the men and, in a whisper, commanded, "When I exit this doorway, guard it securely. Do not allow anyone in or out unless you are sure of their identity."

"Yes, Patir Hamel," each guard responded in turn.

He had not expected the honorific from anyone in the lower sections, but his time with Eddel must have given them pause. It should have been obvious from the start, but in that moment, he was shocked to realize he could have had Eddel's empire when the criminal died.

It was far from a tempting option. He would not give up the opportunity to return to his place of honor for the worthless position of ruling a group of criminals, but the thought was intriguing.

His time with Eddel had taught him many things. He had learned much about the lower sections, and he had found out how little Eddel knew about and was involved in matters of the upper sections. The man had visions of establishing either himself or his successor as a new emperor of sorts over the People of the Ridge, but he posed no true threat.

By the time he had exited Eddel's compound, it was already dark. He walked with his hood raised to hide his identity and moved at nearly a run through the area.

Few wandered through the streets of the lower sections at night without nefarious intent. Eddel had at one point explained that one thief would rob a man, only to turn and be robbed by two other thieves, who in turn would be robbed by four. There was no safety in the streets at night.

He knew if he wanted, he could drop his hood and let those looking for a target know who he was. Since he had tied himself to Eddel, few would be foolish enough to rob him. He did not, however, wish to be identified.

Ten minutes into his journey, he noticed four hooded men on his tail. They looked small in the dark, and Hamel did not wish to take the time to deal with them, but a threat ignored was a death sentence in the lower sections.

He rounded a corner and leaned back against the wall in a dark area behind a pile of trash. When the men came around the corner, they hesitated, then broke into a run.

Since they were more or less heading in the direction he wished to go, he joined the men, running along behind the last man in their group. Now and then, one would look back and see him, but it was dark enough in the shadows of the buildings that it was hard to tell who was behind and who was in front. He found himself laughing at the absurdity of such a thing. He spent a few minutes, running left, then right, then left again. He ran up and down the streets with the four men, looking for himself.

Finally, the group of hooded men stopped. The four men leaned against a wall, gasping for air. Hamel stood with them, trying to control his laughter and pretended to be just as exhausted as they were.

They began to discuss where they thought their target had run off to. Hamel joined in now and then, offering suggestions as to where he might have turned. He could understand why they would not recognize him as they all wore hoods. He could not, however, believe they did not notice one more in their number.

While it was quite dark, it was far from that dark.

Finally, the man on his left did the math. "Wait! There are five of us!"

Hamel pulled out his knife and jumped into position next to the only man who appeared capable of counting. He hissed, "There are five of us! One of you is not one of us!"

The other three men turned and eyed one another suspiciously, not suspecting either the man who had counted first or Hamel who stood beside him. Hamel struggled to contain his laughter.

One of the men reached for a knife, and the other two attacked him before he could get it out. Once they had him down, they knocked him out. The one man emptied the pockets of the unconscious man before pulling back his hood. They strained to see in the darkness, but they recognized him.

The two men then each drew the conclusion that the other man was the impostor. They attacked, beating one other and yelling out curses.

In the noise and commotion, Hamel took down the man standing next to him. As much as he had enjoyed himself, he did not have time to engage in any more distractions.

He rushed away as the other two men fought hard to overpower one another. They appeared evenly matched and fought without discipline or skill. Hamel knew the fight could be over in seconds or go on for an hour.

In another block, the lower sections came to an end. He climbed the hill and felt a familiar comfort wash over him. He felt as if he were coming home. The occasional guard stood watch on corners along the way or patrolled along the streets, but no one stopped him. In the upper sections, it was not uncommon for a hooded man to walk at night.

Hamel moved south for over an hour until he reached his destination. The house was a very different layout than his own. The wall surrounding the building offered little privacy and served more of a decorative purpose than anything. It was a common two-story design with large windows all around.

It had been nearly three weeks since he had last been at the Honored Matir Karotel's home. The house was in darkness, but Hamel knew Karotel would be awake. She often read or researched late into the night after her husband and children were asleep.

He wished to speak with her.

Hamel slipped quietly over the wall and past the guard. He was grateful the boy hadn't noticed him. He did not want to hurt the young man. A guard was not required to stay up all night. Few considered entering the home of another without permission.

Hamel walked around to the back and found the den. It was the only room in the house with its lights on. Sure enough, Karotel was hard at work, pouring over a book and some papers.

He stepped to the side of the den window and took hold of the door handle. It was unlocked, and he made his way silently inside. Her floor, like most floors in the upper sections of the Ridge Capital, were made of stone slabs. The solid floor made it easy to walk without sound.

Hamel stood inside the den. The woman had not yet noticed his presence. He remained motionless, watching her work for a moment. It had been far too long since they had spoken one-on-one. For the last two years, their interaction had been almost entirely conducted in public settings over matters of state. The discussions rarely remained civil. Hamel's heart ached for better days.

"Hello, Honored Matir."

Karotel jumped and dropped her pen. "My Patir!" she said loudly before catching herself. She calmed herself down and whispered, "Hamel, what are you doing in my house? I had heard reports you were in the lower sections."

"It is true what you heard," Hamel said, smiling at her.

"I had heard as well that one of the criminals there had taken you in," she said, leaning forward in her chair.

"You heard the truth there as well."

"Well, may I ask if you fit in with Eddel?" Karotel asked with a smile on her face.

"You may, and I did not," Hamel replied, a slight laugh entering his voice. He paused for a moment and stared at the floor, deep in thought.

"Hamel, what is your next move?" Karotel asked.

"I will go home and then see if I can find a different group to play with," he said with a big smile on his face.

Karotel's eyes examined him for a moment, and he saw sadness. Her voice cracked as she said, "I wish it had not needed to come to such a point in the Council. I wish you could have maintained your honor… Hamel." She struggled to speak his name, but it was necessary not to offer the honor of a title. "The last number of years have been far too painful. I… I miss you."

Hamel had not been prepared for such kind words. He had needed to harden his heart and had done just that. Her words, however, broke through the walls he had set up, and tears began to flow. He clenched his fists and growled, "I will not deviate from this plan."

"No, Hamel, I know you won't," she said. "And neither will I. I will give you thirty minutes before I report you to the soldiers."

"It is no worry, Honored Matir," Hamel said, finding his smile again. "They will not slow me down." He then turned and left through the same door he had used to enter.

CHAPTER 13

THE DAY OF DEATH

Hamel needed supplies, and he had little time. Karotel would wait the full thirty minutes before calling the guards. He suspected she would wait even longer out of compassion for him, but he did not have time to waste.

The last few years had been difficult. They used to be so close, spending much of their time together. He used to hold her children in his arms and… he pushed the thoughts from his mind. He could not afford sentimentality. There was no opportunity to wallow in the grief of what had been lost. He hoped the price he had paid would be worth it. He would find the answers he needed. His people would not fall to the onslaught of the Beasts.

The soldiers on watch did not stop or question him along the way. They had no reason to suspect he had been consorting with criminals. Once the soldiers were alerted, however, he would become a target. He knew he could overpower most soldiers, but he did not want to hurt them. Even if he could best any one or two of them in hand-to-hand combat, that would not protect him from a squadron or from a single bullet in the back. He had to keep moving.

Hamel rounded the corner and saw his house ahead. Just the sight of his home made him smile and long for different days. His heart broke at the memory of his wife. It had been nearly twenty years, but he had missed her and the children every day since. He imagined his wife, son, and daughter waiting inside for him and even pictured them at the end of the front hallway, Lillel looking for her husband and the children their Patir.

He would even have been happy to see Markel waiting inside. To spar with the young man or have breakfast with him would be far better than the road he was on. But none of that could be. He was on a path, and he would walk it.

He was nearly at the house when his eyes caught movement in the upstairs window. It wasn't much, but he had seen it. Without slowing his gait, he began to scan the house for any sign of change. Nothing on the outside of the house was different. The door was shut, and the gate was closed. The only sign something was wrong was that one of the curtains on the lower level was hanging at a slightly different angle. Since Hamel had not left any windows open, it could not have been the wind. There was someone inside.

Those inside were not acting in response to his meeting with Karotel. They were either men from the lower sections, or they were assassins sent by someone who wished to put an end to him after his great disgrace. He had been well loved before, but to fall from such a height was more than many could handle. For some, it was perhaps an opportunity.

Although there could be many in the city who wished him dead, he did not think that was a realistic option. He also did not think those inside had come from Eddel. The man would grow suspicious, but not enough to try to kill him after only a few hours.

If someone knew where to look, they could always find assassins for hire. No member of the Council would ever make use of such a person. As a soldier, he would never stoop to such a shameful action either. A soldier faced his enemies head-on, not by sending someone to kill in the dark.

The assassins he had heard about were somewhat of a mystery. What he did know, however, was that they were rumored to come in twos, and they did not leave a mark. That was useful information.

He had not slowed or turned away. He suspected whoever was inside was watching his approach, and he did not want to let them know he was aware of their presence. He had to think fast. From the decades he had spent as a soldier and as a member of the Council, he had learned to think quickly and evaluate all possibilities. He raced through his options in his mind.

He could not turn away. He only had a short amount of time to get inside his house, get the supplies he needed, and get out of the city. What he needed lay on the other side of that door. If he turned away, he might not survive the next leg of the journey. His only option was to face whomever had come.

He was almost at the gate, and his well disciplined and focused mind moved logically through the possibilities. There would be a minimum of two assassins. He did not trust the rumors, but he knew his reputation as a fearsome opponent would require a backup in case the first one failed.

He also knew they typically did not leave a mark. Hamel had been disgraced, but to murder a disgraced man was no different than murdering a man of honor. The assassins would not want an investigation. That ruled out needles, bullet wounds, knives, and physical attacks.

That would mean they would need to make it look like an accident. If they tried to kill him by knocking him down the stairs, he might hit the bottom and rise up ready to fight. They would then have a battle on their hands, and there was a chance Hamel would survive and a chance there would be signs of a struggle. He would not be attacked on the stairs.

They would also not strangle him as it would leave a mark, and he could do much damage to the house on his way down. A fire could be effective, but if he escaped or put out the fire, word would get out that Hamel was attacked.

Hamel reached the gate and passed through it. He continued to walk as though nothing was out of the ordinary.

His mind worked quickly when it came to strategy. Years of training and discipline paid off.

He concluded their best option would be some kind of gas. If they used one that might stop his heart, it would come as no surprise to anyone. Hamel was old—far older than anyone had lived in recorded history. He was old enough that people could believe his heart had failed. He had also experienced more stress in the last week than most people experienced in their entire lives. To be publicly dishonored was a punishment far worse than death. A heart attack would be easy for most to accept.

He was only a few steps from the door. He thought through the possibilities of how they would administer the gas. He did not think they would fill the entire house. For one thing, if there was even a slight odor to the gas, Hamel would recognize it when he entered the house and turn back. He also knew that soldiers would come to his home, and if there was a residual smell or effect to the gas, it would alert the soldiers to the possibility that Hamel had been murdered.

He figured the gas would have to be released in a short burst and be fast-acting. They would not, however, stand on the other side of the door as they might miss his face, and he might have the chance to either escape or return the favor.

His hand landed on the handle of the door, and he turned it, pushing open the door. He decided the most realistic place for an assassin to attack was his kitchen. He would walk down the long hallway and reach two doors, one on either side. The door on his left would lead to his sitting room. He never went there first after being away from home. Most People of the Ridge upon arriving in their homes would go straight to the kitchen. For that, he would turn right.

The assassins, however, would not be in the kitchen. If they were, he might see them before they could attack as the kitchen was built with an open design.

They would come from behind. They would be in the sitting room, well concealed, ready to come for him.

He would make his way to the counter where he could grab a cup and fill it with water. Since the floor was solid, there would be no sound as the assassin approached from behind. He would stand and wait for the attacker to come. The man would come alone as the second would remain hidden in case the first failed.

He was now inside the house. He closed the door behind him and walked forward.

He would have to hold his breath to protect himself from the poison. He knew he could hold it for nearly a minute and a half. He hoped the assassin would attack within that time. He would stand at the sink, pretend to drink his water and wait, holding his breath. While standing at the taps, he would discreetly loosen the knife from his belt and prepare to pull it out quickly if necessary. When he saw the movement of the assassin's hand as he brought the poison around, he would attack.

Hamel was nearly at the kitchen. There was still no sign of an assassin. Nothing in his house appeared amiss. He quietly drew in a deep breath and held it as he finalized his plans.

The assassin would need to have a means of protection for himself against the gas. The typical mask would clasp at the back. When he saw the movement and heard the release of the gas, he would turn, drive his fist into the man's throat, reach behind his head, pull off the man's mask and quickly secure it on himself. If the other assassin followed, he would throw his knife at the man and attack.

He turned into the kitchen, maintaining his speed as though nothing was out of order. He reached the counter and casually pulled out a glass, setting it down before him. With his left hand, he filled the cup from a jug while using his right hand to loosen the knife and make sure he could pull it out quickly.

He could not be sure, but he thought he felt a slight movement in the air. He kept his back to the door and hoped he was right that the assassins would not want to leave a mark.

Hamel set his cup down and stood still. He raised his shoulders up just slightly to suggest he was taking a deep breath. He tried to relax himself and slow his heartbeat. His lungs were beginning to burn, and he hoped the assassin would attack soon.

A moment later, his hope was realized. A man's hand reached into his field of vision with a canister, and he felt the blast of poison rushing onto his face.

Hamel turned sharply and slammed his hand into the man's throat. The other assassin was not in sight, and the sound of his partner going down would be indistinguishable from Hamel's body hitting the floor, if the first assassin had been successful.

As the assassin stepped back, grasping his throat and making choking sounds, Hamel reached behind the man's head and unlatched the mask. It came off, and the man went down. Hamel pulled the mask over his head and blew out all the air in his lungs to clear any gas out of the mask that remained. He sucked in a breath and felt the relief in his lungs. One assassin was down.

He bent down and took the man's knife and pulled the cloak off the man, securing it on himself before making his way toward the sitting room. As he entered, he pretended to stumble into the other room. At first, he did not see the second assassin.

He pretended to stumble some more, dropped the dead assassin's knife on the ground, and fell to his knees. The other assassin stepped out from behind a large cabinet and raced toward the one he thought was his partner. As he approached, Hamel grabbed the knife lying just within reach and brought it up toward the man.

The man was fast and knocked the blade out of Hamel's hand. Hamel pulled back and leapt to his feet just out of reach as the assassin's own blade narrowly missed Hamel's chest.

The assassin stepped forward, and Hamel knocked the knife out of the man's hand and then blocked attack after attack. He did not have time to waste, but the man was unlike anyone he had ever fought before. He would sacrifice a few seconds in order to learn.

Once Hamel had an idea of how the man fought and the extent of his training, he drove his fist into the man's side hard enough he heard a crack. A moment later, Hamel plunged his own blade into the man.

The fight was over. He was still alive and ready to move. The whole confrontation had taken less than three minutes. While it may turn out well to have learned something of the assassin's style of fighting, he needed to hurry if he were to get all his supplies and move out before the soldiers arrived.

Hamel stood to his feet and went to take off the cloak when he realized he had pulled a muscle once again in his shoulder. He was sore, and he knew he would be very limited if he needed to fight his way out of a bad situation.

There was, however, no time for worries about pulled muscles or age. He needed to collect his supplies.

Before he moved on, he examined each of the assassins to confirm that they were dead. He then did a quick search of the house to ensure no other assassins were lying in wait. He did not want to be caught off guard. He came back and searched the bodies of the assassins, finding nothing of use. Hamel had not expected to find any means of identifying the men, but he needed to check.

He had two small packs ready to go in a closet off one of the back rooms in the house. The one had clothes, a bedroll, and some medical supplies. The other pack had ropes and knives and a sidearm with ammo. He also ran into the pantry to collect some salted meats and other foods for the journey along with a large waterskin. He filled it and, moving his shoulder around to loosen it, made for the door.

He was out and on the street when he heard the sound of the soldiers. They would have had to organize quickly to reach his house in such a short amount of time. He turned down a side street just as they came around the corner near his home. He paused and peered around the corner out of curiosity. The soldiers reached his home and charged inside without knocking.

Most of the soldiers who entered his house were men or women he recognized. It was difficult to see soldiers he had trained in the past so quick and willing to seek to arrest him.

He did not, however, have time for grief. He had to move if he were to get out of the city.

CHAPTER 14

THE DAY OF ESCAPE

Hamel rushed along the streets, heading east toward the edge of the city. Word, by that point, would have spread to many of the soldiers. Every second he spent in the city decreased his chances of getting away. Soon, every soldier would be on the lookout for the man who dared to break into the Honored Matir's home.

As a General, he had the advantage of knowing the guard rotation and placement—unless Cuttel had changed it all. He did not think he would have. The Captain's attention would be on his new wife.

Hamel felt a pang of guilt. He could not believe the course of action had cost him his chance to be at his daughter's wedding. He knew he would do the same thing again, given the need, but it did not ease the pain.

He pushed the thought out of his mind and focused on the assassins he had met. He considered their faces, trying to think if he had ever seen either man before. Neither one looked familiar in any way, and there had been nothing on their persons to suggest any affiliation or provide means of identification.

The only thing that stood out to him was their movement. He had only seen the second assassin in action, but the man had moved with grace and skill, yet in a very

103

unfamiliar fashion. Hamel had been trained in different styles of fighting and had trained countless others in those same disciplines, but at no point had he ever seen or experienced someone who fought as that man had. The assassins had received their training outside of Ridge.

That thought disturbed Hamel.

He pulled his mind back to the matter at hand. He needed to get out of the city and into the wilderness. It was time to leave the Capital.

The greatest challenge was not the city. If he were careful, he could make his way past the guards with little difficulty.

The challenge lay at the boundary. There was always a solid guard posted to watch for threats from the wilderness.

Unlike the western side of the city, which had two walls to protect the people from Beasts in the valley, the eastern side of the city had no natural or structural defense. The guards often used the empty houses on the border as checkpoints and command posts out of which the officers on duty could operate.

Beyond the houses ran a road that circled much of the city, and beyond that were Karotel's new houses. On the other side of Karotel's houses was the vast wilderness separating the People of the Ridge from their allies, the Olmosites.

The guard patrolled the road, and it would be difficult to cross unseen. His only hope was to move fast and keep low.

Hamel climbed to the roof of an empty house within sight of the edge of the city. He examined the guard and was pleased to see nothing had changed.

The soldiers stood on every seventh house and kept watch on the open area. Their role was to make sure the guards on patrol were consistent and to fill in any holes.

The position was more tradition than anything. They had no declared enemies to the east. Only the Olmosite Nation lay in that direction, and they had been allies for years. Other enemies lay far to the north and had not approached the Capital in generations. To the south was nothing but wasteland and to the west was the Valley Floor.

There were rumors of other nations on the far side of Olmos, but while relations with Olmos remained solid, they stood as a shield against possible threats. Every battle Hamel had fought in over the years had either been at the Valley Wall or far from the Capital.

He climbed back down to the ground and changed his cloak to a deep blue, matching the cloaks the guards wore. He knew if he were to get too close to a guard, the uniform would not hide his identity. Most guards would recognize him on sight. In the darkness, however, the cloak would be enough for his purposes.

Once he had his disguise, he approached one of the houses right at the edge of the city and climbed the stairs. The guard saw him approach but did not react. Hamel kept his head down and his hood raised as he stepped onto the roof. He saluted the man and walked forward. The darkness continued to work in his favor.

He took a quick glance to the left and the right. The sentries on either side were just visible in the darkness. They would not notice a problem unless they were looking right at him.

The guard quietly said, "We've been given warning that the disgraced Patir is out among the city and must be apprehended. I know I wouldn't want to meet up with him," the guard said with a chuckle as he turned his eyes back to the road. "You're a bit early to relieve me, but I don't mind. I'd like to…"

Hamel attacked, and the man crumpled to the ground. He checked the guards on the houses to his left and right again, but neither of them had reacted. He hoped that meant they had not seen anything.

He crouched low and pulled a small rope and a gag out of his pack. He tied the man securely and stuffed the guard's mouth full of the cloth before tying that in as well.

Years ago, in his first year after joining the military, he had awoken tied and gagged as a prank by the other soldiers. He had not enjoyed the experience and did not wish to cause the man such discomfort, but he needed to get out of the city.

Hamel made his way north to the next house with a guard and, in a similar fashion, disabled the man and tied him securely. Two guards removed would leave an unguarded distance of twenty-one houses. In the dark, that was more than enough space for him to make his way through.

He moved back to the middle of the newly unguarded area. The night was overcast, but the moon peeked out now and then. He would have to be quiet, stay low, and move fast, but he would make it through. He waited until the two guards on patrol along the road were far enough away that they would not hear him as he moved. Stealing his way to the other side, he reached the fields and rushed through to Karotel's houses.

The houses Karotel had built were of an unusual style. Most homes in the Ridge Capital were large, two-storied homes. Karotel's houses, however, were different. They had virtually no property to them such as grassy areas or trees in which children could play in safety and peace. The houses were built almost right upon one another with just a narrow space between each one. There were also no windows on the side of the wilderness. Hamel had to admit, the wilderness was not much to look at, but it was odd that all the windows should point toward the city. The houses were also quite tall. Each house stood nearly forty feet. No homes were built in such a manner in the Capital.

His shoulders rubbed the solidly built house on either side as he made his way between them. In another moment, he stepped out into the wilderness. Behind him lay not only what was left of his family, his home, and his entire life, but also all that he loved in the world. Ahead lay danger, the unknown, and solitude.

It was a high price to pay, but he would find his answers. His people would not fall to the Beasts.

CHAPTER 15

THE DAY OF RELEASE

Hamel tipped his waterskin back and took a long drink, careful not to spill even a drop. After nearly two days in the wilderness, his feet ached. He had found the occasional spring or creek and had topped up his water supply, but most of the wilderness was dry and empty. It had been years since he had been that far east in the wilderness. He had studied maps of the area and was familiar with the lay of the land, but his knowledge of the area was based on what he had memorized, not recent experience.

He did, however, know there was an oasis hidden in the hills and crevices of the land ahead. He had to be careful for fear of missing it. He would need the chance for refreshment and to get some fruit which grew on the trees in that area.

Hamel's eyes scanned the area for what felt like the hundredth time, looking for the landmarks he had read about. Aside from traders traveling to and from Olmos, few traveled so far to the east. Often their descriptions of the area contradicted one another. He had gone over the notes of everyone he could find, but he was still not sure where the oasis might be.

As he crested a small hill, his eyes landed on a large rock, shaped somewhat like a fist sticking out of the ground.

It had been named, The Hand in the Wilderness. The name was far from creative, but it was accurate.

Hamel shook his head and turned back. The Hand in the Wilderness was a helpful landmark, but it was on the far side of the oasis. He had missed his objective.

He turned around and tried to remember all the landmarks for finding the oasis from the other direction. He had paid equal attention to those details and hoped he could find his place of rest.

As he picked his way through the rocks and hills, his mind went to how far he had fallen. He was intent on returning one day to the Ridge Capital and regaining his honor. He would not meet his end in disgrace. He had more to accomplish.

He wandered through the rocks and crevices and began to wonder if he had, yet again, missed the oasis when he smelled the scent of wet soil. He was close. He searched and found a small crevice that led into an area where the air was moist. With each step leading down, the sound of rushing water grew louder. He had found the oasis.

At the bottom, he stepped into a small valley. He could see why he had missed it. It was long, but not very wide. He thought from above, walking through the wilderness, the oasis would look like a deep crevice and something to avoid. Unless explorers were to come to the very edge of the crevice and look down, it would appear to be of little interest.

The river ran through the center of the small area. He followed the flowing water upstream with his eyes and saw it poured out of a small cave. Looking downstream, he saw the rushing waters disappear into yet another small cave, flowing deep into the earth. The entire area was green. It was a stark contrast to the wilderness above.

The oasis itself had eight or nine trees, all of which were fruit bearing. Just the sight of the trees put Hamel's heart at ease. The trees, the sound of the flowing water, and the smell of life calmed his heart. He found a tree with low hanging fruit and picked a few apples.

Hamel sat on the grass next to the river and leaned back against a tree. The apples were just shy of being ripe and still had a bitter flavor, but it felt good to eat the fruit.

Hamel closed his eyes and relaxed every muscle he could. It had been many days since he had truly rested. He thought the last time was just before his meeting with Mariel in the courtyard.

Every muscle in his body ached. The last two days, he had ignored the pain and focused his energy on finding the oasis, but the journey through the rocky wilderness had taken its toll. His legs were sore, his feet covered in blisters, and his back hurt even when he sat still.

His mind, however, remained on Mariel. With his eyes closed, he could see her weep, and his ears still rung with the sound. He shook his head and tried to force the image out of his mind, but the memory of her pain was too much to bear.

Hamel felt himself slip into a familiar depression. So much had been lost.

He had lost his beautiful Lillel. They had only been married six years when she had died. She should have lived another seven or eight before the Dusk took her. He had lost her so young. He had lost his beautiful Keptel. She had been four years old. If she had not died, she would be twenty-two and married. He had lost his fearsome little Draggel. He would have been nineteen. If he had not died, he would have been advancing up through the ranks of whatever his chosen profession might have been. At nineteen, he might even have been looking for his Matir's blessing for his future wedding.

The grief and pain washed over him for what seemed to be the millionth time. He still could not believe his wife and children were gone. Eighteen years and he longed for them every day. The longing was second only to the sense of guilt. He had never admitted it to anyone, but he could no longer remember their faces without a photo in front of him.

He had spent many years since the accident doing his best to be strong. He had presented himself as someone who could rise above the pain. He had shown himself as a man who could not be deterred from his mission, not even by the deaths of his entire family.

Hamel collapsed onto the grass and wept. He had not cried like that since he was a child.

He felt empty and alone. He so desperately wanted Lillel by his side. He so desperately wanted his children in his arms. He so desperately wanted to stand with his adopted daughters. He longed for his lost adopted son. He yearned to hold his daughter's children.

He thought of poor Mariel, and the image of her tears invaded his thoughts once again. He could not believe what he had put her through. He had felt he had no choice, yet there was always a choice. He had thought there had been no other way, yet perhaps he had not looked hard enough.

He lay on the ground and wept, his shoulders heaving up and down with each sob. He called out his wife's name, his children's names, his children's children's names.

He hoped to see them again. He hoped to return and regain his position as an Honored Patir and be welcomed back into their lives. He wept until he had no tears left and fell asleep.

When Hamel awoke, it was dark. He could hear the sounds of some of the animals in the wilderness but was shocked to think not one of them had accosted him while he had slept. He ate another apple, drank from the stream, and sat back down on the grass.

He felt lighter. It was as if a weight had fallen from his shoulders. His family was still dead. His son and daughters were still lost to him. His honor was still gone. But he had needed to weep. He smiled as he realized that letting go no longer seemed impossible.

He took a few moments and did something he had never done before. He said goodbye to his wife, his daughter, and his son. He spoke out loud and confidently. It was time to move on. He said goodbye to his adopted son as well. He longed for Lemmel and still struggled to believe the man had betrayed the People of the Ridge, but it did not matter. Lemmel was his son, and the offense no longer mattered.

He did not say goodbye to his adopted daughters, their families, or Lemmel's living wife and children. He would return, and he would regain his honor. He would take his place once again in their lives. He was reminded of his resolve and committed that he would not give up. He would regain his honored title of Rezin and once again be Honored Patir Rezin Hamel.

"I am not alone!" Hamel declared, speaking loud enough for his voice to echo off the walls of the oasis. "I will regain my honor!"

"It's true, Honored Patir," a voice said behind him. "You are not alone."

Hamel jumped to his feet and pulled out his knife. He stood facing the direction from which he had heard the voice.

In the darkness, it was difficult to make much out in the oasis. While the moon and stars were out, what light they offered did not easily find its way to the oasis floor.

He could, however, see the one who had spoken to him. Sitting on the grass about four paces away, was a man. His face was shrouded under the hood of his cloak, and a rifle lay across his knees.

"I also suspect, Honored Patir," the man continued, "that you do not have honor to regain. Only the title is missing."

"Honored Patir?" Hamel asked as he slid his blade back into its sheath. It was not necessary to hold a knife while the man held a gun.

The man who sat before him was from Ridge, unless he could disguise his voice. Few Olmosites could master a Ridge accent. But if the man were from Ridge, he could have been away for a time. He might not have heard of Hamel's fall.

Hamel continued, "Perhaps you are not familiar with the events of the last number of days. I am no longer an Honored Patir. I have been disgraced."

"I had heard something of the sort, Honored Patir," the man replied.

"Then you know that you should call me Hamel," Hamel said. He could not imagine what might be happening. The man was speaking to him with respect and giving him honor, yet he deserved none. That kind of thing was unheard of. Hamel wondered if the man might be mocking him.

"I know the people demand you be called 'Hamel,' yet I have always struggled with certain demands. Let the Council and let the People of the Ridge see you as disgraced, but I see you as honored. I will call you Honored Patir, and I think it wise for you to believe it is true."

The man set his rifle aside and pulled back his hood. Hamel could not make out his face in the darkness.

The man added, "Please, Honored Patir, sit down," and pointed to a tree just a few steps from where he was sitting. "I will not hurt you. Sit there across from me and lean back against the tree. It will ease your sore muscles and help you relax."

Hamel accepted the man's invitation and sat down. Once he was leaning against the tree, he saw a small pile of fruit on the ground next to him. He picked one up and found it to be smooth with a stem at the top.

As if the man could read his mind, he said, "They are a strange fruit. They only grow here in the oasis, up among the bushes along the walls. They are sweet and plentiful and grow all year round, although this time of year they are the most flavorful. I don't know what others call them, but I decided to call them charis. Have as much as you want. I have plenty."

His first reaction was to set aside the fruit. He did not know the strange man, nor did he trust him. It could be poisonous. After a moment, he discarded the thought. The man could have shot him with the rifle if he wanted Hamel dead. There would be no one nearby to hear.

Hamel turned the fruit over in his hand and examined it as well as he could in the darkness. It did not appear to have a peel, and he took a careful bite. It was sweet, and it was different than anything he had ever tasted. He felt refreshed but remained on guard.

"May I ask who you are?" Hamel asked.

"Absolutely," the man replied.

Hamel waited for a response. The man sat still and took a bite of a charis fruit that had been sitting on a pile next to him.

Hamel smiled back. Somehow, he liked the man and appreciated the little bit of humor amidst a painful time. "Who are you?"

"My name is Mellel. I don't believe we've met, although I'm quite familiar with you," the man said.

"Not to sound arrogant, but most people are. Surviving the Dusk makes a man stand out," Hamel said.

"It's true," the man replied. Even in the darkness, Hamel could make out a large smile.

"How long have you been sitting here, Mellel?" Hamel asked.

"Oh, not too long. I saw you come into the oasis and stayed out of sight. I knew you needed a bit of time. I could tell you were carrying a heavy burden on your shoulders," Mellel explained.

"So, you watched me eat, drink, weep, and sleep?" Hamel asked, and the man nodded. "You don't think that's somewhat creepy?"

The man laughed, and the sound put Hamel's mind at ease. "I guess you could say that, although I meant only kindness. You needed the time. While you slept, I gathered some charis fruit, and I kept the animals away. They have not come near you."

"Thank you, Mellel," Hamel said.

"You're welcome, Honored Patir," Mellel replied.

"Please," Hamel said, "call me Hamel."

Mellel leaned back against his tree and laughed. "Call you Hamel? Why would I do that? You have forgotten who you are! You are Honored Patir Rezin Hamel, husband of Lillel, Patir of the two children born to you and your wife and adopted Patir of two daughters and a son. I think I'm the only one in the world who remembers who you are. If I stop calling you Honored Patir, who will remind you of your honor?"

Hamel felt the tears well up in his eyes and a heaviness on his chest. He lowered his gaze and took a few deep breaths to stave off the grief.

"Honored Patir, I watched you weep earlier. You cried like a baby, and did I mock you? Did I tell you to stop?"

"Well, you're kind of mocking me now," Hamel replied with a sheepish smile.

"Maybe, but you should feel free to weep before me. I am your friend."

"I am not only disgraced, but I am a wanted man. The soldiers have orders to arrest me. I broke into the Honored Matir's home," Hamel said. "Are you sure you want to be associated with me? It seems foolish to be my friend." He was enjoying the man's company, but he did not want to wear too many masks.

"I doubt that. I doubt that very much. I know Honored Matir Karotel. I may live out in the wilderness some of the time, but I'm not blind to all that goes on in the city."

"Fair enough, Mellel. Tell me, what are you doing out here?"

Mellel shifted on the ground and found a more comfortable spot. He pulled up a flask and took a long drink, set it down, and picked up another charis fruit. He turned it over a few times in his hands, examining every part of the fruit. Finally, he turned his gaze back to Hamel and asked, "I'm sorry, what did you say?"

"I said, what are you doing…" Hamel began.

"I know what you said, Hamel. I'm just trying to be very difficult and mysterious with you. How am I doing?" Mellel asked with a huge grin on his face.

"Quite well," Hamel replied. "And I notice you called me Hamel."

"Yes, I guess I did. Perhaps a slip of the tongue or perhaps I'm just growing comfortable with you. All right. Here's the situation," Mellel said. "You asked what I'm doing out here. I'm simply not going to tell you. I do many things out here. I will tell you this, however: I've been waiting for you. I'm here right now at this moment to be a support to you and to make sure you are well equipped for the next leg of your journey."

"And what is the next leg of my journey?" Hamel asked. He could not imagine Mellel would know his plans.

"You're heading into the Olmosite lands," Mellel replied. "I suspect you'll try to find someone you know. You're probably going to try to track down Churoi. He was only nineteen when you last saw him, standing faithfully by Pulanomos's side. You're thinking he might still be alive. I would say you're going to go right to Pollos City and see if you can track him down."

Hamel struggled to understand how it was possible that Mellel could know his plans and asked, "How do you know all this?"

"I'm not going to tell you that, either," Mellel replied. "There are no more questions and no more answers tonight. I know you had a good rest already, but I suspect you are still tired. I have two mats in a small, dry cave, hidden behind two large charis plants. Come! Let us get some rest before tomorrow."

With that, he stood up, spit the seed from the charis fruit at Hamel, and walked off through the oasis toward one of the cave walls. Hamel felt the seed hit his leg and shook his head. The man was strange.

He climbed to his feet, grabbed his bag, and followed after the man. Mellel led him past two or three smaller trees and right up to a large bush. It was hard to see in the dark, but Hamel was sure he could make out small fruits in varying stages of growth.

When Mellel reached the bush, he used his arms to push aside a few leafy branches to reveal a small, dark opening on the cave wall. He slipped inside, headfirst.

115

The man's feet disappeared into the tiny cave. The sounds of Mellel moving and grunting as he scraped his way deeper into the rocks drifted out. Hamel did not think it wise to climb into a dark hole in the wilderness. He knew there were poisonous snakes and scorpions and did not care to disturb one. He also knew a cave could collapse.

It went against his better judgment, but he decided to trust the man. Mellel had a way about him, and Hamel felt he was willing to take the risk. He did not normally trust a man based solely on feelings, but he would this time. He knelt down and pushed his way into the hole.

Hamel's shoulders were broader than Mellel's, and he found the cave to be tight. He moved through the passageway, sliding on his belly. The rocks and the gravel below scraped his back, arms, chest, and legs. Although it was difficult to know in the dark, he suspected the cave reached four to five paces into the cliff.

A light appeared ahead, and Hamel assumed his new friend had lit a lamp. He pushed on and came to an opening. Hamel rolled out onto the hard ground and pulled himself to his feet. His feet and muscles had ached before, but his little climb through the cave had added scratches, cuts, and bruises.

The room inside the rock stood taller than either Hamel or Mellel's heads and at least three paces across. There were two mats, rolled up against the one wall, along with a small stove, a table, and two chairs. There were bookshelves in the room, with dozens of books, and for light, three lanterns hung from hooks and wires, coming down from the ceiling. Next to a cistern full of water was a shelf filled with fruits, salted meats, bread, and more. Mellel himself was slicing bread.

The man was well prepared for whatever he had in mind, and the cave was well suited for him. The walls were solid stone, and there was a small hole near the roof of the cave through which any smoke from the stove could escape.

Hamel could hardly believe his eyes. He had not known what to expect on the other side of that small passageway, but he certainly had not foreseen such a room. "Mellel, how long have you been living in the oasis?"

Mellel let out a small chuckle. "Correct me if I'm wrong, but that sounds like a question, and you probably are looking for an answer. No more questions. No more answers."

The man turned and handed a slice of bread to Hamel along with a small piece of salted pork. Hamel thanked him and began to eat as Mellel pulled out the mats and spread each on the floor. One of the mats was right at Hamel's feet. Mellel walked around and blew out each of the three lanterns, plunging the room into darkness.

Hamel stood in the dark. He chewed on his bread and pork. He could hear Mellel crawling onto his own mat, and within seconds, the man's snores drifted through the cave. He was a strange man, but Hamel could not help but like him.

He finished off his small meal and lay down on the mat. He felt the safest he had felt since before his disgrace. He closed his eyes and allowed himself to drift off to sleep.

CHAPTER 16

THE DAY OF ENCOURAGEMENT

Hamel awoke to the smell and sound of eggs sizzling on a grill. He turned over and in the dim light noticed Mellel's mat rolled up by the wall. The lanterns were all lit but turned down low.

He greeted Mellel with a "good morning," and the man smiled back at him. Mellel gestured toward the lamps, and Hamel assumed he meant he should turn them up. After he finished with the lamps, he rolled up his own mat.

Mellel pointed at one of the chairs at the table and scooped some eggs he had cooked out of a small pan and onto two small plates. The two sat down at the table to eat.

Mellel led them in a time of thanksgiving for the food. It was a custom Hamel had missed while spending time with Eddel. The criminal seemed less inclined to take part in matters of either tradition or faith.

They ate in silence at first. Hamel found himself lost in his own thoughts until Mellel interrupted his daydreaming.

"Stop thinking about your disgrace, Honored Patir," Mellel scolded. "There is nothing that can be done about that. It came as you knew it would. When you made up your mind to refuse Mariel's blessing, you decided on this result. Stop wallowing in grief." As if to drive home the point, he reached over and took some of Hamel's food right off his plate with his hand and shoved it in his mouth. It was an odd thing to do, but the man was odd.

"It is hard not to reflect on such things," Hamel said, drawing his plate closer to himself. He was hungry and didn't want Mellel to take another handful. "I have lived my life among a people who have always pursued honor."

Mellel stood up, walked around the table until he was near Hamel's plate, and took another handful, shoving that one in his mouth as well. Hamel couldn't help but notice the man's plate was nearly full and wondered if he could take food from Mellel.

Before he could act on that thought, Mellel said, "Hamel, look at me!"

Hamel looked up into the face of Mellel. It was the first time he had taken a serious look at the man in any kind of light. He was an odd looking fellow. His facial features were all either too large or too small. His hair was neither messy nor neat. His teeth were deeply yellowed, and his clothes were rags. The eyes, however, were clear and full of life. He had heard it said when he was a child that the eyes were the window to the soul. If that were true, Mellel's soul was deep and very much alive.

Mellel gripped Hamel's shoulder with one hand and said, "I have gained far more than you and lost far more than you, Hamel. Yet I am content. Believe me when I remind you of the truth you know. You may have been declared a disgrace among the people, but you do not stand alone. You face the world with many at your back, Honored Patir."

Hamel felt the man's words reach in and nourish his soul. His eyes welled up once again with tears, but not out of grief. He felt refreshed and stronger. He felt ready to move forward.

Mellel turned his attention to Hamel's plate. Abandoning any form of etiquette, the man began to eat off Hamel's plate with his hands.

"Are you hungry?" Hamel asked with a smile. "Would you like some of the food on my plate?"

Mellel stopped mid-bite and looked at Hamel in shock. "What a strange question? Of course I would like some of the food on your plate! I'm eating it right now. You should be able to deduce from that action that I want to eat your food. Do you think someone is forcing me to do such a thing? Do you think I would do this if I did not want to?"

Hamel's smile grew, and he said, "No, I suppose not."

He decided the best thing he could do was to eat at least a little more of what was left on his plate before it was all gone. He reached for some of the egg, but Mellel pushed his hand away. The man picked up Hamel's plate and walked out of reach as he finished off the last of the breakfast.

Mellel put the plate down on a counter and turned toward a corner of the room. He grabbed a bag and said, "It's time for you to go, Hamel. You have a long journey ahead of you. It'll take you until nightfall to reach the border, if you travel by horseback."

"Yes, I suspect you are right. On foot, I believe it'll take me closer to three days," Hamel replied.

Mellel's face filled with confusion, and he shook his head. "Yes, I suspect *you* are right about that. On hands and feet, I believe it'll take you close to twelve days. Would you like to tell me how long it'll take you if you dance there? Or perhaps if you roll there? Or maybe if you skip like a child all the way to Olmos?"

Hamel felt he should not answer those questions. He really did not understand the man. Instead, he turned and grabbed his pack and wandered over to Mellel's nearly full plate. He grabbed a few handfuls and shoved what he could in his mouth. When he finished, Mellel was grinning like a fool.

"There you go, Honored Patir! Now you're catching on!"

Hamel felt nothing but irritation at the man's response. He wasn't sure what he needed to catch onto but turned to the exit. He climbed into the cave. With the bruises

120

and scratches from the night before, every move was agony, but he eventually rolled out into the oasis.

The way out of Mellel's hideout, although more painful, felt as if it took less time than it had the night before. When he emerged, he had to squint from the light of the sun. The valley was still bathed in shadow, but the light was brilliant compared with the darkness of the cave.

Mellel squeezed out right after him and took Hamel's bag from his hands. He wandered to the rushing stream and filled Hamel's waterskin along with another one. When they were filled, he handed both to Hamel along with the bag he had brought out of the cave.

"Open it!" Mellel ordered. "I'll take your cloak, and you take the one in the bag."

Judging from the condition of the cloak Mellel was wearing, Hamel did not think he would want whatever was in the bag, but he pulled the bag open. Inside was a light brown cloak in perfect condition. It was thin and ideal for the climate. It would keep the sun off his shoulders. It was an odd style, however. He had never seen a cloak designed in such a way.

"It's an Olmosite cloak," Mellel said in answer to the question going through Hamel's mind. "It's a riding cloak, too. It will allow you to sit on a horse without the sides riding up your legs too much. It'll also keep the sun off you. Since it's Olmosite, it'll help you blend in. They won't let you past the wall if they don't believe you are from Olmos."

Hamel's heart filled with gratitude toward the strange man. He had not yet figured out how he would get into Olmos. No outsider was ever allowed past the gate. The cloak would help. He was about to thank Mellel when he looked up to see his new friend offering him some papers.

"These will get you past any soldiers who wish to question you about your identity, or at least you should have a good chance of making it through," Mellel said. The moment Hamel took the papers, Mellel turned and walked toward the far side of the oasis.

121

Hamel followed, and the two jumped across the rushing stream at a narrow spot. Mellel led Hamel to a crevice in the rock. He stepped through, and Hamel was surprised to see a gate cutting off their path. His new friend opened the gate and led Hamel inside and around a corner.

Before he saw what was behind the gate, he recognized the smell of a stable. Mellel had horses. The man's comment about the time it would take to get to Olmos on horseback made more sense.

Both horses were saddled and ready to go. Hamel expected the man had been awake for some time that morning.

Mellel took each of the horses by the reins and led them out of the stable. He told Hamel to change his cloak and pointed to a path leading through the rocks. "When you're dressed as an Olmosite, meet me up there." With that, Mellel wandered up the path, leaving one horse behind.

Hamel changed into his new cloak and stuffed his old one in the pack. The night's rest, the food, Mellel's encouragement, and the new cloak left him feeling refreshed and at peace. He reminded himself of the words he had spoken many times, leading up to those days. "I am not without family. I do not face the world alone. I must continue. There is work to be done," but added in, "and I am not without honor." It felt strange to say such a thing, but Mellel's words gave him confidence.

He still felt the grief, pain, and confusion over the loss of his wife and children, but he felt as if he had a short reprieve from the weight of it all. He had work to do. He would not give up.

He mounted the horse and rode up the path. It wound around back and forth, but always moving upward. He could see the open sky above him as he made his way out of the oasis. The air grew warmer, and Hamel knew it would be a hot day.

Just before he reached the top, the rocks closed in over his head. When he finally exited the path, it was as if he had ridden out of a cave. The wilderness was barren and dead.

It was hard to believe there was a thriving oasis hidden in the crevices.

Mellel sat on his horse a few paces away. He looked comfortable, yet impatient. Hamel rode to him, and the man pointed at his bag.

"Give me your old cloak. You won't want to ride into Olmos with a Ridge cloak in your bag. If it is discovered, you will be thought to be a spy," Mellel said.

"I'll just tell them I came from Ridge. They are allies of Ridge Nation. We are not at war," Hamel replied.

"Hamel, I think you'll be surprised at what you find in Olmos. We indeed have an alliance with them, but do you not think it odd that not even the Ridge Ambassador has made it past the wall?" Mellel asked.

"They are a private people, Mellel."

"That is true, Hamel. But do not think that my words are baseless. Where do you think I got that cloak?"

Hamel nodded his head. He had grown used to being the wisest around. Since no one lived as long as he had, and he had been a man of such honor, few questioned his words. He found the situation reversed with his wilderness friend. The man seemed to know and understand much that was new to Hamel. He wished he could spend a few days with Mellel, just asking questions and receiving answers, but the man gave no indication that he would tolerate such an arrangement.

Hamel reached into his pack and pulled out the cloak. He turned it over in his hands and examined the collar, the stitching, and more. It had been a gift from his daughters when he had turned forty-one years old. It was a high-quality cloak, but its real value to him was that it had come from them.

He handed it over. Mellel was right. He could not take chances. "I'd like to get that back from you when I return, Mellel."

"No. It is now mine," Mellel said.

Hamel assumed the man was joking and laughed, but from the look on Mellel's face, the man had no intention of returning the cloak.

"Give me your dagger as well. It is a Ridge blade."

"This dagger was a gift from Markel. He is like a son to me. He was my guard…" Hamel began. Once he knew he would not get the cloak back, he was hesitant to give up the blade.

"Yes, yes, yes. I know Markel," Mellel replied. "He is a strong, intelligent young man. I know the two of you were close. I know he looked up to you as though you were his Patir. I know the cloak came from your daughters. I know it all means a lot to you. Give it all to me, and it will all be mine. If you wish to have these things back one day, you may ask, but I make no promises." Mellel moved his horse right next to Hamel, reached over and began to untie the belt on which Hamel's blade hung.

Hamel pushed his hands away. "Alright! Enough. I will give you my blade, but you will not untie my belt. I am not a child who needs help getting dressed, nor am I in the final days of the Dusk and unable to care for myself."

He undid the belt and separated the dagger. He held it for a moment and let his thoughts return to the day Markel had given it to him, but Mellel reached out and took it along with the belt. Mellel reached into his own pack and pulled out another belt with a dagger attached.

Hamel accepted the belt and dagger and examined both. They were familiar to him. He had seen Pulanomos and Churoi wearing similar belts, and he had even had the privilege of examining Pulanomos's blade at one point. It was a high-quality blade. Pulanomos had often spoken of Olmosite workmanship. The blade Mellel had handed him was of great quality.

His admiration of the blade was interrupted by Mellel. "Hamel, I know the cloak you wore and the dagger you carried were of great sentimental value to you. I know it is difficult to give them up." The man reached over and put his hand on Hamel's arm before continuing. "That is why I have given you this cloak and this blade. Since they come from me, they will have significantly more sentimental value for you than anything your daughters or former guard could have

given you. They are now special to you beyond measure, ar
you will doubtless treasure these gifts far beyond what you
have given up."

Hamel opened his mouth to tell Mellel what he
thought of such an idea, but he stopped. He could see the
humor in the man's eyes. His new friend leaned back in the
saddle, laughed, and said, "Hamel, this is a stressful time for
you. You need to spend a bit more time laughing."

With that, Mellel turned his mount and pointed to the
east. "Olmos, as you know, is due east from here. If you head
straight toward the rising sun, you will eventually, assuming
you are not detained by Olmosite border guards, come to the
wall. If you get past the wall, you will need to continue east to
find the city of Pollos. Once there, you should be able to find
those you are seeking."

"Thank you," Hamel said but was interrupted.

"I'm not finished," Mellel said with a smile on his
face.

Hamel began to think the man had been far more
difficult than he had needed to be simply because he had a
playful spirit. Hamel said, "My apologies. Please continue."

Mellel chuckled to himself. "You will not, however,
want to take the direct route. First of all, that is not the road
into Olmos. If you are found entering the nation through the
wilderness, you will have a difficult time convincing the
Olmosite guards you are not a spy or assassin trying to
infiltrate the nation. You will need to head northeast until you
come across a road heading east and west. That is one of the
main trade routes between our nations. You may even come
across a few traders along the way. If the traders are from
Ridge and recognize you, that might be awkward, but I think
you could manage that one okay."

Mellel turned his horse in a northeasterly direction
and began to move his way through the rocks and cracks
along the ground. Hamel finished tying up his belt and then
brought himself up beside Mellel's horse and matched his
speed as best he could.

"When you get to the road, follow east. It's not an overly direct route as the road turns and rises and falls with the land, but it is the way you will be expected to travel. In six or seven hours, you should reach Benjelton. It's one of the ancient abandoned cities. I would recommend you stay there for the night. Neither the Olmosite nor Ridge traders enter the old cities. The cities are thought to be haunted."

"I had heard that. I had intended to explore one of the cities on my way through. I wished to see a bit of our history. I have never had cause to enter one of the abandoned places of our land," Hamel said.

"Yes, I know you were going to stop there," Mellel said.

Hamel wondered again how much the man actually knew of his plans. He seemed to have an eye right into Hamel's mind.

"I would recommend you choose the old Benjelton Council Chambers," Mellel continued. "It is a solid structure, and you will not have to worry about the roof caving in on you while you sleep and move about. You can recognize it because it is right in the center of town and one of the largest, most impressive buildings in the city. It also resembles the Council Chambers in Ridge Capital, just on a smaller scale. Just outside the building is a working fountain. You will be able to wash up and refresh yourself there."

With that, Mellel handed Hamel another pack. Hamel looked inside and found enough food for two days and a few medical supplies. With the food Hamel had in his own pack, it would be plenty to get him into Olmos and perhaps even to Pollos.

"There's a bit of Olmosite gold and silver in there as well. You won't be able to spend Ridge currency while you are in Olmos. It won't be considered unusual for you to have money from Ridge as the traders come back with it all the time, but if you try to change it to Olmosite gold, you will get a very poor exchange."

With that, Mellel wished Hamel a safe journey and, without another word, turned his horse toward the west. In that direction was the Ridge Capital, and Hamel wondered if the man was going to report to someone. He did not think Mellel would betray him, but there was far more to the man than he knew.

He pushed his horse to go as fast as he felt he could on the rough, uneven ground and settled in for the journey ahead.

CHAPTER 17

THE DAY WITH TRADERS

The dust from the road caught in Hamel's throat, sending him into yet another coughing fit. Though the sun was sinking toward the horizon and his first waterskin was nearly empty, there was still no sign of Benjelton.

Once he had left the oasis and Mellel behind, he had reached the road within an hour and had made good time. He had only stopped once along the road to give his horse a break and have a mid-day meal, but his lack of time spent on horseback in recent years was slowing him down. Every muscle and joint hurt.

"It's okay, boy," Hamel said to the young stallion. He was concerned as he listened to its breathing. Between the sun's heat and the dust, he feared the horse would find it difficult to make it the entire way.

Travel on the road was far easier than through the wilderness. When he had first left the oasis, the way was rough and dangerous. With the rocks, cracks, and crevices in the ground, he had needed to move at a crawl to make it through. Once he reached the road, everything changed for the better, aside from the dust and heat.

Hamel bent his head low, allowing the hood to droop over his face as he passed a few more traders moving along their routes. Their dress and accents revealed them to be from

Olmos. While most of the Olmosite carts were covered, Hamel knew they likely carried salt or various household goods.

A few miles before, he had passed a group of Ridge traders, heading to the Olmosite border. They would exchange their fruits, vegetables, and other wares at the border. He kept his head low and disguised his voice as best he could when he greeted anyone from Ridge.

Hamel's military mind always noticed the presence of soldiers, whether they were dressed as such or not. Most traders either traveled in large groups or hired men for protection. From under his hood, he examined each man he passed. While many had broad shoulders and carried large rifles, their faces suggested that they had lost a few too many fights. Not one of them moved with the confidence and control of a Soldier of the Ridge.

Neither Ridge nor Olmos tolerated thieves along the trade routes in any measure. Hamel had only once recalled a report of thieves harassing caravans. He had immediately dispatched four battalions, and his men soon discovered the Olmosites had dispatched a similar force. The thieves were rounded up within a day and been tried immediately by Olmos.

He had heard the Olmosites gave the death penalty to thieves. Hamel was not sure if that were true. He knew very little about their ally. The Olmosite people were very private.

Ridge only gave the death penalty for treason or for slave-trading. As he reflected on such a thing, he realized either Eddel, if he lived long enough, or whoever took over for him would be receiving the death penalty if Hamel ever were to regain his honor. He had witnessed the death penalty once before. A man serving under him had been charged with treason and was convicted by the Council. He had been thrown from the wall. It had been a mercy, compared to the punishment for slave-trading. If one were caught treating a human in such a manner, they were lowered slowly down to the Valley Floor—in the middle of an attack.

He had never observed such a thing, but he had read about it in the archives. The man who had written the account had stopped part way through his description. He had written, *I cannot finish. Despite the heinous crime, I feel compassion for the man and wish the Beasts would simply kill him.*

An image of the young boy in Eddel's compound flashed into his mind, and anger boiled inside Hamel's chest. The child had sat with his mother, covered in bruises and scars—some old, some fresh. It had taken all of Hamel's restraint not to rescue the two.

Hamel closed his eyes and took a deep breath. He hollered out, "They were slaves!" Hamel's fingers hurt, and his nails dug into the palms of his hands. The horse came to a quick halt as the reins pulled up tight. He screamed as loud as he could and then yelled, "They were slaves, and I left them there!"

Hamel's eyes opened. His breathing came in ragged gasps, and the sweat poured down his face and back. The road ahead was empty, and the landscape before him was all wrong. It should have been on fire. The sky should have been collapsing. People across the world should have been screaming and clamoring for his throat. No man should ever walk away from a slave when it is in his power to rescue him.

"No!" he spoke aloud, hoping the sound of his voice and the wisdom he knew to be true would pull his mind back to reality. "I could not rescue them." While he knew the words were true, he could only manage a whisper. Taking a deep breath, he cried out, "But I will go back!"

Hamel shook his head to help focus his thoughts. His stomach turned with all the grief he felt, but he could not dwell on the woman and the young boy. He had a long journey ahead, and it would be foolish to let his mind drift from his task.

Hamel lowered his head once again and allowed the hood to fall low over his face. Off in the distance, there was movement on the horizon. As he drew closer, he noticed the clothing was in the Olmosite style with long flowing cloaks and little detail or design. There were four men, as was the custom for traders—two on horseback and two on the wagon.

The Ridge traders followed the same pattern. Four was enough to handle repairs, allowing for one to go for help if needed. If they did meet a thief, four people were difficult to overcome.

The occasional trader had tried to strike up a conversation, but he had kept his head down and not engaged them. He would reply with grunts or shrugs, and eventually, the traders would cease their attempts to engage him. The hardest ones to deal with were those traveling the same direction as himself. He had spent an entire mile trying to get around a cart while the trader had talked non-stop about a concerning spot that had shown up on his horse's flank. Hamel had not paid much attention to the man, but he did hear the man explain in the end that the spot had turned out to be nothing other than a splatter of mud from the road. Hamel had grunted a response to the man and then found his way past the cart, quickly leaving the man behind.

By mid-afternoon, the walls and turrets of Benjelton took shape in the distance. He pushed his horse a little harder in the hopes of reaching the city. It had been years since he had ridden for longer than fifteen or twenty minutes at a time, and the proof was in how every muscle hurt and the way the saddle wore on his legs.

The road continued beside the city. In his study on the area, he had found the maps to show a large roadway heading from the trading route into Benjelton. His concern was that the passage of time might have made the roadway impassable.

As he came upon the road into the city, he was pleased to find it was relatively clear. There were plants and trees growing along the way, but no large rocks, and the road was still in relatively good condition.

He brought the horse to a halt and looked up and down the road. Only one group of traders was visible in each direction, and they were making their way toward Hamel from the direction of Olmos. Traders considered the city to be haunted, causing Hamel to feel it would be the perfect place to spend the night.

Hamel climbed down off his horse and pulled out some food and one of his waterskins. Until the traders passed, he could not enter the city. The sight of a man traveling into a place believed to be haunted was cause for a great deal of gossip. He found a large rock just on the edge of the road and sat down to have his evening meal as the traders approached. The hood on the cloak Mellel had given him was ideal for keeping his identity hidden.

"Ahh, an evening meal! What a great idea," the man holding the reins of the cart called out. "Do you mind if we join you?"

Hamel offered a noncommittal grunt.

"Excellent! It will be good to enjoy some new company," the man answered.

It was an Olmosite caravan. The four men spoke in the thick accent of Olmos and did not seem to notice or care when Hamel did not speak to them.

The hood fell low enough over his face to work as a disguise, but not so low that he could not watch the four men. Ridge traders would undoubtedly recognize Hamel, former Honored Patir of their people. He did not think it likely that men from Olmos would recognize him, but there were two other problems. For one, the Olmosite and Ridge accents were distinct. Hamel had been practicing the Olmosite accent for years, doing his best to perfect it. He had not, however, had the chance to try it out even once on a native Olmosite speaker. He suspected he would soon have his moment. Since he wore an Olmosite robe, he could not speak in his regular accent.

The other problem he faced was his looks. Since he had survived the Dusk, he had learned that his face was changing. Most men or women gained the occasional line on their faces as they reached their thirtieth year or so, but since no one had ever passed thirty-four years of age except him, they did not know that the lines continued to appear. He had far more than anyone he had ever met. Some said he looked better as the years passed, others looked for ways to say he looked worse, but in a kind way. Better or worse, he looked different. He might be able to fool them with his accent, but not his age.

The men gathered around on rocks, taking seats where they could find them. They each pulled out food and water, and then stared at Hamel.

Hamel waited himself, examining each trader one by one. He did not have time to socialize. He wished to get into the city before nightfall. He had work to do.

The men held their tongues, and not one took a bite or drink from their waterskins. They looked upset, and the leader of the group, or at least the man who had been driving the horses, wore a frown. Hamel noticed as well that there was fear in his eyes.

The Olmosite people were private. Even with all the years he had spent with Pulanomos, he knew little of their culture. He wondered if perhaps he was considered a guest among them. As such, he might need to say something or do something.

The man who had spoken got to his feet and bowed low before Hamel. His voice began to shake, and he said, "Forgive me, Master. We are simple traders, unaware of some of the finer etiquette required of the elite. Please, tell us what we must do to receive your permission."

Hamel's mind raced through what he had just witnessed from their actions and words along with all he had learned over the years through observing Pulanomos. The Olmosites were not a people driven by honor. They were a people driven by power. The People of the Ridge expected to show honor to all, but especially those of greater honor. The greater the honor, the more trustworthy the Matir or Patir. It was so because a Matir or Patir gained their honor through trustworthy actions.

The people of Olmos were not inclined to such patterns. If a man or woman climbed to a higher rank, it was due to power and control and money. It could even come as a result of fear.

He looked down at his robes and, for the first time, noticed that they were of very high quality. The dagger at his side was masterfully made with three or four jewels on the handle. His clothing and dagger might suggest a man of power. The trader had called him, "Master," which Hamel suspected was not because they knew him but was a title offered to people of rank.

He knew he would not be able to pretend he knew what the man was talking about, so he decided he would make them tell him what he needed to know. It was time to test his accent. He spoke up with a stern and angry voice saying, "Young man, why don't you tell me what just happened and what you were expecting from me?"

The man bowed low and held his arms out to the side. Hamel was pleased to see the man had not reacted to his accent.

"My apologies, Master. We have acted the fool. We approached you and, seeing you were a man of rank, wanted to join you for a meal. We did not wish to offend you. We have sat down, and we are awaiting your permission to eat."

Hamel nearly smiled. He did not realize the solution could be so simple. "You have my permission."

The men took their seats, and all four dug into their meals. They did not speak, nor did they look at Hamel. He did, however, notice each man's eyes moving to scan the area. An uneasy feeling began to grow in the pit of his stomach.

Hamel reached down and discretely pulled slightly on the blade to ensure it was loose. He also pretended to be looking for something in his pack and moved his sidearm to the top, sitting just inside where he could grab it in a moment of need.

The meal continued in silence until all four men had finished their food and nearly emptied their waterskins. The man who had spoken before then stood up and bowed. In a loud, formal voice, he said, "Thank you, Master, for allowing us to share in your presence. We are grateful you welcomed us into your meal."

Hamel took a guess that he should respond but decided not to say much. "You are most welcome."

The man paused for a moment as though he expected more, but then asked, "May I ask, sir, if you are traveling alone?"

Hamel thought the question was out of place, but he knew what it meant. The men had been looking around as if they had expected Hamel to have friends or others with him. He was about to be attacked. He decided to face the issue head-on, rather than try to find a way around it.

"Yes. I am traveling to Pollos alone," he said. He was still seated, but he positioned his feet to allow himself to spring forward in a moment. His mind slipped into old habits as he evaluated the threat level of each man. Out of the four, only one appeared to be a concern. He was large, and his face suggested many fights over the years.

Hamel held back a smile. Men such as that man fancied themselves to be dangerous. They generally had no training and little skill; hence, the face that looked as if he had been on the receiving end of many fists. The only danger a man such as that posed was if he was able to get close. A single well-placed strike by even an unskilled fighter could be the end of Hamel.

"Yes, we thought so, Master," the man replied.

"Why is that any of your concern?" Hamel asked coldly.

His mind raced through his options. If they were to attack, he would use his blade to take down the man who had been doing all the speaking. He was closest, and Hamel would not have any difficulty dispatching him by throwing the knife. The other three were far enough away that Hamel would be able to get his sidearm out of his bag before they could reach him.

Hamel had never enjoyed taking a life. Even on the battlefield, he had often searched for ways to allow an enemy to live. Sadly, if the four men were to attack, they would all need to die. If he were to allow anyone to escape, he risked that man coming back at a more opportune time, perhaps even while he slept. He also risked the survivors telling others about him.

"Why is it any of my concern?" the man replied in a mocking voice, and the others laughed. All pretense of respect was gone. "It is my concern because we are in the business of profit. If you could hand over that cloak, your blade, and your packs, we will allow you to walk away with whatever you are wearing under that cloak… assuming it's not of value."

Hamel still hoped he could talk his way out of the situation. "Please, my friends, this is not a wise choice. Why don't you get back up on your wagon and horses and ride off? There is no need for violence."

"I beg to differ, Master," the man said, but that time the title he used for Hamel was said with disdain. He then stepped forward as the others rose to their feet.

Hamel threw the knife and caught the man just below his heart. As the apparent leader of the four dropped to the ground, the others stopped in their tracks. Two of the men's mouths hung open, while the large man with the abused face sneered.

Hamel's hand closed around his sidearm, but he did not draw it from his pack. He still hoped they would walk away. It would be foolish to risk the story getting out, but he thought perhaps they would keep it to themselves out of shame for attacking a man of rank such as they suspected him to be.

He remained crouched low to the ground with his hand in his pack. Without taking his eyes off the three men, he slipped the safety to the off position. They had not seen his face. His hood had remained up the entire time. He knew he was looking for an excuse to let them go and for hope— hope that they would walk away.

The large man charged, and Hamel drew his sidearm. The man went down, and Hamel was confident he would not rise. The others had not moved, nor had they closed their mouths. One of them had not even taken his eyes off the leader who had fallen first. Hamel wondered if perhaps they weren't aware of the plans the leader and the large one had made to rob Hamel.

"If you walk away right now, I will let you go. The men turned their heads to one another for a moment, and he saw a slight nod between them. The one on the right began to weep, and the one on the left dropped to the ground and begged for mercy.

Hamel accepted the fact that the men would die at his hand. The one who begged for mercy took two steps on his knees toward Hamel. The other one discreetly took one small step.

Hamel brought himself to his full height. He had always been taller than most men. Even the large man who had just fallen had still been shorter than the former Honored Patir. "I will not fall for this charade," Hamel warned. "One more step, and I will fire."

The second man fell to his knees. The one on the left inched closer as he begged for mercy and wept. Each move he made toward Hamel was subtle and appeared innocent.

By this point, both men were crying out for mercy, and the one on his right was reaching toward him and waving his arms. As he cried out for mercy, he slowly fell onto his face, just out of reach of Hamel.

Hamel almost missed it. The man on the right who had fallen to the ground was the distraction while the other man reached behind his back. Hamel had just happened to move his eyes back to the man on his left in time to see a flash of steel.

Hamel put a bullet in the man's head and turned back to the man on the ground. The final man let out a scream of rage as he climbed to his feet and charged. Before he had taken two steps, his lifeless body hit the ground.

None of the men had needed to die. Hamel was beginning to think he did not want to enter the land of Olmos. He had heard rumors of their violent tendencies, but the few men and women he had met in his lifetime were nothing like the four traders. The others had been peaceful, calm, and trustworthy.

He took a deep breath and reminded himself, "I am not without family. I do not face the world alone. I must continue. There is work to be done."

He bent down, retrieved his blade, and cleaned it off before he moved to the wagon left by the four traders. It was full of bags of salt to be sold in Ridge.

He shook his head at the waste of life. He wondered what lay ahead for him in Olmos.

CHAPTER 18

THE DAY OF MOSAIC

Hamel retrieved the cart and pulled up next to where the four men had fallen. Three of the men were light and easy to lift into the cart, but the larger man gave Hamel some trouble. His shoulder still ached from his fight with the two assassins, and he cried out in pain as he pushed the man's bulk up and over the side of the cart.

He collected the two guards' horses, as well as his own, and secured all three to the back of the cart. He then hopped onto the seat of the cart and grabbed the reins. The best place to hide the bodies and deal with the cart was in the abandoned city.

The road into the Benjelton was in great condition. There was the occasional rock or boulder that had rolled onto the road, but the way was relatively clear and wide enough for four carts to travel side-by-side, if needed.

While the city was not as large as Ridge Capital, it was still massive. He had always marveled at the size of the abandoned cities. His people could now barely fill the Capital, but there had been a point in their history when they had once filled not only Ridge Capital but also Benjelton and eight or ten other large cities in addition to many small towns and villages. The ruins of the cities were a testament to their long lost glory.

The People of the Ridge had been coming up with theories as to what had caused their downfall for generations. The best theory he had heard was really no theory at all, just an assumption. Something had happened in their history a little over three hundred years before. It was assumed that prior to that point, the People of the Ridge had filled the cities. The earliest records they had showed a mass migration away from the cities and towns throughout the region and into the Capital. The assumption was simply that something "had happened." It was a disappointing and empty assumption, but it was all they could manage.

The majority of people had long since given up on caring, although Hamel had always felt the matter was crucial to their understanding of who they were and how they could move forward. The original generation who had gone through the event gave conflicting reports—everything from the casual mention of sickness to a very detailed and overly dramatic description of a wave of death washing over the nation. Whatever had happened, it had happened fast.

Once the people had realized they were losing numbers in their population, they sought to have many children. Sadly, few could have any more than two, while many could only have one or no children. With the deaths through the many battles with the Beasts, wars in the North, and with few children born, they had experienced a steady decrease in their population for many, many years.

Everyone knew they were a people on the way to extinction. It was just a matter of time.

Hamel reached the edge of Benjelton. The city was entirely walled in, unlike the Capital. As he passed through the open gate, he examined the crumbling buildings. They were still solid and in relatively great shape considering the lack of care over the years, but they showed signs of needed upkeep. The architecture was quite similar to the buildings in the Capital. The buildings were tall, multi-storied, built out of stone, and each wall contained many windows.

The streets were wide and, similar to the Capital, made of stone blocks. The open space allowed for easy travel, and many of the buildings had large courtyards in the front, surrounded by knee-high walls or rusted iron fences. Now and then he came across a fountain. The occasional one had a bit of slow-moving water trickling out, but most appeared as though it had been decades since water had flowed through them.

The shadows grew longer until he could no longer see the sun over the tops of the buildings. He hoped to settle in for the night well before dark.

Most of the buildings were in a similar condition to one another. They were well built and had stood the test of time. The only buildings he found that had not survived were the libraries. Their blackened walls and open, gaping windows revealed a hollowed-out interior. Whoever had destroyed them had wanted the people not to have access to certain information.

Hamel considered that thought for a moment and wondered what information had been kept from them. It was obvious they had lost a lot of knowledge of their past. However, the burning of the libraries suggested more than just random information lost, but an intention to remove all access to knowledge. Perhaps it was their history, perhaps something else.

He reflected back on the libraries in the Capital. They had not shown any obvious signs of a fire, yet the shelves inside were sparsely filled. It had always been said that the architects of the libraries had designed them larger than needed to allow for many books to be written, but Hamel began to wonder if the library shelves in the Capital were empty not in anticipation, but as a result of an act of removal. It was a concerning thought.

He rounded a corner past the third burnt down library and came to a stop. Before him was the City Center. It was as large as the Center in the Capital with as many buildings around the outside of the open area. The Council Chambers were easy to recognize. They were almost identical in style to the Chambers back home, including the steps leading up to the doors. The surprising part about the courtyard, however, was the life. There were no animals to be seen, aside from birds, but the fountain in the center of the courtyard was not dry, nor was it showing a trickle of water. The water it produced flowed out of the fountain like a stream. In contrast to the rest of the city, the entire area around the fountain was green. There were even three apple trees.

He expected to remain in the city for at least two days. The oasis would be a welcome source of water for him and the horses.

He turned the cart to the left to travel around the side of the courtyard away from the Council Chambers. He needed to dispose of the bodies and felt the Treasury was likely his best option. He pulled the cart in front and climbed the few steps to the doorway. The door, made of solid wood, stood wide open and was in good condition.

He stepped inside and took in the empty building. The place had been ransacked. It was not surprising. Even if the gold and silver had been left when the city had been abandoned, someone over the centuries would have looted the place eventually. The building itself, however, was solid. No walls were down. Hamel decided it would be the perfect place to dispose of the bodies.

He used one of the traders' horses to move each of the bodies of the men from the cart to the building. He then closed the solid door and led the horses to the water. He left them there while he looked for a stable in decent condition. Upon finding one tucked behind an old theatre, he retrieved the horses one at a time and placed each one in a stall, providing food for them from the cart. He appreciated the skill of the ancient architects. They had built their structures, even their stables, to last.

The cart itself he left in the open as he made his way across the courtyard toward the Council Chambers. The fountain had created a small pond in the center of the area with a river flowing off between the theater and the city's military headquarters. He crossed the small flowing river and approached the Council Chambers.

142

As he climbed the steps to the Chambers, his stomach turned. He longed for simpler times. He had loved his years as an Honored Patir and missed serving his people in that capacity. He had so many fond memories, but that was behind him. For now, he had more important matters to attend to.

He pushed open the great doors. Inside was a large foyer where people could stand as they awaited an audience with the Council or where Council members, when not in session, could meet with the people. The foyer appeared as though it had once been richly decorated, but the years had not been gentle on the room.

Hamel left the large outer doors open for a moment while he opened the Inner Council Chambers. The Chambers inside were much like the foyer—a poor image of its former glory. At one point, the leadership of the city would have met there, offering counsel and guidance and direction for the people. Three hundred years later, it looked more like a dungeon.

He returned to the courtyard and collected dry sticks and logs from some of the few trees that grew in that small area. The light was failing, and he would need to move quickly.

Once back inside the Inner Council Chambers, he built a fire and then turned to close the outside door. There were few animals in the wilderness, but he suspected so close to a water supply there was a greater chance of meeting a predator.

Hamel sat down and soaked in the light and warmth of the fire. He leaned back against one of the raised platforms set up high for the Council members. He had struggled so much over the last few days, but he felt in this place, he could relax. His meeting with Mellel had helped to take the pressure off his heart, and the sense of safety and security that seemed to fill the Council Chambers was encouraging.

His mind went back to Lillel and his children. For the first time in many years, he thought of them in terms of good memories, rather than pain and a sense of loss. He longed for them to be with him and deep inside, he felt the grief of their

143

loss but smiled instead at the joy he found in their memory. He pulled out some water and took a drink while he continued to reminisce.

His mind drifted to Markel. The look on the boy's face when Hamel had commanded him to go to Captain Cuttel was a painful memory, but it was the right decision. Not only was it the best place for him to be, but Hamel also needed to know Markel was with the Captain. Cuttel would keep him close.

The thought of Cuttel brought him back to Mariel. If the look on Markel's face was a painful memory, it was nothing compared to what he felt for his daughter. He had put her through a lot in recent months.

It was necessary. He could not have given her his blessing. He had held back the Patir's Kiss and would do it again.

His mind then drifted to Karotel, but he stopped his thoughts and brought his mind back to the present. He would not go down that road in his mind—not until his heart was more settled.

On the wall opposite the Council seats was a large tapestry. It was a familiar pattern. It was similar to one of the tapestries that were often displayed in the Council Chambers in the Capital. It was largely red and black and showed a picture of a great battle, the details of which had been lost to history.

But it wasn't the tapestry that had caught his eye. Unlike his own Council Chambers, the Chambers in Benjelton contained an image on the wall behind where the tapestry hung.

He rose to his feet and walked to the tapestry. It was in shreds, but Hamel suspected it was not from vandals. The material appeared weak from the years it had hung on the wall. A light pull from his hands and most of it came down. The room filled with dust, and he quickly retreated to the other side, covering his mouth and coughing repeatedly.

Once he could breathe comfortably again, he examined the image on the wall. In the flickering light of the fire, he could see it was a mosaic. It was beautifully crafted, and it appeared as though not one of the tiles were missing. Hamel stared in awe at the craftsmanship of the work. He had seen the occasional mosaic in the Capital, but nothing that even came close to the beauty that lay before him.

He sat back down and grabbed his waterskin. The mosaic was truly marvelous, but he could not understand the meaning of the image. It was simple enough in one sense. It was a picture of people—of a family. But what made it confusing was the artist appeared to be trying to represent something, the meaning of which must have been lost to time.

In the center, down near the bottom were three children playing. They were young with the oldest only just on his two feet, while the other two looked to be infants. There were stories told of two children born at one time from the same Matir. They said the children would then be the same age and often they would look identical to one another. He wondered if the legends had come from an image such as what he saw before him.

Crouching down next to the children were the Matir and the Patir. They appeared happy and proud of their children. Next to them, on either side, were another four or five other adults, all of whom looked on as though they were proud of the children before them. He did not understand what that part of the image could refer to. He wondered if perhaps it represented cousins or brothers and sisters of the Matir and Patir.

The part that was strangest to him, however, was the two people above the Matir and Patir. Not only did the design of the mosaic make it look as though they were a Matir and Patir of the ones below, but the artist had drawn them as though they were ill. They were each bent over, just slightly, as though they were too tired to stand up straight. Both had white hair. The Matir had long hair, down nearly to her waist, while the Patir's hair was mostly gone.

There were, of course, many men and women among the People of the Ridge who found their hair had grown white. Hamel himself had a fair amount of white growing on his head, but rarely did anyone experience completely white hair. He thought about his own hair and for the first time realized something that should have been obvious. With each year, he had gained a little more white hair. If that continued, eventually he would have only white hair.

Hamel took in the image of the Matir and Patir with white hair once again. He wondered if perhaps the two people in the image were like him. Perhaps they had both escaped the Dusk and lived well past their thirty-fourth year. If that were so, then he was not the first to have done this. Perhaps he would not be the last. Perhaps the mosaic was a tribute to two people such as himself upon whom the Dusk had not fallen.

He continued to examine the image. It was truly a work of art, regardless of its meaning. One thing was for sure, it was a testament to seeing one's children's children. Many would see their adopted children's children, but to see the infants of the children born to you was a miracle beyond what anyone had thought possible.

Hamel smiled. He imagined Lemmel, had he still been alive, meeting the children of his children. The faces of all his living children moved through his mind, and he pictured each one holding an infant, born to their own children. He wondered briefly if there would be some way that others could live past the Dusk as well.

He shook his head at the absurdity of it all. It was clearly nothing more than a dream by a creative artist. It was perhaps even a picture of how much people relied on the teachings and influence of their Matirs and Patirs. Maybe it was a way to point out their influence living on past the Dusk. It could not be an image of people surviving that long. While he had somehow survived, the idea of not only one parent, but both surviving was ludicrous.

Hamel pulled out his bedroll and spread it on the floor. The stone was uncomfortable, and the room smelled musty, but he was ready for a good night's sleep. He would need his rest for the days ahead.

146

CHAPTER 19

THE DAY IN THE COURTYARD

Hamel stood in the sitting room, looking out the window. The anticipation in his heart was overwhelming. It was a day of great honor and privilege.

He heard Lillel's light footsteps come to a halt beside him and felt her soft hand slide into his. When he looked down into her eyes, there were tears of joy.

It was a day of joy and sadness. The children they were to adopt would be their children, and they would love them and care for them. The reason, however, was because of loss. They were coming to Hamel and Lillel because they had lost their parents to the Dusk. It was a day all expected would come, but there was great pain.

"I hear my son is thirteen. I wonder if he is taller than I am," Lillel said. A Matir always received a son to raise, while a Patir always received a daughter. "If he is rebellious, he might be a lot to handle."

"You do not stand alone, Lillel. I will be a Patir to him as well," Hamel said. His heart was bursting with pride. "Do not worry, my dear. You will be a wonderful Matir to him. He will grow to be a man of honor from your teaching. Besides, I have heard great things about this young man."

He placed his hands on her swollen belly. She was due in less than a month. It was a lot to take on the birth of a child as well as a

147

newly adopted son, but Lillel would manage. He felt his face break out into a large grin, and his heart burst with pride, knowing his wife would succeed at such a venture.

The gate squeaked open and drew Hamel's eyes back to the front walkway. "I told you to oil that gate, Hamel," Lillel said. Hamel could hear the smile in her voice.

"I like knowing when people are arriving," he replied, also with a smile.

Three people approached the door. The Matir's son always came first when children were adopted. Hamel's new daughter would come soon after.

The two adults walked in front, blocking Hamel and Lillel's view of the boy coming up behind them. They came to the door and, in line with tradition, stepped aside and allowed the boy to enter on his own.

Hamel turned and walked to the back of the room. It was proper to give Lillel the chance to meet her new son without distraction. It was a moment to remember, and while he would watch intently to share in her joy, he would not intrude.

The boy came around the corner and stood, facing Lillel. He bowed low to her, bending his knees, then stood up straight while she bowed her head, just at the neck. Lillel was not a tall woman, and the boy towered over her.

"Welcome, my child; I am Matir Eatal Lillel," Lillel said. Hamel could see she was nearly shaking with joy, but the formality was necessary.

"Thank you, Matir; I am a boy without a parent," the young man said, his voice cracking with emotion.

Lillel approached the boy and knelt down on one knee. She looked tiny before the young man. Hamel noticed the boy appeared to be at the end of a major growth spurt. "You are not without a parent, my son," Lillel said. Hamel had never heard her voice shake with such nervousness. There were few privileges greater than the adoption of a child. "I am your Matir, and I love you. I am tied to you and you to me. We are one. We are honored family."

The boy bowed again before his Matir and when he spoke, his voice shook as well. "I believe you, my Matir. I am not alone. You are my Matir. I commit to you to follow you to the ends of the earth and back."

Lillel opened her mouth but closed it again. She took a deep breath but was overcome by emotion. She dropped her chin down onto her chest and then laughed. "Forgive me, my son. I am just so honored to take you in that I am losing control of my speech."

The boy nodded, but Hamel noticed the sides of his mouth curl upwards. He reached out and placed a hand on her shoulder and said, "It is okay, my Matir. I am honored too. When I heard I was being adopted by Matir Lillel, I could not believe I could be honored so."

Hamel's face broke out into a grin. The young man was already a man of honor.

Lillel took another breath before she continued. "Thank you, young man." The adoption ceremony was a beautiful moment in a family's life. Rarely did it ever happen perfectly according to tradition. She continued on as best she could. "And I commit to you, my son, to lead you faithfully, and I will give my life to get you to the ends of the earth and back again. As a token of faithfulness to you, I give you my name, Eatal. It will be yours forever and a seal of my promise to you."

The boy smiled. It was a moment of great honor to receive a family name. "If this is true, will you give me my Matir's kiss?"

He bent his head down. From her kneeling position, he was too tall even with his head bent. He smiled, and Lillel laughed. He bent down low at the waist for her to give him his Matir's kiss on his forehead, the kiss of blessing.

Once the blessing was given, she rose to her feet and asked, "Who are you, my son?"

The boy stood straight with a proud smile on his face and said, "I am Eatal Lemmel, son of Matir Eatal Lillel."

The ceremony was complete. Lillel embraced her new son. The difficult days still lay ahead as they learned to be one, but this day was a day of joy.

There was the sound of the door opening again, and Hamel realized his daughter had arrived. His stomach lurched, and he broke into a sweat. He had faced enemies and even Beasts and risen up victorious, but even on the battlefield, he had never felt so weak. He was about to meet his new daughter.

He moved to the center of the room. Out of the corner of his eye, he watched as Lillel and Lemmel stepped off to the side. They would give him his space but share in his joy.

The young lady stepped around the corner. She was only nine years old and quite tiny for her age. Hamel stared in awe. She was a beautiful young girl who stood straight and confident. He could, however, see the fear in her eyes. Her life had just been turned upside down in the loss of her parents. She was about to be adopted into a family, not even meeting her new Patir until that moment. It was often the case that even the two adopted children would not have met prior to the moment of adoption.

While her face betrayed fear, he could also see a strong intellect. Her eyes bore into him, and he felt for a moment that she could look into his very soul. She would grow to be a woman of great honor. Perhaps even an Honored Matir one day.

She bowed before him, bending her knees and then stood up. He returned the gesture with a slight bow of his head.

"Welcome, my child, I am Patir Rezin Hamel," Hamel said. He shook with joy and felt tears forming in his eyes.

"Thank you, Patir," she replied. "I am a girl without a parent."

Hamel approached the girl and knelt down on one knee before her. "You are not without a parent, my daughter. I am your Patir, and I love you. I am tied to you and you to me. We are one. We are honored family."

The girl bowed low again before Hamel and spoke. While she had managed to keep her voice steady until that point, he could hear a shake in her voice as she said, "I believe you, my Patir. I am not alone. You are my Patir. I commit to you to follow you to the ends of the earth and back."

Hamel smiled. The family bond was precious. "And I commit to you, my daughter, to lead you faithfully, and I will give my life to get you to the ends of the earth and back again. As a token of my faithfulness to you, I give you my name, Rezin. It will be yours forever and a seal of my promise to you."

The girl blushed and lowered her eyes for a moment before catching herself. The ceremony was difficult to get quite right.

"If this is true, will you give me my Patir's kiss?" She leaned forward, and Hamel kissed her on the forehead.

Hamel was overcome with joy. The kiss of blessing was an honor to give. He leaned back and asked, "Who are you, my daughter?"

The little girl stood proudly and said with a big smile on her face, "I am Rezin Karotel, daughter of Patir Rezin Hamel."

Hamel awoke with a start. His dreams were often troubling for him.

It had been twenty years since they had adopted Karotel and Lemmel. It had been such a wonderful time and filled with so many joys and challenges. Now, twenty years later, Lillel and Lemmel were dead; Karotel had proclaimed Hamel to be a man without honor; and his Mariel had rejected him as her Patir. Even his name, Rezin, the very name he had given to each of his adopted children had been taken from him. He shivered at the memory.

He pulled himself to his feet. Most mornings, he awoke feeling sore, but the hard ground of the Council Chambers seemed to have added to the aches.

He opened the door to the hallway just enough to see through the windows that the sun had not yet risen. He wasn't sure it would be safe to go outside until the sun was up in case there were night predators. He closed the door again and added a bit more wood to the fire, stirring it to bring it back to life.

Once the fire had grown enough to see clearly in the room, he stretched and began a time of exercise and training. It felt good to do his morning routine.

After a good hour, he stretched each of his muscles. His muscles felt tired and sore, but he always enjoyed the feeling after exercise. What he was not prepared for, however, was the smell. He rarely allowed himself to get to such a point. It was so bad that he wasn't sure he even wanted to be around himself.

Hamel picked up his waterskin and made his way outside. The early morning air was dry and cool. The sun had come up, and there were no signs of predators, so he made his way to the fountain. He took the time to refresh himself, clean up, and top up his water before wandering over to check on the horses.

The five horses were all safe and sound. He led the two horses that had pulled the cart out and hooked them up. He needed the cart closer to the Council Chambers, and once the cart was moved, he released them in the area around the fountain. He then led the other three horses out and released them as well. The animals grazed and drank deeply from the pond while he set to work.

The wagon turned out to be an unexpected benefit. He would be able to make use of nearly all of it. He started by carrying the sacks of salt into the Chambers, setting them down just inside the doorway to the left. There were four layers of sixteen sacks. It would be far more than enough.

He focused on one layer at a time and carried all sixteen sacks inside before starting into the second layer. By the end of the second layer, his legs, arms, and shoulders felt like jelly, and his back ached. He pushed himself and finished off the third layer before taking a seat down by the water.

The horses themselves were tame and had not gone far. They seemed content to remain by the water and continued to eat and nibble on the vegetation. He still had not yet figured out what he would do with the extra horses. It would not do to wander into Olmos, dressed as a man of authority, leading four horses, two of which were cart horses without a cart. He suspected showing up in such a manner would raise many questions.

He allowed himself to doze off for a few moments, soaking in the warmth of the sun which had crept up over the buildings and shone down on the small oasis. When he awoke, he returned to the cart. There were sixteen bags left, one full layer. Hamel wrapped his arms around the first of the sixteen, but the weight was wrong.

Hamel shifted the bag and set it on the tail of the cart to examine it. He leaned in and took a sniff. The smell was familiar. It seemed to have a refreshing scent. The smell gave him an overwhelming sense of thirst. Part of him wanted to rip open the sack and eat whatever was contained inside.

152

He used his knife to cut open a corner of the sack. It had been sewn shut, much like the sacks of salt had been and, unless someone tried to pick it up, it would appear to be salt.

The substance inside was a light brown powder. He felt the urge to taste it but shook off the thought. It would be ridiculous to eat something when he didn't know what it was.

He picked up the sack and carried it into the Council Chambers, careful not to spill the sack or even breath in the powder. The other fifteen sacks were likewise filled with the same powder. He set all sixteen aside, away from the salt. He wanted to save the powder for closer examination when he had more time and others to help him.

Hamel then returned to the cart and set to work on disassembling it. It was hard work as the cart was well built, but he wanted to make use of the wood. Most traders from Ridge carried some weapons, tools, and a few small parts, just in case something broke along the way, and he was pleased to see Olmosite traders did the same. The tools came in handy as he pulled piece after piece off the cart.

When he had finished disassembling the cart, it was nearing the supper hour. He wandered around and collected the horses, returning them to the stable. The traders had some oats in their cart, but he saved it for a later time. They had moved freely for the day and eaten their fill. He secured them within their individual stalls and closed up the building before returning to the courtyard.

He grabbed a few apples from the trees to give him a bit of energy before setting back to work. He wanted all the pieces of the cart inside the Chambers before nightfall.

When he had finished carrying all the parts from the cart into the Inner Chambers, he closed the door and took a look around the entire building, checking each and every room. The Council Chambers were quite large and built to allow people to move from one room to the next, flowing throughout the building. Only the Inner Council Chambers, the room in which the Council would meet, had only one door, although the Inner Chambers in the Capital had a small door built behind the Honored Matir or Patir's seat to offer the Council members a way of escape in an emergency. He suspected the Benjelton Council Chambers had a similar exit.

He was able to move through most of the building without too much trouble. The structure was surprisingly solid, considering the years of neglect. Only one room in the entire building appeared to be anything but structurally sound. The windows around the outside of the building gave a great deal of light for his exploration.

When he had finished his exploration of the building, he returned to the Inner Chambers and lit a fire before closing the door. There were small windows at the top of the room to let the smoke escape, but they did not offer much light. He took the opportunity to check on the door behind the Honored seat and, sure enough, it was not only there, but simple to open. It led into a hallway, opening behind a ripped tapestry. He stepped back inside and closed the door behind him.

It was time to think matters through and lay out his plan. He took some food and water and climbed into one of the top Council seats. From his position high above the area, he could see all his supplies at once.

The cart had provided a great deal of wood and even some extra rope and more, which would all prove to be helpful. He wished to set up traps throughout the building. He needed to use the materials well and efficiently.

As both a General and as the Honored Patir of the nation, he had developed the skill of looking over his list of resources and quickly laying out a plan to make efficient use of everything available to him. He stared at the materials in the flickering light of the fire and mentally walked through each room of the building, laying out traps, along with how he would make use of them.

He wasn't entirely sure he would need such a thing, but he wished to be prepared. If he ran into danger and could return to the Council Chambers, it would be good to know he would be ready.

By the time he had laid out his plan, mentally making use of every piece he could, the sun had set. Hamel committed the plans for each trap to memory and settled down for the night. The next day would be busy. He hoped he could complete his tasks and be on his way the day after that.

CHAPTER 20

THE DAY OF PREPARATION

"My Patir, why do you read so many reports from your soldiers?" Karotel asked.

Hamel's heart warmed as it did every time she asked a question. She was as curious and intent on learning everything she could as he had been at her age. However, her ability to retain information at twelve years of age was remarkable. He was convinced she would be an Honored Matir by her early twenties. It didn't hurt that her own adopted Patir had been made Honored Patir at age twenty-three.

"What kind of information do you think a report contains?" Hamel asked.

Karotel's eyes drifted to the floor for a moment. He could see she was mentally moving through all the information she had collected about the military. Her eyes shifted toward the ceiling as she imagined possibilities outside her gathered knowledge. He smiled again. She would be a great Honored Matir.

"I would expect the reports would include all information about everything that happened during an event, such as who was there, what battles were fought or not fought, what issues were faced... even including the unimportant details," Karotel said.

"Why would it include the unimportant details?" Hamel asked.

"Because what's unimportant to the soldier at the moment is not necessarily unimportant to the nation in the days to come. Extra information will not hurt. Lack of information could be deadly."

Hamel knew his eyes were beaming. He never hid his pride for his children from them. "Exactly right. To answer your question, as General, I need to be fully aware of all that is happening among all the soldiers. It is a large task. Few have ever held the title of not only Honored Patir but also General at the same time. Because of that, I need to be very disciplined to be fully aware of all that is going on."

"Yes, that is why you are a good General and a good Honored Patir," Karotel said.

"Thank you, my child. And because I see the same discipline in you, I expect you will be an Honored Matir one day," Hamel said.

Karotel blushed. She enjoyed compliments, but rarely took them well. "But I would not want to be a General. I think Lemmel will be my General when I am Honored Matir."

"I think that would be wise," Hamel said. Lemmel was already proving himself to be a capable soldier. He would be advancing up the ranks in short order. It would not surprise Hamel if Lemmel would…

Hamel sat back in his chair with a start and examined his daughter's face. Something wasn't right. What he was seeing wasn't real—couldn't be real. The conversation with Karotel had happened, but he could not be there at that moment. He was dreaming. He knew everything was about to change.

In his dream, his little girl's gaze turned from adoration to a serious, yet cold expression. That part of the dream had not happened. She opened her mouth and screamed at him, "Your wife and children are going to die in a year, Hamel. Lemmel will betray us, and I will do my part to see that you are disgraced!"

Hamel awoke with a start. He had had many similar dreams. Fond memories interrupted by the realization that much would be lost a short while after the memory took place.

His heart ached for Lemmel. When Lillel had died, the boy had been seventeen years old. He was too young to have to undergo the loss of a second Matir. Hamel could remember the fear in the young man's eyes. He was so strong and so confident, yet he feared without his Matir he would have no one. He feared he would be left to face the world alone.

Hamel had explained to the young man that his fears were unfounded. He had considered the boy to be his own son from the moment he had arrived at their house. The apprenticeship of the Matir had not merely been a contract. They were family. Hamel had continued his son's training until he had reached the rank of High Colonel.

Hamel blinked away the tears. He could never understand what would have caused Lemmel to go over the wall to the Beasts. There was nothing in any of their investigations to show a sign of struggle or that any of the traitors had been forced into that course of action or even out of their homes. They had simply packed up some of their clothing and gear, then disappeared.

Hamel pushed the thoughts out of his mind. If he continued down that road, he knew he would be thinking about the day he had found Lemmel's uniform, wrapped around an infant Beastchild. The thoughts and memories were too much to bear.

He decided to be productive in the hopes of keeping his mind off painful memories. The sun was not yet showing through the windows, so he added some wood to the fire before stretching and doing his morning exercise.

Once he had finished, he sat down for breakfast. The thought of the powder he had found in the cart had been troubling him. He did not recognize it as something that was commonly imported into Ridge Nation. Since he had never come across anything like it before, it suggested to him the substance was illegal.

He could not imagine what it could be used for. In his experience as Honored Patir and as General, he had never come across a drug that resembled anything like that. It also wasn't a medicine, as far as he could tell. Since it was so well disguised underneath the salt, it was clear it had harmful or, at the very least, illegal purposes. He would certainly want to investigate the matter, but the matter would need to be discussed after he had regained his position as Honored Patir.

He pulled his mind back to the task at hand. He needed to set traps throughout the building.

The first order of business was to secure the Council Chambers. He examined the main door and saw it was solid enough to keep even the most intent of adversaries out for a significant amount of time. On the inside of the door were brackets set into the solid wood archway. As he dug around through the debris to the left of the door, he found the beam used to brace the door from the inside.

He picked up the beam and, while his muscles strained under the weight, it dropped without resistance into the brackets. Once set in place, Hamel could see it would secure the door.

It would not, unfortunately, work well in a rush. He would need to have all his strength to get the beam into place. As a soldier, he had learned early on never to develop a strategy which relied on the full capacity of a soldier. If he were injured in any way or did not have the time to place the beam, his weakness could cost him his life.

He studied the door for a moment and considered his options. The beam was far too heavy to pick up and move in a rush, but perhaps he could arrange it so he would not need to lift it.

Hamel grabbed a smaller length of rope and tied one end of the beam onto the bracket on the one side of the door. He secured it in such a way that the beam could twist in the bracket but not slip off.

He then found an old spike in the supplies left by the traders. He took a hammer from their toolkit and drove the spike into the door frame above where he had tied the beam to the bracket. The rope held the one end of the beam in place, working as a hinge, while allowing the other end of the beam to move in and out of the brackets. When he swung the loose end of the beam up, it hit the nail and held.

The beam now stood upright, held at the bottom by the rope and at the top it leaned against the nail. He gave it a push back toward the brackets, trying his best to guide it down and found it slipped right into the other bracket. He had a system to secure the door in a simple manner, even if he were injured or weak.

He slipped the beam back up and examined the rope, acting as his hinge. It appeared to be solid with no fraying and no slippage. It would serve its purpose.

Hamel then moved all the sacks of powder into the Inner Council Chambers. He set them behind one of the tables set for the Council members in one of the spots far off to the right in the room. It would hopefully remain out of sight if anyone moved through the building.

He checked the door in the back of the room again and saw that it was solid and had a lock on it, secured from the inside. The room could function as a safe house in a time of need.

He then moved into the hallway and throughout the rooms of the Council Chambers. It was hard, tedious work, and he hated the thought that it might be necessary, but he needed a way to incapacitate a group of enemies if he were pursued. He suspected Mellel knew Hamel had that in mind when he had suggested that particular building. With the layout of the hallways and rooms and with the security of the Inner Council Chambers, the building was ideal for his purposes.

He went from room to room, setting up traps and snares. He set up a snare in one room, held by tension and intended to be set off when someone stepped on the trigger set into the floor. In another room, he placed four heavy sacks of salt high above the doorway, capable of falling when a rope was pulled. He hung the wagon wheels by a rope and set them to swing down to hit someone entering the room. The wheels were heavy enough on their own, but he added some sharpened pieces of wood as spikes to guarantee their effectiveness. He needed only to pull a rope to release them.

He continued through the rooms, setting snares and traps. In the unstable room, he weakened what supports were in place. He then set a rope on tension to pull the strongest remaining support out from under the ceiling to collapse it on those inside the room.

When he was finished, he did not think anyone who chased him into the Council Chambers would survive. It would be the perfect defensive position, assuming he was not being chased by an army.

Hamel stepped outside and took a deep breath. The sun had made its way to the west and was nearly disappearing behind the buildings. As he thought about a meal, he realized he had forgotten the horses. He rushed to the stables and checked on them. They were antsy and irritable from being cooped up all day. He led each one out to the grass to graze and to refresh themselves. He ate his supper meal in the cool of the evening air, sitting by the flowing water coming from the fountain. He would be ready to leave the next day.

CHAPTER 21

THE DAY OF INJURY

The next morning, Hamel awoke early. His eyes cracked open, and he stared into the dark. From the dying embers of the fire, he could just make out the shapes of the Council benches, but not much more. He wasn't entirely sure where he was, but he waited patiently while his mind settled on the events of the last three weeks.

He could hear something happening, but he was not quite awake enough to know what it was. It wasn't nearby, but it was disturbing. He knew he needed to act, but he was so tired.

He shook his head and pushed himself up with his arm. It was far too early, and he was no longer used to jumping up alert at the sound of danger. Outside... the problem was outside.

He grabbed the rifle that he had found in the traders' cart and rushed out through the Inner Council Chamber doors to the outside doors, but he paused to listen for just a moment. He could make out snarling and barking. He suspected it was a pack of wild dogs, and they sounded as if they were across the courtyard. The pack had picked up the horses' scent, likely while stopping at the river for a drink.

He cracked open the door just enough to see outside. It was dark, but he could make out movement on the far side of the courtyard. He wasn't entirely sure if he would be able to do anything until the sun began to rise, but he suspected the horses would be safe, albeit quite disturbed. The stable was solid.

Hamel closed the door and made his way down the hallway to the stairs. He had to be careful as he moved through the Council Chambers. The building was well set up now to do a great deal of harm if a man were to step in the wrong place or trip on a rope holding back a trap ready to spring. He did not want to be injured or killed by his own work.

On the second floor, he opened a boarded-up window and felt the cool, evening air wash over him. The sun was creeping up in the east, and he could make out at least eight dogs, perhaps more. They were all around the stable, barking and jumping at the windows. There was not much chance that one might find its way inside. The stable was made of stone, the windows too high, and the doors too solid for a pack of dogs. The greater concern was the state the horses would be in.

His own horse, the one Mellel had given him, moved and acted as a warhorse. It was obedient, intelligent, and ready for action. There were scars on its flank and one on its nose. The dogs would upset his horse, but if he had evaluated the horse properly, it would be more anxious to join the battle than flee from it.

He took aim with his rifle. There were few packs of wild dogs in the wilderness. No trader tolerated them. The animals killed off horses, occasionally attacked people, and if they roamed too close to a village, they could attack a herd. When that happened, the villagers would send a hunting party after the dogs. They were a nuisance no one tolerated.

He fired the rifle, and a dog went down. The others jumped and spun around as they searched for the new threat. Two of the dogs rushed to the side of their fallen member, sniffed him, and spun around, looking for the danger.

He fired again, then a third time, each time killing another dog. By the time the third one went down, the remaining dogs bolted down the street. As they raced away, he took another shot and killed a fourth. It would not do to have the pack on his tail as he made his way to Olmos. Four dogs escaped, and he hoped the experience was enough to scare them far away.

Hamel made his way down to the Inner Council Chambers and grabbed his belt with a knife, secured it to his waist, and slung the rifle over his shoulder. The horses would need to be checked, but he did not want to be caught by the dogs if they came back. As an afterthought, he grabbed his sidearm and tucked it in his belt.

He stepped out into the morning air. There was no sound at first of dogs or any other animals. As he neared the stable, the sound of the horses reached his ears. They were in a frenzy, and one of the horses was screaming in pain. He wasn't too keen on stepping into a stable with four or five panicking horses, but if they did not calm down, they could seriously hurt themselves. From the sounds inside the stable, one was already injured.

The handle to the stable was heavy, as was the door. He began to unlatch it when movement to his left caught his eye. He whipped out his sidearm and fired, killing a dog that had stayed behind, but he could not get a shot off at the second one. Hamel threw himself against the side of the stable, and the dog sailed past. In the movement, he lost his sidearm.

The animal turned and was on him in a second. He felt the pain in his calf as the dog bit down and shook its head, trying to incapacitate Hamel. With the pain, his military training kicked in, and his hand grasped the dog by the scruff of its neck, slamming his knife into the side of its chest.

In the light of the early dawn, his eyes landed on his sidearm, and he lunged for it. Hamel scanned the shadows and watched for any movement.

Once back on his feet, he set himself a new plan. The horses were crashing about within the stable, but he would not be of much use to them if he did not care for his injury.

Hamel cried out in pain with the first few steps as he hobbled his way across the courtyard to the rushing water. Once there, he washed the wound. The water felt refreshing, but it also stung. He had lost too much blood in the few short minutes and decided to pull off his tunic and use it as a bandage. He used his knife to slice the material into long strips and tied the cut on his leg. Within a few minutes, he had managed to slow the bleeding.

His thoughts continued to be drawn to the horses, but he set that concern aside for the time being. An untreated wound could be the death of a soldier. He had not paid much attention to the medical supplies he had received from Mellel, but it was time to put them to use.

Every step felt like fire burning through his left leg as he made his way to the apple trees. He scanned the area, hoping to find a thick branch to use as a crutch, but he moved on without finding one. Apple trees were not known for growing strong, straight branches.

When he reached the bottom of the steps leading into the Council Chambers, he shook his head. There was nothing to be done but endure the pain. He gritted his teeth as he moved up the steps.

Once inside, he stoked the fire. The sun was not up enough to shine much light into the room, but in the light from the flickering flames, he could make his way to his pack. As he rummaged through the supplies he had received from the man in the oasis, he found some extra clean cloth and some salve. He immediately set to work on pulling off the bandages and applying the salve before he retied the cloth. The clean bandages he saved for later. He suspected he would need them soon enough.

Hamel gasped for air as he leaned back against a wall. If he didn't move his leg at all, the pain would settle down to an intense throbbing. In the army, they had trained men to calm their hearts and settle their minds during times of danger or injury. There were times when rest was needed whether a soldier felt capable or not. Within a few minutes, he drifted off to sleep.

A short while later, his eyes opened. His leg ached, and as he stood to his feet, the room spun. He had lost far more blood than he had at first thought.

A quick look at the bandage told him the bleeding had not stopped. He pulled off the old cloth, applied more salve, and tied a new bandage around the cut. He made sure the bandage was tighter than the first had been.

It was time to move out. He wasn't sure how the horses were faring, but he hoped they had calmed down somewhat. He picked up his packs and grabbed the cloak he had received from Mellel. It was a perfect traveling cloak, and he hoped the status such a cloak suggested would give him a bit more space to move around in Olmos. His accent had held up well with the traders, and aside from the new injury, he felt his chances of making it through the border of Olmos were good.

The sun shone brightly by the time he walked out of the Council Chambers and hobbled down the steps. The courtyard seemed strangely quiet after the events of the early morning, and Hamel made his way across to the stables. On his way, he stopped at the river flowing away from the fountain, drank his fill, and topped up both waterskins. He had less than a day's ride to get to the border of Olmos, but he wasn't sure how long it would be after that to get to Pollos. He had assumed it to be a fair distance from the border, based on various comments he had heard from Pulanomos years ago, but Olmosites were very private about their nation.

When he reached the stable, he pulled out his sidearm. He didn't think there was much chance that more dogs were hiding around the corner, but the pain in his leg was hard to ignore. It was difficult to so quickly forget its cause.

He grabbed the latch and unlocked the door. The sight inside was worse than he had expected. Three of the horses in their fright had broken out of their stalls. Two stood at the back of the stable, wild-eyed and snorting loudly. The third had obviously not only broken out of the stall, but one of the boards of the gate had broken in a sharp piece, and the horse had fallen on it. It had not survived.

His own horse and the final horse from the traders were both in their stalls. Only his own horse seemed relatively unaffected. The other horse had the same wild look in its eyes.

Hamel did not want to approach the two horses standing at the back of the stable, so he swung the door open wide and stepped out of the way. He walked a short distance away, back from the stable, and waited. He hoped they would come out and perhaps some time at the river might calm them down, but it was not to be.

A few moments after he stepped back, the first of the two horses poked its head out the door, with the second stepping up next to it. They looked skittish, but he thought they might calm down. Hamel relaxed for a moment, but at the sound of a crow cawing nearby, both horses bolted into the courtyard, racing away down the street.

Hamel hoped they would stop once they reached a certain point, but they turned the corner and disappeared from sight. He hobbled back into the stable. His leg was causing him much grief, but there was nothing that could be done about it for the time being. He ignored the pain as best he could and approached the stall his own horse was in. He pulled open the gate and stood out of the way. The horse snorted a few times and stepped up beside him as if nothing were out of the ordinary. He saddled his horse and led it to the grassy area in the courtyard, leaving it to graze for a few minutes while he went back for the other horse.

The horse breathed normally. It stood tall and appeared calm, but its eyes revealed a different story. He pulled open the door to the stall and stepped out of the way. The horse didn't move. He hobbled into the stall next to it and reached through the slats to give the horse a little push. He did not want to stand anywhere near the animal while it was so terrified.

The horse did not respond at all to the touch. He gave it a harder push, then a slap. The slap moved the horse, but far too much. It bolted, as had the others, out of its stall and then out of the stable. Moving as fast as he could, he followed it out, but it was out of sight by the time he reached the courtyard.

He hoped the horses would return to Olmos. It was possible three horses returning to Olmos without their owners might cause questions to be asked, but he assumed the border guards would have no reason to associate the horses with him.

He wandered back to the fountain where his horse grazed. The sun had climbed into the sky. It was mid-morning. With a well-rested and well-fed horse, he hoped he could make good time and reach the border before it was too late in the evening. He pulled out the oats he had collected from the trader's cart, and while the horse ate, he took another look at his leg.

The bleeding had stopped, and the bandage did not yet need to be cleaned. The pain was still intense, but he knew it would hurt for quite a few days. The journey to Olmos would not help, but he hoped he could get some better care while there. A lot was riding on the unknown when it came to the Olmosites.

He let his horse eat and drink for another half hour, then pulled himself to his feet and led his horse away from the water. The climb into the saddle hurt more than he had thought it would.

As he moved through the streets, he distracted his mind from the pain by memorizing the turns. It was a simple, familiar layout as it resembled the Capital, but he did not want to make a wrong turn in a moment of crisis. He had long since learned that being well prepared was as valuable as being well disciplined.

At the exit to the city, the gates and walls caught his eye. He had not paid them much attention on his way in, but he was surprised to see they were as solid as the Valley Wall at the Capital. There were turrets every fifty paces or so, and the wall was thick. As he rode outside, he looked back and saw a great deal of scarring on the wall, indicating they had faced many battles. The wall, however, appeared as though it could withstand any abuse thrown at it.

He wondered what enemies his ancestors had faced in the wilderness. The Beasts were not likely a threat that far inland. The Olmosites had been allies for centuries. He did not think any of the other nations would come so deep into the old Ridge territories. It was a question he suspected might never be answered. The lack of historical records left many questions.

Hamel pushed the thoughts out of his mind. He had spent the last number of years reflecting on many such matters, but he was on a mission. He had to focus.

Once back on the road, he turned east and moved at a fast pace. The horse was strong and quite attentive to the road ahead, adjusting its course to avoid any problem sections of the road. He made good time, stopping only when necessary and was pleased to see by late afternoon, the border of Olmos was visible in the distance. He had once been that far before, just to the border, but because of the private nature of the Olmosite people, he had not made it past the gates. Even the Ridge Ambassador to the Olmosites could not go past the gate.

CHAPTER 22

THE DAY OF POWER

The Olmosite border town was a mess. On the edge of the town were buildings and tents that served primarily as loading docks for traders. Carts could be loaded and sent out along the highway leading into Ridge. There were three border towns such as that one, each of which had its own road leading to Ridge Nation.

Olmos was a large nation and spread out over a vast area. Their domain was walled in on all sides.

Hamel had always been so impressed by their ability to build a wall covering hundreds of miles. It was solid and well-guarded all along its length, although he had never learned more than that. He did not know for sure what kind of army they had, what size of a population, or what sort of armaments or defenses they had.

He had suspected their military was not as disciplined as his own. When Pulanomos had been in the Capital, many years before, he had observed some of the military training and drills. Hamel had seen the shock on his friend's face at the effort put into ensuring a well-prepared, well-disciplined military.

While Ridge rarely, if ever, dealt with soldiers questioning or disobeying orders, the few Olmosite soldiers he had observed seemed more than willing to turn on a

170

commanding officer in a moment. He smiled to himself. He had told Lillel he thought the Olmosite soldiers were all grumpy. Not one ever appeared content.

The thought brought him back to the moment. He would soon have to stand before one of those "grumpy" soldiers. He hoped he could find one having a good day, but he was not feeling optimistic about his chances.

After the section with loading docks, he passed guard stations and the Ambassador's section as well as a meeting hall. No one, aside from the Ridge Ambassador, his staff, some Olmosite soldiers, and the occasional family lived outside the walls. Most crossed through the gates every evening to return to their homes and to whatever lay on the other side of the wall.

In the area past the loading docks, three soldiers' barracks stood apart from one another, spread out over a distance. In between two of the buildings was a meeting place. The Ambassador's home was off to the north. It was obvious that it had been built far from the actual gate into Olmosite territory. With the barracks near the gate, it sent a clear message to all outsiders.

He rode his horse toward the gate. There were soldiers on top of the wall with rifles pointed down at the people, and each of the border guards was heavily armed. Similar to the Olmosite soldiers he had met in the past, everyone looked "grumpy."

Hamel brought his horse in behind another man, also mounted and wearing a relatively nice looking cloak. No one from Ridge had ever gone through the border that he had been aware of. He was not sure how to navigate his way past the guards. He decided to observe how each person interacted with the guards and follow the example of the man in front of him.

The guards waved the man on the horse ahead of him to a halt and walked up beside him. "Hood down!" the guard screamed.

So far, Hamel did not think the border crossing would be an amicable experience. He examined the guard closely, his every movement, eye twitches, where he looked and when. The man in front bowed slightly to the guard and lowered his hood. The instant he did that, the guard squared his shoulders and yelled, "GET DOWN OFF YOUR HORSE!"

As the man dismounted, the guard screamed again. "Where are your papers?" and then proceeded to strike the man on the side of the head just as his feet hit the ground. Two other guards came up and ripped the paper out of the man's hands as he desperately pulled them from an inner pocket. The first guard screamed some more while the other two knocked the poor man to the ground. As he lay on the ground, they examined his papers.

The man lay motionless, and to Hamel, his position and lack of movement did not suggest injury, but submission. The guards began to laugh. One of the guards kicked the man while the other two read through his papers in detail.

Hamel's mind raced through all he had seen in that short interaction as well as what he had experienced over the years. Olmosites did not respect position, nor did they value compassion. He had learned years ago that Olmosites only feared power. For Hamel to get through the gate, he either needed to submit as the man ahead had, or he needed to be powerful and strike fear in the hearts of the soldiers.

Hamel smiled. He had it. The moment everything had changed had been the moment the man had first lowered his hood. He had submitted to the guards, and the guards were, from that point on, entirely in charge. Though the man was dressed as if he were a wealthy man of power, it had not helped his situation at all. Respect toward the guard was taken as weakness.

The other danger Hamel faced was that he could see the guards examining the man's papers in detail. They were looking for problems or issues. Mellel had said that Hamel's papers would not hold up to scrutiny.

Hamel had to approach the situation in a different way. He needed to remain in power from the start through to the finish. The only way through those gates was if the guards feared him and were afraid to keep him any longer than was necessary.

The three guards each took one more kick at the man and then scrunched up his papers, throwing them at him, before screaming for him to move on. The man had been granted passage through the walls.

They watched him go and then turned to Hamel. All three stood waiting for their next victim.

Before they could wave him forward, he brought his horse into the center of the three guards. The approach forced two of the men to jump out of the way. Once he was satisfied he had caused a stir, he dismounted.

The guard wearing Sergeant's stripes began to yell, "Did I tell you to dis…"

Hamel turned to him in a flash and raised one fist in the air with his index finger held up. The guard stopped mid-sentence, but his mouth remained open. Hamel hoped his outfit, the value of the blade on his belt, the warhorse behind him, and the way he carried himself was enough to convince the Sergeant to hold his tongue. The other two men, one a Private and the other a Corporal, stood on either side of their Sergeant, but neither spoke or made any move.

Hamel, with his hood still in place, stepped close to the Sergeant. The edge of his hood nearly touched the man's face. When he spoke, his voice was just above a whisper, but he filled it with malice, speaking through clenched teeth. "I will not speak to a Sergeant," Hamel began. He stepped even closer, forcing the man to take a half-step back. "You will get for me your commanding officer, or I will remove you from active duty today."

The Sergeant opened his mouth to speak, but only a stammer came out. He cleared his throat and said in a calm voice, "You are not in charge here, I will not…"

Hamel grabbed the man by his shirt and lifted him right off the ground. Hamel had noticed the man was thin and hoped he would be able to lift him easily. If the man had been too heavy, it would have severely diminished the effect Hamel was going for.

He pulled the man in close and said, "These are the last words you will hear from me. If you do not obey me instantly, I will show you what I meant when I said I will remove you from active duty today."

He dropped the man and, in the process, gave him just enough of a push to send him sprawling backward. He resisted the urge to watch the two other guards in case they attacked. The issue before him was power, not safety. He would need to take his chances that they would not attack. Confidence would declare more power.

If he was attacked by the soldiers, he would be finished. The riflemen on the walls would drop him in a moment. The only hope he had was to remain in charge and to give the impression he was not to be trifled with.

The Sergeant crawled to his feet and rushed off through the gates. Hamel crossed his arms, standing firm. His leg continued to throb, but he had learned over the years to ignore pain.

The two other men had not moved since Hamel had begun his interaction with the Sergeant, but once he crossed his arms, they stepped away from him. He could hear them whisper to one another, although he could not make out anything they said. The Corporal was quite a large man compared to the Sergeant, and Hamel suspected the man was evaluating whether or not it was worth challenging the stranger in the hopes of establishing himself above his Sergeant.

Hamel's suspicions were confirmed when the man stepped in front. He looked mean and confident and even a little excited about his chance to rise above the threat that sent his Sergeant running in fear.

Hamel ignored the man and stared straight ahead for a moment until the man began in a loud voice, "You will show me your pa…"

Hamel drove his fist as hard as he could into the man's chest, right above his heart. The Corporal gasped in pain for a moment before Hamel knocked the man unconscious with a left hook to the jaw. Hamel then relaxed, stood up straight, and crossed his arms, returning his gaze to the gate as if nothing had happened. Out of the corner of his eye, he watched the Private take two large steps back and hold his position.

Most people in the lineup had grown quiet and the guards, even the ones on the walls, remained still. It was as if no one dared speak above a whisper.

After about ten minutes, a man walked around the corner and through the gate. Hamel looked at his shoulder and saw the man was a Captain. He appeared to be in his early twenties.

Hamel could not submit to the Captain. With a Sergeant running in fear and a Corporal knocked out cold on the ground, the Captain would be looking for a reason to detain him. He had to remain in control.

As the Captain approached, he had a large frown on his face, and each fist was clenched. The officer looked down at the Corporal, and his jaw muscles rippled.

The Captain needed to be overpowered immediately. Before the man could speak, Hamel turned his head toward him and spit at his feet. "A Captain?" Hamel said in a voice that would carry even to the top of the wall. He laced his voice with no lack of disdain. He then turned to the Sergeant who had returned with the officer. "You brought me a Captain? Is this honestly the highest ranking officer at the wall today?"

The Captain stopped in his tracks. His mouth dropped open, and his fists unclenched. Fear had entered his eyes. When the man spoke, it was with a clear, steady voice, despite the unease Hamel could see in him. "I am in charge of the wall today and over all the officers. You will not find a higher ranking officer within ten miles."

Hamel stepped forward and spoke in the same quiet voice he had used on the Sergeant. His hood remained over his face, and Hamel hoped it had the added effect of giving him a menacing look. He tried to put as much rage into his voice as he could and quietly said, "Listen closely to what I am about to say to you, Captain. I did not expect to be faced with such an unfriendly welcome at the gate today. I have

175

been away on the kind of business that Captains such as yourself are not even aware goes on in this world."

He let that sink in for a moment and then followed it in the same quiet, sinister voice, "You now have two choices. One choice will end your career. The other choice will not affect you at all. You will be able to go back to work and forget about this whole incident."

Before the man could respond, he pulled out his papers, slammed them on the Captain's chest, and said, "Make your choice, Captain."

The Captain's face went white, and he gulped as he took the papers, opened them for a moment. Hamel could see the Captain's eyes did not focus on anything on the page, glancing at it for less than two seconds. He then neatly folded the papers in half, handed them to Hamel and said loudly, "Welcome home, Master. Is there anything else we can do for you while you are here?"

Hamel took a small step closer to the man and growled through clenched teeth, "Nothing, Captain. Nothing at all," before he turned back to his horse and climbed into the saddle. He noticed the guards gave him a wide berth as he moved through the gate. He was in. He had made it through the gates and was perhaps the first man or woman from Ridge Nation to ride through into Olmos.

Hamel was not prepared for what he saw on the other side of the gate. For the first few minutes, he rode his horse down walled areas, empty except for the occasional soldier. The walled areas turned left and right, and Hamel realized they were designed not only to slow people down but to prevent someone on the outside of the gate to gain even a glimpse of what might be on the other side.

When the passageway came to an end, and he stepped into the city which lay on the other side of the wall, he nearly fell off his horse. There was so much to take in, and little of it made much sense.

His first thought was shock at the level of poverty and despair. Within a stone's throw of his position, there were perhaps twenty men, women, and children along the streets, begging any of the dozens of people wandering through the area for bread, money, or anything of value. Soldiers moved through the crowds, and Hamel watched as those begging for food scurried out of their way. The streets themselves were nothing but mud. The buildings were in disrepair, and he could hear yells and screams of anger coming from just about every direction at once. To add to it all was the smell. He could not imagine what might cause such an odor. He suspected it was the smell of everything from human waste to rotting vegetables to perhaps even death. By comparison, the lower sections of the Ridge Capital bordered on paradise.

But the poverty, mud, screams, and even the yells were not what troubled him the most. There appeared to be a sickness upon some of the people. He tried not to stare and did his best to hide his shock. Some of the men and women had a look to them which he had never seen before and could not comprehend. Their skin sagged on their faces and arms. Their hair was either all white or had a lot of gray to it.

The few men and women with such a condition walked as though they were tired, and two of them used small sticks as crutches as they moved along. Some of those affected by the sickness walked as though their backs were too tired to keep themselves straight, or perhaps as if they had injured their backs. Some of the men had even lost large sections of their hair.

He turned his horse along the road to the right, hoping it would lead him somewhere useful as he collected his thoughts. The poverty, the mud, and the sickness were a lot to take in all at once. His immediate thought was that Olmos was so private because they were trying to hide a disease which had fallen upon their people.

If that were the case, however, he couldn't understand why they would allow some Olmosites to interact with the People of the Ridge. A sickness with a contagion typically led to a quarantine. He had noticed one of the men, walking with a stick and with his back bent over, was being helped along by a young boy who by all appearances remained healthy.

While he knew he should ignore the sickness for the time being and focus on the task at hand, the people he had seen troubled him. He allowed his thoughts to continue a little further.

He wondered briefly if, perhaps, the Olmosites were embarrassed about the sickness. He did not think that likely. They were a people of power. He did not think they would offer such compassion as he had witnessed in that young boy if the disease were thought of as an embarrassing weakness.

His mind drifted back to the mosaic he had seen in the Inner Council Chambers in Benjelton. There were people in the image that appeared to be representing parents of parents. They had been displayed as somewhat bent over. The man and woman in the picture each had white hair.

He nearly fell off his horse as a thought struck him. The people he had seen when he first came in through the gate's passageway and continued to see as he rode down street after street bore quite the resemblance, in certain ways, to the man and woman in the mosaic. He wondered for a moment if perhaps they had somehow escaped the Dusk and were not ill, just old.

The thought disturbed him. On the one hand, he thought it would be wonderful if people did not die in their fourth decade and could live to see their children's children or even to see their children's children's children. On the other hand, it seemed wrong. The Dusk was when people were meant to die.

He looked down at his hands for a moment and reminded himself that he had not died. He had noticed his skin change, and he looked different than others. He had also noticed he had developed a few lines on his skin such as he saw in great supply on the arms and faces of some of the men and women. A question crept into his mind, "If they were people who outlived the Dusk, how old were they?"

Hamel shook his head and pushed all thoughts of the Dusk from his mind. He had to concentrate on the matter at hand. He needed to find the city of Pollos. If Pulanomos's young assistant, Churoi, was still around, perhaps Hamel could find him in Pollos.

Churoi might be the one who could help him find the answers he needed.

CHAPTER 23

THE DAY OF OBSERVATION

As Hamel moved deeper into the border town, he began to notice the houses were cleaner, there appeared to be less poverty, and either the smell had improved, or he had grown used to it. He shook his head as he considered that even the nicer, cleaner homes were in worse condition than many houses in the lower sections of Ridge.

His first priority, he knew, was to find either a map to Pollos, the Capital of Olmos, or at the very least find directions. It was difficult to know how common maps were among the Olmosite people. If maps were not often used, they could be difficult to find or purchase without raising suspicion. To ask for directions, however, would declare himself to be an outsider. His accent would not save him from a people who recognized uncommon ignorance.

He decided his best option might be a library, if he could find one. There might, perhaps, be a map of the entire land in such a place. He thought it was also possible that he might even find a map of the city of Pollos.

The town turned out to be larger than he had expected. Thousands of people lived among the mud and poverty.

As he continued pushing farther inland from the wall, he came upon an area he suspected might be the town center. Olmosite architecture was unfamiliar with its extra spires and domes, but one such building had a large inscription which read, "Master Turoi." He suspected that was, at the very least, a sign of importance, if not authority and leadership.

A short distance from Master Turoi's palace, there was a large building which had a statue in front with a man and a woman looking over a large scroll. He hoped it was either a place of education or a library, either of which would have information. The possible library was situated next to a small stable with a hotel on the other side. Seeing as it was nearly evening, he decided to spend the night.

He rode his horse to the stable and dismounted. Immediately two young men raced out of the stable doors and up to Hamel. The one boy took the reins and led the horse into the stable while the other stood with his head bowed and his hand out. The whole process made him uncomfortable. The People of the Ridge were far more relational. Older men were expected to invest in the lives of younger men, to help them, encourage them, and support them. An opportunity to speak into their lives and to bless them in some way was not to be missed. These young men did not expect anything from Hamel, other than money.

He pulled out a small silver coin. He did not know how much money he would need to get to Pollos, but he suspected a coin such as the one he was about to give would carry great value to the young lad, far more than he would typically see in a day. When he placed the coin in the young man's hand, his suspicions were true. The boy nearly dropped it in his shock. He bowed low, landing on both knees and touching his forehead to the ground at Hamel's feet, then stood and rushed into the stable. He could hear the excited voices of the two young boys.

He turned toward the hotel to secure a room before heading to what he hoped was a library of sorts. On the main level of the hotel was a large common room full of tables, chairs, and people. The pub was far from tasteful in Hamel's view.

The men gathered at the various tables watched him closely. He could feel their eyes examining his cloak, his movements, his dagger. Hamel assumed his height and build, not to mention the rifle slung over his shoulder, added to the effect. The moment he looked back in any one of their directions, however, their gazes quickly turned to the floor, their table, or one another.

At the counter, a large man with an apron stepped up. The man was well built across his shoulders and arms, although his belly suggested a love of food. His eyes told the story of a man prepared for a fight, but his nose and jaw declared a man who had lost as many battles as he had won.

"Welcome, Master," the man began. "Are you here for a drink or for a few days?"

Hamel noticed the man's accent was not the same as the one he had perfected. He wondered if perhaps the accent in the capital was different than the accent of the people in the border towns. He decided to stick with the accent he had worked to develop and hoped it would help to carry more authority to a people consumed with a desire for power.

A moment of doubt surrounding his entire plan passed over him. There had been so many unknowns before he had set out, but he had never imagined different accents among the Olmosites. The People of the Ridge all spoke with one accent, although they mostly lived in one city. It raised the question of how many assumptions he would have to discard.

He relaxed his shoulders and focused on the moment. "I am here for at least one night," Hamel said as his eyes scanned the room once more. Not a man had moved or spoken since the moment he had entered the room. "I would like a room—a nice room. And I would like a bottle of the strongest stuff you have."

"Yes, Master," the man replied. "Of course. I will give you my best room and a bottle of Noola." The man smiled and added, "Just be careful with it. It is difficult for men to drink the Noola I serve here and remain on their feet." Hamel could hear a few of the men in the room snicker. "It will all, of course, cost two silvers."

Hamel paid the innkeeper, and the man pulled out a small bottle from behind the counter. He handed it to Hamel before turning toward a stairway at the back of the room. The stairs were narrow, dirty, and little light made its way to the steps.

Ever since he had arrived at the wall to Olmos, Hamel had been doing his best to hide his injury. The cloak covered the bite well, but it took all his willpower to hide the limp. Each stair caused pain to shoot through his leg.

At the top of the stairway, the man led Hamel into a hallway. At the end, there was another flight of steps at the top of which was a large, solid, locked door. The man unlocked the door and stepped through into another hallway, then re-locked the door behind Hamel.

From years of serving as a soldier, Hamel had learned to recognize potential threats. He kept his back to the wall and his face toward the man as he continued down the hallway. Hamel eyed each door they passed, prepared for danger. It seemed unusual to have a set of rooms sealed off from the lower sections. It was either to protect the guests on the upper level from the danger below, or it was to keep Hamel and people such as himself locked in.

At the end of the hallway, the innkeeper unlocked a door. Inside was a large bed, a lavatory, a small desk, and a small window. He bowed low to Hamel and then handed him two keys, one of which he pointed out was for the room and one for the door at the end of the hall. The man then thanked Hamel for his business and stepped out, closing the door behind him.

After locking the door and doing a quick search of the room, Hamel immediately went to the sink. He was pleased to find there was not only running water, but the lavatory was clean. The room itself was furnished with quality furniture, expensive carpeting, and beautiful drapes. It was clean, but nothing had been updated in what appeared to be decades. It had at one point been a quality room, albeit small. He suspected it was the best they had, and they cared for it well. He began to think the locked door at the end of the hallway was to offer a little more protection and a little more privacy to the high paying guests.

Hamel took the chair from the desk to the lavatory and set to work on changing his bandages. The Noola he had just purchased worked well to clean the wound. As soon as he opened it, the smell suggested it was far stronger than anything he had ever heard of in Ridge.

Hamel's eyes began to tear as he cleaned the wound. He could see early signs of infection and hoped he could keep it clean while it healed. Once he was finished, he smothered the bite with the salve he had received from Mellel and put clean bandages on the wound. He washed out the old bandages, using the Noola he had purchased to disinfect the cloth, and hung them to dry.

When he rose to his feet, he quickly grabbed the wall for support. The pain was more intense than it had been before the latest cleaning. Stepping out of the lavatory, he stared longingly at the bed. He wanted nothing more than to take the weight off his leg and relax for the night.

"I am not without family. I do not face the world alone. I must continue. There is work to be done," Hamel said. The old quote from his favorite author had been a great source of comfort to him. He walked back to the mirror in the lavatory and said it again, "I am not without family. I do not face the world alone. I must continue. There is work to be done."

The day was not one for rest, but for action. He needed to keep moving. He had to get to Pollos soon.

CHAPTER 24

THE DAY OF LEARNING

Hamel decided to leave one of the packs in his room. He secured the sidearm underneath his cloak and slung the rifle over his shoulder. He moved all his money into an inside pocket of the cloak, tying it so it did not jingle. He also took the one pack filled with some of the medical supplies, a portion of the ammunition, one waterskin, and some food. He did not trust the security of the room and took what he least wanted to be stolen, but not so much he would feel burdened.

Hamel locked the room securely on his way out and forced himself to walk without a limp. Every step hurt, but he was not willing to show weakness at such a crucial moment.

At the end of the hallway, he paused before the large, solid, locked door. Little sound carried through the doorway, but from what he could hear, there were people on the other side.

Hamel unlocked the door and swung it open, standing off to the side to avoid any direct attack. At the top of the stairs, heading down to the second floor, three young boys stood. Their faces drained of all color, and they each let out a small yell before they bolted down the stairs.

Hamel smiled to himself. He remembered trying to go places he was not allowed when he was a young boy. He ignored the incident and locked the door securely behind him.

The way out of the hotel was similar to the way in. As he reached the pub, silence overtook the room, and men eyed him closely. Each one tried to give the impression they were not looking in his direction at all. He continued out and into the street. It was nearing the supper hour, but he hoped he could get an hour or two at the library before returning to the hotel room.

The building he had suspected of being a library or school turned out to be the main library for the town and perhaps the area. Two people worked in the library, both of whom suffered from the same condition he had witnessed when he first came through the gates. They were the first two white-haired, bent-over people he was able to observe up close. Each walked quickly through the library, but the man walked with a limp, and the woman's back was hunched over.

"What may I help you with, Master?" the woman asked, eying the rifle slung around his shoulder. "Is there information you seek?"

"Yes," Hamel replied. He found the title, "Master" to be difficult to adjust to. "I am interested in maps."

The man with the limp stood up straighter, and his face lit up. "Yes, Master! Excellent! That is in the north wing of the library. I oversee all the maps, building plans, and more. Please follow me."

The man led him to what Hamel was sure was the south end of the library, but he did not comment on the matter. The room they entered was full of books and old scrolls and smelled of dust and age. Hamel was surprised to see two soldiers stationed outside the room.

"We have plenty of maps in this area," the man explained. "The most popular, of course, are the maps of Ridge Nation, but we have some of Olmos and the nations to the East as well. We also have a few of the Valley Floor."

Hamel tried to make sense of what he had heard. He thought it strange that the popular maps were of Ridge

186

Nation. He did not think the average person he had seen in the streets would have visited Ridge, especially considering the difficulty he had observed in getting back through the gates. It was worth further research.

"I'd like a detailed map of Ridge Nation, one of the most accurate maps you have of the Valley Floor, and two detailed maps of Olmos, one of the nation as a whole and one of the city of Pollos." Hamel hoped if he asked for so many maps, he would be less likely to arouse suspicion than if he asked for only one. Before the man could respond, he had one more idea. "Do you also have a map detailing the entire region, including from the valley right through to Olmos?"

The man's face lit up again. "Yes, Master, I have a large map of the area drawn up by a local cartographer. He finished it based on the latest data collected in recent exploratory trips. I will, of course, need to see your papers. The information would not be classified to a man of your obvious status, but I need to check to make sure."

Heavy footsteps and the sound of chainmail rubbing against leather reached his ears. From what he could tell, the soldier stood not more than two steps behind him. The familiar sound of sidearms drawn out of leather holsters let him know he was in no position to challenge anyone.

As he reached for his papers, he felt a hand land firmly on his shoulder. "Your rifle, please, Master," the soldier said.

Hamel did not think from the man's expression, nor from his tone of voice, that the taking of the rifle was anything but a matter of security. He did, however, remember the interaction at the gate. It would not do to offer the soldiers any form of submission that might indicate weakness.

He turned to the man who spoke and stepped close to him, clenching his fists and his jaw. The second soldier reacted by shoving what felt like the tip of his sidearm into Hamel's back, but Hamel ignored it. "Listen very closely, Corporal," Hamel began. "I am not accustomed to handing anything over to men such as yourself, let alone my rifle. I do, however, wish to see these maps. I also suspect you wish to still have your rank tomorrow. I will hand you my rifle while I show this man my papers. If I turn out to be less than what is expected, I will not be surprised if you seek to arrest me. If, however, I turn out to be someone you do not want to cross, I will not be surprised if you hand me back my rifle, apologize for insinuating that I might not have the authority to be in here, bow with your forehead near the ground, and return to your position."

The man's eyes filled with fear, and he swallowed three times. Hamel knew he hadn't said anything unusual, but he had learned years ago that the best threats included little that was not expected.

The Corporal's eyes moved quickly to the other soldier, and Hamel felt the barrel of the gun pull away from his side, followed by the sound of the sidearm sliding back into its holster. Power seemed like the only language Olmosites understood.

Hamel unslung his rifle and handed it forcefully into the arms of the Corporal. He glanced at the second soldier, just long enough to determine his exact position and distance away. He then turned back to the librarian.

The white-haired man's mouth hung open, and sweat trickled down the side of his face. Hamel handed him the papers, and the man took it with trembling fingers. While the librarian read, Hamel waited with arms crossed, facing the man, but keeping an ear out for any change of position with the soldiers.

The man closed his mouth and swallowed as he looked over the paper. Hamel hoped what he had received from Mellel was detailed enough to get him through the man's scrutiny. He did not understand much of what was on the paper, other than that his name was Wos Hamtia.

When the man finished, Hamel could see tears forming in his eyes. He managed to keep his voice steady as he said, "My apologies, Master. This was but a formality, of course. We need to keep this information secure. It is the only information we have in the library that remains under constant guard," the man explained.

"I would not expect anything else from you, my friend," Hamel said. The man's face relaxed at Hamel's words. "It is not you. It is your friends standing behind me that I am concerned with." He retrieved the papers from the man who then turned to the soldiers.

The librarian addressed the two men standing guard and spoke with authority as he said, "This man has the authority to be in here. He is…" At that point, the man choked on his words. He cleared his throat and tried again. "This man is a Colonel. He is also a Naromite."

The Corporal's eyebrows shot up at the title, "Colonel" but nearly dropped his rifle at the word, "Naromite." Hamel could see panic fill his eyes. The soldier quickly looked to the other guard as if he thought the man could help him know what to do.

"Please forgive me, Colonel," the soldier said as he respectfully handed the rifle back to Hamel. He then bowed, bending his knees and dropped his forehead nearly to the floor. When he stood again, he backed away along with the other soldier and resumed their positions at the door.

Hamel did not realize Mellel's papers indicated he was a Colonel. He also could not imagine what a Naromite was and why it would cause such fear in the soldiers. He turned back to the white-haired man to see him busy collecting the maps Hamel had requested. When he had collected everything and set it on a large table in the center of the room, he bowed and turned to the door.

Hamel stopped the man by asking, "Librarian, what is your name?"

"It is Os, Master."

"How long, Os, have you been working here at the library?" Hamel asked.

"Since I was assigned to my wife, Master. I was sent here when I was twenty-one and told to report to the Chief Librarian. He married me to his daughter, and then we were both placed here as apprentices."

Hamel considered Os's answer for a moment. He had not known that Olmosite marriages were assigned. He had assumed it was a choice. He decided he wanted an answer to the question of age. If the man looked the way he did, he wanted to know. "How long ago was that, Os?"

"That was just over fifty-one years ago, Master," Os replied, his eyes held firmly on a spot near Hamel's feet. Since he had examined Hamel's papers, he had not raised his eyes even once.

Hamel feared the sound of his heart beating could be heard by the librarian or even the two soldiers standing guard outside the room. He felt grateful for the hood which still hung down over his face.

It was true. The Olmosites lived much longer than his own people. Such knowledge raised many questions. He did not, however, feel he could justify interrogating the poor man for answers. As important an issue as it was, he set it aside for another matter. "Tell me, Os, is there information in this library on Naromites?"

The man's eyes shot up to Hamel's with a look of disbelief and all color drained from his face. "No, Master, of course not."

Tears began to stream down Os's cheeks. Hamel did not want to torment the man, but he needed to know. "Then I have one more task for you, Os."

"Anything, Master," Os replied.

"Tell me everything you know about the Naromites."

The man collapsed on the floor and wept. "Please, Master. I will do anything you ask. Please do not kill me."

"If you tell me everything you know, I will not kill you," Hamel replied. It tore him apart to threaten the poor man. His mind drifted to all the things of late he had not wanted to do.

The man's eyes remained on the floor for another moment before he reached up with his hand to the table and used it to pull himself to his feet. When he spoke, all life had left his voice, and Hamel had to lean forward to hear the man. "I know the Naromite Clan is small, but they are everywhere. They are assassins of the highest order and can kill a room full of people within seconds. I know that no one survives once a

Naromite decides they will die, and if you find out someone is a Naromite, it is said they will often kill you and your entire family. I know if you are caught speaking of the Naromites, it means certain death. Please, I do not know anymore." The man's shoulders slumped as he finished, he let his head roll forward onto his chest.

"If no one is allowed to speak of the Naromites," Hamel began, "how is it that you have come to know so much about them?"

The man's body stiffened for a second, and what little color he had left in his face drained away. He drew in a long, deep breath before he squared his shoulders and looked Hamel directly in the eye. Hamel could see the man had not gained confidence but had the look of a man who had resigned himself to death. "That is as far as I will go. I will not betray those I love. I have told you what I know, but I would sooner die the worst death you could give me than to turn over to you those who have told me this."

Hamel smiled and stepped up to the man. He had gained all the knowledge he could from the librarian.

Hamel put a hand on each of the man's shoulders and stared him in the eye. "Os, I can respect that. No harm will come to you for telling me this. I will not ask who told you, nor will I harm them for telling you even if I do one day find out. I am impressed by your courage."

The man's eyes grew large, and relief flooded his face. "Thank you, Master. Thank you." The librarian began to look around the room as if he were not sure where he was. "Thank you. Is there anything else you need before I leave you to your maps, Master?"

"No, Os, you may go," Hamel said.

The man scurried away and closed the door behind himself. Hamel was pleased with all he had learned, despite the fear he had struck in the man.

He began to pour over the maps, starting with the one covering the entire region. He wanted to make sure that he wasn't missing anything in his knowledge of the area. He was pleased to see Olmos did not have any more details than Hamel had about the layout of the land.

Next, he looked at the map of Olmos. The country was far larger than he had thought. He examined it in detail, doing his best to commit it to memory. He quickly found Pollos and considered the route he would need to take to get there. He could see it was a long day's ride by horseback. He would need to leave early in the morning to arrive by nighttime. As he examined the country as a whole, he saw there were many cities and towns spread out over the area, and the wall did appear to surround the entire nation. It was hard to imagine constructing a wall of such a size.

Next, he moved on to the map of Ridge Nation. At first, he didn't see anything he had not expected, but then he noticed something unusual. There was a lot of detail about the city, but what details appeared to attract the most attention were related to defense. The lack of a wall on the eastern edge of the city was noted along with arrows pointing out various routes into the city. The locations of all the barracks and all government buildings were clearly marked. Even the small valley to the south of the city just on the edge of the wilderness was marked as a training ground for soldiers as well as typical times of the day when training and drills regularly took place.

In addition to those concerning details, there were marks on the map where Hamel had not thought there to be anything of interest. Just to the north of the city were two small mountains along with a few hills. The more westerly mountain had several notes with marks and a pathway going partway up the far side away from the city. Hamel made a mental note to explore that area of the mountain when he returned to his role as Honored Patir. There was obviously something there of interest to Olmos, but something of which the People of the Ridge were unaware.

The final map was of the Valley Floor. As he pulled it out, he was mentally preparing to head back to the hotel. There was not much information available regarding the valley. There was only one known path in, and it was walled off and well defended by Ridge. The other three sides of the valley were cliffs of such a height, no one in recent history had dared try to descend them. Even if someone were to climb down one of the cliffs, they would not survive their encounter with the Beasts.

He glanced at the map quickly but then turned his full attention to it. The map was far more detailed than he would have thought possible. Not even the People of the Ridge knew much more than that the area was full of trees and Beasts.

Hamel spread out the map on the table and leaned over it. It took him a moment to even accept what he saw. The map laid out in detail locations of about eight groupings or tribes or villages of Beasts. The People of the Ridge had never ventured into the area, but it appeared as though the Olmosites had somehow entered the valley and explored it. Right in the center of the valley was a large area marked simply as "ruins" right next to a small lake. He could see rivers marked through the area and on the northwest side of the valley, there was what appeared to be an entrance of sorts. He could not quite make out everything on the map, but from the arrows and the drawings of roads and paths, the Olmosites had a way into the valley.

Hamel let the information sink in. It was hard to work through it all in his mind, but he had to accept it. He would take the time later to evaluate the information. As he quickly reflected through some of the implications of the issue, he noticed something else not too far from the Valley Wall. Just a short distance inside the forest, a spot was marked. He could not make out what it all meant, but he committed the exact location to memory, along with the entrance on the northwest side of the valley. The details on the map of the valley troubled him greatly.

Despite the shock at what lay before him, he smiled. He still did not know much of what was happening, but he had finally made some progress.

It was time to head back to the hotel. He had collected enough information for the time being. He needed his rest before setting out early the next morning.

He opened the doors to find the guards still at their positions. Neither guard said a word, but each guard bowed low as he passed. There was no sign of either librarian on his way out. The place was quiet.

CHAPTER 25

THE DAY OF THIEVES

As Hamel stepped outside, he paused for a moment as the cool air rushed over his body. Had he not been in Olmos and had he not been in terrible pain from his leg wound, he would have enjoyed a nice walk in the fading light. He figured he had been in the library for a little over an hour, but in that time, the sun had set.

Before climbing down the steps, he gazed out over the large courtyard. The streets were bustling with people, and merchants were out selling their wares. The border town came alive at night.

He headed directly for the hotel. He did not want to interact with people, nor did he need anything from the merchants. He wanted his rest.

About twenty paces from the hotel, he saw a flash of movement just to his right. A hand went for his knife at his belt, and he reacted more on instinct and training than anything. Hamel's fist shot out, while the other hand grabbed the wrist of the person trying to slip his blade out of his sheath. It all happened so fast that he hadn't realized who had attacked him until the thief was lying on the ground in front of him.

Hamel did not seek out fights or battles. He had been taught there was always a better way. As such, he usually felt a certain amount of grief at injuring an opponent.

This time, however, was not like any other time. He stared down at the person who had tried to take his blade and struggled to believe what he saw. There, lying on the ground in front of him was a young boy, not much more than eight or nine. Hamel's mouth dropped open, and his breath caught in his throat. He had injured or perhaps even killed a child. In his head, he could still hear the sound of his fist connecting. The horror he felt was so incapacitating, he barely noticed as someone else slipped the blade out of his belt, and the rifle strap was cut neatly from his shoulder.

He had been disarmed, but it did not matter. If he had killed a child, he no longer wanted to live. He would be happy if someone drove the blade deep into his back at that very moment. He would have welcomed such an event—perhaps even thanked his killer if he had been able to speak on his way to the ground.

He could hear the light footsteps grow quieter as the thieves ran off. Somewhere, deep inside, it registered that they had not been trying to do him any harm. They had only wanted to steal the jewel-encrusted blade and the rifle.

Hamel's mind drifted back to the young boy in Eddel's compound. He had been about the same age as the boy who lay before him. He had allowed a child to remain in slavery and struck down another child in the streets.

Hamel took a step closer to the boy. The young child lay motionless on the ground, and Hamel felt like emptying his stomach. If the child were dead, it would not matter if the entire Ridge Nation pleaded with him to be their Honored Patir, he would never take such a position. One who killed a child had no honor.

He vaguely noticed someone step up next to him. A man's voice spoke, "Ahh, I see you caught one," the man began. "They are a troublesome lot. It is good to see that there is one less running the streets."

Hamel turned his head to examine the man who had spoken and tried to make sense of what he had said. It had sounded as though the man was pleased to see a child harmed. "It is... good?" Hamel asked. The shock and disbelief inside were overwhelming.

"Absolutely!" the man replied. "They should give you a medal. There have been more and more as of late. They say their numbers are growing because more people are hungry, but I say it is because they are lazy, and that they enjoy stealing."

Hamel imagined the man's body lying on the ground in place of the young boy. It took a great deal of his discipline to turn away and address the matter at hand. He reached down and checked the boy's neck for a pulse. Relief flooded his entire body as he felt that for which he dared not hope.

The contact seemed to arouse the child from his unconscious state. The boy sat up and looked around in confusion. When he saw Hamel leaning over him, his face flushed, and he jumped to his feet before stumbling off down an alley.

"Pity, that is," the Olmosite man said as he turned away. "Oh well, they are hearty folk, you must give them that. It's a wonder the spirits don't get them in the alleys."

As relief over the boy's condition flooded over Hamel, he reflected back on the man's comment. He recalled some of Pulanomos's aides making comments about spirits in dark places. The Olmosite belief in ghosts had always seemed strange to Hamel, but he had respected it.

He took a few deep breaths and evaluated his situation. He had lost his knife and his rifle, but the money inside his cloak as well as the sidearm had both been left untouched. He was not too concerned. It was a significant hit to have lost two weapons, one of which gave him a certain status in the eyes of people, but he did not think either weapon was necessary.

He turned toward the hotel, this time remaining vigilant to watch for thieves. It would not do to be taken twice.

When he entered the inn, the common room was much as it had been the last time he wandered through, but more crowded. When he had first walked in, the patrons had eyed him closely but had avoided his gaze if he had looked their way. That was, however, when he had been wearing the knife and carrying the rifle. On his present walk through the crowded common room, it was a different story. Everyone watched him, and no one looked away if he glanced in their direction.

He walked past the man at the bar and made for the stairs. Hamel's senses were alert to every glance in his direction and every movement of the men in the room. He was confident an attack was on its way. He reached the top of the first stairway and was halfway down the hall before he heard multiple feet on the stairs.

He rushed forward to the second set of steps. He did not want to face them in the hallway. There was always a chance someone in one of the rooms might step out and attack from behind. He knew the safest location would be in his room while the second was at the top of the stairs on the other side of the door. He did not, however, feel that reaching either location in time was realistic. The safest reachable position for him was at the top of the stairs with the locked door at his back.

He raced up the steps and reached the top. The men had just reached the bottom of the stairs as he turned around. He counted six men.

The stairway was wide enough for two at most to run side-by-side, if the men were thin. If they fought one at a time, Hamel would have no difficulty with them. He had not met a man who could best him in hand-to-hand combat in many years. Fighting from the higher ground found at the top of the stairs only helped. He did not think a crowd of nearly drunk men would pose a threat. The concern, however, was if one of the men was armed.

Before they reached the half-way point on their climb up the steps, he pulled out his sidearm and pointed it at the man in the lead. The men came to an instant halt.

"I do not wish to kill any of you," Hamel said in his Olmosite accent, "but I do not think any of you will survive if you come much closer."

The two men in front stood side-by-side. Each held out their hands as if to ward off any danger. The looks on their faces told the story of two men who knew they had made a fatal mistake. The men behind, however, seemed less concerned. One of the men in the very back moved just slightly, and Hamel realized he could be going for a weapon.

He picked the largest of the two men in front and aimed his gun right at his head. He then spoke in a calm, confident voice and noticed while he spoke, the man in the back stopped moving. He said to the large man in front, "Understand that one of the men behind you is going for his weapon. If he pulls it out, I will have to shoot you to get you out of the way so I can shoot him before he shoots me. If he does happen to get me before I get to him, it will not likely be before I take out you and the man directly behind you. You have to ask yourself if it's worth it to you for you to be shot so that your friend can shoot me."

"Kolos!" the man shouted. "Are you going for your gun?"

"Um... maybe..." Kolos replied.

"If you are, stop it!" the large man commanded. The pitch of his voice had gone up.

The man in the back, Kolos, shifted just slightly, but then slowly raised his hands. Hamel took a quick glance at each of the men and felt the threat of being shot was over. He did not, however, lower his weapon. "Now, each one of you, except for the big guy here in front, turn around, raise your hands where I can see them, then slowly walk down the stairs—in that order. Turn around; raise your hands; walk away."

The men did as they were told. He did not want anything from the man in front, but he was the only thing keeping the other men in line. If he were no longer in danger, Hamel would be. The five men reached the bottom of the stairs, and Hamel told them to keep walking. They continued on until they were out of sight.

"Now, you turn around," Hamel barked at the man.

"Listen, we shouldn't have followed you. It was a mistake. You don't need to worry. I'll just walk away," the man said.

"I have no intention of shooting you," Hamel began. "But I will if you do anything that makes me nervous."

The man nodded and turned around. He stood on the step while Hamel grabbed the key for the door and unlocked it. He kept his weapon trained on the man as he swung open the door. He took a quick look into the upper hallway to make sure it was clear, stepped through, and slammed the door closed. Within seconds, the door was locked again, and he was on his way to his room. He would need to leave in the night. He did not expect to make it out of the hotel alive if he had to use the front door in the morning.

Once in his room, he confirmed nothing had been touched and then checked the bandages he had cleaned. They had dried in the short time since he had left for the library. In the hot, arid climate of Olmos, Hamel suspected most things dried in short order.

He changed his bandage again, cleaning the wound as best as he could. He was pleased to see that the redness had not spread. The pain was intense, but he could manage.

Hamel packed his bags, loaded them on his shoulders, and turned out the lights. He walked to the window to examine his exit. His room was on the third floor, and he did not think he could climb that distance down without falling.

On the ground below, the crowd had dissipated somewhat, but there were still many lights. Even if he could manage the climb without slipping, he knew for sure someone would spot him. He would need to wait.

He wandered to the desk and moved it against the door. He then went to the sink and drank as much as he could manage, then filled his canteens. He would need some sleep before he set out.

Over the years as a soldier, he had developed the skill to take a two-hour nap, but there was always the chance of oversleeping. He was tired and sore enough that he worried his discipline would not wake him at the appropriate time. His Matir, however, had taught him another little trick. If he drank enough water before a nap, the water itself would wake him.

He settled into the bed and within moments was sound asleep.

CHAPTER 26

THE DAY OF ESCAPE

Hamel watched the boy. He shook his head and corrected himself. Lemmel was no longer a boy. He was a young man. He had trained hard for the army and would be a Lieutenant by the time he was nineteen. He was intelligent and strong.

Hamel felt the tears on his cheeks. The young man also wept, tears streaming down his face. It had only been a day since Lillel and his two young children had died. Nothing had seemed real since the accident that left him alone with Lemmel and Karotel—until the moment he was confronted by Lemmel.

Hamel quickly rushed through the possibilities. Lemmel's face was red; his hands were clasped tight; and he clenched and unclenched his jaw. He would feel a lot of anger at the loss of his Matir and younger brother and sister. He would also feel fear, wondering what his future held.

That was it. Lemmel was afraid. A boy without a Matir to guide him was a boy without family. He would fear being Parentless. He would appear free, but he would be left to face the world alone. He did not understand that Hamel had, from day one, seen Lemmel as his own son, not merely Lillel's.

"Do not fear, my son," Hamel said. "You are my son. I will make you my son."

Lemmel furrowed his brow before hope overcame his confusion. Finally, his face fell again. When he spoke, his words came out in just

202

above a whisper. *"I do not remember the words of the adoption. I cannot take part."* He hung his head. The tears he had shed a moment before gave way to weeping. Hope had been lost.

Hamel grabbed Lemmel firmly with one hand on each shoulder. *"Welcome, my child, I am Patir Rezin Hamel."*

Lemmel shook his head and said between sobs, *"I don't remember what I am supposed to say."*

"You are not without a parent, my son. I am your Patir, and I love you. I am tied to you and you to me. We are one. We are honored family," Hamel continued, ignoring Lemmel's confession that he could not remember the tradition.

"I commit to you, my son," Hamel said, *"to lead you faithfully, and I will give my life to get you to the ends of the earth and back again. As a token of faithfulness to you, I give you my name, but you may set it aside to keep your Matir's name. The name you choose will be yours forever, and it will be a seal of my promise to you."*

"But Patir, the tradition… I haven't fulfilled my part!"

Hamel set aside the tradition for a moment. *"Lemmel, do you not understand? I am adopting you as my son. You do not need to do anything or say anything. Adoption is mine to give. It is from a parent to a child, and my adoption of you is my promise to raise you to be a man, not your promise to be raised. You need only to receive."*

Lemmel shook his head slowly. Hamel could see in his eyes that he was processing his way through everything that had happened and was coming to grips with the idea that Hamel was taking him as his own son. He furrowed his brow once again and appeared to set his face on a course of action. Lemmel smiled and then bowed his head low, dropping down to one knee. He had remembered one part of the tradition.

Hamel leaned down and gave him his Patir's kiss on the top of the head. The blessing was given, and the adoption was complete.

"Who are you, my son?" Hamel asked.

Lemmel stood up straight and smiled, his face still wet with the tears of grief. *"I am Eatal Lemmel, son of Patir Rezin Hamel."*

Hamel awoke and rushed to the lavatory. He could not be exactly sure, but he suspected from the angle of the moon shining through his window that roughly an hour had passed. His Matir's trick had worked.

He felt the weight of the dream on his heart as he used the lavatory, then collected up his packs. He missed Lemmel so much his heart ached. It had been four years since he had betrayed the People of the Ridge. Hamel could not find peace with the betrayal, but he did not care. He would give just about anything for a few more minutes with his son.

He had lost so much over the years. He had lost Lillel, Keptel, and Draggel to an accident. He had lost Lemmel to the Beasts. He had lost Karotel and Mariel to a decision. He felt so alone. He cleared his throat and whispered, "I am not without family. I do not face the world alone. I must continue. There is work to be done."

He returned to the window and was pleased to see few people in the streets. The moon was bright but was just a sliver in the sky. The sky was partially clear of clouds, but one would cover the moon soon. Once that happened, it would be time to move.

He opened the window. The way down was not realistic, but the way up appeared to be a viable option. His room was on the top floor of the building, and he was confident he could scale the short distance to the roof. He examined the outside wall of the building and loaded up his packs. He needed only to wait for cloud cover.

While he waited, he pulled the sheets and blankets off the bed and tied them end to end. He did not want to have to use them, but it was his backup plan. When he had finished, he had a rope of around three paces in length.

When the moon moved behind the cloud, he moved fast. All Ridge soldiers were experienced climbers. He had seen to that himself when he had been actively overseeing the military's discipline. He put that skill to use as he made his way out onto the tiny ledge and used the cracks and joints in the stone wall to make his way to the roof. It was slow going, but he made steady progress. At one point, the moon peeked out from behind the clouds, but he did not think he had been seen. If anyone was watching for him, it was more likely they would be looking for him on the stairs or at the front door.

Reaching the ledge, he pulled himself over. He ran along the small parapet that had been designed into the roof of the building and examined the four outside walls. The side opposite his room lowered down onto an addition built onto the building. It was only one floor down, but he did not think he could risk the jump.

He secured his makeshift blanket rope to one of the crenellations along the parapet and lowered himself. When he reached the roof of the lower building, he dropped and felt the pain shoot up his leg. It reminded him yet again of the desire to be home where he could take the time to heal. When he searched the three sides of the lower building, he found the corners on the new section of the building had quoin built into them. He used the slightly protruding stone blocks to scale down the final two floors.

At the bottom, he stepped into the street and made his way to the stable, avoiding the front of the hotel. He knocked on the door of the stable for a few minutes before one of the boys called out. He tried to remain quiet, but the boy had no such concerns.

"I have come to take my horse," Hamel hissed.

"Go away!" the boy hollered. "We release no horses at night."

Hamel feared the attention the boy's voice would draw. He did not want to face the six men in an open area. "Listen closely, boy," Hamel hissed again. "I'm the man who dropped a horse off last evening and gave the young man a silver. Do you remember me?"

"Yes, Master," the boy replied. His voice took on a respectful tone. "Have you come to retrieve your horse?"

Hamel bristled inside. He did not like to repeat himself, and he despised foolish questions. "Yes, boy, I have come to take my horse. If you saddle my horse and bring him out to me and do so quietly, I will give you another silver."

There was silence on the other side of the door while Hamel listened to urgent whispering. A small amount of light shone through the cracks of the stable, and he could see movement. He hoped they were hard at work preparing his horse. He fished a silver out of his bag and waited.

In less than ten minutes, his horse was led out. It was saddled and appeared to have been hastily brushed down. Both boys bowed respectfully, and he handed the silver to the taller of the two. Without a word, he climbed into the saddle and moved off.

Hamel had not realized how close he was to the edge of the border town. There were only another four blocks before the border town ended abruptly. He rode along the outskirts of town until he found what appeared to be the easterly road leading to Pollos, based on his memory of the maps in the library.

By that point, the clouds had moved on from covering the moon. His path ahead lay clear before him, and he was pleased to find the road in excellent condition. He decided to push his horse to a trot and settled in for a long ride. Based on the position of the moon, he figured it was around two o'clock in the morning. He hoped he could maintain his speed and reach Pollos by early afternoon.

Hamel brought his horse to a halt by a small stream not long after sunrise. They had maintained the trot for just under an hour from the city and then slowed to a walk. He figured they had covered nearly twenty miles through the night but would need to cover another twenty before they reached Pollos. It would be hard on both Hamel and his horse, but he hoped they would find rest once there.

He cleaned his wound and changed his bandage. The bite was in a difficult spot to examine properly, but he thought it did not look too much worse than it had in the night.

As he mounted up, he spent some time thinking ahead to a meeting with Churoi. He hoped to find a friend in Pulanomos's former assistant, but it was difficult to know. It had been many years. Churoi might not be the same man he had been.

He wished Pulanomos was alive. The two of them had been close, and Hamel knew he could count on his friend to care for him in his time of need. The grief of his friend's passing washed over him again. As someone who had outlived most other people, he would have thought he would eventually grow accustomed to the death of others around him, but each loss took its toll.

With learning that the people of Olmos did not appear to die in their thirties as did the People of the Ridge, he had briefly imagined Pulanomos had survived, but then remembered the letter he had received from Churoi. The letter was to share the news that the former Ambassador, Pulanomos, had passed away at age thirty-four.

It had been so many years since he had seen or heard from Churoi. The man should be alive and well, assuming no accidents had taken place. He had been so young when Pulanomos had served as Olmos's ambassador to Ridge. He just hoped the small friendship he had developed with the young man would be enough.

CHAPTER 27

THE DAY LEADS TO THE SQUARE

As the morning passed, Hamel grew sore from being in the saddle so long. He had spent much time as a soldier riding a horse, but not as much in recent years. By the time the sun was at its highest, everything hurt. The pain in his leg, however, made the ache from riding pale in comparison.

He stopped for lunch and tried to walk it off but found no success. He only felt pain with each step. When he sat down to clean the wound and change the bandage, he was disappointed to find red lines running away from the cut. An infection had set in, and he would need serious medical care. He had a sudden fear rush over him that he might lose the leg if he could not find the help he needed. Rumor had it that Olmos was more advanced in their medical sciences than Ridge, and Hamel hoped it was true.

He cleaned the wound with the Noola. The pain he felt using the alcohol to clean the wound was far worse than the pain he felt in the leg while riding the horse, but he needed to clean it as well as possible. He then packed the open cut full of Mellel's salve and bandaged it again. He decided to clean the other bandages as well with the Noola and hung them up on a small branch to dry. They would be ready to go by the time he finished his lunch.

He sat down and ate his lunch and drank from the canteen while he went over the plan he had laid out for finding Churoi. The matter with the men in the inn, forcing him to head out in the middle of the night, had turned out for his benefit. It meant he would arrive early enough in the day to begin an exploration of the city. He hoped he could find the man before nightfall, rather than find a hotel.

The matter of his leg was also of concern. He knew his leg was in rough shape. The lack of cleanliness and proper medical care was beginning to show. If Churoi could be trusted, perhaps Hamel's leg could get the needed care.

Aside from his goal of finding Churoi, he was without a plan. He was not one to move forward in such a manner, but so little was known about Olmos. He would have to figure it all out as he went along.

He climbed back on his horse. As he rode, he realized his belt might give him some grief. He had lost the knife and been left with an empty sheath. An empty sheath, of course, was nothing but a sign to all who saw it that he had lost his weapon. It could be taken as a sign of weakness among a people who sought power.

Hamel undid his belt as he rode and pulled off the sheath from the blade, tossing it into the dead grass and weeds lining the road. He tied his belt back on and continued on the way. He could not afford to show any weakness among the Olmosites. They were like a pack of wolves, waiting to attack.

He came upon a steep rise in the road and climbed to the top on his horse. When he reached the top, he came to a halt and stared out over the valley ahead. Most of Olmos, at least the part he had come through, was not much more inviting than the wilderness had been. It was dry and dusty and not conducive to successful farming. The valley that lay before him, however, was far greener than anything he had witnessed since he had passed through the walls surrounding the country.

It was still far from what the Valley Floor in Ridge could offer, but he could see miles and miles of farms stretched out. While most of the crops looked sickly and dry, they were at least growing. In the center of the fields was a large city. It was smaller than Ridge Capital, but even from a distance, he could see wealth. The buildings stood high, and the architecture was beautiful. The place looked clean and spread out with everything from palaces to larger estates. He could even see one section with a large wooded area. It was contained within the wall of the city, but it spread out over many, many acres of land. He thought he might like to explore that area at some point in his visit to the city.

Hamel set off down the road at a trot. There were many people on the road. Most heading into the city were leading carts full of wheat or fruits or vegetables. Those coming out were often pulling empty carts. There were soldiers on the road as well. The people leading carts in and out of the city avoided them, giving them a wide berth.

He decided to give them space as well. He knew if it came down to it, he could get through the situation as a Naromite Colonel. The Naromites obviously were feared by everyone, soldiers included. The papers could be very useful to him. He also suspected they could be a death sentence. If the papers were thought to be false, one bullet could end it all. It would not matter how hard he fought. Any man could die from a gunshot.

The other problem he faced was the actual Naromite clan. The librarian had told him the clan was small, but it was impossible to know how far their reach or influence extended. It was always possible word may spread about a Naromite Colonel—even if no one was supposed to talk about them. If the clan heard a Colonel was wandering the land, they might look into the matter. He did not want to push his good fortune.

He also wondered what it might be like to run into an actual Naromite. If they were so feared, that could mean they were dangerous. It would also be difficult to convince someone in a secret order that he was part of that order when he knew nothing of their ways.

The wound in his leg continued to throb. He wanted to stop and give it a rest, but there were too many people. Weakness could not be shown in the presence of Olmosites. He hoped Churoi would welcome him, and Hamel could find the medical care he so desperately needed.

When he reached the city, he found it well guarded. Soldiers lined the tops of the walls. Each man was armed to the teeth and looked as though he were anxious to find an opportunity for a fight. The gate itself had what appeared to be nearly two dozen soldiers standing guard. As people moved through the gate, they held their tongues and kept their eyes on the ground.

He noticed most of the soldiers kept a close eye on him as he rode through the gate. He was the only one on horseback within sight who was dressed in fine robes and with his hood up. One of the Corporals stepped forward at one point, but a Sergeant grabbed his arm and shook his head. Hamel suspected the robes and the warhorse he sat upon was enough to convince the soldiers to let him pass without question.

Once inside the walls, he looked around in awe. The city was beautiful. Few buildings were anything less than majestic in their design. He had never seen such architecture and thought to himself if circumstances were different, he would invite some of their craftsmen to come to Ridge to build even a few structures. They would be a marvel for the People of the Ridge.

The streets themselves were wide and paved with flagstone. The crowds moved orderly and with purpose, and soldiers stood every twenty paces. The soldiers watched the crowds, and Hamel could see it was their presence that was keeping the people in line. No one made eye contact with a single soldier. If a soldier looked at a man or woman, they stopped speaking and continued to walk in a straight line.

The people of Olmos lived in fear. They were calm and contained, but it had come about through the close oversight of armed guards.

The traffic moved slowly but steadily on the street. Those heading the same way as Hamel kept to the right side of the road, and Hamel followed suit. He observed how people moved and acted. Their eyes never drifted to a soldier, and their conversation was never in a whisper.

He wandered the streets of the city for hours, memorizing the layout. It was not difficult to find a pattern. Most main roads traveled inward to the center of the city where there was a large Square. He thought perhaps a few thousand people could gather there. The City Square itself was open, completely paved with flagstones, and had few structures. There were two large fountains near the center of the Square and surrounding them were a dozen pits.

At first, Hamel could not make sense of what he saw when it came to the pits. He had never heard of anything quite like it. The pits themselves were built of stone, somewhat similar to a well but much larger. Most stood by themselves, but three or four had a crowd around them. The men, women, and children standing by were yelling down into the pits and throwing what appeared to be fruits and vegetables.

Hamel directed his horse in the direction of one of the pits with only seven or eight people gathered. Two soldiers stood nearby, sneering and laughing as the men and women tossed their food into the depths.

As he drew near, one of the soldiers turned to him, bowed low, and took the reins to his horse. The man simply said, "Master," and waited while Hamel dismounted. The soldier continued to hold the reins while Hamel walked to the edge, careful not to limp.

The pit itself was, as he had observed, surrounded by a stone wall the height of his waist. As he approached, he could see the mortar between the stones on the inside of the pit was packed full of broken glass and metal shards. It was clear that whatever was in the pit was not expected to get out without paying a great price.

212

When the people surrounding the pit noticed him, they parted and stepped back. One of the children offered him a rotted tomato and asked, "Master, would you like to throw this?"

Hamel noticed the boy's accent was the same as the accent he had learned to mimic. He shook his head to the boy as he stepped up to the pit. His first reaction was to gag, but he composed himself. The smell of rotten fruits and vegetables and meats was unbearable, and the flies and bugs were so thick, he struggled to see what lay below. As he focused through the swarm, he could see lying on the bottom was a woman in rags.

She lay on the floor of the pit, perhaps three and a half to four paces down. At first, he thought she must be dead, but then he noticed the slight movement of an arm. He judged she must have been in the pit for months, and her leg lay twisted at an odd angle. He could only imagine the pit was some form of punishment or torture.

His accent needed to be tested in the capital, and his cloak did seem to afford him a certain level of privilege. It was time to understand more about Olmosite ways.

"What is this woman's crime?" Hamel asked.

The soldier who had taken the reins of his horse answered, "Master, the woman was caught with stolen bread. A baker was robbed early one morning just over a month ago, and we found this woman and her husband eating two loaves of bread just over by the fountain there."

Hamel paused for a moment as the answer settled in his mind. He could not imagine a punishment so severe for stealing a loaf of bread. He also could not imagine a conviction based solely on finding her eating a loaf of bread. Once again, abuse lay before him, but he could do nothing to address it. He had to keep moving, but there was another question that needed to be asked. "And what became of her husband?"

Both soldiers and the crowd laughed before the man answered, "When we threw his wife into the pit he…" the man paused, and both soldiers laughed again before the man explained, "…he didn't seem to be happy with the idea of his wife ending up in the pit. He fought so hard when we threw him into his own pit, he didn't go in very well. He was snagged on the sides and died before he hit the ground."

Hamel's breaths came in ragged gasps. He was once again grateful for the cloak. His face felt as if it was on fire, and he was sure it was a deep red. He focused on his breathing and forced his heart to calm. Every move he made would be observed, and he could not give himself away. A poor reaction could be disastrous.

"How long will she be kept in there?"

The other soldier spoke loudly in reply. "Do you have someone else scheduled for the pit, Master?" Everyone laughed again. "She's in there until she dies. With her broken leg, she just can't make it to the side of the pit to take her life."

The pit was a death sentence—a very cruel death sentence. A man or woman would be dropped in there to suffer until they gave up and took their own lives. It was a disgraceful way to treat even an animal, let alone a person.

He nodded his head to the soldiers and the people and returned to his horse. He wished to do something for her, but he could not imagine what. His mind drifted back to the young boy in Eddel's compound. He had left another person to suffer.

As he mounted, he heard one of the women say to the rest of the crowd, "If she stays in there much longer, she might last as long as the Ridger." Everyone laughed again before resuming their barrage of rotten fruits and vegetables.

The words of the woman rang in his head. He had only heard that term twice before, and even then, he had overheard it from the Olmosite soldiers assigned to Pulanomos. He had assumed it was some sort of slang used for the People of the Ridge. With each of the times he had heard the term, he had not been left with the impression that it was a term of endearment.

He did not know for sure what the woman had meant, but he had his suspicions. He would need to explore the other pits—and soon. If there was someone from Ridge held captive, he would need to address the matter.

CHAPTER 28

THE DAY OF SLAVERY

Hamel rode out of the City Square feeling both angry and ill. The thought that someone could be treated with such abuse and that both the common people and the soldiers were willing to take part was appalling. Before he had entered the Square, he had wondered if the people were oppressed, but he was beginning to think they were content with their way of life. It was not the soldiers who were forcing the men and women to treat the poor woman in such a disgraceful manner.

He spotted what appeared to be a small restaurant with an open patio not too far from the City Square. He had not eaten since he had stopped at the small stream just after sunrise. He needed to sit and think for a moment. He dismounted just in front of the restaurant, and a young boy came and took his horse away. He did not pause for Hamel to give him any money which was just as well to Hamel. He was too distracted to worry about such matters. He sat down at a table and within seconds, a young girl stood at his table and poured him a glass of wine while a young man set down a bowl filled with small rolls of bread.

Hamel's stomach turned, and he had to force himself to unclench his jaw. He closed his eyes and concentrated on slowing his breathing and relaxing his shoulders, back, arms, and legs.

He was always on mission. He had been on mission since his adoption at thirteen.

Everything else had always taken second place to whatever mission he had been on at whatever moment. Some missions had been assigned by his commanding officers. Some missions had been assigned by the Council. Some missions had been to love and raise his children. He had always given his all for each and every mission. He felt as if the weight of each one of those countless missions bore down on his shoulders.

Hamel grabbed a piece of bread and took a bite. His stomach had begun to settle but was still twisting, and he feared he could lose his meal. A soldier, however, learned to eat when necessary. He had developed the ability to eat in the worst of situations, yet the situation he was in at that moment tested his limits.

He made a mental note to return to the Square. The other pits needed to be explored to find the "Ridger." He could not imagine what circumstances might have brought the man or woman to such a place, but he would find out. The person had apparently been there longer than the woman. His or her suffering must have been great.

He briefly thought through any reports he had heard of someone going missing four to eight weeks before, but he could not think of anyone. That, in itself, did not surprise him. He could not remember every detail of every report he read. Someone could have gone missing during that time, and he might have forgotten. He had had so much on his mind in recent months.

He turned his thoughts back to the woman in the pit. It would be difficult to get her out. Her current health, along with her broken leg, had likely guaranteed her death, but he felt it would be better to die outside the pit.

He did not think he would be able to move her without her crying out in pain. He would have to act at night, but if she could not be silent while he pulled her to freedom, she would only be thrown back in, and he would be given his own pit.

He was pulled from his thoughts by the clearing of a throat. The young girl who had given him his glass of wine stood in the same place she had when she had filled his glass. He wondered briefly if she had not left. "Yes, young lady?" Hamel asked in his Olmosite accent.

The girl's brow furrowed, and her mouth opened just slightly. Her eyes betrayed confusion, but she composed herself quickly. "Master," she said and bowed low before him. "Is there any food you would like me to bring to you?"

Hamel examined the young girl. She was young, perhaps thirteen or fourteen years old. Her cheeks were sunken and what he could see of her forearms told a story of far too little food.

He had spent a great deal of effort until that point trying to be careful not to act in any way which might betray him to the people of Olmos, but he was not sure he could manage much longer. The sight of this starving young girl working at a restaurant made him fear that he was at a breaking point. It had all been too much. The poverty in the border town, the thieves he had faced, the woman in the pit… he closed his eyes and pictured the young boy in Eddel's compound along with his mother. When he opened them a moment later, the young girl was still before him and still starving.

Hamel had reached his limit.

After all the disgrace he had faced and the loss he had experienced, he wanted to scream. Deep inside, he wondered how many cruel people in the city he could kill before they stopped him. He suspected he could manage quite a few.

Hamel let his eyes drop to the table. He took two deep breaths. The pain in his leg continued to throb and did not help his demeanor.

He would not allow himself to slide into unnecessary violence, but he could not ignore another injustice. He decided to take the middle road. The child needed food. He might draw some attention, but he would risk it.

"Yes, I would like some food, but I would also like some company. I would like you to bring me a meal fit for

218

two people, and you will join me. I would like to warn you, though, I am a big eater, so bring enough food."

The girl's confusion turned to fear. He suspected he had broken several social boundaries. He hoped it would be worth it. The girl needed to eat, and he needed information. It was perhaps an ideal arrangement.

Hamel leaned back in his chair and closed his eyes. The message was clear: the conversation was finished. He would wait for his food and her company.

He heard the girl's light feet fade as she scurried into the restaurant. The sun was warm, and it felt good to lean back, soak in the sun, and clear his mind. It had been nearly three weeks since he had experienced much peace. He looked forward to a day when he could rest.

About ten minutes passed before he heard another throat clear, but this time it was a man. Hamel opened his eyes to see not only the young girl standing by his table but also an older man dressed in fine clothing. As thin as the girl was, the man was her complete opposite. The girl's arms shook as she held two large platters, far more than even the two of them could eat.

Before the man could speak, Hamel decided to take charge. He turned to the girl and said, "Put the food on the table."

She bowed her head but did not set down the platters. She turned to the man, and he frowned. He nodded his head, and she set the food down before stepping back to the man's side. Hamel considered the interaction for a moment. Until that point, people had deferred to him based on his outfit, warhorse, and perhaps his demeanor. The situation at the restaurant was different. His mind raced through the possibilities of what could have caused a different reaction.

"The girl tells me you have invited her to sit with you for dinner," the man said. His face appeared well acquainted with his frown.

Hamel hoped he could smooth things over. He feared he had sent the wrong message. "I am merely looking to have some company. Nothing more. She will not be harmed in any way."

The man's shoulders relaxed, but he shook his head. "She is mine. She will work for me and for me alone. I have purchased her, and the ownership grants me full control until she is forty years old, at which point she may begin to save money to purchase her freedom. That is the contract we arranged. I will not have her sitting when she should be working. It is not right."

The image of the boy in Eddel's compound flashed into his mind yet again, and he imagined the man before him lowered alongside Eddel into the waiting arms of the Beasts. He knew he would have a great deal of difficulty convincing the man to return to Ridge with him to be tried for his crimes, which left his mind to drift to various ways of killing the man.

Hamel shook his head to force the thoughts away. "Perhaps you do not realize who you are speaking to." He hoped he could convince the man to give a little. It might be another foolish move, but he was angry enough that he was not willing to let the matter go.

"I do not care who you are. I do not care if you are the High Chancellor himself! I own the rights to her. She is mine and not a man or woman in the entire world can question my decision on this matter."

Hamel was learning a great deal about the people of Olmos. Slavery was legal, and the rights of an owner were paramount. Those rights could override any authority. He would have to find another way to address this matter. He knew he should probably leave. If he pushed too hard, he might not survive to find Churoi.

Once again, he remembered the young boy. He also remembered words his Matir had once shared with him, "There are times when it is worth risking everything to do what must be done." It was one of the reasons he had been willing to disgrace himself to pursue the matter of the Beasts.

He would not walk away. He would not let this one go.

Hamel turned his head to the girl. Her face was expressionless, but her eyes declared her fear. As he looked closely at her face, he could see faint bruises which had mostly healed.

Hamel had crossed some sort of cultural line. He did not know exactly where, but he was confident the girl would pay the price if he could not change the situation. "Would you consider selling her to me?"

Hamel's insides twisted at the thought. It was not that he was unwilling to pay for her freedom; it was that he could not imagine paying a price for a human being. People were meant to be free, but this one needed freedom to be purchased for her.

At the question, the man's expression changed from irritation to joy. He pulled back the chair on the other side of the table and sat opposite Hamel. The young girl continued to stand as she waited patiently for whatever decision was made. It was as if she had no concern for whom her master might be. She had accepted her lot in life.

"I paid one gold for her when I purchased her, but she was only eight years old at the time. She could barely carry a tray. Her former master had been a cobbler. You can see how much more there is to offer at this age. She is stronger, a hard worker, and I have invested countless hours in her training and money into feeding and clothing her for so many years. I will not take less than ten golds." The man sat back in his chair and rested his clasped hands on his rather large belly.

Hamel once again found his mind filled with violent thoughts. He had never enjoyed injuring another, even in battle. As his mind flew through various images, a smile crept up on his face. He had to push the thoughts away. He was not a violent man at heart, nor did he think such a course of action would be helpful in his current situation.

He took a mental count of his assets. He had four golds and six silvers. He also had a horse. He did not know what a horse might be worth in Olmos. He thought he would find out. "I will trade you my horse for her. The horse is in

221

your stable. It is a strong stallion, well trained, and solid. You will find him worth a great deal."

"I have seen your horse. It is quite valuable, but not as valuable as that," the man said, pointing to the girl. "I wouldn't give you more than four golds for the horse. Maybe four golds and three silvers at the most."

Four golds and three silvers for the horse plus his four golds and six silvers gave him nearly nine golds to work with. "Then I will give you four golds, six silvers, and my horse."

The man leaned forward and slammed his fist on the table. "Are you trying to rob me? Shall I call for the soldiers?" the man hissed. "I told you ten golds. I will not take a silver less."

Hamel pushed down the fire building inside his chest. The woman in the pit and now this. He had no more to give, other than his sidearm. He did not, however, think it wise to sell or give up a sidearm in public. He wondered if the status of "Naromite" might force the man to acquiesce. He briefly thought about showing his papers to the man, but then remembered that Mellel had warned him the papers would not hold up to scrutiny. If he were found out to be in possession of forged papers, he suspected the girl would remain in slavery, and he would find himself in the pit.

"I would not think of robbing you," Hamel said in a growl. "What I have offered is all I have. I would still like to purchase the young woman, but I have no more. Certainly we could come to an arrangement."

The man's face broke into a huge grin, and he laughed loudly. "Of course we can," the man said. "I will take your cloak. It appears to be of great value." He laughed again. "I certainly hope you are wearing something underneath."

Hamel closed his eyes. He did have something on underneath, but not much. He had used his tunic as bandages. He had on some trousers, but they were not much more than undergarments. A lack of a cloak would also reveal his injury. He had not wanted to meet Churoi in such a dishonorable state.

He opened his eyes again and raised his head. "Since my cloak is of such great value, I will give you four golds, my horse and my cloak. You will give me the girl and one of those plates of food."

The man nodded his head slowly and exclaimed, "Agreed!" He raised a hand, and a young man rushed out of the restaurant with a pen and a piece of paper. It was the young man who had brought out the bread earlier. Hamel assumed he had been watching the entire interaction.

Hamel wished he had found a way to purchase the boy's freedom as well. He appeared to be in no better condition than the girl. He was thin with sunken cheeks and had a glazed-over look in his eyes.

Hamel would never have enough to save them all.

The contract did not take long to draft up. The man tossed it to Hamel, who read it over carefully. It was clear, and it lined up with what they had agreed upon. The man then signaled for a soldier who came over.

The soldier read through the agreement. He laughed to himself and nodded his head. The restaurant owner signed it, followed by Hamel. The soldier then asked the restaurant owner for his papers, confirmed his name and status, then asked Hamel for his papers. Hamel had not wanted to draw too much attention to himself, but he feared he was beyond that point. He would need to follow through with what he had agreed upon.

He handed the papers to the soldier and watched as the young lieutenant's face drained of all color, and his knees wobbled. He looked up for just a moment at Hamel before he dropped to one knee and lowered his head nearly to the ground. He then stood up, turned to the restaurant owner, and backhanded him.

The man rolled off his chair and nearly landed on the young girl in the process. The soldier screamed, "You moron! Do you realize who this is? You would be better arguing with the High Chancellor than to challenge this man!"

The restaurant owner's face filled with shock and a total lack of comprehension. He had gone from thinking he had won to having no idea how bad the situation was.

The soldier leaned down close to the man, and Hamel could just barely hear him whisper, "You should have found out who you were bargaining with before you agreed to humiliate him. You will be fortunate if you are still alive by morning. Now get up and act with whatever humility you can muster."

The soldier turned and bowed once again to Hamel. When he spoke, his voice shook. "I am sorry, Colonel. Please forgive me. A contract must be followed. I have no choice in the matter. If I could find a way, I would give you the girl for no money. Please do not hold this against me." He then took the paper and signed it before saying, "It is complete, and it is binding."

"Your robe, Master," the soldier said. His eyes remained on the ground, rather than on Hamel.

Hamel handed over the four golds and pulled off his robe. He was grateful for the short pants he still had, but he could hear people across the road laugh. He took a quick glance at the young woman. Her face twisted in a look of confusion, shock, and disgust.

He was not surprised by her reaction. The little he knew of Olmosite customs and from what he was learning, none of what had happened would have made sense to her. He suspected she was more afraid than anything. She likely did not understand the concept of actual freedom, nor would she know she had it. It would come in time, but it would not be an easy concept to grasp for one who had spent her entire life in bondage.

The restaurant owner, with the help of the young man, had found his way to his feet. His eyes darted between Hamel and the soldier. When he looked at the girl, it was with an expression of hatred. He took the cloak from the soldier and bowed to Hamel before he grabbed one of the platters of food and rushed away.

224

The soldier also bowed to Hamel before handing the contract to him. Without another word, he turned and disappeared into the crowd.

The young girl continued to stand motionless with the confusion written across her face. Her mouth moved as if she were trying to say something, but no words came out.

Hamel picked up the tray of food and then approached the girl carefully. Her eyes dropped to the ground in a look of submission, and her entire body shook. He gently took her arm but immediately let go in shock. Through her cloak, his hand had easily wrapped around her upper arm. He had not imagined her arm to be so thin. He felt sick to his stomach, and the anger burned even hotter. The girl had been starved.

He had witnessed starvation before, and it had troubled him ever since. He had learned that a starving person did not have endurance. He made a mental note not to push her to walk or run too far until she was strong. Without his horse, they would both need to walk everywhere. The city had suddenly grown much larger.

He gently took her arm again and led her away from the restaurant. The young woman was free, but her heart was still in slavery. It would be a long journey.

She turned to look over her shoulder, and Hamel saw both desire and relief written on her face. The journey to her freedom would be long indeed.

He knew he had done what was right. But he was not sure he had done the right thing for his mission.

CHAPTER 29

THE DAY TO EXPLORE

Once they had traveled a short distance from the restaurant, Hamel found a small fountain and sat the girl down on the side of it. She looked at it in awe, and he wondered if she had ever been that far from the restaurant in her life.

"It's time to eat. You will need your strength, and you will not find it without food and water," Hamel said.

The girl took a piece of bread from the plate and tentatively took a bite. She chewed slowly as though the experience was difficult. She watched him closely, and he noticed if he moved his arm quickly, her whole body flinched.

He dug into the plate of food. There was far more on the one plate than the two of them would be able to eat, and he was confident she would not be able to eat much at all at first. It would take many weeks before she was strong enough to eat what her body needed.

As men and women walked by, they sneered and mumbled insulting comments. Hamel suspected his size and bulk, which was hard to miss considering his current attire, was the only thing keeping the crowds from shouting their insults. He felt the shame of being exposed before the people but felt a smile creep onto his face. The child was worth the humiliation. No one should be left in slavery.

"Do you want my cloak?" the young woman asked, pulling Hamel away from his thoughts.

"Do I want your cloak?" Hamel asked in shock. "Are you offering to give me your cloak, young woman?"

"Yes, my Master."

Hamel had always considered it wise to take his time answering questions. The girl thought she was a slave. A poorly worded answer could do more damage than good. "Why would you offer me your cloak?"

"Because you are humiliated. It is not good for you to be humiliated while I stand clothed."

"Would you not be humiliated if you gave me your cloak?" Hamel asked. He had an image in his mind of trying to wear her tiny cloak, and he almost burst out in laughter.

"Yes, my Master. But I am meant to be humiliated. I am a slave. You are not."

Hamel nodded and took a moment to collect his thoughts. "Let me see if I understand you correctly. I am humiliated because I am left with only shorts. You, however, feel it is better for you to be humiliated to save me from my shame. And you feel it is better for you to be shamed because you believe you are only a slave, and I am a free man. Is that correct?"

"Yes, my Master," the girl said, her head hanging low.

"What is your name, my child," Hamel asked.

At the words, "my child," the girl's head shot up. Her mouth dropped open, and the bread roll she had held in her hand fell to the ground. She quickly composed herself and lowered her gaze. "I am simply the girl slave," she said. "My former Master never called me by name. The other one was the boy slave. I am the girl slave."

There was so much Hamel wished to correct but was not sure how much he could address at one time. "Am I your former Master?" Hamel asked.

"No, my Master, you are not."

"Then let us start there," Hamel said. "I will never call you a slave. I may call you 'my child' or 'young woman' but never 'slave.' I did not purchase you so you could continue in

227

slavery. I purchased you so you could enter a life of freedom. I purchased you to set you free. A free woman must have a name. Were you never given one?"

The girl's eyes remained focused on a spot on the ground, just near her feet. Hamel thought he saw a tear flow down her cheek. He did not mind that he had brought up a painful memory. She would have many in the years to come, and they would all need to be addressed. "The other slaves called me Gollos, my Master."

"Gollos. A name is important, Gollos. Let us deal with matters properly. There is much you will need to learn, but you cannot learn it all now. Do not fear me, Gollos. Instead, you must hear my words. You are mine. You are not mine in the way you think you are mine, but you are mine in the way of freedom and in the way of my people. When you understand that, you will know that being mine means I give you my life so that you may be free, and so you may be strong." He took a deep breath and made a decision. "I make you my daughter in the tradition of my family."

The girl nodded her head as if she understood, but Hamel was confident she did not. Another tear streaked down her cheek.

"It is not necessary that you understand everything now, but one day I hope you will. You are not alone, my child. You are now my family. I am tied to you and you to me. We are one. We are honored family. I commit to you, my daughter, to lead you faithfully, and as I have given my wealth, my horse, and even my cloak for you, I will also give my life to make you strong. As a token of my faithfulness to you, I give you my name. You will now be known as Rezin Gollos. You bear a name that, for the moment, I myself do not bear because of my humiliation, but one day, all will know I bear it again, and we will bear the name together."

The girl nodded her head in submission. She did not understand what had been given to her, but it did not matter. She had been a slave for many years. It would take many years more to help her understand her freedom, and that she had been welcomed into a family.

Hamel had not set out to adopt another child. He knew the customs of Olmos were different, but he would act with the honor he had known from his youth.

"My dear Gollos, do you know what it means to be a daughter?" Hamel asked.

She nodded her head. "I have witnessed many men and women with their daughters. A daughter is free to wander, and her parents only beat her if they are angry. It is different with a slave. A slave is beaten so they know they are a slave."

"Ahh, I am beginning to understand you more, my daughter, but *you* are far from understanding who you are now. A daughter of those men and women are beaten because their parents are angry, but a daughter of mine is not beaten. We will talk more about that later. All I will say at this point is that you are in no danger from me. For now, you must understand one thing. The question you asked earlier, what was it?"

"I asked if you would like my cloak, my Master," Gollos said as she wrapped her arms around herself.

"I will not take your cloak. In fact, one day, if I am able, I will give you a better cloak. One that is not torn, and one that is far better than that one. I sit here in humiliation, yet my humiliation is something I gladly bear for you. It is not for you to take away my humiliation because it is the price I have paid for you. You must instead observe my humiliation, for it is your place to watch me and learn from me. One day, you might need to bear humiliation or pain or to pay an even greater price than humiliation for another. You must learn from me so you can learn what it is that drives me to act this way. One day, you will understand what motivates me, and you will be able to act the same way for another."

The girl glanced briefly at Hamel and then lowered her eyes again. She opened her mouth but struggled to get the words out. He waited while she took the time to form the question she needed to ask, "What is it that motivates you, my Master?"

"It's love," Hamel said.

As he answered, her head dropped low, and a quiet sob shook her shoulders. He could see she was not shedding tears of relief or joy, but sadness and fear.

Hamel smiled and put a hand on each of her shoulders. "Gollos, listen to me. I think perhaps you have believed a lie. What is it you fear when I speak of love?"

"You wish to harm me," Gollos answered.

Hamel laughed before he could catch himself. He did not wish to embarrass her, but the thought was so absurd in his mind. "Did I not say you are not in danger from me? I will say it another way: I will not harm you, Rezin Gollos. You must learn to believe my words. You should start by looking into my eyes," Hamel said.

She glanced up briefly and met his eyes for only a second. She tried again but could not manage to hold his gaze. When she tried a third time, he could see she was looking just below his eyes. It was enough for now.

"If you look a man in the eyes," Hamel explained, "you can often see the truth of what he is saying. I speak the truth; you will not be harmed by me. The love you speak of is selfish and seeks only to take. That is not love. Love that is true is giving. It is what drives me to give my cloak, my money, my horse, and even humiliate myself for you. I will not require anything from you as payment. It is my gift to you. My love for you means you are safe with me."

As Hamel extended his hands to her, she flinched but managed to stay in her seat. "Look at my hands, my daughter. Tell me what you see."

She stared intently at them and shuddered. He had to admit, they were not attractive hands. Years of hard work and many battles had left them scarred and rough. His hands were somewhat gnarled and rough looking.

"I see the hands of a man who has been in many fights," Gollos explained.

"You see correctly. But what you don't see are two things. These hands tell a story of a man who has not lost many battles and has won every war he has fought. The hands also tell the story of a man who will never use his fists to harm

230

those he loves but has always used them to protect." Hamel paused in the hopes that she would be able to grasp what he had told her. "While you are with me, you will be safe."

She nodded her head, but he was confident she did not yet believe what he had told her. He hoped she would one day, but it would take time, and he would be patient. He had fought many battles for the freedom of his people and not one of them had been easy. To fight the battle for the freedom of Gollos's heart would not be easy either. He would take the time he needed. Victory was rarely found in one day.

"Have you had enough to eat, my child?" Hamel asked.

Gollos nodded, and he handed her some more food to hold. He then put some of the food which would keep into his pack. He did not own much, but he still had his papers, his sidearm, some Ridge money, six silvers, some of his medical supplies, and the contract which declared his ownership of Gollos.

He took a quick look at his leg. The red lines had spread beyond the bandage. There was not much he could do about it, but he took a moment and changed his bandage right there by the fountain. He quickly cleaned the area with the Noola he had purchased and packed the wound full of salve before putting on a clean bandage.

The sun would soon fall below the buildings, and they would need a place to stay for the night. He did not think they would find Churoi before darkness came, so he looked around for a merchant who might exchange his Ridge money for Olmosite money. Mellel had told him he would get a terrible exchange for it, but he did not have much choice anymore.

He took the plate with the leftover food and handed it to two men begging on the side of the road. He could see Gollos watch him out of the corner of her eye. She looked distressed that he was giving it away, but as they walked on, he explained, "It is good to give to those in need, Gollos. Do not worry about yourself. We will have enough."

As they walked down the road, Hamel continued to receive many glares from people as well as quiet insults. He was grateful no one moved against him. He did not want a confrontation.

After a short distance, they came across a market which was just about to close for the night. Hamel found a man selling clothes and material and even a few rugs. The man claimed the rugs were from Ridge craftsmen, and Hamel recognized the styles and designs. He hoped the man would have use for Ridge money.

When he explained that he needed to exchange some Ridge currency, the man smiled nearly from ear-to-ear. "Of course I can exchange that money for you, my friend," the man exclaimed. "How much do you have?"

"I have three Ridge golds and two Ridge silvers," Hamel explained.

The next few minutes were spent haggling over the amount. The man insisted at first that all Hamel's money was only worth one Olmosite silver, but Hamel would not hear of it. They went back and forth repeatedly until they finally agreed upon nine silvers for Hamel's money. He did not think that amount would get them far, but with the six he still had, he hoped it would be enough to provide for them until they found Churoi.

From there, they set out down the street again. Hamel wanted Gollos to think and act as though she had always been a free woman, but he knew he could not expect such a transition in less than an hour. It bothered him that she walked just a step behind him and would not look him in the eye unless he demanded it of her, but some matters would only be solved by time.

Hamel moved toward the east end of the city. He had made his way through the north, center, and west sections of the city on horseback and wanted to cover the east next. He had decided to leave the south end, where he had seen the giant park, until last. It was growing late in the day, and Hamel found an inn to stay for the night.

As the two walked into the inn, Hamel's mind drifted to his injury. It was a constant throbbing pain, but the more immediate danger was that it would make him an obvious target for thieves. When they walked through the common room of the inn, the sneers and comments he heard reminded him that his injury was not the biggest concern. He was wearing only shoes and a pair of short pants. It was difficult to move unnoticed when you walked around in shame.

At the counter, Hamel turned and scanned the room. He counted eighteen men. Most were his age or older. The sight of people older than himself was still a challenge for him to comprehend. None of the men appeared to be a threat in any way in terms of their physical builds as they appeared to have spent a great deal of time in their respective seats over the years. He picked a spot to stand in case someone did seek a confrontation. He did not think it would be realistic to get Gollos to the door if they were threatened, but there was a spot with a wall where he could stand in front of her and perhaps lead her up the stairs if needed.

The sound of the innkeeper's chuckle brought Hamel back to the matter of needing a room. The man stood taller than Hamel and weighed far more, but not in a manner which suggested speed and agility. "Did you forget something?" the innkeeper asked, and every man in the room laughed.

"Yes, large man standing behind the counter and observing the most obvious details for all to see and hear," Hamel replied with a smile. No one laughed. He thought perhaps he had crossed the line, but there were times in his life when he did not wish to play games. "I'd like a room with two beds," Hamel said.

The man's smile disappeared, and he growled, "No rooms with two beds. Only one bed. You'll have to share." The men in the room laughed again.

"How much?"

"How much you got?" the man asked, and the room erupted in laughter yet again. It appeared as though the men in the room spent most of their time drinking and laughing at the rather unhelpful man behind the counter.

"I'll give you three silvers for the best room you have," Hamel said confidently.

The room erupted in laughter once again, and Hamel wryly observed that he appeared to be developing the same ability the innkeeper had. Perhaps the room was far too drunk to manage anything other than laughter.

"Ahh, you are a funny man," the innkeeper said with a frown on his face. "I don't have time for this."

"Neither do I," Hamel said, but this time he spoke with authority. As a General and as an Honored Patir, he had learned many years ago how to control a room with his voice.

The room grew silent, and the man at the bar stepped back. The innkeeper took a moment and composed himself before naming his price, "Eight silvers. And I'll want you out of the room just after first light."

"Done," Hamel replied. He wanted to be on the move first thing in the morning to find Churoi. If they did not find him the following day, they would only have seven silvers to work with at the next hotel.

He paid the man and received the key to his room on the second floor of the inn. As he turned to head up the stairs with Gollos, he noticed a man stand up and move toward them. Once the man reached the foot of the stairs, he turned and crossed his arms.

"How about you give me your pack," the man said as he wobbled slightly on his feet. "It looks like you've lost just about everything else. If you give me the pack, I might be convinced to find my way to my seat again."

Hamel turned to the man at the counter. "What's your policy on stealing in your inn?"

The innkeeper frowned again and shouted loud enough for everyone to hear, "I don't mind, as long as no one steals from me. They steal from me, and I turn them over to the soldiers."

The crowded room filled with laughter once again. Hamel suspected anyone handed over to the soldiers for stealing from the innkeeper would end up in the pit. The man before him, however, did not seem concerned that Hamel

234

would be turning him over to the soldiers. He suspected many witnesses in the room would side with the man wobbling at the foot of the stairs.

"What is your policy on fighting in the bar?" Hamel asked.

"I don't mind that either, as long as my bar isn't damaged in any way," the man growled, and everyone laughed.

As the laughter faded, three more men came from the first man's table and stood beside him. Hamel did not see any other way around the situation. He handed the pack and key to Gollos and stepped forward to face the men.

The first man took a swing, and Hamel felt guilty. They were drunk. Their reflexes were slow, and their judgment was impaired. He did not like to fight men in such circumstances.

He decided to take the man down quickly and hoped the rest would understand they were in a dangerous situation. He reminded himself, however, that their judgment was in fact quite impaired. When the man hit the ground, the other three stood with their eyes on their friend for what seemed like ten minutes before they slowly turned their gaze back to Hamel. One of the men grunted, and all three charged.

Hamel did not like the situation. He could easily incapacitate all three, but he was concerned for Gollos's safety if one of the men were to land on her. He focused on taking down the men, dropping each one straight to the floor rather than throwing them. It was more challenging, but he noticed the movements hurt his leg less than it would to toss the men over his shoulder.

When he was finished, he quickly scanned the room again. No one had moved. Hamel suspected they were all still trying to comprehend what had happened. Only the innkeeper looked aware of the fact that Hamel had easily incapacitated four men without one of them laying a hand on him.

235

He turned back to Gollos and retrieved his pack. Her face was drained of all color and was once again filled with fear. He did not think she feared the fallen men.

He led her upstairs, and they found their room. Once they entered, Hamel locked the door behind them. She watched as he moved a small table and firmly wedged it against the door. He nodded to himself as he checked to make sure the door would not budge.

When he turned around, there were tears in Gollos's eyes, and her entire body trembled. It would take a long time for her to understand she would never be in danger from him. He knew he needed to cover the ground again.

"Gollos, please sit down." She instantly obeyed and sat down on the edge of the bed. She looked even more defeated than she had looked when he first met her.

"What did I tell you by the fountain today, my child?" Hamel asked.

"You told me you would never harm me," she answered in a voice just above a whisper.

"Have men lied to you before?" he asked.

She nodded her head quickly in response. Her hands and chin trembled.

"I have never lied to you, Gollos. We are one. We are family. I would give my life for you." He watched her as she nodded her head, but he could see the doubt in her eyes. "I understand that it will take time for you to learn to trust, but you are no longer in the clutches of the man who owned the restaurant. You are now a free woman and will be treated with dignity and respect."

"But free women are beaten as well," she replied.

"Not by men," he said quite firmly. "They are beaten by dogs who call themselves men. A man protects. You will never be struck by me."

She smiled for the first time since he had met her. He was not quite sure what had caused the grin, but he was happy to see such a response.

"Listen," Hamel said in a soft voice. "You need to learn to recognize the truth from a lie. I tell you this truth: I will never harm you. All I will ever do for you will be for your good and for your benefit. You have seen what I am capable of. Tell me, did I use my strength and skill to harm you or protect you?"

She shook her head in confusion and said, "I don't understand."

Hamel smiled at her, and he saw her relax. "That is fine. Let me say this. You have seen that I can defend you. The strength I have is for two things: for those who are a threat to you, my strength is something to fear; for you, it is something to give you confidence. I know you feel weak right now, but we will make you strong."

He glanced back at the barricaded door. "Young lady, do you see this table wedged securely here in the doorway?"

She nodded her head and once again began to cry.

"Gollos, let me ask you a question. From what you have seen of me and of what I have given for you, does that not tell you how much you are worth to me? I have given all I had and even suffered humiliation and shame for you. And now you have seen a little of what I am capable of. Should that not give you confidence? If you are worth that much to me, and you have witnessed me standing between you and danger down in the room below, I must ask you this question. Do you think I wedged that table in the doorway to keep you in or to keep danger out?"

She sat on the bed and examined the door in silence. Hamel could see the confusion and the internal struggle written on her face. He decided he would leave the thoughts with her for the time being and spent a moment cleaning his used bandages and reapplying the salve. He was nearly out of salve and Noola. He could not manage without medical care for much longer.

Hamel settled down on the floor in the doorway, near the barricade. Despite the pain in his leg, he was confident he would be asleep in minutes. Just before he felt himself drift off, he stole a glance at Gollos. She was still seated on the edge of the bed, her eyes fixed on him. The look on her face, at least what he could see in the dim light coming through the

237

window, was still one of confusion. It would take a while for her to see herself as free.

He was glad he had purchased her freedom. The risk to the mission was worth it. It would merely be more difficult from that point on.

CHAPTER 30

THE DAY OF LIFE

Hamel awoke to a loud banging on the door. Years of training took over, and he found himself on his feet, off to the side of the door, ready for action. He glanced over his shoulder to see Gollos standing in a corner, her thin frame shaking in the early morning light.

As his mind raced through the possible dangers facing them on the other side of the door, he briefly considered the fact that she stood helpless in the corner. She did not stand in a defensive or offensive position. If he went down, she would be taken. When they had time, he would need to address the matter. He made a mental note to begin her training as soon as she had the strength. Perhaps sooner.

The banging came again, and Hamel called out, "What do you want?" in his Olmosite accent. He had grown used to speaking in the accent and no longer had to think about the matter.

"I told you I wanted you out by first light! Now get out, or I'll have the soldiers remove you."

Hamel heard the footsteps of the innkeeper thump on the floor as he made his way back down the hall toward the stairs. Hamel made note that he also heard the footsteps of at least two other people. They were either looking for a fight, or the innkeeper was not willing to take his chances with Hamel alone.

He smiled. He was confident none of those footsteps belonged to any of the men who had been in the common room the night before. From what he had witnessed of the quantity of drink consumed, not one of them would be up for a fight so early in the morning.

He checked the barricade once again and turned to Gollos. She had pressed herself into the corner, and even in the dim light coming through the small window, he could see tears.

Hamel walked slowly to her side, took her hand, and said, "My child, you do not need to fear. I will protect you with my life. I have given my all to take you from slavery. Do not think you will so easily be given up now."

She nodded and stared at the floor. Hamel did not feel they had much time, but he wanted to address two matters. "Gollos, you must look me in the eye. Remember you are free."

She raised her eyes. This time, she focused in on his forehead. "Yes, my Master."

"Gollos?"

"Yes, my Master?"

"I do not want to be called 'Master' by you."

"Yes, my Master. What would my Master wish me to call him?"

"My papers say my name is Wos Hamtia. You may either call me Wos or Hamtia, I do not mind either name, but I do not want to be called Master."

"Yes, my Master," the girl said, before she realized her mistake and drew back. Her arms went up over her face as she cried out, "Wos! No, I mean, yes, my Wos."

"Gollos, I said I do not want to be called Master by you, but I did not say I would harm you if you called me Master," Hamel said with a smile. He watched the confusion in her eyes. She had lived too many years as a slave. He would be patient to help her stand strong. He wished he had Mariel by his side. She had a way of calming fear and pouring strength and confidence into people.

"We do not have much time. We will leave in a moment. I will just need to quickly change my bandage," Hamel said before rushing to the lavatory where he had left the bandages he had cleaned. He cleaned the wound and applied a portion of the remaining salve from Mellel and from his own supplies brought from Ridge. He tried to ignore the burning pain in his leg. The infection had spread.

He hoped Churoi would help him. Since he had known next to nothing about the interior of Olmos, he had based his plans entirely around meeting the younger man. If Churoi could not help him, he would have to find another route.

When he was ready to leave, he turned again to Gollos. She had not moved from her place in the corner. "Gollos, we will need to leave. Will you come with me?"

Hamel was growing used to the confusion in her eyes. He paid close attention to every expression she made, as each one helped him to understand her more.

"Will I come with you?" she asked. "Do you mean that if I wanted to stay here, I could?"

Dread filled Hamel's heart. He had thought asking her might help her to understand she was free, but he would never leave her there. She would be in terrible danger if she remained in the room. He was torn. On the one hand, she needed to learn to make decisions. On the other hand, a poor decision at that moment could be deadly.

If she stayed, he would as well. But he could not stay.

"Gollos, it would be wise for you to leave right now, but if you will not leave, I will stay and protect you. I will stand in your defense as long as I have strength." He was not sure that was the right response, but it was as far as he could go.

"But I am a slave," she said.

"Not to me, Gollos," Hamel replied.

She smiled again, and he noticed she raised her hand and touched the back of her neck. He began to wonder how often she had smiled over the years. He hoped he would see many more. He noted as well that her comment about being a slave had come just moments after he had told her once again that she was free. He suspected she wanted to hear him say it again.

Gollos stood up straight and said, "I will go with you."

"I'm glad, my child. Let's go."

She moved toward him, and he directed her to stand off to the side of the doorway while he moved the table he had wedged against the door. He pulled his sidearm out of his bag and watched Gollos out of the corner of his eye. She looked frightened but less so than she had in times past. He hoped that was progress.

Hamel unlocked the door and stepped to the side. He stood just in front of the young girl before swinging the door open. In the flickering light of the hallway, he could not see anyone waiting for them. He took a good hard look up and down the hall before waving for Gollos to follow him.

The two made their way to the stairs and gently descended. Hamel thought it was unrealistic to think he would be able to leave without at least one challenge, but upon reaching the bottom of the stairs, he found the inn empty except for the innkeeper.

"You're late!" the man growled. "Get out of my inn before I call in the soldiers!"

Hamel did not care to argue with the man. Instead, he made for the exit with Gollos close behind. When they stepped into the cool, morning air, Hamel found the streets as deserted as the inn had been.

He turned east. He hoped to explore as much of that end of the city as possible before noon and then make his way to the south. As they walked, Hamel handed Gollos a waterskin, and he listened as she sucked back gulp after gulp. He had not known she was as thirsty as she was. He had also not thought to ask her if she were thirsty.

When she finally paused long enough to catch her breath, he handed her some of the food he had stored in his pack and took back the water. She began to eat it in the same manner by which she had been drinking, and Hamel feared she would choke.

He held his tongue. Manners and proper eating were not important at that moment.

He raised the skin to his mouth to drink what little she had left him when she gasped and dropped the food in her hands. "No, my Master!" she shouted. "I mean…." She closed her mouth, and her eyes dropped to the ground.

"You may call me Wos Hamtia or either one of those names, Gollos."

"Wos, please do not forget that I just drank from that skin," Gollos said.

"I don't understand, Gollos," Hamel said. "I cannot forget you drank from the waterskin. You drank like a parched camel and left me very little." He did not know if she could pick up on his humor.

"I just drank from that waterskin," Gollos explained. "Do you not know that slaves are dirty, diseased creatures?"

Hamel stopped walking and examined her face. He did not think someone could be dirty or diseased simply because they were a slave, but on the other hand, it was always possible that she did have a disease that she had picked up over the years. He looked down at the canteen and wondered if it were a stigma or a truth.

"Are all slaves dirty and diseased, Gollos?" Hamel asked.

"Yes, Wos." When she pronounced his name, it sounded like it was difficult for her to form the word. "Masters do not drink from the same cup as a slave because we are…"

Gollos stopped mid-sentence, and her eyes drifted off to a spot somewhere to the left of Hamel. He could see she was thinking through what she had always believed.

Hamel nearly shouted for joy. He hoped she was starting to think through matters as a free person.

"Gollos, think through the matter. Take your time."

Her eyes continued to wander, but Hamel could see she was not focusing on anything in particular. Her mind was moving in a direction it had never traveled before. When she spoke, her words came slowly. "Although, Wos, I do not believe I have any diseases that free people do not have. I do not show signs of disease. I am not ill." Gollos raised her eyes to meet Hamel's and held his gaze, eye-to-eye, for the first time. "I do not think I have a disease."

Hamel smiled and nearly wrapped his arms around her but caught himself. He did not know how to treat Gollos in a respectful manner. Among the People of the Ridge, an embrace declared love, respect, and hope for the relationship, but in Olmos and for Gollos, he did know what message that would send to her. He did not want to do something wrong and hinder her progress.

"I do not think you are dirty or diseased, Gollos," Hamel said.

She rushed to him and wrapped her arms around him. He did not think for one moment she truly understood what freedom she had received. The bondage had been written on her heart for many years, and it would take years for the truth to be written over the lies, but they were moving in the right direction. She held on tightly and did not let go. He wrapped his arms around her and held her just as tight. After a few minutes, he could feel her shoulders and arms shaking and heard quiet sobs. The two remained in place for what seemed like an hour as she sobbed in his arms.

Her tears drew his mind back to his late wife and two lost children. A wave of grief washed over him as he pictured their faces and was reminded yet again of his loss. His mind then went to Karotel, Mariel, and Lemmel. So much had been taken from him over the years. He thought of the poor young girl, sobbing in his arms. He did not even know how old she was, but for all those years, she had lived in slavery. He wondered how much fear, tension, and anger she had built up over the years. He hoped the sobs and tears were a way for her to relieve the pain.

When she finally pulled away, she looked around as though she had forgotten where she was. When she turned her eyes to Hamel, her face had turned a deep red. "Wos," she said quietly, "you are a very different man than my former Master."

"I will take that as a compliment, Gollos," he said and put his hands on each of her shoulders. "I hope you will learn that there are many people who are different from your former Master. But for now, let's keep moving."

As they walked, Hamel observed his surroundings closely but wanted to invest in Gollos at the same time. The Ridge way was for a Patir or Matir to pour their lives into those who were younger. He would pour himself into her.

"Tell me, Gollos, what you see when you look at me. I wish to know what you can observe."

Gollos examined Hamel as they continued along the street. "You walk straight."

"Yes, that is the way I was taught to walk by my…" He paused. He was well aware that the terms Patir and Matir were exclusively Ridge terms for parents. He was familiar with the term "Mother," but that term seemed to lack the weight of the Ridge tradition carrying both compassion and investment. He would have to settle for the word and hope it would make sense to her. "My Mother taught me to walk that way. Good job, Gollos."

She looked at the ground and smiled again. This time, the smile did not leave. "My child, what does it tell you about me when you see that I walk with my shoulders squared, my back straight, and my head held high?"

"You look strong to me," she said.

"Correct." He stopped and turned to her. He gently reached for her shoulders and pushed them back from their slumped position. He then lifted her chin up.

When he was finished, she looked rather awkward and uncomfortable. He did not think she would be able to maintain the posture for long, but he wanted her to understand something. "You, Gollos, are free to stand like me. Decide you are strong and stand like it."

"But I am not strong," Gollos replied.

Hamel laughed. He was not sure how to respond. He knew very little about her to point out her actual strength.

245

Physically, she was perhaps one of the weakest girls he had ever seen, but that would change with a proper diet and consistent training. "One thing at a time, my child. If you do not believe you are strong yet, you may walk as though you are strong because you stand with me. In time, you will walk strong even when you do not have me to walk beside you."

He forced down a smile as they continued down the street. She managed to keep her shoulders and head up as she walked, but she moved like a marionette, controlled by strings above her. From the smile on her face, he suspected she was entirely unaware of how awkward she looked. He held his tongue. She would learn to stand and walk strong one day but learning something foreign was never easy.

"What else do you observe?" Hamel asked.

"Your accent," Gollos said, her body jerking along in her attempt to walk with confidence.

"What do you notice about my accent?" Hamel asked.

"It is slightly different than everyone else's," she explained.

"Interesting," Hamel said. He had thought he had the accent down perfectly. No one else had commented on it until Gollos. "What does that tell you? Please, answer honestly."

"It tells me that you are either a man who has traveled far and lived there long enough for your words to change or that you are pretending to speak as though you are from Pollos."

Hamel laughed out loud, and Gollos joined in with her own nervous laugh. "Well, that is interesting, Gollos. I will admit, I am impressed. Now, if you are right about one of those possibilities, what are the ramifications?"

"Ramifications?" she asked.

"Yes, ramifications," he said. "Those conclusions could raise questions, concerns, and more."

Gollos grew quiet again as they walked. Her eyes remained down as they often did. After about a minute, she said, "If you are someone who has traveled far and lived away, then you are less familiar with the city than others may be. That might explain why you are exploring the city."

246

Hamel smiled again. She had a mind like Karotel. He was confident the young lady would go far.

"However, if you are pretending to have a proper Olmosite accent, then you are not from here. That would also explain why you are exploring the city. It would also tell me that you are hiding something."

At those last words, he came to a stop. She had a quick mind.

The girl's eyes moved to Hamel, and she held his gaze. The fear had returned, but alongside it, confidence. "Wos, I think that is it. It would explain why you did not appear to understand the process of slave transfer, and it would also explain why you are treating me as though I am not a slave."

"Gollos, if I were not from here," Hamel said in his Olmosite accent, "what would you do about it?"

She paused again, but this time did not look down at the ground. "I don't know what I would do."

"Young lady, if you found out I was not from Olmos, would you hand me over to the authorities?"

Gollos's face took on an expression of incredulity. Her mouth opened and closed once or twice, and her eyes darted around. When she spoke, her voice was just above a whisper. "You are not from here. I am confident of it, my Mas... Wos. But I will not hand you over to the authorities. I may have lived my entire life as a slave, but I am no fool. If I were to do that, I would betray the first person who has ever shown even a small amount of kindness to me. Not only have you protected me, but you have even allowed yourself to suffer humiliation for me. No Olmosite I have ever met would do such a thing. No, you are not from Olmos, and no, I will never betray you."

Hamel put his hand on her arm and was once again shocked by how thin she was. When he spoke, he matched her whisper. "Then I will take the chance of trusting you, Gollos. I am not from here. My accent does not match my country of origin. I will need you to keep this information secret."

247

"Yes, my Ma…" Gollos began. She had almost called him "Master" twice within a few minutes' time. Old habits were not easily lost. "Yes, Wos, I will keep your secret."

"Excellent," Hamel replied. "Then let us continue. We have to finish exploring the city so I can find the man I am looking for."

"Who are you looking for?" Gollos asked.

"I am looking for an old friend. Actually, a friend of a friend. His name is Churoi. He was the assistant to the Ambassador to Ridge many years ago."

"I know of Churoi," Gollos said. Her face took on a look of pride, and she squared her shoulders. "I can help you find him."

"How do you know of Churoi?" Hamel asked. "I was left with the impression you had not left the restaurant often."

"I rarely left the restaurant, but my former Master required that I memorize all the political, financial, military, and influential people of the city and many details about them," Gollos explained. "It was helpful in his business practices and for the purpose of extortion. My knowledge helped to procure many advantages for my former Master and to protect him from quite a few threats."

Hamel noted the ease and comfort with which Gollos spoke of such shameful practices.

She continued, "Churoi is the assistant to the High Chancellor. He is a man of great influence and power in the city. He is feared nearly as much as the High Chancellor himself."

"Where would we find him?" Hamel asked.

"He would be with the High Chancellor," Gollos said. "The High Chancellor owns the estate on the south end of the city."

Her smile had grown into a toothy grin and had spread to her eyes. She shook as she bounced on her toes. The sight of the smile stretched across her face was a joy for Hamel, but it also grieved him. His mind drifted to the years she should have spent smiling but had instead spent cowering

248

in fear from her Master. He hoped to see many smiles flowing from joy in the days ahead.

"Then we head south," Hamel said as they turned in the direction of the large estate he had seen.

His mind drifted to Churoi. The young man had climbed to the position of assistant to the High Chancellor. Hamel hoped Churoi's power and influence would not have changed him from the kind, compassionate man he had been.

As they made their way south, Hamel struggled to keep his walk steady. His lower leg felt like fire, and his upper leg ached. Even his back ached. He longed for relief from the pain. The thought that Churoi might be able to help gave him the drive he needed to push through the ache.

Gollos, however, was a different matter. He noticed the young girl breathing heavy. He was not the only one struggling to walk. If she had not been outside the restaurant often, physical exercise, even something as simple as walking, would not be easy for her.

They found a small area in the shade of a large building to stop and drink some water and eat some more food. He knew Gollos's only hope of building strength was to eat often and get the exercise she so desperately needed. He hoped they would have the opportunity for training under Churoi's care.

When they had finished a small meal and rested for a few minutes, they resumed their journey south. While Gollos had little endurance for the walk, her excitement over figuring out where Hamel needed to go seemed to drive her forward.

They reached the south end of the city just before noon and quickly found their way to the High Chancellor's estate. As with much of Olmos, Hamel did not have his plan all worked out as to how he would navigate his way through each interaction. His meeting with Churoi would be no different.

The High Chancellor's estate was not difficult to find, nor was there any question as to whether or not it was the home of the Olmosite leader. Soldiers lined the steps leading to the front doors, and the wall around the palace looked solid enough to protect a city. He did not think his lack of cloak would endear him to the soldiers, but he did not see any other way.

"Gollos, we will now see if we can make contact with Churoi. I was close friends with the Ambassador to Ridge years ago. Churoi and I spent a great deal of time together during those years. When I am with him, I will speak in my normal accent. I will not speak as an Olmosite. I need to know that you will not tell them I have mastered… or nearly mastered…" Hamel said with a smile on his face, "the Olmosite accent."

"I will not betray you, Wos," Gollos said.

"I will also need you to keep some other information secret as well. If you recall, the soldier who oversaw the contract exchange for you made comments about my status. I need that information to be kept secret. My papers must not be mentioned."

"I will not betray you, Wos," Gollos said.

"One more thing," Hamel said. "My name is not Wos. I need you to make sure you never call me that name around anyone in the palace."

"Yes, Mas…" Gollos said before catching herself yet again. "What shall I call you?"

"My real name is…" Hamel stopped mid-sentence. Something just outside the palace had caught his eye.

At the bottom of the steps, just to the side, was a large statue of a man. He was wearing Ridge attire, rather than an Olmosite cloak, and he looked familiar. Hamel took two steps toward the statue, thinking his mind was playing tricks on him. There was no doubt about what he saw, and he felt his heart stop in his chest.

"Gollos, do you know anything about that statue there?" Hamel asked, not taking his eyes off the sight before him.

"Yes, I believe so," Gollos replied. "That is a statue of a man from Ridge. He was a leader among their people many years ago. His name was Hamel, but the Ridge People do not live very long, so I expect he is dead now."

250

"Why is there a statue of Hamel in front of the High Chancellor's palace?" Hamel asked. Few things confused Hamel to such an extent that he could lose his focus on the task before him. The sight of a statue of himself in front of the Olmosite Palace was just such an experience.

He vaguely noticed the sound of a procession of horses moving toward the front doors of the palace. Whoever was coming was very important.

"It is a sign of the High Chancellor's greatness," Gollos explained. "He befriended Hamel while living among the Ridgers."

"Why would that make him great?" Hamel asked. "And when did he befriend…"

He stopped himself and abandoned the line of questions. The procession of horses was too close. The soldiers stood straight, and each soldier scanned the courtyard. They were looking for threats, and no one escaped their notice. He could see half-a-dozen soldiers at least eying their position. Hamel had grown accustomed to recognizing when a situation had grown dangerous. They would need to conduct themselves carefully, and he would need to wait until a later time to find his answers.

Hamel grabbed Gollos's shoulder and hissed, "Listen closely. My name is Hamel. I am the man the statue is fashioned after. You must only call me Hamel from now on, but only around Churoi. I do not know who this High Chancellor is or how he befriended me, but no one can know I used the name Wos Hamtia."

Gollos shook her head. She appeared to be accepting most of what he was saying, but one part wasn't sitting right. "But if you are Hamel, he did befriend you. That is why he is the High Chancellor."

The procession of horses came to a halt in front of the palace doors, and Hamel's attention was drawn to them. He noticed Churoi right away. He was older. He had been but a youth when Hamel had last seen him, but the man seated on a horse near the front of the procession was definitely Churoi. His first thought was that Churoi had risen to the

251

position of High Chancellor, and his heart was instantly filled with pride and joy for the young man.

But something about Churoi's position in the procession suggested he was not the man of honor. He looked to the well-dressed man sitting on the horse next to Churoi, and his mouth dropped open. He had met that man before and had indeed been friends with him.

It was Pulanomos. His friend was alive.

CHAPTER 31

THE DAY OF MEETING

Hamel's mind raced. In seconds he went through disbelief and shock, all the way through gratitude that his friend was alive and moving along to anger at being deceived. He shook his head and pushed the anger away. Such a reaction would not help. There would be a reason why his friend had allowed such a lie. For ten years he had thought Pulanomos had died from the Dusk, but there he sat on his horse.

He opened his mouth to call to his friend but caught himself. He did not want to reveal that he had been posing as an Olmosite, but to reveal himself as a citizen of Ridge, or as the Olmosites called them, Ridgers, would be unacceptable. Citizens of Ridge were not allowed past the walls of Olmos.

"Gollos, remember what I told you. Do not reveal that I was speaking in a false accent and do not reveal the papers I have for identification in Olmos," Hamel said.

"Yes," Gollos replied. "But is your name truly Hamel?"

"Yes," Hamel replied. Time was short.

Gollos examined his face, then the statue. They did not have the time to discuss the matter, but Hamel needed to allow her a moment to take it all in. "You are... the man... the statue?"

"Yes, that is me. My name is Hamel, and that is the name you must use when you speak with me and when you refer to me around the High Chancellor or Churoi. When we are around any other people, however, simply call me…" Hamel paused for a moment. "…simply call me 'friend.'"

"Yes, Hamel, I will do that for you," Gollos smiled. She squared her shoulders and held up her chin as she spoke.

"One more thing for now," Hamel said, and Gollos nodded in reply. "I need you to holler out to the High Chancellor. Just call out his title."

"My Hamel," Gollos said quickly. Her eyes had grown large, and her mouth quivered. "A slave may not speak to someone of his position."

"Trust me, Gollos. It will be okay," Hamel said.

She nodded slowly then turned back to the procession of horses. By this time, Pulanomos had dismounted and made his way half-way up the stairs. The doors were opened to welcome him inside. They were nearly out of time.

Gollos took a deep breath and called out, "High Chancellor!"

Every soldier within sight drew their weapon. The roof of the palace was lined with eight men, and each one had a rifle trained on Hamel and Gollos. Out of the corner of his eye, he saw men on either side of the courtyard take up position, and he assumed there were more behind him. If they attacked, there would be no hope of escape.

Hamel watched Pulanomos glance over his shoulder. Their eyes met for just a moment, but his friend turned back and continued up the stairs. Hamel had taken quite the risk, and it appeared to have turned out poorly.

As Pulanomos's pulled himself to the top of the last step before the door into the palace, his walk slowed, and he came to a stop. The High Chancellor turned, and his mouth dropped open.

Hamel did not want to rush his friend, but the soldiers in the courtyard were nearly upon him. He could not fight them, nor could he allow himself and Gollos to be taken as prisoners.

Two soldiers grabbed Hamel by the arm, and he could hear Gollos cry out. The men were not gentle.

"Wait!" Pulanomos called.

His friend stood with a look of utter disbelief, holding out an arm. His head shook back and forth.

Hamel smiled, imagining what must be going through Pulanomos's mind. Not only had it been over ten years since they had seen one another, but there before him, standing in a land where he was not allowed and wearing next to nothing, was his friend.

Pulanomos composed himself, and Hamel heard his friend's voice carry over the short distance between them. It was good to hear his voice after so many years. The High Chancellor turned to one of the guards and ordered, "See that man and that young girl over there. Go fetch them for me and take them directly to my Chambers. And get that man a robe."

The guard moved toward Hamel but was stopped by Churoi who was still with the horses. In his surprise at seeing his old friend, Hamel had forgotten about Churoi. The younger man spoke loudly to the guard and said, "Treat them well, soldier, or you will pay for it with your life."

The guard rushed to Hamel and Gollos and bowed. Hamel watched Pulanomos quickly move inside the palace, rather than wait for them. "Welcome, Master," the soldier said. "Please, follow me."

Hamel nodded his thanks. He wished to avoid speaking and revealing either his Ridge accent or his Olmosite accent.

The guard turned and led Hamel to the steps and to the doorway. The door was held open by four more guards, each of whom bowed.

Hamel's eyes drifted to Gollos as they moved into the palace. Her face held a look of wonder. He was not sure if her surprise was from the richness and architecture of the building, or if it came from the fact that the guards bowed.

"Remember to stand straight," he whispered. "Walk and talk with confidence."

She pulled back her shoulders and stood a little taller. He smiled, knowing she would do well.

The building itself was both large and beautiful. Hamel suspected the walls were not painted a gold color but were, in fact, plated with gold. The hallway before them stood taller than his house in the Ridge Capital and had to be fifty paces long. The ceiling itself was painted in detailed designs and every four or five paces a giant chandelier hung from the ceiling.

Once inside, the guard who had led them up the steps turned to two men standing just inside the door. He whispered to them and then paused for a moment as he sized up Gollos. He appeared to be considering the matter and then whispered some more to the two men. When he turned back to Hamel, he bowed once more before leading the way down the hallway.

The guard led them to a large, carpeted set of stairs. As with the first set of stairs, each step ached, but Hamel held his tongue. When they reached the top, a hallway led both left and right, and the guard turned to the right. The hallway was long, and there was only one doorway right at the very end.

In front of the door stood two tall men. They were not dressed as the regular guards but were wearing long brown cloaks with hoods that covered much of their faces. Through the open front of the cloak, Hamel could see armor. He could not help but notice the armor appeared not only expensive and detailed but solid. They stood ready; eyes fixed on Hamel, Gollos, and the guard. Hamel could tell they were of a different sort than the regular soldiers.

The guard leading them down the hallway approached the two guards and bowed before them. "The High Chancellor has requested an audience with this man and his slave," the guard explained.

Hamel held his tongue. He wasn't entirely sure what it would mean for Gollos if he announced that she was a free woman. He knew as well, both accents needed to remain a

256

secret. He decided to learn more before he shared that information.

The two men guarding the door stepped aside with suspicious glares. Hamel noticed each man's hand rested on the handle of the knife at his belt.

Past the door, the walls were covered with large paintings, curtains, and elaborate carvings. The room had doors leading off in all directions. At the one end of the room, sitting nearly ten paces from Hamel, was a large ornate desk with a chair behind it and three chairs before it. Hamel suspected it was the High Chancellor's office or meeting room.

Before he could examine the room in detail, two men rushed in. They were both elderly, quite thin, and wore stern expressions on their faces. The one man carried an expensive and well-crafted robe for Hamel. Hamel quickly slipped it over his head and tied on a belt which was also provided.

The other man approached Gollos with a new robe and belt for her. Hamel watched as the man reached for her old robe as if to pull it off rather than let her dress herself. She looked on in fear at first, but the fear turned to shock as the man dropped to his knees, his hand twisted in an unnatural position.

Hamel leaned in close as he gripped the man's wrist, twisting it nearly to the point of breaking. He hissed in a voice loud enough for the soldier and other servant to hear, "This young lady is not to be touched by anyone. Is that understood?" He hoped by hissing the words, the man would not recognize either a Ridge or Olmosite accent.

The man's head nodded up and down, and he choked out, "Forgive me, Master."

Hamel let the man go and rose to his feet. He kept his eyes fixed on the man with an angry glare, clenching his jaw for added effect.

The man wilted under Hamel's gaze. When he stood, he cautiously handed the small robe and belt to Hamel and rushed out the door, accompanied by the other man.

He did not want to terrify the men, but he hoped he could send a clear message early on that Gollos was to be treated with respect. In a land driven by power and fear, a young, thin, former slave would face nothing but danger at every turn.

Hamel turned to the guard. The man had his head bowed low to the ground. "Soldier!" Hamel barked. He spoke loud and quickly in the hopes of hiding any accent. In a hiss, he asked, "Is there a private room close by where this child may change into this robe?"

"Yes, Master," the guard replied and led Hamel to a doorway.

Hamel pulled open the door and stepped inside. There was only one way in, and the windows were locked from the inside. It was a small sitting room, and Hamel nodded his approval to the guard. He set the robe down on a chair, waved Gollos into the room, and whispered, "You may change in here. If you have any problems, call for me, and I will come."

Gollos smiled and nodded her head, after which Hamel stepped outside, closed the door, and stood sentry. As he stood, he did his best to form an angry, suspicious look, eying the guard and his every movement. He knew he was acting in a dramatic fashion, but he wanted to send a clear message. He had learned there was much about Olmos that he did not understand. The incident with the servant and Gollos's robes confirmed in his mind that he could not be too careful when it came to her safety.

After only a minute, Gollos came out. Her face was red, and she had a sheepish look, mixed with confusion. In her hands was the belt.

Hamel did not quite know the proper way to tie an Olmosite belt, but he had guessed based on what he had seen of Pulanomos and Churoi's belts when they had lived in Ridge many years ago, along with the style he had seen among the people over the last day or so. He suspected slaves did not wear belts. It was likely the first time she would have ever worn one.

He quickly tied the belt for her. Once finished, the guard led them across the room to the chairs before the desk. "Please, Master, sit here while you wait."

Hamel nodded to the man and sat down. He directed Gollos to sit in the chair beside him and could not help but notice the guard's look of disapproval. Hamel suspected not only had he broken some sort of cultural expectation, but that Churoi's threat to the guard outside had convinced him not to challenge Hamel in any way.

They waited another ten minutes before one of the doors behind the desk opened, and Pulanomos and Churoi stepped out. "Leave us!" he commanded the guard, who turned without a word and left the room, closing the door behind him.

Pulanomos waited until the man left and then rushed toward Hamel. The two friends embraced one another, and the High Chancellor, despite his position, wept as he held Hamel. Hamel felt overcome by emotion and cried nearly as hard as he had in the oasis.

It had been over ten years since they had seen one another. Hamel had missed his closest friend dearly and still often read the letter from Churoi telling him of Pulanomos's death.

When they let go, Hamel choked out the words, "I was told you were dead. I grieved for you for years. I still grieve your loss. I'm struggling to believe you are alive, even though you stand before me!"

Pulanomos nodded his head and more tears flowed down. "I know. It was an unfortunate necessity. I am so sorry, Hamel. I will explain it all. Not yet, though. For now, we must simply enjoy the fact that we are together once again."

Hamel smiled. It felt good to smile and to feel joy. There had been so much grief in recent times.

"It is good to see you again, Honored Patir," Churoi said, stepping up next to Hamel.

"Churoi!" Hamel exclaimed and grabbed the young man by his shoulders. Churoi's eyes bulged as the larger man pulled him into a tight embrace. "I have missed our walks together along the Valley Wall and our talks as we spoke about life and strategy and friendship."

Churoi laughed. "I have missed you as well, Honored Patir."

Hamel's gaze dropped to the floor for a moment. "I am not an Honored Patir anymore. I have fallen greatly. I have been disgraced among my people."

"We have heard," Pulanomos said. "Our Ambassador sent word almost immediately. It grieved me greatly to hear of your disgrace. I am so sorry. I considered pulling out our Ambassador and cutting all trade relations with Ridge immediately when I heard. I wondered if I could force the Council to reinstate you, but I remembered you had taught me never to make a decision out of anger. I decided it would be better to honor you by following your example than punishing them for their actions."

"I am glad you did not, my Pulanomos. It is not worth disrupting the peace between my people and yours," Hamel replied.

"Always the man of wisdom!" Churoi said with a laugh. "If it is acceptable to you, I will continue to call you Honored Patir, regardless of the decision of the Ridge Council. As long as you are here, you are an Honored Patir to me."

"Thank you, Churoi," Hamel said. "It is good to be honored by my old friends."

"And who is the child sitting in the chair?" Pulanomos asked. His expression turned from joy to disgust as he examined her.

"This young woman is with me," Hamel said. He was not sure how to explain to an Olmosite that he had purchased her freedom.

"She is a slave," Churoi said. "I did not think that the Ridge People took slaves for themselves."

"She is no longer a slave," Hamel said.

"But she is marked as a slave," Churoi said. "The servants told me."

Hamel looked at Gollos. She did not look surprised at the comment about being marked as a slave. "How is she marked?"

"Show him," Churoi said.

At the sound of Churoi's command, Gollos jumped to her feet and turned around. She pulled her hair apart at the base of her neck, and Hamel saw a tattoo of a large ring. He had caught glimpses of the mark the day before but had assumed it was either dirt or a birthmark. He had not understood that the ring represented slavery.

"It is okay, Gollos," Hamel said. "There is no need to show me that anymore. It is a thing from a former life. You are a free woman."

She dropped her hair back in place and turned back to face the three men but did not return to her seat. Instead, she stood off to the side of the desk. Hamel suspected she was slipping back into her role as a slave. It would take time.

"I am sorry to do this, but I have to slip out," Churoi said. "The High Chancellor has asked me to oversee all matters of state while the two of you reacquaint yourselves with one another and as he helps you settle in. I will see you at a later time, Honored Patir."

"It is good to see you again, Churoi," Hamel said.

The man smiled and nodded, "It is good to see you as well, Honored Patir." He then turned and walked out the door he had come in a few moments before.

"Please, come with me," Pulanomos said. He then turned off to the side of the room and led the way through a hanging curtain. On the other side was a small room. There were four or five chairs, and Pulanomos offered one to Hamel and took another. Hamel waved Gollos to the chair next to him and watched as she carefully sat down. He was pushing the limits of what she was comfortable with while she remained a slave in her mind.

Pulanomos watched the interaction with a large smile. "So quickly I forget the desire of the Ridge People to pour their lives and souls into another. In Olmos, a man is born or sold as a slave, and a slave he remains. We do not seek to give

261

them anything, just take what we can from them. But I know it is not that way with you. I am glad that you remain true to your ways, old friend."

"If a man does not hold his integrity, he is no man at all," Hamel said, quoting his Matir.

"You are always full of those little sayings for each situation, my friend," Pulanomos said and smiled yet again. "I can't believe you are here. I want to hear all about how a half-naked Hamel managed to get through the Olmosite border and show up outside my front door. I also want to tell you everything, but ..." Pulanomos's eyebrows shot up, and he leaned forward. "Wait, I forgot. You are injured!"

He jumped to his feet and rushed out through the curtains. Hamel heard a door open, and his friend call out, "Slave!"

Gollos nearly jumped to her feet at the command. She caught herself just before she left her seat and made an effort to lean back in the chair. The sound of footsteps rushed into the large room outside the curtain, and Hamel listened as Pulanomos ordered the man to get a doctor immediately.

The footsteps faded away, and Pulanomos came back into the room. Instead of sitting down again, he knelt before Hamel and raised the cloak to take a look at the leg.

Pulanomos groaned when he saw the infection. "This looks terrible, Hamel. Why did you not get it looked at earlier?"

"I'm in Olmos," Hamel said with a smile. He had learned years ago to ignore pain when it stood in the way of a task. The pain in his leg was intense, but he managed to speak and act as though nothing was wrong. "I don't exactly have a doctor I can turn to."

"No, I don't suppose you do," Pulanomos replied, his eyes remaining on the leg. "But I do. In fact, I have some of the best doctors in the country at my disposal."

"Pulanamos," Hamel began. "I am a soldier. I have seen many wounds. I can recognize a wound that is beyond help. You and I both know I am going to, at best, lose the leg, and at worst, my life."

At the mention of the potential loss of his life, Hamel noticed Gollos grip the armrest of her chair. He glanced at her hands, and her knuckles were white.

"I need a favor of you, my friend," Hamel said, turning back to Pulanomos. "I wish for this young woman to be free. I do not want her to be returned to slavery in any form."

Pulanomos glanced briefly at Gollos, and Hamel took special note of the hint of disgust he saw in his friend's eyes. He would need to make sure he had secured provisions in place for the girl in case something happened to him.

"I don't think it will come to that, Hamel," Pulanomos said with a laugh. "I can see the infection and see that it has spread, but what you do not know about us is that we are far more advanced medically than you might think. Our doctors will be able to bring down the infection. I do not think you will lose your leg and certainly not your life. The doctor will be here in a moment, and we will see what he has to say."

Pulanomos lowered the cloak down over Hamel's leg and walked to the third chair. He dropped into it as though he were exhausted and said, "It is so good to see you again."

Hamel searched his friend's face. He had changed and in a similar way to Hamel. There were a few lines on his face, perhaps more than on Hamel's. His hair was nearly all gray, and his belly suggested a more sedentary life. His eyes, however, were sharp. Hamel could see his friend's intellect shining through.

"I expect you have many questions," Pulanomos said to Hamel's silence.

Hamel laughed. "I have far more questions than I am comfortable with!"

"Yes," Pulanomos replied. "You were never one to be satisfied until you understood exactly what was going on. I will try to answer them soon. I have some questions of my own, of course. The least of which is what brings you to Pollos." The High Chancellor smiled and raised both hands and added, "Not that I'm not thrilled to see you. I never

263

thought we'd be together again. I am glad you made it into Olmos." His friend smiled again, then leaned forward and said with urgency, "I would suggest that you not speak around anyone. It would raise many questions to have a man from Ridge among us in Pollos."

Hamel nodded his agreement. He had assumed as much.

At that point, a doctor rushed in the room. Pulanomos gestured toward Hamel, and the man approached him, bowed and waited. Hamel raised the cloak to his knee, careful not to say anything. He knew once word got out that there was a man from Ridge with Pulanomos, it would be difficult to put the rumors away. On the other hand, he was not sure it would be wise to announce he had mastered, or nearly mastered, the Olmosite accent.

The doctor examined the wound, taking the bandage off. He examined each of the puncture wounds and asked, "Was it a dog bite, Master?"

Hamel nodded yes, and the man continued his examination while he asked, "How long ago?"

Hamel glanced at Pulanomos, and his friend asked, "Doctor, can you heal the infection?"

"Yes, High Chancellor," the doctor said, bowing to Pulanomos. "Forgive me. I have spent many years asking questions. I did not mean to offend."

"There is no offense. I do not, however, wish for conversation between this man and anyone else," Pulanomos said.

"Yes, High Chancellor. I will need him to visit your clinic. I have everything I need there to treat his wound."

"I will see that he is there shortly," Pulanomos said. "Please head down to the clinic and prepare for his arrival."

The Doctor bowed again, then rose to his feet and rushed out the door. Hamel could not help but notice once again the difference in the way people treated one another in Olmos. In Ridge, men and women were motivated by honor and sought to act in a way which offered honor to others. In Olmos, men appeared to act out of fear of those greater than themselves. He suspected women acted the same way, but he had seen few women outside of crowds or in roles of service.

Once the doctor had left and the men outside had pulled the door closed, Pulanomos said, "It is wise of you to hold your tongue, my friend. I think it best not to let too many people know you are from Ridge. Olmosites are not comfortable with outsiders among them. I will summon a soldier to take you to the clinic. You will be well cared for, but I suspect you will need to remain there for a little while."

Hamel opened his mouth to ask about Gollos but was cut off by Pulanomos raising his hand. "Do not worry. I will care for the young woman. I see that you do not treat her as a slave. Since you treat her as a young woman from Ridge, I will see that she is treated with the same dignity and protection that you would offer her."

"Thank you, Pulanomos."

Hamel stepped close to Gollos. "Do not worry. I will see you soon. The High Chancellor and I were very close when he was an ambassador in my country. He will be true to his word to care for you." As he spoke, he took her hand and slipped the forged papers from Mellel to her. She took the papers without a word and slipped them into the fold of her new cloak.

As he stepped away from Gollos, she bowed deeply to Hamel and then to Pulanomos. When she had finished, she stood on the side of the room with her eyes on the floor.

CHAPTER 32

THE DAY OF HEALING

The two men walked to the door, and Hamel stepped out. Pulanomos looked at the guard on the right and commanded, "Take this man to the clinic. You are not to speak to him at all, nor are you to let anyone speak with him other than myself, my assistant, or the slave who arrived with him. Is that understood?"

The man replied with a simple, "Yes, sir."

Hamel took note that he was the first man he had seen in Olmos who did not bow to a superior. The man did not give the impression that he was disrespecting Pulanomos in any way, but it was clear to Hamel that the man was not expected to bow. Hamel realized as well that the man had called Pulanomos, "sir." Most Olmosites called their superiors "Master," or in Pulanomos's case, "High Chancellor."

The guard led Hamel back to the stairs and down again. At the bottom, they turned right and entered another small hallway leading past a series of doors. He could hear voices behind some and sounds of strange machinery behind others. Some of the doors looked solid, and some were even reinforced with steel. He was moving through a secure area.

As they walked, Hamel paid close attention to the other man. He was certainly a soldier but of a very different caliber than the others he had seen and met in his short time in Olmos. The man walked with a certain deadly grace that suggested a wrong move by an adversary would be the last move they would ever make. The soldier's eyes scanned every detail, and Hamel was well aware that the man was taking note of Hamel's own scrutiny.

He decided it would be wise to be wary of the man and all those who were of his order. It would be foolish to underestimate this soldier or any of his fellow warriors.

Until that point, Hamel had been able to ignore the pain in his leg, for the most part. As he thought about the possibility of treatment, the pain felt as though it intensified, and he noticed he had begun to limp. He hoped the sight of weakness would not cause problems for him later on.

At the end of the long hallway, they turned right again, followed by a left turn. The hallway ended shortly after the turn at a large open doorway through which Hamel could see the doctor hard at work ordering men and women around.

The guard led the way into the room and came to a halt just inside the door. The man scanned the room, his hand on his blade, and Hamel noticed people avoided looking in his direction.

Hamel had spent decades watching, considering, and strategizing his way through every situation. He had grown accustomed to evaluating the slightest movements, gestures, actions, and choices of those around him. The pain in his leg, however, so close to treatment, felt unbearable. He could no longer maintain control and stumbled into a chair.

No one moved to his aid. Hamel wondered if it was because the chair was next to the guard. Every man or woman in the room kept their distance.

The soldier drew his knife and screamed, "Now!" The doctor dropped the papers he was carrying and jumped.

He ran to the soldier and bowed, then to Hamel and bowed before him. "Please, Master, come this way."

The doctor helped Hamel to his feet and led him to a bed in the corner. The moment Hamel collapsed onto the bed, the soldier turned and walked out of the clinic. The doctor motioned for Hamel to lie down on his stomach as the injury was on the back of his leg, and one of the assistants removed both Hamel's sandals and raised his cloak to just above the knee.

Hamel hoped they would be able to save the leg. He had not mentioned anything about his concern of losing the leg earlier to Gollos for fear that it would upset her, but he had been slowly coming to accept the idea that it could not be saved. His friend, however, had given him hope.

"Master," the doctor said. As he spoke, he knelt on the floor and placed his forehead nearly onto the thin mattress of the bed. "I will need to begin your treatment almost immediately. It will not be pleasant. We will need to inject medicine directly into your leg to stop the infection and begin the healing. Since your leg is so deeply infected, you may feel a greater pain than you have ever experienced. I can give you a sedative if you would like."

Hamel had experienced a great deal of pain over the years as a soldier. He did not think the pain would be as severe as the doctor suggested. He shook his head to indicate he would not need the sedative. He wanted to remain sharp.

When the injection came, Hamel screamed. He had never experienced pain on that level before at any point in his life. He had not thought such agony was possible. He grabbed the mattress and squeezed, hearing it rip along the bottom where it had been attached to the bed frame.

The last thing he remembered before he lost consciousness was a shake in his hands and a sound erupting from his throat that he did not recognize.

When Hamel awoke, he stared at the wall for what seemed like an hour. He could hear noise behind him, but nothing in him suggested he should look or consider it. He could make out voices but did not care to listen.

The pain in his leg throbbed with every movement, every sound, every heartbeat. Even his thoughts felt as if they added to the pain.

As his mind cleared, he noticed his grip on the mattress and that he had soiled himself. Although the shame of such a thing would have been great among the soldiers in the Armies of the Ridge, he did not care how much shame it placed on him in Olmos. The pain was all that mattered. It was all he knew.

A voice said, "Master, I will need to inject more medicine into your leg, and we will need to drain more of the infection. We were able to do much while you were unconscious, but now that you are awake, it will be quite painful again. I am sorry, but it is the only chance we have to save your leg."

Hamel could not respond. He felt an overwhelming dread, mixed with apathy.

When the injection came the second time, he shook violently. He did not scream, but only because he could only inhale.

Hamel passed out again.

Hamel wondered how many times he had passed out. He could not think. The pain did not seem natural. He was hungry. He was also aware that his thoughts were not merely inhibited by pain. The medication had affected his mind. He could not think clearly, nor could he decide how he should act or what he should do. He just knew he had to endure.

One thought that did land in his mind was a memory about a sedative. He wished he had taken it. He did not know if he could ask for it, or if it was too late. He did not know who to ask.

He heard voices again, and pain rushed through his leg.

Everything went black.

Hamel sat in a chair and looked around. He did not know how he had come to be seated. His arms felt heavy, and his brain sluggish. They had, at some point, given him a sedative. He did not mind.

His eyes moved across the room, down to the floor and to his leg. The wound was bandaged, but while the skin around the area was still red, it did look to be in better condition than it had before he had received the medicine.

He leaned a little farther to get a better view of his leg but pulled back. His head felt like it weighed as much as a stone block. He feared if he leaned too far, he would roll right out of the chair.

He noticed that he wore different clothing. His new clothes were plain and simple. He suspected they were gowns used by patients.

A young man noticed Hamel's movements and rushed out of sight. A moment later, the doctor came in with the young man on his heels.

"It is good to see you awake, Master," he said.

Hamel nodded in reply. He remembered something about how he had decided not to speak.

"I know you are silent, Master," the man said. "The High Chancellor came to visit you. He is the one who authorized a sedative, contrary to your own wishes. He explained to me that I was not to seek any answers to any questions, beyond a nod or a shake of the head."

Hamel nodded to indicate he understood but immediately regretted moving his head.

"Are you in much pain?" the doctor asked.

Hamel nodded slowly.

"Are you thirsty and hungry?"

Hamel nodded again, and the doctor quietly informed the young man who rushed away.

"I have been instructed to tell you that you have been in the hospital for two days. Your slave is fine and well cared for. I have been told as well that the High Chancellor is anxiously awaiting your return." The doctor nodded as though he was pleased with himself for remembering all the instructions, but then added, "Your leg will be fine. We were able to stop the infection, and you should be able to walk on it as soon as your head clears from the sedative. The food and water will help with that. For your leg, you will need to come back once a day for another injection for three or maybe four days to ensure it heals well, but I believe we caught the infection in time."

At the mention of another injection, Hamel's eyes widened, and he leaned back in his seat.

"Oh, do not worry, Master," the doctor said. "The injections will not hurt much now. The pain you felt before was because of how severe the infection was. Now you should not feel too much discomfort."

Hamel smiled, and the doctor's facial features relaxed.

When the young man returned, he carried a plate of very simple food. After setting it before Hamel, he rushed off to get a large jug of water and a cup.

"I expect your stomach is quite unsettled, even though you are hungry," the doctor explained. "This food is not to the liking of most people, but its bland flavor and texture should go down easily, and it will give you the strength you need. You should also drink all the water in the jug. I know it is a lot, but you will need the liquids to refresh your body and to flush the sedative out of your system." The

271

doctor turned to the young man and commanded him to inform the High Chancellor that their patient was awake but needed a few hours for the sedative to clear.

Hamel did not want to wait a few hours, but not only could he not communicate without revealing more than he wished, but he also knew the sedative was still heavy in his system. Instead, he focused on his food and drank all he could of the water. Eventually, the doctor and other man walked him to a comfortable bed. Within seconds, he drifted off to sleep.

When he awoke, he found his mind clear and sharp. His head still hurt and felt heavy, but he was grateful to have his mind back.

He pulled himself into a seated position and stepped down onto the warm floor. It was rough on his bare feet, but it felt good to stand. Every muscle felt tight, and his back ached.

Once on his feet, the room shifted slightly, but he was steady. His injured leg felt sore and weak, but he was grateful he still had it.

"Friend!" Gollos hollered, using the term he had asked her to use, as she rushed into the room. She came up close and wrapped her arms around him.

He smiled at her and leaned in close to her ear, whispering, "Have you been well cared for?"

"Yes," she whispered back. "The High Chancellor has taken great care of me. He has informed all the people that I am to be treated well and with great respect."

Hamel smiled and whispered, "I am glad. I was worried about what it would be like for you when I could not protect you, but it is good to learn that my friend has cared for you."

He stepped back and looked her over. Already her skin had a healthier shine to it, and her eyes were bright. Even a couple days of a good diet and living without fear had accomplished much in a short time.

"The High Chancellor sent me to take you for a walk. The doctor has told him you need to get up and move," Gollos said.

At that moment, the young man assisting the doctor approached with a new outfit. He handed it to Hamel and directed him toward a small room where he could change.

Once dressed in a more respectable outfit, Hamel let Gollos lead him through the corridors to a door leading outside. When Hamel stepped out, he gasped. What lay before him was a beautiful, lush, green area of land. Since leaving Ridge, he had not seen anything so well cared for and so well watered. He could not see how far it went into the distance for the trees blocked his view, but he remembered how it looked from the outside of the city. The High Chancellor's estate covered a large area.

"Can I call you Hamel now?" Gollos whispered as she looked around. No one else was within earshot.

"Yes, but do not let that name slip out around anyone else. Only the High Chancellor and Churoi may hear that name spoken," Hamel said.

"I understand. I have kept your secret. I have kept all your secrets and will continue to do so," Gollos said with a smile. He noticed she was forcing herself to stand straight, hold her chin high, and keep her shoulders square.

"I am proud of you, Gollos," Hamel said.

Gollos's expression twisted into shock, then disbelief, then tears. "How can a man of your greatness be proud of a thing like me?" she asked with a look of genuine confusion.

Hamel's shoulders slumped, and he felt a weariness wash over him. "That is something you will need to learn in time, Gollos, but I do not think I have the strength to teach you now. Perhaps time will be a better teacher anyway,"

Hamel said before turning toward a path. "Let us walk, and you can tell me of your experience over the last two days."

The path was wide and well shaded. Hamel appreciated Gollos's attempts at supporting him, but he was aware that if he fell, she would be able to do little to stop it.

As they made their way through the trees, Hamel listened to Gollos tell him of all she had experienced. To her, it was as if a world of wonders had suddenly been created before her very eyes. She spoke about the comfort of the bed and the servants taking care of her. She spoke of the soldiers and how they would stand guard outside her room each night, protecting her from any danger. She spoke about how Pulanomos invited her to speak with him three times, asking about Hamel. She could not believe the High Chancellor would want to speak with her.

Hamel listened intently. He was glad she had been treated well, although most of what he heard concerned him on one level or another. He wondered at the motivation for posting soldiers outside a room in the High Chancellor's house.

The two continued their walk, and the path led them around a small lake. Hamel caught sight of fish in the lake and the occasional deer in the forest. Either Pulanomos hunted, or he kept the animals as part of a nature preserve.

When she finished sharing every detail she could think of from the names of the servants to the food at each meal, Gollos's face held a grin from ear to ear. "Are you strong enough to continue our walk?" she asked.

Hamel smiled and let Gollos know he had reached his limit, so the two turned back toward the High Chancellor's palace. He was pleased to see the former slave skip beside him. She was experiencing a taste of freedom.

"I am glad you had a chance to spend a great deal of time with the High Chancellor. The two of us were quite close years ago," Hamel said. "What kinds of things did he want to talk to you about?"

"He wanted to know everything we had done and everywhere we had been. He wanted to know all about how you had purchased me and if I knew how you crossed the border into Olmos. He told me he is very concerned for your safety, Hamel," Gollos explained.

Hamel considered what she had said for a moment. "Did he find out that I can speak in an Olmosite accent?"

Gollos looked at the ground. "Do not worry. I lied for you," Gollos said. "I told him that when you spoke, you growled. I said you were hard to understand, and I pretended I did not know you were a Ridger."

Hamel was torn. He did not want her to lie. He also did not want it known he could speak in an Olmosite accent. He decided he was unprepared to navigate the matter. He hoped as he recovered, he would be able to reflect on the issue.

When they reached the palace, it was time for the evening meal, and Hamel wished he could sit with Pulanomos and Churoi. Gollos informed him that Pulanomos had needed to slip away for the rest of the day, and Churoi was gone most days on matters of state.

The two returned to the clinic, and the doctor informed Hamel he would be okay to retire to his own room but should return the next day for a quick examination of the wound and for another shot. The two then made their way to a small dining room where Gollos ate each meal.

As they sat down, Hamel leaned in close and whispered, "Do not talk of any private matters in here. There is too great a chance of being overheard."

During their meal, Hamel asked Gollos if she would tell him a little bit about herself. There was much she would not speak about, but what she did share nearly cost Hamel his appetite. It was difficult to hear of a person being treated as nothing more than an animal. He was surprised to find she was not bitter. She had not known anything else, and it did not surprise her to think she had been treated so poorly. He

275

made another mental note to address the matter of her worth at some point. While he was relieved that she was not bitter, the thought that she could believe she deserved such treatment was horrendous.

As the evening wore on, they went for another short walk to help Hamel regain his strength. The guards kept their distance from him. He suspected Pulanomos had been quite clear that the guests of the High Chancellor were not to be bothered.

Eventually, Gollos led Hamel to the apartment which had been set aside for them. There were two bedrooms, and Hamel noticed she had taken the smaller one. He considered offering to switch with her, but the exhaustion overcame him.

"Gollos," Hamel began. "I am tired, so I will retire to my room. If you are up in time for breakfast and I am not, please wake me so I can eat with you."

"Yes, my Master," Gollos said and turned to her room before Hamel could correct her.

He closed the door to the bedroom and collapsed onto his bed. Within moments he was asleep.

CHAPTER 33

THE DAY OF TRAINING

Someone was in the room.

Hamel tried to wake up, but the night's stupor was still upon him. He had never struggled so much to clear his head and come out of his sleep. He wondered if he had been drugged. His arms felt heavy, and he struggled to breathe.

As he came to, something registered in his mind about his leg. He had been injured. He was not yet strong. Perhaps that was it. Perhaps that explained his weariness.

But someone was in the room.

The sound was slight, but it was there. As his mind cleared, he thought he heard the sound of movement, but no steps. It was as if what was in the room did not touch the floor.

A sudden fear rushed through his heart. What if the Olmosite belief in ghosts was more than a myth? There was no such thing amongst the People of the Ridge, but that did not mean there could not be such an evil in Olmos.

He did not remember where he had put his knife, but he knew he would normally have placed it under his pillow where his right hand could reach and grab the handle. He would have to move quickly. The knife might not do anything against a spirit, but he would not stand unarmed. He would take his stand between the bed and the wall and face the demon head-on.

His heart felt like ice, and his face froze as an eerie melody came forth from the entrance to his room. The song was light and beautiful, yet sad and evil.

It was ready to attack.

He shoved his hand under the pillow, and his fingers wrapped around the familiar handle of his blade. He rolled toward the wall and off the bed, away from the spirit's song.

As his body turned and his feet dropped toward the floor, he saw it. It was small, but it held its arms out to the side. The white mist of the apparition flowed behind it as though it were blowing in the wind. It had been a child in life, and grief mixed with terror filled his heart.

He did not think his knife would do anything, but he could hope. He pulled back his arm and prepared to throw the blade, picking the center of the ghost as his target.

At the sight of the knife, the spirit's mouth opened wide, and it reached out toward him. The song turned into a shriek, and the ghost backed away.

Something stayed his hand. Something inside caused him to hesitate.

"Please, my Master! I meant no harm!" Gollos screamed, tears flowing down her face.

Hamel's breath came in ragged gasps as he tried to understand what was happening. His mind moved slowly, and he knew he was not quite awake. The injury and healing had taken its toll.

The child dropped to the floor and crouched in the entrance to his room. Her sleeping clothes were of a strange style. In the wind, the light material flowed, and her bare feet had made little noise on the stone floor.

"Gollos?" Hamel asked. Rage flooded through him, but he calmed his heart. He knew he was scared, not truly angry. "What are you doing?"

"Please, my Master," she said through her tears. "My former Master wished to be awakened by song. I assumed you would want the same. I meant no disrespect."

He was still not sure what had happened. He only knew he had never been so afraid in his life.

"What…" he began. "How did your former Master wish to be awakened?"

"He wanted me to sing him awake," she said, and broke down and wept. She remained crouched on the floor as if she were trying to make herself as small as possible.

Hamel slowly made his way over to her and sat down on the floor next to her. His hands still shook, but he wrapped his arms around her. She did not move but remained where she was.

"I'm sorry, Gollos," he said.

"You said you would never hurt me," she said in a barely audible voice through her tears. "But you were going to kill me!" It was difficult to make out her words between the sobs and her thick accent.

"I'm truly sorry, Gollos. I didn't know it was you."

"Who did you think I was?" she asked, exasperation evident in her tone.

"I…" he began. "To be honest, I thought you were a ghost."

Her face shot up, and she met his eyes. A new terror filled her eyes. "Ghosts are real?" she screeched.

"Well…" Hamel said. He still could not think with total clarity. "Umm…." He took a deep breath and shook his head. "No, Gollos, I don't think ghosts are real. The People of the Ridge have never believed in ghosts. I just thought that Olmosites did and when I saw you, I…." He shook his head again. "I'm sorry."

He felt her body relax, and he let go. He still felt the battle rush flowing through his veins, and everything in him wanted to fight. He focused on calming his breathing even more and rose to his feet.

Gollos stood up as well, and her face bore an expression of embarrassment, mixed with fear. She lowered her head and turned away from him and toward the door. She took one step, then stopped.

He saw her shoulders shake, and his heart broke. He knew she must feel so betrayed. He felt in that one moment that everything he had told her had proved to be a lie. She might not ever believe she was safe with him. And it would be his fault.

Her shoulders shook even more. Her head remained down. She began to make some noise, but it sounded less like weeping and more like laughter.

He thought he must still be groggy and shook his head again. He blinked his eyes a few times, doing his best to wake himself up. He stepped beside her and leaned over just enough to see her face. Her face held a large grin, and she was laughing.

Gollos turned toward him and laughed some more before pointing down to her sleeping gown. The light material blew in the breeze coming through the window.

"You really did think I was a ghost," she said as she laughed. "My gown looks like a ghost. My singing must have sounded like a ghost's wail." At that comment, her face fell. "Is my singing that bad?"

Hamel felt like he had been knocked back and forth between two Beasts and almost thought he'd prefer to face an enemy army than to try to make sense of what was happening.

"Um…" he began. He just wanted the moment to be over. "No, Gollos. At least, I don't think so. I don't actually remember. I just remember hearing something, and I thought it was a ghost and reacted and…. I don't know what else to say. Maybe some time you can sing for me when I'm awake. I might enjoy that."

Her smile came back, and she nodded her head. Another quick glance down brought back a laugh, and she walked out of the room.

Before he could close the door behind her, she turned back and said with a grin while she wiped a tear away, "I believe breakfast will be ready for us in one hour. I did not know how long you would need to prepare yourself for the day, so I wanted to wake you in time."

"Thank you, Gollos," he said and closed the door. He sat down on the edge of his bed and closed his eyes. He hoped once he was fully recovered, he would not take so long to regain his wits after waking.

Before leaving his room, Hamel checked his bag. He had suspected that his sidearm would have been removed but was still disappointed to find it missing. When Gollos emerged from her room, dressed for the day, he asked her about it. She explained the soldiers had insisted on searching his bag.

Hamel understood. He would have done exactly the same thing had someone come from another nation to stay in the Honored Matir's home. It made sense.

Hamel paused for a moment and considered the time they had before breakfast. He did not know what the days ahead would be like and thought he had better make the most of every opportunity. He glanced around the main room. It was furnished with expensive furniture, and the floor itself was solid stone. It would be perfect for their needs.

"Gollos, have you had any combat training?"

Gollos's expression suggested she wondered if he were speaking a different language. She shook her head and said, "Honestly, Hamel, I do not know what you mean."

"I mean have you been trained to fight with a knife, or hand-to-hand combat, or how to fire a rifle?"

"No, my Ma… Hamel!" Gollos hissed. She glanced around as if she feared they had been overheard. "My former Master would not allow any of his servants to even hold a knife, except for the chefs in the restaurant. We were not permitted to fight in any way. He told me if I was ever attacked, I was not to fight back."

"I have told you repeatedly that I am not your Master, Gollos. But you need to know as well that I am not like your former Master. It is time for you to understand that I will teach you things not for my benefit, but for your own."

Gollos nodded her head and said, "I understand, Hamel," but he suspected from the look in her eyes that she did not.

"We will start by spending some time this morning learning the basics of hand-to-hand combat," Hamel explained. He took a moment to examine her once again. She was far too thin to have much strength, but he knew with a better diet and exercise, that would all change.

For the next 30 minutes, Hamel taught Gollos how to defend herself and even how to strike her opponent when necessary. He did not think she would be ready to fight for many weeks, or even months, but she would never be ready if they did not start her training. He wished she would never have to use any of what he taught her but suspected the time would come.

When they were finished, the young girl could barely raise her arms. She gasped for air and appeared ready to collapse. They took a few moments to clean themselves.

Before they left the room, Hamel explained, "For now, we will keep your training to ourselves. It may be wise for us to keep it a secret that you are learning to fight, and that I see the need for you to learn."

"Yes, Hamel," she said with a silly grin on her face. He had noticed an increase in her confidence with each new move she learned. As they made their way to the dining hall, she walked straighter, and her eyes drifted less frequently to the floor.

A little too late, Hamel realized Gollos faced a new problem. As someone who had spent her life with lowered eyes, she was not accustomed to walking with her eyes not on the ground. He tried to catch her, but she tripped over her own feet and went down hard on the stone floor. When she pulled herself to her feet, she hung her head in shame.

Hamel put his arms on her shoulders and whispered in her ear, "Do not be ashamed of a fall, Gollos. It is those who do not climb to their feet again who must bear their own shame, not those who rise and continue on their way." When she did not look convinced, he added with a smile, "Besides, tripping on nothing is kind of funny."

She smiled sheepishly back at him, and the two made their way to their seats. Within minutes, a large breakfast lay before them.

The two ate in silence. Gollos did not appear to have much to say, and Hamel had much to think about.

They were in Olmosite territory, right in the center of Olmosite rule. Although he had been close to Pulanomos and Churoi in times past, there was much he did not understand. He was also continually reminded that he was an outsider in a land that did not tolerate visitors.

The Olmosites had always presented their resistance to visitors as a matter of privacy, but the fact that Olmosites lived decades longer than the People of the Ridge was proof they had secrets. He reflected yet again on the pits, especially the one which contained the "Ridger."

The "Ridger" in the pit was a concern. It meant the Olmosites had held a man or woman captive and had not returned them to Ridge. If the individual had broken a law, they should have been returned, if possible, or at least Olmos should have communicated with Ridge that one of their citizens stood accused. That suggested the person's crime was something the Olmosites wanted to keep secret.

He would have to return to the Square and evaluate the situation. Regardless of the crime, however, he was not sure he could leave the person in the pit. To add to the difficulty, he did not feel he would be able to have that conversation with Pulanomos, at least not yet.

He was also confused about the matter of the Naromites. There was some clan within the ranks of the Olmosite military that was far more dangerous than any other soldier. He suspected the two guards outside Pulanomos's office were Naromites. Their movements and even their eyes declared themselves to be a threat.

His mind drifted again to the statue outside the palace. It seemed odd to him to have a statue of a "Ridger" present outside the palace. There was more there to be explored, and he made a mental note to ask Gollos about it when they had more privacy as well as to explore the topic with Pulanomos.

His mind continued to drift to the many questions for which he desired answers when he noticed Gollos whispering to him. "I'm sorry, what did you say?" he quietly asked.

"Hamel," she whispered, her eyes darting to a spot behind him. "A man has entered the room."

Hamel rose to his feet and turned around. Behind him stood one of the soldiers he suspected were Naromites. He was taller than Hamel, nearly as broad in his shoulders, and wore the cloak and armor of the same style as the men who had stood outside Pulanomos's apartment.

"I have some questions for you, and you will answer them or die," the man said with a lack of emotion in his voice very much in contrast with his threat.

Hamel stepped forward and set his mind to what he had trained countless soldiers to do during a crisis: think. He raced through all the information he had available to him. He did not believe he was in any immediate danger. The man might attack in a few minutes but not likely right away.

The lack of emotion was likely an attempt at intimidation. It portrayed the idea that the man had no reservations about killing Hamel, nor would he hesitate for any reason. Such an attempt suggested that his clan was not only well trained physically, but well prepared mentally and psychologically for battle.

The man was not standing in a pose ready for battle, which suggested he did not expect any resistance. Hamel suspected no one ever resisted these men. That could prove to be advantageous in future confrontations, but Hamel did not wish to reveal that he was not afraid to stand up to the man.

Hamel's mind continued to race through all the information before him. He looked deep into the man's eyes and noticed doubt. While the man was not used to resistance, he did fear that it might come. The doubt and small fear mixed with an expectation that no one would resist him suggested he was not alone. The man was confident that if resistance were shown, someone would come to his aid.

Hamel took stock of his situation. He could not act at that moment because Pulanomos would question why he would resist a soldier in the High Chancellor's own palace. He would also have to be careful because he would not want Gollos to be hurt during a fight. He was also weakened due to his leg. He felt sluggish, and his lower leg was tight. He feared he would pull the muscle if he pushed it too far.

The biggest problem, however, was his voice. He could not use it. If he spoke with his native accent, he would betray his position. If he spoke with his Olmosite accent, he would betray that he was capable of disguising himself well among the people.

He decided to try to speak in a hoarse voice. "Of course," Hamel replied, his voice scratching to such a degree he was nearly impossible to understand.

"I'm sorry, Master," Gollos said as she bowed low to the soldier. "My friend is unable to speak with you. The High Chancellor has commanded him not to speak with anyone. It is our wish not to disobey an order from a man of such power and authority and who is worthy of such reverence."

Hamel nearly smiled. She was surprisingly adept in the Olmosite formalities.

The man's eyes did not leave Hamel's face the entire time Gollos spoke. He appeared to be scrutinizing every movement Hamel made as if he were preparing for a fight.

Hamel had faced Olmosite soldiers at the wall and was not concerned about their abilities. The man before him, however, and the men guarding Pulanomos's apartments conducted themselves as though their training was of a different kind. Until he faced one, he would not be sure he could defend himself or overpower the man.

Hamel noticed a tightening of the soldier's jaw, his shoulder tensed, and his knees bent. It did not seem likely the man would attack, but he had so far failed at intimidating Hamel or even Gollos. His next move would be an attempt at causing Hamel to flinch before continuing on his way.

Hamel relaxed his shoulders, spread his feet shoulder width apart, and held his hands loosely behind his back. He set a small smile on his face and steeled his will not to move.

The man lunged forward, and Gollos cried out in fear. Hamel heard her hit the floor hard. She had not been struck, but the shock of the man's movement had sent her backward. The soldier stood so close, Hamel could feel his breath on his face, but Hamel had not even blinked. He allowed his smile to grow and bowed his head enough that the man had to step back to avoid being struck by Hamel's forehead.

The man turned and stormed away. As he walked out the door, two other men stepped from the shadows and followed him.

Hamel was beginning to enjoy his time in Olmos.

The rest of the day passed without incident. The regular guards continued their pattern of avoiding Hamel and Gollos, and those Hamel suspected were of the Naromite clan made no more appearances. He knew he would have to be careful with their clan, but he also knew the Olmosites only

286

respected power. If Hamel gave the slightest indication of fear, he might find even Pulanomos's protection was not enough.

By mid-afternoon, Gollos was quite sore. The morning's training had caught up to her, and she complained that every muscle and joint hurt. The two returned to their apartment, and Hamel guided her through some stretches and took the opportunity to do some more training with her. He explained to her the pain was a necessary part of the process as her muscles adjusted to the new regimen.

"As the next two or three days go on," Hamel added, "you will begin to find your muscles grow tighter and more sore by the hour. Every time you sit, it will be painful to stand. But you must learn to walk without giving any indication of your discomfort."

Gollos nodded her head, but her eyes betrayed her lack of understanding. Hamel waited in the hopes that she would ask. It would take time for her to understand that she was not merely someone to be ordered around.

After the moment had grown awkward with silence, he prompted her, "Do you know why you will need to learn to hide the fact that your muscles are sore?"

"No, Hamel," she said and bowed her head.

He waited again. The young girl needed to learn she was responsible to pursue her education. "Would you like to know?" he asked. "If so, you could ask me."

Her eyes lit up, and a sheepish smile appeared on her face. "I am sorry, Hamel. I am not accustomed to asking questions. I am accustomed to obeying orders."

Hamel stepped up close and put a hand on her shoulder. "Listen closely to me, Gollos. You have lived your entire life as a slave. It will take time for you to think as a free woman. We do not have slavery in my land, at least among law-abiding people, so while you are not accustomed to asking questions, I am not accustomed to helping someone think and act and live as though they are free. This is a learning experience for both of us."

She nodded her head and smiled again. "Please, Hamel, tell me why I should act as though my muscles do not hurt."

Hamel said, "I wish for you to think it through. Start with this. *What* are we in the home of the High Chancellor?"

"We are guests," she replied.

"Correct. And if a guest refused to eat the food provided to him, what would that tell the host?"

Her mouth dropped open, and her eyebrows shot up. "The High Chancellor would be terribly offended!"

"Why?"

"Because he is responsible for caring for his guests," she said. Her words came fast, and she had an intense look in her eye. "If a guest will not eat the food, it would suggest the host is either not capable of caring for his guest or, worse, that the guest suspects that it is not safe to eat the food. It would be an insult worthy of challenge! But Hamel, we have eaten the food. What does this have to do with how I walk?"

"If our hosts were to find out I was training you to defend yourself and perhaps even to fight, what message would that send to them?" Hamel asked.

She stepped back, and her mouth dropped open. She had begun not only to understand the possible insult but the implications of Hamel's training for her.

"It would suggest to them that we believe we are not safe within their walls. Or it would suggest to them that we are looking to attack them." She wrapped her arms around herself, and she dropped her head down until her hair fell forward and covered her face. When she asked the question running through her mind, her voice came out in just above a whisper. "Do you not believe we are safe here?"

"Gollos," Hamel explained, "there are many reasons why you need to train. I will not explain them all right now, but it is always difficult to know how safe we are in any situation. But back to the matter of our training, I do not think it to be wise at this point to reveal that you are receiving training. If you were in my country, your training would have begun at age ten or earlier, and by your age, you would be well trained to protect yourself and to fight when needed, so it is not unusual for a man of the Ridge to train his..." Hamel paused. "Gollos, I have mentioned before that I will treat you as my daughter. Are you comfortable with that?"

Tears filled her eyes, and a smile broke out on her face. "Yes, Hamel," she said with her eyes on the floor. "I think that perhaps you love me very much. I do not understand why, but you are not like the men of this place. I think if being your daughter means I will be trained and taught and made to be strong, then I wish that very much."

"Then I will continue," Hamel said. He hoped her answer suggested she understood. "It is not unusual for a man of the Ridge to train his daughter to fight and defend herself. In addition to that matter, we do not know what all we will face in the coming days and weeks and months. We need to be prepared."

They continued their training for another ten minutes. After washing, they visited the clinic for the doctor to examine Hamel's leg. He felt weak, but his strength was returning. It was true the Olmosites were far more advanced in their medical care than his own people, and he was grateful for it.

The doctor explained his leg had responded well to the treatment and, although he should come back one more day for a final examination, the doctor felt Hamel had nearly completed his healing. To Hamel, the matter was good news, but he could see Gollos was giddy after hearing the report. He had not realized how much stress his injury had caused her.

Once his visit to the clinic was done, they returned to the apartment. Hamel took the opportunity to lie down for a rest before the evening meal. He felt so much stronger, but there was still such exhaustion.

289

CHAPTER 34

THE DAY OF SECRETS

Hamel awoke from his rest to the sound of knocking on the door to the apartment. He scrambled out of bed and dressed before stepping out into the sitting room, but by that point, the visitor had come and gone.

"I am glad to see you are awake, Hamel," Gollos said. Each time she said his name, rather than use the term "Master," she appeared to relish the experience. "That was a servant sent by the High Chancellor himself. He wishes to have a meal with us and to spend the evening with you."

Hamel's face lit up. He had been awaiting the opportunity to spend some time with Pulanomos. He had missed his friend greatly and longed to reacquaint himself after so many years. He also had many questions.

Gollos opened the door, and the two made their way to Pulanomos's apartment. The servant had informed Gollos that the High Chancellor desired privacy for their meal, for which Hamel was grateful.

When they reached the door, two soldiers stood guard while a third remained off to the side. The third soldier was the one who had confronted Hamel earlier that day. He frowned at the sight of Hamel, although he made no move to interfere.

One of the soldiers knocked on the door. In a moment, it was opened by Churoi. His eyes glowed, and his smile stretched across his face. "My friend! Come in! Come in!" he said and put his arm around Hamel. "I have been far too busy with matters of state, but I have enough time to eat with you and the High Chancellor this evening."

Hamel watched Gollos out of the corner of his eye. She followed them into the room but stood off to the side of the room. Her head was bowed as she took up the position of a servant or slave.

"I am so glad you have the time this evening, Churoi. I have missed you and hoped to find out what has been going on in your life for all these years." He turned and reached out his arm for Gollos, and she approached. When she stepped up next to him, he put his arm around her shoulder and added, "Gollos and I are looking forward to our time together."

Churoi's brow furrowed as he looked at Gollos. An expression of distaste crossed his face for a moment before he looked back at Hamel and smiled, although a certain joy was missing.

"Yes, of course, Honored Patir," Churoi began. He paused for a moment before adding, "Patir, when I was with you among the Ridge People, you had a greater impact on me that you might realize. You taught me many things." He paused one more time for a moment as if considering his words. "One of the things you taught me was to ask questions. It is not common among Olmosites to ask difficult questions. May I, my friend, ask you a personal question?"

Hamel laughed. "Of course, Churoi. What would you like to know?"

Churoi paused again and glared at Gollos before turning back to Hamel. "What is this girl to you?"

Hamel remembered the perpetual confusion on Churoi's face for the first two or three months in Ridge, serving under Pulanomos. Olmosites and the People of the Ridge, although allies, thought very differently about life and people. The young man had often struggled with the concept of honor and respect.

"Churoi, you know the way of the People of the Ridge is different than the Olmosite way. We do not tolerate any form of slavery. We are a people of family. I have adopted Gollos as my daughter in the manner of my people. I wish that she be viewed not only as a free person, but also as my daughter and, as such, be treated as you would treat me."

Churoi's eyes fixed on Hamel. He bit his lip, and Hamel could see an internal struggle was taking place.

"It is okay, Churoi," Pulanomos said, stepping into the room through a small doorway leading deeper into the apartment. "I recognize she is marked as a slave, and no slave woman has ever been freed, but we will today honor Hamel by granting his request. She is declared free."

Churoi turned and bowed deeply to Pulanomos. When he straightened, he smiled. "Yes, of course." He turned back to Hamel and Gollos and said, "My apologies to both of you. I would never seek to speak in such a disrespectful manner to the daughter of Hamel. Please, come and sit while we eat."

Pulanomos led the way through the door he had just used and down a long hallway. Hamel had not realized the apartment was so large. After a few twists and turns, they came to a room arranged with a table in the center and a sitting area off to the side. The table was set, and steam rose from the food.

Within a few minutes, all four were well into their meal. Hamel was pleased to see Gollos's appetite had increased. She would need to eat well if her training was to move forward.

As they ate, Pulanomos took the time to tell the story of how he had risen to High Chancellor. It turned out that after he had returned to Olmos, the former High Chancellor had been looking to retire. Two days before his retirement, he had been assassinated on a trip to one of the outlying cities, and a civil war had nearly broken out. Pulanomos had stepped in and brokered a peace between the two factions before more blood was spilled. It was not long after that he had been asked by the Senate to be their new High Chancellor. He had, at first, hesitated, but at Churoi's encouragement, stepped up to serve his people.

Hamel nodded his head throughout the entire story. It was good to be with Pulanomos and Churoi again and get a glimpse into their lives.

A deep sadness passed over his heart as the story went on. It was a good skill, at times, to be able to read the facial expressions of people and to evaluate conversations, body movements, and more, but it was sometimes a curse. He would have preferred at that moment not to know his friend was lying.

He could see from Pulanomos's eyes that he was leaving out a great deal of information. That, in itself, was not a problem, nor was it unexpected. There was no way to tell everything, and there would be matters of state that would need to be protected and kept private. But his friend was not only leaving out details. There was deception.

In addition to the matter, Churoi's reactions to the story indicated some of it was new to him. It was not much, just a movement here, a twitch of the eye there, but he noticed that the idea of Churoi encouraging Pulanomos to take the role of High Chancellor was unfamiliar to the younger man. He noticed as well from both men that there was something untrue in the story when it came to the former High Chancellor's assassination.

The most telling expressions, however, were from Gollos. She had been well acquainted with the political situation in Olmos, and much of what Pulanomos said appeared to be unfamiliar to her. When the civil war was mentioned, she did not react, but she did to the High Chancellor's explanation that he had negotiated peace and that he had resisted taking on his new responsibilities. She also seemed to react to the mention of the assassination of the former High Chancellor.

Hamel was pleased with her control. It was only his years of working with people and practice at reading body language that gave her away as well. He did not think Pulanomos or Churoi would have noticed. He hoped that he and Gollos would have a good discussion later.

When Pulanomos had finished his story, and the meal was over, they retired to the sitting area off the room near the entrance to the apartment. A servant was fetched to return Gollos to her room, and Churoi stepped away to attend to urgent business.

The two old friends sat on the couch together with the door open onto the balcony. A slight breeze brought in some of the cool air of the early evening.

Hamel felt thrilled to be back together with his friend after all the years. It was so good to see him again. But he was also looking forward to getting some answers. There was much he wished to understand.

"Hamel, go ahead."

"Go ahead?" Hamel asked.

"Yes, go ahead," Pulanomos replied. "I know you well. I have never had a friendship as close as ours. Not before I spent those years among your people nor since. I know you have a myriad of questions for me. So, go ahead and ask. We have complete privacy here."

Hamel did have many questions. The challenge was not coming up with questions; it was a matter of which ones to ask first.

He smiled and said, "It is true I have many questions. There is so much I don't understand, and so much I wish to understand. I want to know how it is that the people of Olmos live so much longer than the People of the Ridge. I want to know why you never contacted me, although I suspect you were not allowed as it would reveal that you too did not experience the Dusk." He paused and decided to start somewhere else. "Why is there a statue of me outside your house?"

Pulanomos laughed. "Yes, that is, I'm sure, a small question compared to the bigger ones but must seem odd to you. It is simply this. Our people value diplomacy. We are not strong diplomats with one another. That is why there is so much war and infighting among us. But when it comes to other nations, we are proud of a peaceful relationship. The Ridge People are our closest allies, and we value your friendship. My people have recognized my part in building that peace between our two nations, and they see our friendship as a testimony to... well... this is embarrassing. They see my friendship with you, personally, as a testimony of my greatness. Shortly after I became High Chancellor, they insisted the statue be built as a way to honor me. I resisted at first, but then I nearly had a riot on my hands. Neither of us are men who seek glory, but sometimes it is thrown upon us. You have received much glory yourself. At least until recently."

Hamel felt his face flush as his mind raced through the night of the Council meeting. It was just over three weeks since his disgrace, but it seemed like an eternity had passed. He did not allow himself to dwell on the thought. The faces of Mariel and Karotel were too much to bear. Even the thought of how he had treated Captain Cuttel weighed heavy on his heart.

"I see the memory of such an event is hard for you. I apologize, my friend. I did not want to bring your pain to the surface," Pulanomos said.

"It is fine," Hamel said but decided not to dwell on the matter. Instead, he chose to go right for the big issue before them. "How is it that your people live so long? I have seen people that might be as old as seventy or eighty." For such a large matter, Hamel felt the question seemed so small. "And why have we not learned of this matter before?"

Pulanomos smiled, but there was sadness in his eyes. "This is a most difficult question to answer. It's not simple, Hamel. There is history there; there is pain; there is fear; there is stubbornness; there is ignorance. All of these things are a factor in the second question. As for the first question, we simply don't know."

"You don't know why your people live so long?" Hamel asked.

"Well, I guess it's not that simple," Pulanomos replied. "It's not that we don't know why our people live so long. It's that we don't know why your people don't. Our people do live to seventy or eighty years of age. We even have the occasional person who lives past one hundred."

Hamel could not conceive of someone living past one hundred years of age. They would see and know four generations of family. He did not, however, find the idea that his people were dying young to be a shock. It was something he had already begun to suspect. "So, you believe that your people live the proper amount of years, but our people die before their time?"

"Yes, that is correct," his friend explained with compassion in his voice. "But we have no idea why. We have been researching this for many years. One of the reasons our medical sciences are so far advanced beyond your own is because of the effort and time we have put into researching this matter. We have secretly taken blood samples from your people and tested your food and water. We have even tried to develop some medicines that might work on your people, but so far, we have had no success."

Hamel sat back heavily in his seat. His friend had not been entirely honest about many things that evening, but much of what he shared about the theories about their lifespans rang of truth.

The mosaic in Benjelton had continued to bother him since he had studied it. Finally, he understood with certainty that it was a picture based not on mere hope, but on reality. The problem of the Beasts was no longer his primary mission.

CHAPTER 35

THE DAY OF REVEALING

Hamel leaned forward again and held his face in his hands. His friend remained silent. This was not a time for speech, but a time for acceptance.

His people had been left alone to suffer the consequences of this early death, and their only allies had said nothing. Hamel felt a sense of betrayal germinate in his heart.

"Why have you done all this in secret? Why not tell us? Why not bring us onboard? You would not need to conduct your research behind closed doors. We could have worked together." Hamel found the whole matter difficult to believe, but it was a relief to finally receive some answers.

"If I had my way, I would have done so, Hamel. I greatly wished to tell you. Even before I went to Ridge as Ambassador, and before we met, I fought hard to encourage our leaders to tell your people what we knew, but I have only met with resistance."

"What is keeping your people from sharing this information?" Hamel asked.

"Fear."

"Fear of what?"

"Fear of the same sickness," Pulanomos explained. "Our people believe you are dealing with some form of contagion—a sickness that infects your people. They are convinced that if we reveal what we know, the Ridge People will storm our walls and enter our nation in the hopes of avoiding the onset of the Dusk." He paused for a moment before saying, "They believe if that happens, our people will contract whatever disease or sickness you have."

"But you do not believe this is the case?" Hamel asked.

"No," Pulanomos said with a chuckle. "Not at all. Our research has shown that it is not airborne, nor is it in your blood as far as we can tell. It does not appear to be in your food or in your water. It is a mystery to us. What we are confident of, however, is that it is not contagious. That is why I was so willing to be an Ambassador to the Ridge People. Actually, not only because I did not believe your sickness to be contagious, but also because I wished to create a closer presence among your people to facilitate greater research into the matter. And because I wished to create a greater peace between our people."

Hamel nodded his head. He did not like much of what had been shared with him, but he understood. Often fear drove people to terrible ends, and leadership needed to work with people through the matter. It also fully explained why Pulanomos had to lead Hamel to believe he was dead for all those years. If Hamel knew his friend had survived, many questions would have been asked.

But the explanation raised an obvious question. "What about me?"

"Yes, Hamel," Pulanomos said. "What about you? That is the question our researchers have been asking for nearly ten years. We have no idea why you are still alive. Do not misunderstand me. It has given me great joy that you survived, but it is a perplexing matter. We have studied you closely as a result. I am embarrassed to say that we have taken blood samples, food samples, observed your habits, and more."

"How did you get blood samples?" Hamel asked. "I would think I would notice such a thing."

Pulanomos laughed again. "Yes, I would think so. We have access to some of your research facilities where your own people have tested you to see if they could figure out why you are still alive."

"Yes, that would make sense. It would also answer why they have come to me many times over the years telling me they have lost samples and need more blood," Hamel said with a laugh. In his mind, he made a mental note to evaluate Ridge's security measures—if he ever returned home and to his former position.

"So, you can see why we have been so secretive when it comes to your people. The Olmosites are a passionate people. It is difficult to change their minds on this matter," Pulanomos explained. "This brings me to another matter. I see you are growing stronger? Is your leg fully healed?"

"Yes, thank you. Your doctor is an excellent physician. I assume while I was asleep, he took more blood samples from me?" Hamel asked with a smile.

"That he did," Pulanomos said, returning the smile but looking embarrassed. "But, he was unaware as to why he would need to do such a thing. The blood samples were given to our researchers, who, of course, do not know that you are here."

"What would happen if they did know?" Hamel asked.

"Well, they would likely petition me to do an autopsy on you," Pulanomos explained. "That, of course, is out of the question. I would rather not have that discussion. Besides, they are not my greatest concern. If the general population finds out that we have a man of the Ridge here, or as our people call you, a 'Ridger,' they will likely storm the palace, take you out into the street, and kill you. Fear does strange things to people."

"So, they believe if a... Ridger... is among them, they will be infected?" Hamel asked.

"Exactly. Once, a few years ago, a man was suspected of being from Ridge Nation, and before the soldiers could come to his rescue, his own friends killed him in the street and burned his body. Even some of the soldiers first on the scene took part. It was a sad day." Pulanomos's eyes drifted to the floor and grief filled his face.

Hamel felt compassion for his friend. He and Pulanomos were close, but one thing he knew about his friend was that he was an expert manipulator. He knew the expression of sadness following his explanation was false. The people did not fear a man from the Ridge. In the pits in the City Square, there was a man or woman from Ridge, and no one was concerned about a contagion. In addition to the person in the pit, Gollos had never mentioned a fear of contagion around him, and yet she was well acquainted with the political and cultural situation of her people. Not only was his friend keeping information from him, but he was speaking lies.

"This is why," Pulanomos continued, "you cannot leave the palace under any circumstances. I am impressed that you made it this far into Olmos and right to my door without being found out, but if you leave and someone hears your accent, a simple slip of the tongue could cost you your life. I will need you to remain on my property as long as you are here. You are welcome anywhere within the safety of my walls, and I will continue to instruct my guards not to approach you."

Hamel wasn't entirely convinced that plan would work for him, but he held his tongue. He was not one whom traditionally found that walls could contain him. The good news was Pulanomos's reasons for lying had been revealed.

The man wanted Hamel to remain within the estate. He decided to shift the topic slightly.

"On that matter, I should mention I had a bit of a confrontation today," Hamel said.

Pulanomos laughed. "Hamel, I've seen you in battle. I've seen you face a Beast and come out the other side with only a few scratches. I do not think there could have been a 'confrontation' as you call it on my property without someone telling me that I was down a guard or two."

Hamel added his laugh to the conversation. "It was small and simple. One of the guards—the kind that stands outside your door, not the regular kind—came up to me and demanded to know the answer to certain questions. He told me if I did not answer his questions, I would die."

Pulanomos leaned forward. He could not hide his anger at the news. "What did you do?"

"Gollos came to my rescue," Hamel said and watched as his friend's eyebrows shot up in surprise. "She told him that I have been ordered by you not to speak with anyone."

Pulanomos sat back and stared out the open balcony door into the darkening night. "She is a smart child for one who has grown up in slavery. Yes, I believe I will have to think more highly of her in the future. But this soldier, describe him for me."

Hamel took the time to tell his friend of the man's height, build, facial features. The soldiers guarding Pulanomos's apartments wore no insignias of any kind that Hamel could see.

When he was finished, Pulanomos frowned deeply. "That is the Captain of the Guard. You are right in pointing out that he was a different kind of soldier. His cloak and armor give him away to most people, but it is their training that truly sets them apart from other soldiers. They are deadly on the battlefield."

Pulanomos sat back on the couch and crossed his foot over his knee with his eyes fixed firmly on a spot on the ceiling. He appeared deep in thought. He took a slow breath before saying, "Their clan is called the Naromite clan. You would not have heard of them. They do not leave Olmos. They are feared by all for their skill, and even the officers in the army will not dare to question a Naromite Acolyte. I am upset that one accosted you today."

"There was no harm done, Pulanomos. Think nothing of it," Hamel said.

"No, this cannot be allowed to continue," his friend said with authority and decision ringing loud and clear in his voice. "If the Naromites begin to challenge my authority by questioning you, it will not stop there."

Pulanomos stood up and made his way to the door. Once there, he opened it and said to the guards, "Summon the Captain of the Guard to come here immediately."

One of the guards rushed off down the hall while Pulanomos made his way back to the couch. Less than a minute later, the Captain strolled in. He had not been far from the room. Hamel began to suspect either their quarters were close by or this meeting was planned.

"Captain," the High Chancellor called out. "Close the door behind you. I wish to speak with you."

The Captain nodded to the soldiers who closed the door and then approached Pulanomos. Hamel watched every step the man made. He was tense and ready to spring into action at any moment. His movements were controlled and confident. Hamel also noticed that while the man did not look directly at him, he was watching Hamel closely. When he stopped before the High Chancellor, he stood with his hands behind his back and his feet shoulder-width apart. He was a soldier, but not one who stood at attention—even before the High Chancellor. The soldier was used to his high position, and the fear he often struck in people.

"I understand, Captain, that you spoke with my friend here today," Pulanomos said.

"Yes, High Chancellor," the Captain replied.

303

"Are you aware that I had given orders that my friend was not to be spoken to at all?" the High Chancellor asked.

"Yes, High Chancellor. My apologies. I had questions to which I wished to know the answers. I feel it is my responsibility to know who is walking among us," the Captain said.

Hamel observed the soldier closely. He had disobeyed a direct order, yet there was no true remorse in his eyes, nor did there appear to be any fear at all. Something was not right.

Leaning forward in as casual a manner as he could, Hamel pretended he was scratching his injured leg. In the process, he prepared himself to spring into action if necessary. The scratching would have the added benefit of drawing attention to his injury, perhaps even causing the Captain's confidence to grow.

"It is not within your authority to ignore my commands, Captain, unless I am mistaken," Pulanomos said in a threatening voice.

"No," the Captain replied.

Pulanomos leaned back in his seat and began to pick at one of his nails. "Captain, perhaps it would be helpful for me to introduce you to my friend. Would that be acceptable to you?"

The Captain bowed slightly to the High Chancellor. "That would be quite acceptable to me, sir."

Hamel eased to his feet. He was not sure what Pulanomos had in mind. His friend had just explained the necessity of keeping his identity a secret from the people.

"My friend here is not from Pollos," Pulanomos explained. "In fact, he's not from Olmos at all."

The Captain's hand went to his knife at his side, but he did not draw it. "I see, High Chancellor. May I ask where he is from?"

304

Hamel did not like where Pulanomos was taking the conversation. He feared within a few moments, either he or the Captain would be dead. He did not wish to kill the man.

Pulanomos simply said, "His name is Hamel," before placing both hands behind his head and smiling.

Hamel examined the Captain. The Naromite's eyes were still set on Pulanomos. On the outside, Hamel knew he could maintain a calm and unconcerned presence. On the inside, his mind raced.

Pulanomos had just given him away. He did not think his friend wished him to die. If he did, he could have killed him in the hospital, and there would have been nothing Hamel could have done to defend himself. It appeared as though Pulanomos wished the Captain to die. Perhaps it was the High Chancellor's way to punish the Captain for disobeying him, but Hamel did not think that to be so.

"Hamel?" the Captain asked as he drew his blade and turned to Hamel. "Yes, I see the resemblance to the statue outside. I did not notice it before. I have heard of his disgrace, of his dealings with Ridge criminals, and how he broke into the Ridge leader's home."

"Yes, Captain," Pulanomos said.

Hamel noted how much detail the man had about his dealings in the Capital. The Naromites were well informed.

"What do you think should be done, Captain, now that you know we have Hamel of the Ridge in our midst?"

The Captain smiled and said, "We either throw him in a pit or kill him."

"Yes, Captain," Pulanomos said. "Which would you prefer?"

The Captain lunged. While Hamel's leg was still somewhat stiff, he no longer worried it would hinder him. He only wished he had not just eaten a large meal.

Hamel blocked the Captain's knife and easily disarmed him. The blade clattered across the floor as the man attacked again. Hamel pushed the soldier's fist off to the side with his left hand and then used it to backhand the man across the face. A moment later, Hamel had driven his right fist into the man's stomach, dropped the soldier to his knees and, moving around behind him, placed the man in a choke-hold. A few moments later, the Captain lay unconscious on the floor. Hamel had certainly found the man to be well trained, but not up to the level of the elite Ridge training he had received—and taught.

"Pulanomos..." Hamel began.

"Yes, Hamel," his friend answered amidst laughter. He continued to laugh as he walked over to the soldier's knife and picked it up from where Hamel had tossed it.

"Why did you reveal my identity? Why did you lead the Captain to attack?" Hamel watched the soldier closely. He was already stirring and would be up on his feet in seconds.

Pulanomos knelt down beside the man and used the soldiers' own knife to end his life. He then stood, walked to the door, and opened it. "Guards. The Captain is no longer in my employment." He tossed the knife out into the hallway as if for effect. "Call the Lieutenant and have him report to my quarters immediately." He turned back toward Hamel but stopped and added, "And call someone to clean up the body."

He returned to the couch, took his seat, picked up his drink, and motioned for Hamel to join him once again. The two sat in silence while four men came in and removed the Captain's body. As they worked, the Lieutenant came in, and Pulanomos called in the two soldiers at the door.

Without any formality, Pulanomos said, "Soldiers. You are my witnesses. The Lieutenant here has just been promoted to Captain of the Guard. That is all."

He waived the two soldiers and the new Captain out of the room, and a few moments later, the cleaning crew exited and closed the door. To Hamel, the experience was surreal, but from what he judged of Pulanomos's demeanor, it was not something unfamiliar to him. He had not seen that side of his friend before. Years could change people, but that was extreme.

"So, Hamel, this has been a wonderful evening. I hope to do this again soon, but for now, I must retire. Churoi and I have to attend to matters in the south of Olmos. I expect we will not be back for at least two days. Perhaps when I return, we will meet again for dinner."

"That sounds wonderful, my friend," Hamel replied, hiding his revulsion over the soldier's execution.

"You may bring your new daughter with you as well," Pulanomos continued. "I see you are quite fond of her, and I can respect your desire to treat her as though she were a Daughter of the Ridge."

"Thank you," Hamel replied and rose to his feet. "I wish you well as you travel. I trust it is not a matter of great concern."

"No, Hamel, thank you. It is merely a political matter that requires both the High Chancellor and his assistant. It is one of the tedious matters of state we are required to address. I will be happy when it is over. When I come back, perhaps we will go hunting. My property is over two hundred acres. It is all walled in, and there are many deer in the forests. I have not had a holiday in well over a year. I think it is time."

"I agree!" Hamel replied. "It is good for you to rest. Even a leader must care for himself or he will fail to be what the nation needs in its time of crisis."

Pulanomos laughed again. "I see you are still full of wisdom. Good-night, my friend. We will speak again in a few days."

"Good-night, Pulanomos," Hamel said. "I enjoyed our time together." He paused and looked down at the stain on the carpet. "Until, of course, the incident with the Captain."

"Yes, that was most unfortunate, but necessary. I cannot have a Captain challenging my orders. The Naromites report directly to me on all matters. If it were found out that a Naromite officer disobeyed me, I would lose more than you might realize. Olmosites value power above all else. A High Chancellor who shows weakness is, at best, out of a job."

"I do not doubt that, my friend. I will see you soon."

Hamel left the room. As he passed the guards, he nodded to them, but they merely eyed him closely.

The evening had certainly been disturbing for him—especially the end—but he had learned much. Much of what he had learned required more information to understand it properly, but he was beginning to get a clearer picture of what was going on. There were two matters, however, which stood out to him and had shocked him.

The first involved the Captain. Hamel was convinced that Pulanomos had sent the man to accost him. He suspected his friend wished to see if a Naromite soldier could stand against a Ridge soldier in combat. He had wanted to know that himself but did not wish that information to be revealed to anyone else. In addition to that, his friend had put him in the position of having to fight unarmed against a soldier with a blade. Pulanomos had put his life in danger to test out who was stronger.

The second matter, however, disturbed him more. The soldier was a Naromite, under the direct authority of the High Chancellor himself. That would be fine with Hamel, if not for one thing. When Hamel fought against the Captain, the fight, as quick as it had been, had shown him the skill and style of the Naromites. Hamel knew he had fought the Naromites before. It had only been once, but it was undeniable. The Captain fought in the same manner, skill, and style as had the two assassins he had met in his home.

They had been Naromites. It was clear who had ultimately sent them to his home that last night in the Capital.

Pulanomos was not his friend.

CHAPTER 36

THE DAY OF PLANS

Hamel watched his two oldest children closely.

He had trained Lemmel well, and his son had proven to be a capable student. It was an honor to watch him grow. He had shown Lemmel how to defend himself and how to fight. He had taught him strategy and how to lead well. But any child could learn to fight or understand strategy. The test of both Lemmel's abilities and of Hamel's own abilities to teach lay in the next step. The young man needed to know not just how to fight and defend himself, but how to teach another to fight and defend herself.

Lemmel stood before his sister and led her through the training exercises. At eighteen years of age, he was already the equal of many experienced soldiers. His arms were strong, and his body solid.

Standing before him, his fourteen-year-old sister was a complete contrast. Her frame was slight, and she looked as though she could fall and shatter at any moment.

Hamel knew she was far stronger than she looked, but she was no match for Lemmel. The moment, however, was not to see if Karotel could stand against someone twice her size and weight, but to see if Lemmel could teach someone with wisdom and patience.

Some young men in such a position would use the opportunity to prove their strength and to act without compassion. Hamel remembered observing one young soldier teaching a young lady to fight. He snapped her wrist and then tossed her three paces through the air.

Hamel felt the anger well up inside as he thought back to that moment. He had wanted to throw the man from the Valley Wall but had instead taken him behind the barracks. He had challenged the young man to a fight and used the same restraint the young soldier had shown to his own student. The man had not returned to active duty for six weeks. When the soldier had returned, he was humble.

Hamel hoped his training of Lemmel would prove successful. He watched as his son taught with patience. He did not use his strength to hurt or harm but to strengthen his sister.

The tears formed in Hamel's eyes. He had never been more proud of his son than at that moment. To see him teach another with the sole purpose of helping that one be strong was almost more honor than he could bear.

Lemmel would be a good soldier, and one day he would be a good Patir.

Hamel awoke with the rising of the sun. From the quiet in the apartment, he suspected Gollos was still asleep. The girl had been in bed before he had returned the night before, which was just as well. He would have liked to have spoken with her about Pulanomos's rise to power and perhaps even about the Naromites, but she needed her sleep.

He decided to remain in bed for a few moments while he thought through his next steps. Pulanomos appeared content to have him remain within the castle walls, perhaps indefinitely. In other circumstances, such a course of action might be acceptable, but Hamel was not one to sit still, nor was he interested in living out his days hunting and relaxing on a two-hundred-acre estate.

He still had many unasked and unanswered questions, but there were more pressing matters. He wanted to know why his people were dying at such a young age. He did not think his friend had been entirely honest about everything. He knew the explanation that the people of Olmos feared a Ridge contagion was nothing more than an attempt to keep Hamel from leaving the palace. That suggested to him that some of the answers he needed were on the other side of the wall.

He urgently desired to visit the man or woman from Ridge held in the pit. He could not understand how a "Ridger," as the Olmosites called them, could end up arrested and serving out a sentence in the bottom of a pit. He knew there was a matter of urgency. It did not sound as if people in that condition lasted long. He wished to meet the man or woman as soon as possible. He suspected the Ridger might be a source of great information. He also suspected whoever was in the pit would need rescue. Hamel was not convinced the prisoner was there justly.

As he continued to lay in bed, he considered what he would need to accomplish those two goals. He would need a way out of the palace and then back in again. That would, of course, be the most challenging part. He had two days while Pulanomos and Churoi were away and wished to make the most of it, but he strongly suspected the soldiers would have orders to keep him in the palace.

He would also need Gollos to remain behind with a good story for his cover. He would not have her lie for him, but he did not think it would be necessary. She might need to assist him as he exited the palace and assist him as he returned.

Finally, he knew he would need a decent disguise. If a man or woman from the palace or a soldier recognized him, it could cause a great deal of grief. If he had his choice, he would wish to have another cloak similar to the one he had worn while entering Olmos. He would then find his papers from Mellel to be quite useful again. After his conversation with Pulanomos, he knew papers declaring him to be a Naromite Colonel could open many doors.

The memory of his conversation with his friend brought with it a wave of sadness. His friend had lied to him repeatedly. Not only that, but his friend had tried to kill him by sending assassins and then Pulanomos had risked Hamel's life with the Naromite Captain. Pulanomos, sadly, was no longer someone Hamel trusted.

After losing his honor, his status, his family, and leaving his people, the loss of his friendship with Pulanomos was overwhelming. He found the tears flowed freely down his face. Perhaps there was a reason he cared so deeply for Gollos. Perhaps he felt she was all he had left.

He climbed out of bed and stretched his leg as he pushed the grief out of his mind and went over his mental list once again. He needed to acquire a cloak, find a way out of the palace, reach the man in the pit, and return. It would be a full day, but it needed to begin properly. Gollos's training could not wait.

He knocked on the door to her room and smiled. He was tempted to wake her by singing, but he set the thought aside. He thought she might not see the humor in it, and he did not wish to embarrass her. He also had never been able to carry a tune.

When she emerged from her room, she seemed happy and well rested. They each drank some water before he led her outside for a run. He was impressed at how well she kept up with him, especially in light of how tired she had been while walking not too many days before. Good meals, some exercise, and exploring the forest on the palace estate had proven to be of great benefit.

Hamel made sure they ran close to the outside walls so he could examine them as they ran. While it felt good to get out and move his leg, he did not think the wall was a good option for finding his exit. He would need to find a better way in or out.

When he noticed Gollos reaching her limit with the run, they returned to the room and spent another 30 minutes in training. By the end, she looked ready to collapse.

After cleaning up and having a quick breakfast in the dining hall, they returned to the room. He took the opportunity to explain to her that the more she pushed herself, the stronger she would become and the more endurance she would have. He could see the doubt in her eyes, but she accepted his words.

He then asked her to tell him everything she had learned about the palace itself while he was in the clinic. He was impressed by her knowledge. She had an uncanny ability to learn and retain information.

Gollos explained the layout of the palace in detail. She spoke of the administration offices, the serving staff quarters, the kitchens, the soldiers's barracks, and more. She shared how she had found out where the barracks were but avoided that area as soldiers were well known to be dangerous toward young women. She even shared where she believed the Naromite barracks were located.

"So, in the serving quarters," Gollos explained, "there are twenty-two serving staff on a rotation and ten cooking staff. In the administration offices…"

"Wait," Hamel interrupted. "You know exactly how many serving staff there are?"

"Yes, I believe there are twenty-two."

"How do you know that? Did you go in there and count?"

"No, I watched what they were doing, whom they served, and so on. I was in the kitchen at one point and saw what was needed in order to run the kitchen properly and then evaluated their staffing needs in terms of who might be working at various times, considered the three dining halls, and how many would be needed if the dining hall was filled and…"

Hamel cut her off. "And with the information you had, you were able to piece that number together, even though you only saw a few kitchen staff at a time?"

"Yes, of course. It is not hard. My former Master had me evaluate how many workers were needed for various business ventures…"

"Would you know how many soldiers are present in the palace?"

"Of course. Which ones? The guard or the Naromites?"

Hamel shook his head and laughed. He enjoyed the fact that Gollos was a continual surprise. "Tell me both."

"Well, it is said in the city that an entire battalion of soldiers remain in the palace at all times, but as I have observed, there are not likely more than fifty or perhaps sixty at most, including the men who patrol outside. As for the Naromites, there are not many stationed here. I would say six or seven at a time, but the Naromites are always coming and going. I would expect there is a larger Naromite barracks nearby in the city."

Hamel considered the new information. "So, if two of the Naromites are always standing outside the High Chancellor's apartment, there are only four or five in the Naromite quarters?"

"No," Gollos said. "The others patrol the palace, mostly staying out of sight if you are not looking for them. They often stay more to the north side of the palace. I would say in the Naromite quarters, there is only one or two present at a time."

Hamel smiled and shook his head again. He wondered if she would consider a life in the military one day. If she were willing to take her place among the People of the Ridge, she would be an excellent officer. "Where is the Naromite barracks?"

"It is just down the hall from the High Chancellor's apartments," she explained.

"And do you know what is to the north side of the palace?" he asked.

"No, when I tried to enter that area, I was always stopped before I could get too far," she said. "I'm sorry, Hamel. I wish I could have retrieved this information for you as well."

Hamel laughed. "Gollos, I had no idea you were so adept at collecting information. You do not need to apologize for anything. You are full of surprises."

Gollos shied away at the compliment but appeared pleased. "Thank you, Hamel."

Hamel sat back and let his mind move through the information and drift over the next steps. He needed to move quickly but carefully. He had his answer as to how he would exit and enter the palace, but he needed to be careful.

He explained his plan to Gollos and asked her for her opinion as to the chances of success. Once she overcame her shock at being asked for her opinion, she agreed with him. It was a good plan.

CHAPTER 37

THE DAY OF THE RIDGER

Hamel and Gollos set out. Each carried a bag as Gollos led the way through the palace toward Pulanomos's apartments and the Naromite barracks where Hamel hoped to find his means of free travel.

When they reached the entrance to the Naromite barracks, Hamel stopped for a moment to examine the door. It appeared to be a normal door. There was nothing fancy, solid, or unusual about it. It was entirely without markings and entirely unimpressive.

Hamel noted two things. First, it was a sign of the fear the people had for the Naromite clan. It would be known that it was a barracks by all those who worked in the palace, and no one would dare enter. The second thing he realized was that it was to his advantage that it was unmarked. He and Gollos were new to the palace, so it would be understood if they were not aware that they were forbidden entrance.

Hamel stepped forward and opened the door. Inside was a short hallway with three open doors. The first led into a large room he suspected was used for training and practice purposes. There were weapons of all sorts on the walls, and

Hamel took a knife. He hoped its absence would go unnoticed.

The second doorway led to a series of rooms with bunks. One of the rooms held cloaks and armor, and Hamel stuffed the armor in his bag and the lighter cloak into Gollos's bag. Gollos continued to look around for a moment while he quickly stepped through the third doorway. The room he found was empty of people, as had been the other two, but the final room was used as an office of sorts and had a table with maps. He suspected it was a room for strategic planning.

He took a quick look around. Not much in the room was of interest, aside from the maps. As he quickly glanced over the maps, he couldn't help but notice how many were of Ridge Nation, specifically the Ridge Capital.

It was not difficult for Hamel to recognize plans of attack and routes laid out for both a frontal assault as well as a covert attack. While the official relationship between their nations was one of peace, the Naromites had other plans.

The sound of the door sliding open drew Hamel attention back to the risk they were taking. He pressed himself against the wall, behind a large cabinet. He did not wish to be found in the barracks. They had wandered too far into the rooms to pretend they had just taken a wrong turn.

He knew he could overpower the man. His experience with the Captain the night before had taught him that. But if he incapacitated the man or killed him, it would alert the Naromites and Pulanomos that someone had broken into the Naromite barracks. He feared it would not be too great a leap to reason out that Hamel was behind it.

He hoped the person would enter the training area. If they did, it might give Hamel and Gollos the chance to slip out unnoticed. He listened to the footsteps, and his heart sank as he heard them turn into the strategy room. He could remain unseen for a moment or two as he hid behind the cabinet, but not for long.

Hamel knew his only option was to step out and play the fool. If he could convince the soldier he was simply lost or had taken a wrong turn, he might get out of the situation. He was not sure yet how to get Gollos out, but he hoped they would figure it out along the way.

He was just about to step from behind the cabinet when he heard Gollos address the soldier. "Excuse me, Master, but can you tell me how to find my way back to my apartment?"

Hamel's heart stopped, and he nearly cried out in fear. He did not want Gollos harmed in any way and did not think the Naromite would have any inhibitions against harming a child.

"What are you doing here?" the man shouted.

"Please, Master," Gollos replied with a tremble in her voice. "Do not be angry with me. Please tell me how to find my way back to my apartment."

Hamel considered revealing himself in order to protect Gollos, but he hesitated. Gollos often surprised him with her ability to move through difficult situations. He remained hidden behind the cabinet.

"It is forbidden, child, to enter the Naromite barracks. I could kill you now for such an offense, and no one would question me," the soldier said. Rage was evident in his voice.

Hamel prepared himself to act, if necessary. He would not allow Gollos to be harmed.

"Forgive me, Master," Gollos said. "If you will just point the way to my apartment, I will not return."

"You are most fortunate, child," the man said, "that the High Chancellor has placed his protection upon you and your friend. If it were not for that, you would be used for training purposes to teach the young Acolytes how to kill without a weapon."

318

"Thank you for your kindness to me," Gollos said, her voice choking on the words. "I will leave now. But please, show me the way to my apartment."

At first, Hamel did not know why she would not run out of the room, but then he understood. She was trying to force the man to lead her out of the barracks, thus clearing the way for Hamel to find his way safely out as well. He smiled again and shook his head. He suspected the shake in her voice was nothing but an act.

"Follow me!" the man barked, and Hamel listened as the footsteps led down the hallway to the door. Once the door was opened, he heard the man growl, "Find your own way."

Hamel took the opportunity to slip across the hall through the doorway leading to the sleeping quarters. When the man returned and entered the strategy room, Hamel heard him ruffling through the maps. A moment later, Hamel was down the hallway and out the door.

The two met back in their apartment, and Hamel put on the armor and cloak. With the hood up, his face was well hidden, and he would pass as a Naromite. He filled a waterskin and put some food in a small bag. He explained to Gollos that she could tell anyone who asked that he was out exploring. He knew they would assume he was walking through the two hundred acres of wooded land in Pulanomos's estate.

Before he left, he gave her his Patir's kiss on the forehead and told her he hoped to be back by early evening. His primary goal was to see the "Ridger" in the pit. He hoped the man or woman was still alive.

Once he had retrieved his papers from her showing him to be a Naromite Colonel, he left the apartment and tried his best to walk as he had seen the Naromites walk. They moved with a certain stealth that he felt was more dramatic than practical. He felt silly moving as they moved, but it appeared to work well. As he walked down one hallway, not too far from his apartment, he passed another Naromite who nodded at him but showed no indication he noticed anything out of place.

Hamel stepped out of the palace and walked down the steps to the street. No one stopped him, and no one questioned him. People on the street avoided eye contact with him, and many even changed their paths to avoid walking too close to him. At one point, as he wandered through a small market, a young man turned around after having purchased some bread from a vendor and dropped it all on the ground the moment he saw Hamel.

The Naromites were feared by the people. Hamel suspected the fear was warranted. In a nation driven by power and control, people like the Naromites would not hesitate to use their power.

He found the Naromite walk to be exhausting. It took a great deal of effort to maintain the movement. It was a walk that suggested both stealth and danger. He looked forward to the day when he could walk, speak, and act freely as Hamel, once again. He longed for the day to be welcomed back among his people.

It was just before lunch when he arrived at the City Square where the pits were located. He immediately moved to the pit where he had seen the woman only a matter of days before, but even before he reached the edge, he had his answer. There were no people gathered around, which was a complete contrast from his previous visit. A quick glance into the pit showed him the woman was no longer there. He could not dwell on her but wondered if he had come back sooner if he would have been able to do something for her. He still was not sure what he might have done.

A voice interrupted his thoughts. "Master, may I help you?"

He turned to see the same two soldiers he had met his last time in the Square. Neither one would recognize him as the hood of the cloak was an effective disguise. Each soldier had their heads bowed low.

"What do you wish to help me with?" Hamel asked.

"Forgive us, Master," the soldier said, bowing even lower than before. "It is not often that a man of your status comes to the Square to look at the prisoners. Is there a specific prisoner you wish to interrogate?"

Hamel smiled. In such a horrific place, he hoped something was about to work out well.

"Yes," he said in his Olmosite accent. "There was a Ridger in one of the pits. I wish to speak with that prisoner."

"Of course, Master," the man said. "But many have interrogated him over the years. He will not answer a word. All he does is speak Ridge parables and proverbs and tell Ridge stories. He even refuses to take his own life. He survives by eating the rotting food and dirty water thrown to him. He is a most difficult man."

Hamel pondered what the soldier said. The prisoner was a man. He had been in there for years. It was difficult to imagine someone surviving years in such conditions. The fact that he would refuse to give any information suggested he was either an honorable man or a man without information—or perhaps insane.

"How many years has he been in the pit?" Hamel asked.

"Forgive me, Master," the soldier said. "I do not know. I have only been assigned to the Square for two years, and the man had been in his pit for a long time at that point."

"Which pit is he in?" Hamel asked.

"He is in the large pit," the soldier said and pointed to an area near the center of the Square. The pit was perhaps twice as big as the other pits.

321

"I wish to speak with him," Hamel said. "Do you have the means to draw him from the pit and a place where I may interrogate him in private?"

"Master, please do not test us," the man said. "We do have the means to remove him from the pit. We have ladders in the guardhouse. But we cannot remove that prisoner. The High Chancellor himself has ordered that he never step out of the pit. He has even declared that if the Ridger sets foot outside the pit, the entire guard will be thrown into the pits along with their families. We dare not remove him, even for a moment."

Hamel nodded his head to the soldiers. Pulanomos had known there was a man from Ridge in the pit. Whoever it was had displeased him enough to see fit the Ridger never escaped.

"Very well. I will interrogate him while he remains in the pit. But I wish for complete privacy. I require access to the ladder that I may enter the pit."

The soldiers each fell to their knees. "Please, Master, I beg you not to test us. We are faithful servants of the High Chancellor. We would never do such a thing. The High Chancellor has commanded us that the man never receive visitors in his pit without the High Chancellor's written permission. Please, Master, we are faithful servants."

Hamel was not sure he would have complete privacy if he needed to speak to the man from the side of the pit, but he did not have any choice. "Well done, men. You have proven yourselves to be faithful servants of the High Chancellor. I do, however, need to interrogate the prisoner in complete privacy. Since you will not offer me the privacy of a room or the pit, I will require that you keep all people away from me. If I suspect anyone hears a word of what I say, you will die."

"Yes, Master," the soldier said with a shake in his voice. "We will see to it immediately."

322

The soldier who had spoken gave a quick order to the second man to retrieve the other soldiers from the guardhouse. When they arrived, the four soldiers cleared the Square of anyone present and took up positions patrolling the perimeter. Hamel feared his words would carry to them, but he would do his best to speak in a quiet voice.

He approached the pit, and as he neared the edge, he was hit by the stench. It was far worse than the smell of the woman's pit. His heart still ached for her, but he had to put her out of his mind.

The sun was bright in the sky, directly above the pit, offering a great deal of light for Hamel to examine the man. The Ridger remained on his feet, moving around. He was tall and, though he was thin, he was muscular. The man worked through various Ridge military forms and exercises. He had been a soldier. That might explain why he was still alive. He would not break down as he would see his arrest and imprisonment as a foe to defeat. He would also never take his own life while the Olmosite guards walked free.

Having served in the military for many years, Hamel wondered if he knew the man. A soldier's disappearance was rare, but Hamel could not recall any such disappearance in many years. The only ones to have left the military were through death, retirement, or betrayal to the Beasts.

The man had either not noticed Hamel watching him or did not care. Hamel's shadow fell on the bottom of the pit, so it would not take long before he was noticed. With the sun behind him in addition to the cloak pulled over his head, he would not be recognized. He had already decided to use the Olmosite accent at first. If the man were a soldier, he would invariably recognize Hamel. If he were a traitor to Ridge, he would not hesitate to barter the knowledge of Hamel's presence in Pollos for his own life.

The man noticed Hamel's shadow. He turned his bearded face upward and squinted into the sun. "What do you want, Naromite?" the man said in his Ridge accent.

323

Hamel nearly fell into the pit. He knew the man. He had never seen him with a beard and certainly not in such a disgusting state. The man had been perhaps sixty pounds heavier the last time they had been together, built as solidly as the average Ridge soldier. His hair was bleached from the sun and perhaps malnutrition, but the voice, the eyes, the face… there was no doubt about it.

It was Lemmel. Hamel's son was alive.

Hamel's mind raced. He had thought, as had everyone else, that Lemmel had betrayed the People of the Ridge by entering the land of the Beasts and provoking them. His uniform had been found wrapped around a Beastchild. He had mourned for his son and had thought him to be dead for four years. He had thought his son was a traitor.

Hamel's breathing came in gasps, and he gripped the side of the pit as if his life depended on it. His strength drained from his body, and he feared for a moment he would fall. He had longed for his son for so long. Deep inside, he wanted to fall into the pit. They could be together again.

Hamel tried to make sense of it all. Lemmel was alive. Lemmel had been a prisoner for four years. If he had known, he would have rallied the Ridge Armies and attacked. Ridge Nation was evenly matched with the Olmosite Army. While the Olmosite Army was larger than the Ridge Army, Ridge soldiers were far better trained and far more disciplined. But the rage the army would feel over one of their own held in such a dishonorable state would have given the People of the Ridge the drive they needed to reach Pollos and bring the Olmosites to their knees.

Hamel had to pull himself back to the moment. He had begun to dream of wiping out the entire Olmosite people to reach and free his son. The thoughts flowing through his mind were not honorable. Revenge was never an honorable course of action.

His mind raced to one more place—the Dusk. When he had last seen his son, he had been twenty-nine years old.

Four years had passed, and Lemmel should either be dead or at least show signs of the onset of the Dusk. Instead, he looked healthy and strong.

"I said, what do you want, Naromite?" Lemmel asked again.

Hamel discarded all his thoughts and questions for a moment. He desperately wanted to climb down into the pit and wrap his arms around his son, but he could not. He would need his control and discipline if he were to rescue Lemmel.

Hamel felt both at a loss for words and overwhelmed with what to say. He picked a question he did not need an answer to. He spoke quietly, but with his Olmosite accent, "What is your name?"

"My name is Lemmel, Naromite. A man's name is his honor. If he holds to his honor, his name will be praised," Lemmel said, quoting an old proverb.

"And when an honorable man's name is praised, he will give his praise to another," said Hamel.

"Ahh, you are familiar with Ridge proverbs. You are the first who has been able to speak them," Lemmel said, then added, "Your voice is quite familiar, Naromite. Have you interrogated me before? If so, I truly hope I was a difficult and stubborn subject."

Lemmel smiled up at him, and Hamel found a smile creep onto his own face, despite the longing. His heart ached for the years of suffering and the time lost, but he was proud that his son had maintained his honor and his sense of humor. "We have met before, Lemmel."

"Now that is also something different, Naromite," Lemmel said. "You are the first Olmosite to call me by my name. All others have called me Ridger. Does that mean you wish to show me respect?" Lemmel laughed and returned to his forms and training.

"I wish to speak with you about an important matter," Hamel said quietly in his Olmosite accent, "but it is

325

necessary that you keep your voice down. It is necessary that when I tell you a secret, you keep it to yourself."

"Now, why would I wish to do that?" Lemmel asked as he moved around, stretching his muscles. "What would I gain from keeping your secret?"

"Escape," Hamel said.

"Ahh, you have my attention," Lemmel said with a great deal of sarcasm in his voice. He did not slow his training, even a small amount.

Hamel looked around and confirmed that no one was near. He leaned in and, dropping his Olmosite accent, whispered, "Lemmel, my son. It is me. I am here."

Lemmel stopped what he was doing and turned back to Hamel. Rage filled his face, and he spit out the words, "Do not play with my emotions, Naromite. I have been in this pit for far too long. If I did not think you to be a coward, I would invite you down here to see if you could survive longer than the last Naromite they allowed into my tiny, round kingdom. Why don't you grab a ladder, and we will see if you are my Patir? He would not so easily be defeated by a weak man, imprisoned in a pit."

"Lemmel, forgive me. I did not know you were here. All these years I thought you were dead," Hamel whispered. The tears began to flow, and he choked on his words.

The defiance fled from Lemmel's face at the sound of grief in Hamel's voice. "Patir?" Lemmel asked.

Hamel could hear the skepticism in his voice. "It is me. I have come."

Lemmel stood still for a moment, squinting at Hamel. There was doubt written across his face, but Hamel could see hope as well.

"I am sorry," Hamel said. "I cannot draw back my hood to show you my face or else I would risk exposure, and your hope of rescue might come to an end. You can trust me, my son. It is truly me."

Lemmel nodded his head but looked unsure. When he spoke, his voice was full of hope. "If it is you, tell me the last thing you said to me."

Hamel thought back to that moment. Lemmel had stopped by his office early in the morning. He had a smile on his face large enough that it appeared as though his face would split in two. His son had informed him that his wife was pregnant again. They would be expecting a child in the new year. It had brought such joy to Hamel's heart, and he had clung to that moment over the years.

"Tell me! What did my Patir say to me?" Lemmel said, defiance once again entering his voice.

"I told you..." Hamel began, but found his voice had turned gravelly. "I told you that I was so proud of the Patir you had become. I told you that I wished I had been half the Patir you were."

Lemmel sunk to his knees in the filth lining the bottom of the pit. "My Patir..." he began. "You have finally found me. I knew you would. I knew you would eventually come to my aid."

"Lemmel, I had no idea you were here. If I had known, I would have come sooner."

"I know you would have. I dreamed of this day, and it is finally here," Lemmel said between tears.

The younger man stood to his feet quickly, and Hamel could see in his eyes that his mind was racing through the situation, evaluating next steps. Hamel's mind had been working through the same issues. He would not be able to rescue his son that day. He would not be able to do so until he was ready to leave Pollos.

"I know you cannot rescue me at this moment, my Patir," Lemmel said, his voice quiet, but confident. "I can remain here knowing the day is coming. Do you know how long?"

Hamel felt the grief rush over him once again. He felt weak in the knees but angry toward every Olmosite soldier

327

and every Olmosite citizen, including Pulanomos. He had learned Pulanomos was not the friend he had pretended to be, but to take his son and keep him prisoner for all those years in such a shameful state was beyond what he would have thought anyone could do.

"I think it will be many days, Lemmel," Hamel said in a quiet voice. "I would like nothing more than to release you today, but I cannot. The day I release you is the day that they will turn their eyes to me and suspect my involvement. I will not be able to release you until the moment we are ready to leave. I am truly sorry, my son, but you must endure for a short while yet."

"I understand, my Patir," Lemmel said, but his head and shoulders slumped. "It has been so long. Is my wife alive? Has the Dusk settled upon her yet? And what of my children?"

"Your wife and children are well," Hamel said. "I have taken care of them in your absence. The last I saw of your wife, the Dusk had not settled on her. She will be at least another year."

Hamel examined his son once more, looking for signs of the Dusk. Lemmel had married a woman just a year younger than he was. She would last longer than he, but he should be showing signs of the end. "Lemmel, why are you not experiencing the Dusk now?"

Lemmel smiled, but it was not a smile of joy. There was a desire for revenge in his eyes. "They gave me something to drink before they placed me in this pit. They told me it was an antidote for the Dusk. I took it willingly because I knew if it were true, it would give me more time to escape and more time to pay them back for what they have done."

Hamel let that sink in for a moment. It was as he had begun to suspect. If Olmos had an antidote, it stood to reason they were also behind the cause of the Dusk. Perhaps they had created a poison and were the cause of all the death his people had suffered. He was not sure how that could be, but it made more sense than Pulanomos's explanation. If that were the case, he would need to find a sample of the antidote and determine how the poison was administered. He had a theory about the second part, but he still had no idea where he could find the antidote.

"Do not think of revenge, my son," Hamel said. "The desire for revenge will rot your heart and leave no room for love or compassion. Cast that aside. Your rescue is of greater importance. I will give you my water and the food I have. Please eat it and continue your training. You will need all the strength you have to survive the escape and the journey back to our people."

Hamel scanned the Square. He tried his best to make sure no one was watching. Just in case he was being observed, he leaned over the side far enough that he felt he could slip the waterskin out of his cloak along with the food. He dropped it into the pit, trying to avoid the glass and metal shards on the walls. Lemmel picked up the food and canteen. He took a large gulp of the water, and a look spread across his face as though he had never tasted anything so wonderful.

"I must go now, but I will try to return tomorrow and then every day I am able with some food and water for you. You must strengthen yourself so we may leave when it is time."

"Thank you, my Patir. I will do as you say," Lemmel said. "But first, you must know that Pulanomos is not our friend. He cannot be trusted. The kindness he showed to us in the past was not from a heart of love. The friendship we experienced was nothing but a lie."

"I know, my son," Hamel said. The grief grew heavy on his heart. "I am staying with him in the palace. He has kept my identity and presence a secret from the people, but if there were any doubt as to his loyalty, your situation has confirmed for me what I strongly suspected."

Lemmel nodded and said, "Goodbye for now. I will see you soon."

"Yes, Lemmel," Hamel replied, and his voice choked again. "Goodbye, for now."

Hamel stepped away from the pit and made his way directly to the soldier he had spoken with a few minutes before. When he reached him, he said in his Olmosite accent, "Are you in charge of the guard?"

"Yes, Master," the guard said and bowed low.

"Listen very closely to me. The prisoner has value to me, and I require that he not be harmed in any way in the coming days. I will come back regularly to speak with him, and I will expect the same level of privacy each time. Is that understood?"

"Yes, Master."

"I also require that you and your men keep news of his regular interrogations secret from everyone. If word gets out, I will require your life as payment. Is that understood?"

"Yes, Master," the soldier said and bowed low before him.

Hamel left without another word. The plan to release Lemmel was forming in his mind. He did not think he would be able to rescue his son without the death of each and every guard in the Square. It would be a costly mission. The thought of killing the guards felt pleasant. He pushed the thoughts aside, doing his best to consider the advice he had given his son about revenge.

CHAPTER 38

THE DAY OF PROTECTIONS

The experience of finding his son in the pit had left Hamel's insides boiling. His shoulders were tense; his jaw clenched; and everything in him wanted to scream.

As he left the Square, he found himself longing to stop by the restaurant where he had met Gollos. Her former Master had been a wicked man, and Hamel found himself entertaining violent thoughts. He felt it was best to stay away. It would not benefit anyone for the man to die at that moment. It might even hinder Gollos's chance at returning with him to Ridge. He knew as well that he was angry, and he was looking for a fight.

It was mid-afternoon by the time he reached the palace. His strength had mostly returned to him after the infection that had nearly cost him his leg. The last time he had approached the palace, he was concerned his leg was lost, and the pain had been intense. By this day, he was able to move quickly and with purpose.

Hamel walked through the front doors of the palace. The men standing guard did their best to pretend not to notice him. He had almost perfected the Naromite walk on his trip through the city, but it had left his legs tired. It was difficult to walk in such a strange manner.

As he had suspected, no one spoke to him or approached him on his way to his apartment. He had been concerned he might run into another Naromite along the way, but even if he had, they would have no reason to question him.

Once in his room, he quickly removed his Naromite cloak and armor and dressed again in the clothes he had received from Pulanomos. The room itself had been tidied. He had noticed Gollos was quick to serve. He struggled with that one. On the one hand, he wished for her to learn not to be a slave. On the other hand, it was good and important to serve others and care for them—there was honor and strength in caring for others. He did not know how to navigate through such a matter.

He pushed the thoughts of Gollos's view of her own identity out of his mind. He knew he was merely trying to distract himself from the day's events. To learn to live as free would take her a while, but she was in a good place to learn. Not much was expected of them as guests of the High Chancellor.

His mind drew back to his son. Lemmel was alive. His heart rejoiced at the thought, and he found himself longing to return to the Square to "interrogate" him some more. He wished nothing more than to rescue his son and wrap his arms around him.

In his mind, he could see his daughter-in-law and their children. His face broke out in a silly grin at the thought of presenting their husband and Patir alive.

His heart also grieved at the knowledge that his son had suffered as a prisoner for four years. It could not have been an easy life, but the tenacity of Lemmel to stand firm, to continue to exercise and care for himself, and not to take his life as was expected was a testament of his honor.

The grief led his mind once again to the matter of Pulanomos. The man who had claimed to be his friend had kidnapped his son, faked Lemmel's death and betrayal, and had held the man prisoner for four years. Pulanomos was not Hamel's friend, nor was he a friend of the People of the Ridge. He was the enemy.

The matter, however, would have to be dealt with at a later time. A civil relationship would need to be maintained for the time being.

Hamel leaned against the door leading out to the hall. He needed a moment of quiet to collect his thoughts, calm his mind, and focus. He now knew Olmos was either responsible for the Dusk setting upon his people or at the very least, withholding the cure. He knew as well that they were somehow involved with the Beasts. Perhaps every time they found a uniform of a Ridge soldier left at the wall by the Beasts, Olmos was involved. He did not quite understand why the creatures would wrap the uniforms around their deceased Beastchilds, but it would merely be a matter of time before that question was also answered.

Hamel took a deep breath. He emptied his mind, calmed his thoughts, and relaxed his muscles. If he stepped out of his room before he had settled, he worried he would take his anger out on an Olmosite guard.

Once his breathing had calmed and his anger subsided, he stepped into the hall. He wished to find Gollos and eat the evening meal with her. They were growing close, and she made his heart proud as he watched her step further and further from her life as a slave.

Gollos enjoyed wandering through the estate, so Hamel made his way outside. The green grass and the forested area of Pulanomos's estate was breathtaking. Having grown up in Ridge and spending a great deal of time in the Valley Floor, Hamel had grown used to fertile, well-watered land. Gollos, however, had never experienced anything but the dry, arid city.

Hamel searched the gardens next to the palace and did not find the young girl, so he found the main path leading into the forest. The trees were tall; the air was calm; and the sound of birds put his heart at ease. The walls surrounding the estate cut down the noise coming from the city. The noise of the crowds was replaced by the sound of flowing streams and leaves blowing in the wind. Pulanomos had a sanctuary.

When Hamel found Gollos, he heard the commotion before he saw her. Her angry voice carried through the trees along the path.

He picked up his speed, moving toward the sound. When he arrived, he found Gollos arguing with two soldiers. His first impulse was to attack, but he calmed himself. His fuse was too short to step in without first understanding the situation.

When the guards saw Hamel, both men took a step back. They wore the common uniforms of low-ranking Olmosite soldiers. Their armor hung on their bodies in a way that suggested their builds were not in agreement with the physical demands of the military. Hamel noted as well that neither man had done up all his leather straps. Even their stance suggested they would rather lounge on the edge of the lake than maintain any form of discipline.

They were, unfortunately, armed. Hamel noted the presence of a sidearm on each guard, and he decided to be careful. With a lack of discipline often went a lack of restraint. As Hamel approached, each man placed a hand on his sidearm.

Hamel nodded to Gollos, trying his best to hold his tongue so as not to reveal his identity or his ability with the Olmosite accent. Her face, which had been tense and filled with fear, relaxed, and she smiled in response.

"My friend," Gollos said, avoiding the use of Hamel's name as he stepped next to her. "I do not know what these two guards wish, but they have been threatening me. I have

334

tried to return to the palace, but they refuse to allow me. I told them we were guests of the High Chancellor."

Hamel returned his gaze to the two men. His mind raced through his options. He did not think the men would want to use their sidearms unless he attacked, and they could claim self-defense. Using their weapons would bring many guards rushing to the scene, and questions would be asked. He also knew if he were to attack, he would have to be fast or at least one of them would have the time to draw his weapon, and Hamel would go down. He hoped they would be able to slip out of the situation. His lack of ability to speak, however, hindered his ability to talk his way out.

Both guards appeared to have no ranking on their shoulders at all. Hamel suspected they were entirely untrained, but from the condition of their faces, both were familiar with a brawl.

The taller of the two guards spoke directly to Hamel. "We have heard of you. You are the one they call the Mute."

Hamel smiled. He had been told not to speak to anyone. Perhaps they had been told either not to speak to him, or that he was incapable of speech. Soldiers had a tendency to give nicknames to people. He liked his nickname.

Both men chuckled to themselves, and the shorter one said, "Why don't you just walk away, and we'll forget we even saw you?"

Hamel turned to Gollos, and her eyes were filled with fear and confusion. He suspected she was evaluating whether or not he would leave her. He smiled at her to give her confidence and because he was convinced that he could use the guard's ambiguity to his advantage. Ridge soldiers were taught to speak with clarity or face the inevitable misunderstanding.

He bowed his head low to the guards to signify his agreement with their suggestion that he leave and turned to Gollos. He held out his arm for her, and she took it. The two began to walk away.

"No!" the shorter guard hollered. "I meant you turn and walk away and leave her behind! Not both of you leave!"

Hamel stopped and had to force down his smile. He had feared from the start the confrontation would end in violence. He did, however, need to act properly in the situation at hand—not react out of anger towards the problem with Lemmel in the pit.

He leaned down to Gollos and whispered, "Do you think if you were to face the smaller of the two, that you could incapacitate him?"

She quickly shook her head as panic filled her eyes. He knew she might be able to manage it from the short amount of training he had given her, but hesitation at that point could cost one or both of them their lives. He did, however, wish to show her what she was capable of.

"Ahh," one of the guards called out. "I see you speaking to one another. I guess that means you are not mute. Perhaps it is time for us to teach you a lesson for deceiving the High Chancellor's guards."

Hamel spoke quickly and explained the plan. "This is what we will do. We will turn, and I will approach the taller of the two men and stand within inches of him. You will approach the shorter of the two men and also stand within inches of him. Put on a confident face, and when you see me move, strike the soldier as hard as you can in his throat. Strike the way I taught you to strike, throwing the weight of your full body into your fist. You will not likely incapacitate the man, but you will give me time to do so. Once the man staggers back, watch closely how I deal with him, so you are prepared to respond in a similar manner when the time is right."

Hamel saw the muscles in her jaw tighten. A look of resolve filled her once panic-stricken eyes, and she nodded. The two turned back to the guards, and Hamel approached the one on the right, Gollos the one on the left.

Both men placed their hands on their sidearms, but Hamel wasn't too concerned. He kept a bored expression on his face. Few people saw a look of boredom and recognized strategic threat.

Once they were both directly in front of their own target, Hamel slammed the man in the jaw hard enough to knock him unconscious in one blow. Gollos struck her guard directly in the throat, and Hamel lunged onto him as he staggered back. Before the soldier could raise his sidearm, Hamel had dislocated the man's arm and brought his knee up into the man's jaw. The soldier's body slumped to the ground.

He quickly disarmed both men of their knives and sidearms before checking on Gollos. She had a look of shock on her face, but she was nodding her head.

"I think I can do it," she said. "I think I can protect myself. If you just give me some more training, I think I will be able to protect myself and maybe even others. I think I can do it. I think I can protect myself. I think I can fight if I need to. I think I can manage."

Hamel smiled at her and put his hand on her cheek to calm her down. He remembered reacting the same way when he was around seventeen. His first patrol had ended in a confrontation with two thieves. He had talked non-stop the entire way home while the other soldiers mocked him.

He had never asked her how old she was, but he suspected around thirteen. By her age, most Ridge children had received a great deal of physical training. It was good she was a fast learner. "You have done well, Gollos. Next, we will need to address this issue. These two men are still dangerous. If they are not dealt with properly, we will either face them again, or we will face others. An example will have to be made."

"How?" Gollos asked.

"I'm not sure yet, but we will figure it out soon enough. I think the House Steward will be able to address the matter quickly," Hamel explained. He had not met the man, but he knew Pulanomos would not leave his home without clear instructions as to how such matters should be addressed.

"We will keep one of the sidearms. I will hide it quickly. Pay attention to where I hide it."

Hamel took one of the sidearms and found a short, knotted tree nearby with a hole about his eye level. It would be difficult for Gollos to reach it there, but it was the best spot he could find in the few moments they had. He wasn't sure how long before one of the guards regained consciousness, and he wanted to be back at the palace by that point.

The other guard had dropped his weapon when Hamel had dislocated his arm. Hamel put that sidearm back in its holster. He knew the man would have a difficult time drawing it.

"Here is what we will do. I will drag the two men back to the palace. This will serve to humiliate the guards and will suggest to the House Steward that we are not hiding anything. You will ask for the House Steward when we arrive and then will tell him that these two guards threatened us and would not let us leave their presence. You will not mention your involvement in striking this man, however."

Once the two men were side-by-side, and Hamel could keep a close eye on them, he grabbed both men and dragged their unconscious bodies together.

"Gollos, quick, tell me why you should leave your involvement in the fight out of the explanation to the House Steward?"

Gollos's face broke into a large grin. "Because I am small and appear weak. It is best to allow them to continue to think I am weak and insignificant."

"Are you weak and insignificant?" Hamel asked.

"I am not insignificant, but I am still physically weak," she replied.

"You are correct; you are not insignificant; and you can use their perception to your advantage. As for your physical weakness, we are addressing that matter, and I think you are far less physically weak than you believe. But there is one more matter. You must think strategically. When we return with the soldiers, what will the House Steward and guards notice is missing?"

"The weapon," she said, pointing to the one guard's empty holster. "And if they notice it's missing, they are going to wonder if we kept it."

"Correct. How can we solve that problem?"

Gollos's gaze drifted upward for a moment. Hamel took the time to check the soldiers as he dragged them through the forest. Neither one had stirred.

"We will need to do something which will suggest that the weapon has been lost—perhaps while we were dragging them back... the forest won't do as they will just follow our tracks... it'll have to be... the stream."

"Well done, Gollos," Hamel said. "You have a strong mind."

She blushed and grinned an awkward smile before Hamel checked on the soldiers once again. Both men remained unconscious. He removed their helmets and grabbed fistfuls of their hair. He did not feel it was dignified to drag them by their hair, but it would serve the purpose of making an example of the men, and it would be painful. If they awoke during the return trip, they would not remain quiet, so he would not be surprised by an attack.

They made their way back to the palace as directly as possible, rather than follow the twisting paths. It allowed for them to cross the winding stream twice before they broke out into the clearing near the palace.

They were spotted immediately, and nearly a dozen guards rushed to their side. As they approached, Hamel whispered, "Gollos, remember to speak with anger and authority in your voice."

When the guards arrived, they surrounded Hamel and Gollos. Hamel let go of the two men, and they each landed with a thud. The one began to groan, and Hamel leaned down and assisted the man as he returned to an unconscious state.

"What are you doing?" one of the guards shouted. He had drawn his weapon but was not pointing it at Hamel. From the markings on his uniform, he was a Lieutenant. It was reasonable to assume he was well aware that Hamel and Gollos were not to be harassed and did not wish to push any interaction to a point where there would be consequences.

Gollos spoke up, but the anger and authority in her voice came out more like an angry scream. "These men harassed us in the forest. You will go get the House Steward immediately!"

"Now young... lady..." the Lieutenant replied. His face revealed an internal struggle with the term of respect. It would likely be well known she was a former slave, and it was difficult to overcome bias. "I know this is upsetting for you, but I don't see any reason why the House Steward need be involved. These are my men. I will discipline them."

Gollos screamed again, "If these are your men, perhaps you sent them! I don't think we will want to talk to you about this!"

Hamel hadn't realized it was possible for anyone to scream so loud. It was beginning to hurt his ears, and he feared she would damage her voice. He suspected it was the only way she could think of to show both anger and authority."

The Lieutenant paused for a moment and smiled nervously. "No, young lady, I can assure you that I was not behind anything these two men have done. We will, of course, summon the House Steward."

He sent a Corporal running to the palace. From how quickly the soldier returned with the House Steward, Hamel suspected the man had heard the commotion and was already on his way when the guard met him.

When he arrived, each of the soldiers bowed low to the man. He was tiny, but from the look on his face, he was used to authority. His eyes took in everything from Hamel and Gollos, dripping from their trip through the river, to the two soldiers unconscious on the ground by their feet.

"Lieutenant, what has happened here?" the House Steward asked in a quiet, but firm voice.

"My apologies, Master Steward," the Lieutenant said, "but these two soldiers were harassing the High Chancellor's guests in the forest. The Mu... the respected guest of the High Chancellor must have fought back. The two of them returned just now, dragging the soldiers."

"Is this true?" the House Steward asked Gollos.

"Yes," she screamed before Hamel put his hand on her shoulder and signaled for her to calm her voice. "Yes, Steward," Gollos said in a quieter, yet firm voice. "If it wasn't for my friend here coming to my aid... well... I am glad he came."

The House Steward nodded quickly and turned to the Lieutenant. "Lieutenant, my orders were clear. No one was to speak to this man. He was to be treated well. The young lady has been declared free from her slavery and is to be treated as such. They are both guests of the High Chancellor and to accost them is to insult the High Chancellor himself. I do not have time for your disobedience."

He turned to two of the guards and pointed at the two unconscious men. "Guards, kill those two for defying orders."

Hamel took Gollos's arm to calm her as both men were executed. There was nothing they could do to stop it. Hamel had not foreseen such a result.

"Lieutenant, this is your only warning," the House Steward continued. "If these two are bothered or come to harm in any way, even if it is not as a result of your men, I will order half the guard tossed into the pits, and you yourself will lead the way."

With that, the Steward turned and stormed back to the palace. The guards rushed to pick up the bodies of the

341

two dead soldiers and dragged them in the direction of one of the side gates.

"My apologies to both of you," the Lieutenant said, bowing low. "I assure you, this will not happen again. You are safe within these walls." Turning to Gollos, he said, "May I ask where the other sidearm is?"

"You may ask," Gollos said.

Hamel fought to keep a steady expression. She was playing the part well. He was not sure how she would handle the death of the two guards, but she appeared calm.

"Well..." the Lieutenant began, "where is the soldier's sidearm?"

"You will have to look for it. We followed a direct path through the forest. You can follow our trail," she said.

The Lieutenant called over two guards. He explained the missing weapon and sent them back along the path. He then bowed low to Hamel and Gollos once again before he turned and rushed after his men dragging the two bodies.

Hamel waited until the soldiers were too far to hear him speak and whispered, "I'm proud of you, Gollos. You handled that well. Are you okay? I did not expect them to kill the soldiers."

"I have seen many men executed," Gollos replied.

Hamel struggled to believe that such a thing could be true, but he trusted her. He put his arm around Gollos's shoulder and gave her a side hug.

Gollos leaned in for just a moment before pulling away. She stood in silence for a moment as the guards resumed their post before asking, "Will that happen again? Am I not safe in the forest?"

Hamel took in a deep breath and let it out before they started back toward the palace. They had missed the dinner hour, but he expected the cooks would take care of them. "I'm sorry, Gollos, I do not think you will be as safe as you should be. I misjudged the guards' discipline. Their honor is far less than I thought it would be. You will most likely be

342

safe for a few days as the fear of the Steward's threat rings in their ears, but it will not take long before they forget, and a few guards decide to test their boundaries."

"What shall I do?" she asked in a quiet voice.

"Let us discuss this over supper, Gollos," Hamel said.

Gollos remained quiet as they made their way to the dining hall. It was a relatively private room, but there was no freedom to discuss openly. On their way, he asked Gollos to request that their evening meal be delivered to their apartment, and the two returned to their quarters.

After a short while, a knock on the door announced the arrival of four servants who carried enough food and drink for six people. They set down the meal, bowed, and left without a word.

After a short prayer of gratitude for the meal, Hamel addressed the matter of her safety. He desperately desired to share his experience at the pit with her, but he knew her heart was troubled.

"Tell me, Gollos, what is the solution to the matter of safety on the palace grounds?" he asked.

"I do not know, Hamel." Her face was sullen, and her fists clenched.

"Often in situations such as this, we struggle to find a solution because there is not just one solution. Is it possible there are multiple responses on our part?"

Gollos raised her eyes to meet Hamel's. There was confusion mixed with curiosity in her voice as she asked, "Multiple responses?"

"Yes. There is not one solution to this problem. However, there are several things we must do. Each one will add to your safety. Tell me, what can be done?"

"Kill all the guards," she said flatly.

Hamel was disturbed to hear a lack of concern in her voice, but he understood her anger. "Gollos, did they harm you in the forest?"

She quickly shook her head. "No, you arrived just moments after they confronted me."

"I am glad," he said as he reached over and put his hand on her shoulder. "Then let us assume that killing all the guards will not be on the agenda for this evening."

She smiled, and Hamel saw her shoulders relax.

"I should not go into the forest alone," Gollos said.

"Tell me, is that a solution or a response?"

She looked up at him, and he saw anger flash in her eyes. "It is not a solution. The problem still exists. It is a necessary response for the time being."

"Excellent. What else can we do?"

"We can continue our training so I can defend myself," she said.

"Good—solution or response?"

"Response. It still does not solve the problem," she explained.

"You have a strong mind, Gollos. Can you think of a solution?"

"Aside from killing all the guards?" she asked.

He smiled. "Yes, Gollos, aside from killing all the guards. I understand your anger. There are times when wicked things happen, and we desire revenge. Killing is an act that is final. It cannot be undone. It is certainly a last resort."

"Then I think we are left with nothing but responses," she said.

"Good. I think you are right. We do not have the authority or influence in this place to make the required changes. I also hope we will not be here long enough to affect change on that level. I will return to Ridge in time, and I hope you will return with me."

"Why did you leave your home?" she asked.

"That is a long story. I hope to tell you one day, but not today. It would take far too long to explain our culture and all that happened leading up to the events which drove me here. For now, let me say that our people seek honor. I was disgraced before them and ended up here in Olmos."

"Will they accept me among them?" She hesitated, and Hamel waited. "Will I be safe?"

"Yes, they will certainly accept you among them. Our people have no concept of slavery... or at least the honorable ones do not. They will not consider the mark on your neck to be a mark of slavery. They will consider it to be a mark of your freedom. As for your safety, you will be far, far more safe than you are here in Olmos, but I can never guarantee anyone's safety. I once thought all people in Ridge were safe, then I lost three who were quite dear to me. I will, however, do all I can to keep you safe."

"Who did you lose?" Gollos asked.

"Perhaps that's also a story for another time. Let me bring you up to speed on whom I found in the City Square and then we will train."

Hamel took the time to walk through his experiences of the day. He shared about finding his son in the pit and a little of his discussion with Lemmel. Gollos reacted with horror at the thought of his son in the pit for so long but explained that she had heard rumors of a Ridger who would not die. Hamel informed her that he planned to go see Lemmel every day, if possible, to take him food and water.

When he finished, he decided to settle one question on his mind. "This term you and others use for the People of the Ridge, 'Ridgers,' is it a respectful term or a disrespectful term? It is not the way we refer to ourselves."

Gollos's face turned red, and she looked at the floor. Hamel noticed a tremble in her fingers.

"I am not angry, Gollos. I am simply trying to learn."

"Then you will not strike me when you find out what I have said?"

Hamel was at a loss for words. He felt horrified that she might have been struck for saying the wrong thing, but also irritated that she would think such a thing of him. It was an insult to his honor, but he would show compassion. "Gollos, I am not a man of abuse. I will not strike you, except by accident if we are training, and I slip. You do not yet appear to understand the way of my people. I have taken you in my heart as a daughter. It is a sacred and familial relationship. My heart towards you is always to build you up, never to tear you down. You can expect my actions toward you to always fit within that relationship—nothing else. I have had three daughters before you: one born to me and two others adopted as you are. I have yet to strike any of them… except once during training with my oldest, Karotel. I slipped and struck her shoulder."

"Was she hurt?" Gollos asked, looking Hamel's bulk up and down.

"No," Hamel said with a laugh. "She is a strong one. She used my shock and horror at my slip to get past my defenses. It was the only time she was able to knock me down. She looks back fondly on the day and never seems to let me forget it. But you, my daughter, appear to have taken the conversation away from my question."

Gollos's face went red again. "It is not a term of respect. It is a term we use to speak of your people, but we never speak of the Ridge People with respect. They are our enemies. We are taught from a young age that they beat their women, enslave their elderly, and eat their young."

"Do you think that is true, Gollos?" Hamel asked with a large grin on his face.

"I do not think you would find me all that filling, Hamel," Gollos replied with an embarrassed smile. "I believe I am safe from being your dinner for the time being."

"Excellent! I think it is time for some training. If we keep this up, you will put on some muscle and perhaps if we are short on food…"

Gollos gave Hamel a look which suggested she did not think his comment to be funny. She then set to work moving some of the furniture to the side of the room to give them space.

The two trained for nearly an hour before Gollos asked to quit. Hamel had not expected her to last as long as she did, but she had determination in her heart. They focused on self-defense against multiple attackers. He desperately hoped she would not need such skills anytime soon, but he could not take the chance.

CHAPTER 39

THE DAY TO REMEMBER

The following morning, Hamel and Gollos went for another run through the forest. Hamel paid close attention to the guards. Each one gave them a wide berth, and few dared even to glance in their direction. They returned to the room, spent time in training, cleaned up, and made their way to the dining hall.

Hamel set aside as much food as he could discreetly carry in a small pack. He gathered mostly eggs and meat in the hopes of providing Lemmel with the strength he would need. When they finished, they returned to their room, and Hamel changed into his Naromite armor and cloak. Before he left for the morning, he filled another waterskin for Lemmel and reminded Gollos not to wander into the forest alone. She assured him she would stay within sight of many people. Her goal for the morning was to visit the library and spend her time researching whatever caught her interest.

Hamel moved through the palace corridors. There were few people in the halls and corridors. He did pass a Naromite at one point, but the man did not so much as glance in his direction.

His leg felt strong, and he was grateful to the doctor. He no longer felt any twinges of pain, and he found he could move with speed.

When he reached the City Square, nearly two hours later, the same guard he had spoken with the day before approached him. Hamel nodded at the man, and the guard sent orders for the Square to be cleared.

Hamel approached the pit and leaned over the side. Lemmel was well underway with his daily training. He was thin and malnourished, but Hamel could see his son was still a soldier at heart. What weight he did have was solid.

"Lemmel," Hamel whispered quietly.

"Yes, Naromite?" Lemmel replied.

Hamel smiled. His son was intelligent. It would not do to assume a man dressed as a Naromite was his Patir. He would have to prove his identity each and every time he came or risk Lemmel revealing Hamel's presence by accident.

"It is me, my son," Hamel said.

"You call me 'son?' If it is you, my Patir," Lemmel said, his voice dripping with sarcasm, "tell me of the blessing you gave me on my seventeenth birthday."

Hamel smiled. He hoped Lemmel would not bring a memory forward which he could not recall. "I did not give you a blessing on your seventeenth birthday. I was away with the Armies of the Ridge. I could not give you your blessing for many weeks after that day."

Lemmel's face lost the disdain, and he smiled. "I will admit, my Patir, I had begun to suspect I had imagined your visit yesterday. I have pulled out the waterskin you left many times to look at it in the hopes of confirming or denying your presence."

"I understand. I hope to have you out of here soon, my son. I have brought new food for you and fresh water. I have brought enough food for two days this time as I am not sure if I will be able to visit you every day."

Hamel leaned over and, as discreetly as possible, dropped the food and water into the pit. Lemmel then tossed up a rather soiled canteen and pack to Hamel.

"There is some meat and eggs in there, as well as some fresh fruit. Remember, you need to build your strength," Hamel said.

"Yes, Patir."

"Do you have the strength in your heart to continue for yet a little longer?" Hamel asked.

Lemmel laughed and spread his arms out wide, stretching his neck to one side, then another. "My Patir, before you came, I had my honor to keep me going. Now I have hope."

"Good. I plan to have you out of the pit within a week, but I cannot move too soon. As much as I want to, I have to leave you in there for a while yet. There is much to accomplish in the coming days."

"My Patir, I have been in here for years. I can survive another week," Lemmel said. "Do we have much time together today?"

"I will remain about a half-hour," Hamel explained.

"Excellent. Tell me about my wife and children."

Hamel smiled and began to tell Lemmel everything he could think of regarding his children and wife. Lemmel's youngest son, the one he had never met, was nearly four years old and quite the terror. He shared how the young boy had a tendency to climb anything and everything, and Lemmel's wife had on more than one occasion found him on the roof of their house. He shared how the family was growing, and how Lemmel's wife would often tell stories to the kids of their Patir.

Lemmel listened with a huge grin on his face, but there was sadness in his eyes as well. Much had been lost.

When he finished, Lemmel thanked Hamel. "It brings such joy to my heart. I know there are questions you wish to ask. Tomorrow, perhaps you can tell me how it is you came to be in Olmos."

"Yes, I look forward to that," Hamel said with a smile. "You do not think I would be here unless I was disgraced among our people?"

"I suspected that might be the case. I could not imagine another sequence of events that would lead you here and into the palace with Pulanomos."

"Lemmel," Hamel began, "What do you know of the Beasts?"

"I know very little, actually," Lemmel began, "other than I believe Olmos is somehow involved in the increased attacks on the city."

"Why do you say that?" Hamel asked.

"Because shortly before I was taken, we found the uniform of a young Lieutenant wrapped around a Beastchild. It was after a particularly vicious attack of the Beasts. We, as always, believed she had betrayed us. When I arrived in Pollos after I was taken, they tossed me in this pit, and she was here. It caused me to wonder if my uniform was found wrapped around a Beastchild, and I was assumed to have betrayed the people."

"Yes, that is true," Hamel said. He felt guilty for believing that his son could betray their people.

"Do not be troubled over the idea of believing I had betrayed our people, my Patir," Lemmel said sharply. "We all believed that was the situation."

"Did they reveal anything to you of what their involvement was with the Beasts?" Hamel asked.

"No, nothing at all."

"What of the young Lieutenant? What became of her?"

Lemmel shook his head. "She was barely alive when I arrived. They told me if I killed her, they would release me back to our people. When I refused, they shot her in front of

351

me." Lemmel looked off to the side of the pit. It was covered in rotting vegetables and mud. "I buried her body over there."

"I'm sorry, Lemmel."

"It has been difficult not to grow bitter or go insane. I suspect I may have fallen to each to an extent, but I have maintained my honor."

"It is good, my son, that you have done so." Hamel felt he would need to leave soon. The danger in taking too long was that more people would see the Square sectioned off. He did not want to have to explain matters to a true Naromite. "Tell me, what do you know of the poison—the one they use to bring on the Dusk? And do you know anything about an antidote?"

"No, my Patir. I am sorry. I know nothing of the poison or antidote. I have spent most of my time in this pit—other than short periods years ago in a small prison cell or an interrogation chamber. They have given me no information at all about anything."

"That is fine, Lemmel. Do not worry about it. I must go now, but I will tell you this. I have rescued a young Olmosite girl from slavery. If I am not able to make it here, I may send her one day. I do not wish to do so, but you must be prepared for it. She is around thirteen years old, very thin as she has not been well cared for. Her name is Gollos, and if she comes, she will prove her connection with me by relaying the story you asked me about yesterday."

Lemmel nodded his head slowly. "Do you trust her, my Patir?"

"Yes, completely," Hamel replied.

"Then I will choose to trust her as well," Lemmel said with his eyes on the floor of the pit. "It is difficult to consider trusting an Olmosite after all I have experienced."

Hamel closed his eyes. He longed to wrap his arms around Lemmel and pull him from the pit. He could only imagine the abuse his son had experienced at the hands of such cruel guardians. "It will be over soon, Lemmel."

352

CHAPTER 40

THE DAY OF INSIGHT

As Hamel made his way back to the palace, he felt at a loss on how to proceed. He had a plan mostly formed in his mind for Lemmel's release, but the matter of the Beasts continued to trouble him. He had not yet found the information he needed. The other matter, however, of the Dusk and the antidote was an issue which could not be ignored. He needed to find out all he could and return to his people.

His legs still tired quickly from the exaggerated Naromite walk. The assassins took each flowing step as if they were trying to sneak through a dark alley. Hamel felt silly walking in such a manner. Any respect he had for their clan had long since slipped away. The walk served no purpose but as a show for people—declaring the Naromite to be dangerous. His muscles were exhausted from such an arrogant display.

At the palace, he slipped in through the front doors and reached his apartment, changing back into his regular Olmosite clothing. He relished the idea of walking like a normal human being again.

He wanted to find Gollos. He knew that even if she stayed close to her room, she could still be in danger from the ruffians hired to guard the palace. He checked the library, the dining hall, and many of the rooms before stepping out into the large estate behind the palace. He found her pacing back and forth, just outside the door.

When she saw him, her face lit up, and she rushed to his side. "Hamel," she hissed. "The High Chancellor just returned a few minutes ago. He sent me to get you. I wasn't sure what to do. I've been hoping you would return in time. We must hurry."

The two made their way to Pulanomos's apartment. Hamel had been concerned he would return too late, and his old friend would find out he had not remained within the palace walls. He knew, however, the incident with the guards would turn out to their advantage. He could focus the conversation on that topic anytime it strayed too far in a dangerous direction.

Shortly before they reached their destination, Hamel grabbed Gollos's arm. "Gollos, I suspect the conversation we will have today with the High Chancellor will be very enlightening as to his intentions and goals. Pay close attention to everything you hear and attempt to understand what is truly being said. The High Chancellor is not being honest with us about much. He has hidden motives. It is our job to show discernment during this conversation to determine what he is actually trying to accomplish."

"Yes, Hamel," Gollos replied. Hamel noticed she squared her shoulders and stood tall. A look of intensity entered her eyes. She was thriving under her Ridge mentoring.

When they entered the apartment, Pulanomos and Churoi were both present. They were speaking with the new Captain of the Naromites. He bowed his head slightly to the High Chancellor before leaving the room. As the Captain passed Hamel, he nodded but failed to hide his look of disgust for Gollos.

354

Hamel did not appreciate the look Gollos had received, but he found his heart filled with pride for his own soldiers. No elite Ridge soldier would ever show such disgust for a person of another station, nor would they show such lack of control.

Once the door closed, Pulanomos approached with arms outstretched. Hamel was grateful for the control he had developed over his emotions and facial features. Ridge soldiers practiced maintaining a certain level of stoicism in case the need arose. Every part of him wanted to leap upon Pulanomos and beat him with all his strength until the man was within a hair of succumbing to death, but he knew there was much more to accomplish. Not only would his personal desires need to be set aside, but revenge never provided the satisfaction it promised.

"It is good to see you, my friend," Pulanomos said loudly with a great deal of enthusiasm. Churoi approached as well and bowed low to Hamel.

"I am so sorry to have been away the last two days, but I think you will find this to be common. I expect to be here tomorrow, but I will be quite overwhelmed with my responsibilities, so I doubt we will see much of each other." Pulanomos made his way to the sitting room and onto the open balcony.

As the four walked to their seats, Hamel wondered what his old friend had in mind over the long term. He did not think Pulanomos would let him stay there until he died. He also did not expect his friend would throw him in prison to extract information from him. If Lemmel could not be broken, he would understand that Hamel would not break either.

They reached their seats, and a realization hit Hamel. He had two weaknesses that his son had not had for all the years: Lemmel and Gollos.

He did not think they would use Lemmel against him. Pulanomos would assume Hamel knew nothing of his son's incarceration and to reveal such a thing would potentially enrage Hamel. An enraged man could not be expected to cooperate.

That would leave Gollos as his primary weakness. He glanced over at the young woman—the child. She had a strong heart, and he knew she was brave, but it would be agony for Hamel to remain strong if they used her against him. If she were tortured, he was not sure how he would respond. A child of the Ridge would expect Hamel never to betray his people and that knowledge could give Hamel strength, but what of an Olmosite child?

There was no doubt in Hamel's mind that it would eventually come to that point. He would need to be long gone before that day arrived. He would need a timeline, and finding the timeline was his goal for this interaction with Pulanomos.

"What have you been doing the last two days, Hamel?" Pulanomos asked.

"Your hospitality has been overwhelming, my friend, thank you," Hamel replied, comfortably avoiding the question.

Pulanomos nodded and added, "My people are well trained in the work of hospitality."

Hamel knew he could not leave it there. Pulanomos would expect more detail. He let his face break out in a large grin, careful to make sure his eyes revealed joy as well. "I have been exercising, building up my strength. I have explored a bit of your land and enjoyed some wonderful meals!"

"Excellent!" Pulanomos replied. "I have heard from the Steward of your incident with the two guards in the forest. I apologize for such a disgraceful experience. I suspect if you could kill a Naromite with little difficulty, the regular guards would not be a challenge for you."

Hamel let his smile fade and allowed for some of what he was truly feeling to creep onto his face—although not too much, for fear Pulanomos would become suspicious. He knew the safety of a young girl thought to be a slave would not be of concern to the Olmosites and, while they would understand on a certain level, he knew they would not grasp the rage he felt.

"It was a disgraceful experience, indeed. I am grateful I arrived on the scene on time, but it is disturbing to me that soldiers would have such a lack of control that they would accost a vulnerable child."

Pulanomos nodded, but his eyes showed little compassion. "Our people do not think of slaves as having value. It is not in our custom for a slave to be set free, so the thought that a slave might be treated as anything other than chattel is foreign. I confess I have struggled to look on the young... girl... as free. But it is of no consequence. As long as she stays near your side, she will be thought of as your slave and under your ownership. Within sight of the owner, a slave is rarely abused by another."

Hamel turned his head and coughed. He knew he could not maintain a steady expression in light of Pulanomos's explanation. He longed to be back in Ridge, but until that time, he needed to maintain his control. "We will try not to stray from one another for long, then."

"Excellent, Hamel!"

"There is something which concerns me, Pulanomos."

His friend's smile faded, and both he and Churoi leaned forward. Pulanomos asked, "What is on your mind?"

"It is the long-term, my friend. I appreciate your hospitality, but I suspect this arrangement cannot last forever. Eventually, word will get out that you have a strange, silent man in your palace. Eventually, the Naromites might ask questions as to how one of their soldiers was killed. Eventually, you may grow tired of my presence and the effort it takes to keep me entertained."

Pulanomos laughed. "I will never grow tired of you, Hamel. Aside from Churoi, you have always been my closest friend, and I wish to make up for the time we have lost." His friend then leaned back in his chair and raised his eyes to the ceiling in deep thought. "However, I have been asking the same questions. You will need to learn to speak with an Olmosite accent, of course, but I expect I will be able to secure some housing for you. I have some long-term ideas for us to consider."

Hamel nodded, "Yes, that sounds wise. What do you have in mind?"

"Let me ask you this," Pulanomos said with another smile on his face. "I have seen you easily defeat a Naromite—and not just any Naromite, but a Captain. Naromites are promoted based on their skill, yet that man fell to your own skill in seconds." He paused for a moment before continuing. "Tell me, Hamel, how many Naromites do you think you could defeat at one time? Two? Three? Four? Five? More?"

Hamel did not think his friend was so ignorant to suggest that one man could defeat five well-trained soldiers. The circumstances would need to be just right for him to overcome even two, let alone more. He feared if he gave a number, Pulanomos would test that number with Hamel in the coming days. He also suspected that if he said he could not defeat more than two, Pulanomos would also test that number. It would be best to distract him.

Hamel laughed. "I find it is best not to test those matters. Skill can easily be defeated in the face of one false move. If I were to face two or even one again, I might easily lose my life. But tell me, Pulanomos, what does this have to do with your long-term plans?"

"Your presence, Hamel, has revealed a weakness among the Naromite clan. Their training is obviously lacking. So, I have an idea I wish for you to consider."

"Tell me what you are thinking, Pulanomos. Are we not friends? Tell me what is on your mind."

Pulanomos's eyes filled with sadness. "It is this. I know you have been disgraced from your people, and I know that means you can never truly return. I am sure this is quite

358

painful for you, but I wonder if perhaps you would consider a different life here in Olmos. I could use your help in strengthening the nation. You are a great leader of people, a wise and intelligent military General, and a deadly fighter."

Hamel did not nod. It was not honorable to agree with compliments, only to offer gratitude. "Thank you for your kind words, my friend." He waited. He knew the difference between praise and flattery.

Pulanomos held Hamel's gaze for a moment before he smiled again. "I will come right out and say it, Hamel, as I know you are a man who prefers conversation to be direct. I wish for you to accept your exile and consider your life to be here in Olmos. I wish for you to be an Olmosite."

Hamel wanted to correct the High Chancellor. He had been disgraced, not exiled. He was welcome back to the nation at any time. He was even still the most decorated and respected General in the Armies of the Ridge. If he returned, he would need to address the matter of the two dead men in his home, and there would be questions regarding his entrance into Karotel's home, but those would both be trivial matters to clear up in time. It would not, however, be wise to clarify those details with Pulanomos. Instead, he asked, "What would that life in Olmos entail?"

"Yes, you do prefer direct conversation. If you, Hamel, will set aside your loyalty to your own people and swear allegiance to Olmos, I will make you a General in the Naromite clan. You would, of course, need to learn to mimic an Olmosite accent, as I have already mentioned, but I do not think that would be difficult for a man of your intelligence. You could train my Naromites to fight in the manner of the Ridge soldiers and teach strategy to my armies so we could protect our lands more effectively. I would give you free rein, power, and authority to do as you please. You could have anything you wanted: riches, fame, respect, fear, women, land, and more. I would give it all to you."

Hamel had always felt conversation was similar to battle. A direct attack allowed him to know how to react. He could not, however, pretend as though Pulanomos's offer was even an option for him. To feign a willingness to betray his people was a disgrace too great to bear.

He knew as well, however, that to deny Pulanomos right then and there would force his friend to take another route. He did not yet know what that route involved, but Pulanomos would let him know soon enough.

"My friend, you must know that to deny my people would not be an option."

"No, no, no, Hamel," Pulanomos replied. He held both hands stretched out in a placating manner. "I am not asking you to deny or betray your people in any way. I just want to know that you will settle here and make this nation your home, your focus, your love, and your work."

Hamel did not think rephrasing the offer helped Pulanomos's argument. To offer the Ridge training and strategies and, perhaps, even their secrets, would never be acceptable to Hamel, regardless of how it was phrased. He knew he was inviting immediate arrest, which could mean torture and perhaps death for Gollos and, at the very least, the continued imprisonment of Lemmel. But his honor had to be maintained. He also needed to find answers to both the increasing attacks of the Beasts and the premature deaths of his people.

"That, I still cannot do, Pulanomos."

Pulanomos frowned for a moment, then caught himself and smiled again, yet his eyes revealed anger. "Well, perhaps in time, you will change your mind. But it does not matter. You are still my friend. The next four days I will be here and there, busy with many affairs of state, but on the fifth day, I will set aside my responsibilities. I have cleared seven days just to spend with you, Hamel. I hope to hunt with you, perhaps travel a bit, and become reacquainted. It has been far too long, and I wish to spend some extended time together.

If we travel, you can bring your slave—your friend—with you as well, or you could leave her here, and I will give explicit orders to the Steward for her safety. But, for now, Churoi and I must attend to some urgent matters."

Pulanomos stood and then led the way to the door. Hamel could feel a coldness in their relationship. He had learned much and looked forward to discussing it with Gollos.

Back in their apartment, Hamel sat across from Gollos in the hopes of seeing what she had gleaned from listening to the conversation. He was impressed with how she had recognized the compliments as flattery to manipulate Hamel into doing what the High Chancellor wanted. She did not understand the concept of loyalty and felt Hamel's refusal to swear allegiance to be foolish, but she respected it.

"Do you wish to return with me to Ridge?" Hamel asked.

"Of course, but you cannot return. As the High Chancellor has said, you have been disgraced and are never allowed back."

"That is not true. I have been disgraced, but I have not been exiled. To be exiled is to be driven from the land. To be disgraced is to lose your honor among the people. I can return anytime I wish."

"Oh." Gollos's expression betrayed shock. "But I still do not understand why you would turn down the High Chancellor's offer."

"Yes, I know. But I ask you again, do you wish to return with me to Ridge?" Hamel asked.

"Of course, but it does not matter what I wish; it only matters what…" She paused and stared at him in shock. "Wait… if I am free… does my desire to go to Ridge matter?""

361

Hamel waited while she processed her epiphany. He hoped she would learn to think more as a free woman. He held his tongue while her eyes drifted unseeing through the room. After a moment, her eyes regained focus and lit up.

"I can go to Ridge even if you stay here?"

"That depends," Hamel said.

"On what?"

"On two things. First, whether or not you are free. Second, whether or not other things might prevent you from going to Ridge."

"I am free," she declared and squared her shoulders. "So, what other things might prevent me from going to Ridge?"

Hamel laughed. "You are free. From that standpoint, you can go where you wish. But you are also barely more than a child. Because of that, you cannot simply travel wherever you wish. Wait a few years." He paused and smiled. "Also, you have this little matter of the Olmosite attitude toward you as a former slave, your own safety, and the guarded wall that stands between you and freedom."

"What can be done about those?" she asked.

"About your age, you just need to wait. Time is one of those things that removes our youth," he said with a large grin. "You can't grow up faster than time allows. In terms of your safety, it is not right that Olmos is a dangerous place for you, but it is what it is for now. As for the wall, I think I can get you past it, but time will tell. I do not see how you could get past it on your own. But there is another matter that we need to discuss. What did you learn about our future?"

"That you could stay here and be a great man," she said.

He shook his head. "No, staying here and being a Naromite General would not make me a great man. Besides, that is not an option for me."

"We learned that the High Chancellor wishes to spend time with you in a week."

"Has the High Chancellor been honest with us up until this point?" he asked.

"Not entirely."

"Then perhaps we did not learn that the High Chancellor wishes to spend time with me, but that the High Chancellor will be free in four days."

"I don't understand," Gollos replied.

"I do not think that Pulanomos wishes to hunt with me in four days. Consider what we know. I turned down his offer. He is not my friend. We know that he is willing to keep a Ridge soldier for years for no other reason than to humiliate him. On the morning of the fifth day, he will turn his attention to me. What does that tell you?"

"It tells me that on the morning of the fifth day, we might see a different side of the High Chancellor."

"Yes, Gollos, that's true. It also means that by the evening of the fourth day, we will need to be on our way out of Olmos."

CHAPTER 41

THE DAY OF THE NAROMITE

The rest of that day and the following day was spent at the palace.

Hamel did not dare slip out, even to see his son. While Pulanomos was consumed with matters of state, the chance that he might want to meet for even a few minutes prevented Hamel from moving too far from the palace.

To make full use of the time, Hamel and Gollos trained as often as she could physically manage the regimen. The two took horses from the stable and spent much of the day on horseback. She was a quick learner, and in short order, they were able to reach a gallop.

He was encouraged by her progress. He had assumed they would have far more time before Pulanomos turned on him, but that was no longer the case.

They finished the day sore from head to toe from riding and from their physical training. She complained very little, but he could see her wince every time she sat or moved.

In the evening, he took the opportunity to ask her questions. He tried to learn everything he could about the city, about the political situation, and more. He learned very little which he felt would be useful to him at that time, but he did learn where the main industry was situated in the city, including the location for all exports. He would need to explore those locations and planned to do so in the morning after his visit with Lemmel.

The following day, Pulanomos left the palace for the northern part of the nation while Churoi traveled the city dealing with matters of state. Hamel never received any details about their plans, but that did not surprise him. He did not think they trusted him any more than he trusted them.

He wondered if anything about their friendship was real. They had been so close in times past. Few people had been as great a comfort to Hamel during the loss of his wife and young children. Few had stood by him as faithfully as had Pulanomos. He suspected some of it was real, and that Pulanomos had, on some level, been a friend to him, but there was little of that former friend in the High Chancellor.

Hamel walked out the palace doors, wishing he could take Gollos with him. He did not trust the guards, and he did not think the House Steward would show enough concern to keep her safe. He hoped if she remained in a public enough place, she would be free of harm. The journey to the pits would do her good, but he did not think he could get her out of the palace or justify her presence at the City Square.

Before he left, he gave orders for her training to continue. She was to practice what she had learned in terms of combat in their apartment and to practice riding some more. She knew to stay within sight of the palace and was content with such an arrangement.

The moment he stepped into the City Center, the guards went to work sectioning off the area. Within moments, the Square was closed off to everyone but Hamel. He was about to approach the pit when the soldier in charge of the guard rushed up.

"Master," the man said, bowing low. "I must ask for your forgiveness and your advice."

Hamel smiled to himself. The man sought forgiveness, which meant he had done something Hamel would not be pleased with. He followed it up, however, with a request for advice. Such a request could stroke a man's ego and appease any anger. He was beginning to like the man and hoped the lead guard would not be present in the Square when it was time to release Lemmel.

"Speak, soldier," Hamel replied.

"I have not told a soul of your visits. I have kept your orders in every way, until yesterday. Forgive me, Master, but I had no choice."

Hamel's heart raced, and he took a slow, deep breath. "Tell me everything. And tell me of this advice you seek."

"Yes, Master," the soldier replied. "Around mid-afternoon yesterday, a Naromite approached the Square. I did not notice that it was not you. He was a higher rank than you are, but I thought he was you. I immediately went to work with the other guards sectioning off the Square, and once I was finished, he approached me. It was then that I noticed he was not you. He demanded I tell him what I was doing. I had no choice. I told him everything I knew, which is not much, I assure you."

"What did you tell him?" Hamel asked.

"I told him a Naromite Acolyte had been coming to the city Square most days to interrogate the Ridge soldier. I told him we sectioned off the area for him, and that we were not to tell anyone."

"Anything else?"

"He asked if I knew your name, which I did not, of course. Then he asked what time you usually came to the Square. I told him, and he said he would be back. You are early today, and I expect he will be here shortly."

"And what is this advice you seek?" Hamel asked.

"I wish to know how to proceed. I did not wish to disobey you, but to disobey an interrogation from a Naromite Captain would guarantee my death."

Hamel's mind raced. There was no doubt he was out of time. He had learned much but not enough. He had also learned there was something about his cloak or armor which declared him to be an Acolyte. He knew there was a Captain who would be coming to check on him. He doubted the Captain would come alone. He would need to set the stage for what might come next, and he would need to approach it quickly.

"Tell me, soldier," Hamel began. "How do you know I am an Acolyte?"

"It's your uniform, Master. I do not understand why a man of your age would still be an Acolyte, but your uniform reveals it."

"Explain it to me."

"Your armor is slated side-to-side, Master," the man began. "The armor of all Naromite Acolytes is slated side-to-side."

"How is it different for the officers, then, Soldier? You appear to be well acquainted with the Naromite style."

"Master, I mean no disrespect," the man said and lowered his head.

"Answer my question, Soldier," Hamel ordered.

"Yes, Master. When a Naromite is promoted to Lieutenant, the armor is slated up and down. When a Naromite becomes a Captain, they receive a small red line around the base of their neck. When they become a Colonel, the line becomes green. When they become a General, they receive a star on their chest. I confess, I have never seen such a star."

"How do you know all this?" Hamel asked. He had not noticed the slight differences in armor. A Ridge soldier was trained to notice detail, but perhaps he was too distracted with all that was on his mind.

"We are taught it from a young age, Master," the soldier said. "To not recognize a Naromite's rank is to insult the man and to invite death."

Hamel decided he would take a risk. He pulled out the ID papers Mellel had given him in the oasis. He handed it to the soldier and told him to read it.

The man read the papers and then handed them back, closing his eyes and bowing his head. "Master, forgive me for not recognizing your rank. I based my judgment on your uniform. I did not realize you were not an Acolyte."

"There is nothing to forgive, soldier," Hamel said and watched the man's shoulders relax. "Listen very closely. I am on a mission from a very high authority. I am not willing to tell you who that authority is. I will also not be dissuaded in any way by a Naromite Captain or any Naromite at all. Do you understand?"

"Yes, Master," the soldier replied, bowing his head low once again. As he raised his head, he whispered, "Colonel, the other Naromites have arrived.

Hamel turned his head to look behind him. Three men were entering the Square. At that distance, he could see their armor was slated up and down but could not see the small red line. He assumed the one in front to be the Captain, and the others walking behind him were of a lower rank—likely Lieutenants.

There wasn't much time, and Hamel wished to make the most of it. "Soldier, we only have a few moments. Answer me this question. Do you have a pit without any prisoners?"

"Yes, Master," the soldier replied.

"Excellent. I will meet with the three Naromites in the guardhouse. We have an important matter to discuss. Empty all guards out of the house and ensure we have privacy."

With that, he turned and made for the three Naromites. Once again, he felt silly due to the Naromite walk. If it were not for the stress of the moment, he feared he would

368

crack a smile over the thought of the four men trying to intimidate one another in such a childish manner. He remembered his Matir had taught him there were some situations too serious to find them humorous, but he had disagreed. Humor was a joy in life, and he would not live without it.

"Acolyte!" the Naromite shouted. "Kneel and explain yourself!"

Hamel was not sure he could defeat three Naromites at once, but he had a few ideas. Instead of kneeling, he walked right up to the Captain and stopped only a hands-breadth away. When he spoke, he used the quiet growl he had used a few times before to intimidate Olmosites. He hoped it would work.

"I am no Acolyte, Captain," Hamel said and took a small step closer. In doing so, he raised his head just enough that the man could see a bit of the age on his face. He was pleased to see the Captain's mouth open slightly and his eyebrows shoot up. He suspected no man would remain an Acolyte for so long. "You will listen closely to me, Captain, and obey every word I say. I will speak with you in the guardhouse. If you refuse to come, we will speak out here. I do not think you will enjoy our conversation in either place, but perhaps a less public location may be better."

Hamel enjoyed laying out mysterious threats to Olmosites. He had noticed most Olmosites displayed their power in direct ways, but he could tell that a subtle display of power carried more weight with them.

The Captain's jaw quivered, and he hesitated before giving his reply. When he did speak, his voice was calm and controlled. "That will do, Naromite."

Hamel took note that the Captain did not call him "Acolyte." He knew he had already won. In the confined space of the guardhouse, he would have a greater chance of overcoming all three—if he were careful.

369

When they entered the guardhouse, Hamel made a big show of checking all the rooms to confirm they were alone. He then returned to the main room and stood before the Captain, hands clasped behind his back. He waited for the Captain to explain himself, sending a clear message as to who was in charge.

"Naromite," the Captain began. While his voice was not filled with confidence, Hamel could see the man doing his best to act well. "There has been word of a rogue Naromite Colonel in the land. We are not familiar with you. We do not wish to challenge you as I can see you are no Acolyte, though your armor declares you to be one. If you could simply show me your papers, we could clear this matter up quickly."

Hamel had known the moment the men entered the Square that they would need to die. He never enjoyed killing, but he would not be stopped. He reached in his cloak. He was confident the papers would never pass a Naromite's inspection, but he did not think it would come to such a point. As he reached for his papers, he took a step forward, drew his knife and brought it up under the Captain's jaw. The man dropped, and both Lieutenants sprang into action.

Hamel feinted to the left and charged forward, letting the Naromite on his right stumble for a moment. He quickly took down the man on the left and leapt off to the side in anticipation of the second man regaining his footing and charging Hamel's position. The man flew through the space Hamel had just occupied moments before and hit the wall hard. It was not difficult to finish him off.

Hamel raced through his hastily created plan in his mind and made a few adjustments. He had intended to dispose of the bodies in one of the empty pits, but that would not do. Too many would see the Naromites's bodies, and word would get out. He had another idea.

He stepped out of the guardhouse and called the lead soldier to come to him. When the man arrived, he bowed low and said, "Yes, Master. Were you able to resolve the misunderstanding?"

"I was, although not likely in the way you expected me to," Hamel said.

"Yes, Master. Would you like me to remove the bodies?"

Hamel was grateful the man still had his head bowed low. He was not sure he would ever grow accustomed to the Olmosite way. "Yes, soldier, but I have a specific place in mind for the bodies. Go get two soldiers and have them stand guard outside this door while I deal with a matter or two."

"Yes, Master," the man replied and hurried off.

Hamel walked over to Lemmel's pit and leaned over the side. Lemmel was busy exercising but looked up once he saw the shadow.

"What can I help you with today, Naromite? Would you like to come down here and have a conversation?" Lemmel called out.

"I'm your Patir, my son," Hamel said.

"If you are my Patir, tell me this: when I twisted my ankle at age fifteen, did you or my Matir bind up the joint?" Lemmel asked.

Hamel's mind raced back to that day. He did remember Lemmel spraining his ankle, but he did not remember anything about it. "Truthfully, my son, I do not remember."

"Then it is difficult for me to know if you are my Patir," Lemmel said. "Perhaps if you were to come down here, I could see if you fought like a Ridge Soldier or a Naromite child."

Hamel would normally find his son's banter amusing, but he did not feel they had time. "Lemmel, matters are escalating quickly. We do not have much time. You must ask me about something I remember so I can confirm my identity."

"If my Patir truly has crossed from Ridge to visit me in my squalor, perhaps he would remember the first meal I ever had alone with him. Tell me of that day."

Hamel smiled despite the urgency of the situation. "You asked me to vow never to tell anyone of that meal. I have kept my vow to this day and will not break it."

"Well, then, if you are my Patir, I release you from your vow so you may tell me."

Hamel's face broke out in a large grin, and he bent his head low in case one of the guards were to see. "You were trying to impress me as your new Patir. You opened your mouth to say something profound but belched instead. Your face turned red, and you ran from the room. Shortly after you requested a new Matir and Patir, but such a thing is never done. I consoled you and let you know that I did not think less of you."

"My Patir, forgive me," Lemmel said with a laugh, "but I am short on trust these days. I also doubted yet again if I had seen you or not. What is the urgent situation?"

"I will explain quickly as we have very little time. I expect to release you this evening. In a few minutes, I hope to toss down to you the bodies of three Naromite soldiers. In their cloaks will be concealed your food and water for this day as well as a razor I brought for you to shave. I will try to bring more food this evening for our journey out of here as well as a horse for you to ride. I will also post a guard around your pit so you will not be disturbed. When darkness falls, you must change into the uniform of the Naromite Captain. He will have a small red band around his neck. Take any ID he has. There will be no weapons on the men, but I will bring weapons with me tonight. Right now, you must quickly clear away an area on this side of the pit for the Naromites to land, so their clothes are not dirtied too much by the fall. Finally, I hate to ask this of you, but you must use as much of the water as you can to clean your body. I expect you smell of death, and it will not do to have your disguise discovered due to your odor."

Lemmel nodded his reply. He then quickly rushed to the side near where Hamel stood to scrape an area on the floor of his pit clean.

Hamel turned and walked back to the guardhouse using the exhausting walk of the Naromites. When he reached the doorway, he entered without a word and closed the door. A quick search of the building revealed another waterskin and a large bag. He stripped one of the Lieutenants of his armor and stuffed the entire uniform, along with all the weapons he found on all three of the Naromites. He would have loved to have given the blades to his son, but it would raise too much suspicion. Instead, he secured each knife to his own belt so they would be visible to the guards. He then hid the waterskins, food, and razor in the cloaks of the two dressed Naromites.

When he finished, he opened the door to the guardhouse and called the two guards inside. "Quick!" he commanded. "Drag all three bodies to the edge of the pit containing the Ridger. You will do this as quickly as possible, and any questions or comments will not be welcomed."

The men set to work. Hamel led the way out to the pit and made sure neither of the men looked inside. He did not wish for them to see the area Lemmel had cleared.

When they were finished, Hamel had the two men stand back while he called down, "Ridger! Perhaps having a few bodies to keep you company will loosen your tongue. It may not be so bad today, but if you wait a week or two, it might be preferable to simply shed some light on a few questions." He then tossed the body of the Lieutenant he had stripped down into the pit, followed by the other Lieutenant and finally the Captain.

Lemmel shouted a reply. "I will not betray my nation in any way. It will take a lot more than smell to motivate me."

373

"Soldiers," Hamel hollered. Both men jumped to attention and approached his position. Hamel commanded them to retrieve the entire guard and return to the pit. Once they arrived, he gave his orders to the lead guard in the presence of all the men. "Listen carefully! You are to post two soldiers around this pit. Neither one is to show their face to the Ridger. I do not wish him to see any faces at all until I return. The soldiers are also to prevent anyone from visiting the side of the pit—even a Naromite. If they question your orders, you may refer them to the High Chancellor himself.

At that comment, Hamel heard a collective gasp from the soldiers. Only the lead guard remained composed, but just barely.

He continued, "You are likely wondering if he will put on a Naromite uniform. He is welcome to do so. Let him act as if he is one of us. Perhaps it will convince him not to be so stubborn."

The soldiers tried to smile and pretended to laugh, despite the obvious tension. No one in Olmos appeared to know how to act around a Naromite. He suspected the fact that he had just killed three other Naromites made him all the more terrifying in their minds.

"Do you understand your orders?"

"Yes, Master," the lead guard replied, and all the soldiers bowed low before him.

CHAPTER 42

THE DAY OF THE SILQUE

Without another word, Hamel turned and made his way to the western edge of the city. Gollos had given him information as to where the shipments were collected before their export out of Olmos. As soon as he was out of sight of the Square, he found an alley which offered some privacy and changed his armor to that of one of the Lieutenants. He hoped the rank would give him a bit more freedom, at least until he could get some green material to make himself a Colonel.

The western gate was also where he had entered the city not too many days before. He had not, however, realized at the time what all was in that section, nor had he known how important it was to him and to the People of the Ridge.

Once he found the shipping facilities, he moved through each one in turn. No one looked at him as he wandered through the hallways of the buildings or examined the shipments. Some even rushed to get out of his way. His Naromite armor gave him the freedom to enter and act as he wished.

Most of the storehouses and shipping stations contained salt, some vegetables, carpets, and more. None of it was of much interest to him.

After moving through seven buildings, the eighth contained what he was after. He was not yet sure if his suspicions were true, but he hoped to find out.

A quick glance around gave him the flow of the entire place. Everything was collected on one end and moved toward the west side, at which point a dozen or more bags were loaded in each cart.

Off to the side of the large, shipping area, he saw a man giving orders to the workers and took a gamble that he was the manager or foreman. A quick signal drew the man to his side.

"Yes, Master," the man said and bowed. "How may I help you today?"

"What is your position here?" Hamel asked.

"I am the plant manager. I oversee all operations involving the silque."

"Excellent. We will go into your office right now, and I wish to ask you some questions," Hamel said.

As they moved toward the man's office, he rolled the unfamiliar word, "silque" around in his mind. He knew he was playing a dangerous game, but he did not have much time. If he had weeks or even days, he would have been much more cautious. The urgency of the situation required a different approach.

Once inside the man's office, he began his interrogation. "I wish to understand how much you know about the silque. Tell me everything you know about its manufacture, purposes, quantities, distribution, and more. First, you will start with manufacture."

"Master," the man pleaded, "I assure you I know nothing but what has been told to me by the High Chancellor's office. I have not sought out any information. I have been content to know only what your clan has allowed."

376

"Excellent," Hamel replied. "Then you have nothing to fear. I will not punish you unless I feel you are holding something back. I give you my word that if you tell me something you are not permitted to know, you will not experience any consequence from me or by my direction."

Hamel could see the man was not convinced that he would come to no harm, but he began. "I know... that... it is..."

Hamel slammed his fist down on the desk. "I am a busy man. I will not spend an hour here listening to you stumble through your explanation. Spit it out—all of it. And do so quickly!"

"Yes, Master. The silque is manufactured according to your specifications. I am not involved in that process at all, nor do I know anything about how it is produced. It is produced at the silque laboratory. It is then shipped to us and..."

Hamel interrupted the man by asking, "And where are these labs?"

"They are just to the southwest of the palace, right next to the wall, Master."

"Carry on," Hamel said.

"Once it is manufactured, it is brought here in large vats. We bag it up, load it on the carts, and it is taken by the traders to the Ridge Nation. They, of course, cover the silque with other stock for sale or trading such as salt."

Hamel thought that was far too simple of an explanation. The plant manager had omitted some of the details Hamel had demanded of him. Hamel pulled his knife from his belt and took a step toward the man.

"Please, Master!" the man shrieked. "I have not lied to you!"

"No, I do not think you have. However, you have held back information. Also, I asked you for the purposes and distribution of the silque. I would like more information on

377

the distribution, and I would like you to actually speak to the matter of its purposes."

He took another step toward the man. The manager shook with fear and crumpled to his knees. "I do not know much about the distribution. All I know is that there is a contact within the Ridge Nation. That person accepts all the silque and distributes it as he is ordered. I have never met the man, nor do I know what he does with it, nor have I ever been to Ridge, Master. Please, believe me."

"And its purposes?" Hamel asked.

"I know nothing for sure, but I have heard rumors. Please, forgive me. It is difficult not to hear things—even things one should not hear."

"Tell me the rumors you have heard. Do not hold anything back, and you will receive no punishment from me. Nor will I ask you to tell me who you heard it from," Hamel growled.

"Yes, Master, of course." The man was still on his knees, and any fight he might have had in him had long since disappeared. His face revealed a lack of hope that he might survive the experience. "I overheard someone say, once, that the silque was poison. It was used on the Ridgers to slowly kill them. He said that was why they all had such short lives. I would have thought nothing of this, but I heard it from many people and have come to suspect it might be true."

Hamel took a moment to let the information sink in. It was similar to what he had suspected. "Is there anything else you would like to tell me before I leave? I do not want to come back. If I must come back, I will be less kind."

The man's eyes remained on the floor, and he paused for a moment before adding, "Only that the silque has been flowing through this factory for many years. Whatever its purposes or value, much has been delivered to the Ridgers over the generations my family has worked here."

"Excellent. You may resume your duties," Hamel said. He slid his blade back into its sheath and walked out of the room. He needed to reach the palace without delay. Despite his attempts at keeping his actions in the Square secret, he was confident word would spread, and he did not feel he would have much time.

CHAPTER 43

THE DAY OF THE DIVERSION

When Hamel reached the palace, he turned to the south, hoping to find what the man had referred to as the silque laboratories. It wasn't long before he found a large building, right next to the wall. It was well guarded, but as far as he could see, no Naromites. He hoped that would make the process easier. He would not need a sample of the completed product. The product at the shipping yards was the same as what he had pulled off the cart in Benjelton, but he wished to learn what all he could about the poison that was killing his people.

The two men standing guard outside the laboratory shifted on their feet as he approached. The men turned their heads just enough to make eye contact with one another, and their eyes filled with panic. He suspected only certain Naromites were allowed inside. With Hamel approaching, the men would be left to struggle with the question of how to stop an unauthorized Naromite.

The one man raised his hand and, with a crack in his voice, said, "Halt!"

Hamel came to a halt one step away from the man. "Why?"

"Forgive me, Master," the man said. "It is not allowed for you to enter. Only Naromite Colonels or above."

Hamel did not think it would be wise to force his way inside. He felt that would not only be the end of himself, but also Gollos. Such a turn of events would also prevent Lemmel's escape. He would need to devise a different plan.

Without a word, he turned and made his way back to the palace. He wondered if he could find a Colonel's armor in the Naromite barracks but did not think the disappearance of such a high-ranking uniform would go unnoticed. He had been fortunate, in a way, to come across an Acolyte's armor. The uniform might not even have been missed, or perhaps it would have been considered misplaced.

When he returned to the castle, he noticed servants and guards moving about at a fast pace. His mind went immediately to Gollos, and he rushed to his apartment. When he entered, he found Gollos inside. Her face was drained of color, and she was pacing back and forth.

"Hamel!" she cried and rushed into his arms. "I was so scared!"

"Tell me everything," he said.

"About an hour ago, a group of Naromites rushed into the castle," Gollos began. "Some of the servants overheard them saying the rogue Naromite Colonel was suspected to be in the city. Word was sent to the High Chancellor, and he is returning immediately. I was sure they would catch you."

"We must move fast, Gollos, or we will be found out. Tell me quickly if there are any empty apartments in this section of the building."

Gollos's eyes betrayed her confusion, but she answered, "Yes, they are all empty except this one."

"Excellent. Go grab a book you are enjoying, one which you are currently reading, and can remember much of what you have already read. I must change."

Hamel ran to his room and dressed in his regular Olmosite clothing as fast as he could. He then wrapped up the Naromite armor along with the extra armor he had from the Lieutenant and met with Gollos again in the main room. She held a book in her shaking hands.

He tucked the armor under his arm and gently put his free hand on her arm. Speaking in a soft voice, he said, "Gollos, listen carefully to me. You need to calm your heart. Take a deep breath and relax. Convince yourself that you are not in danger and trust that we will get through this situation. We still have a few minutes, but very soon you will have to show that you are relaxed and enjoying your book."

Gollos forced her breathing to slow and relaxed her face. In a few seconds, only the tremble in her hands remained.

"While you are relaxing," Hamel said, "show me the way to the empty apartment farthest from our own, but on the way to the rear of the palace."

She nodded, then led the way into the hallway. He did not think they would have any time left once Pulanomos returned. They had to move quickly.

Once they found the apartment, Hamel was pleased to find the door unlocked. They went inside and hid the Naromite uniforms before heading down to the exit leading to the estate grounds. They saw few people, and no one paid any attention to them.

Outside, Hamel explained the plan. "Listen closely, Gollos. I need you to find a comfortable seat near the palace, but not in a noticeable place. I would like you to settle in and read your book. If anyone questions you about what you are reading, tell them. If anyone asks about me, tell them you have seen little of me today so far and the last you saw me, I was heading off into the forests of the estate. Do you understand?"

"Yes, Hamel," she replied. "I will read my book and tell anyone anything about it that they want to know. As for you, I will tell them I saw you heading into the forest and that I have not seen much of you today."

"Excellent. Now go find your seat and read. Make sure you relax."

Gollos rushed off to find a chair, careful to stay out of sight of the guards. As she found her spot, Hamel made his way toward the wall. The guards' focus was mainly on the outside of the wall and, if he was quick, he knew he could get past them without drawing attention to himself. Once he reached the edge of the forest, he found a path and followed it to a shallow pool not too far from where they had hidden the weapon the other day. He quickly stripped down to his undergarments and climbed into the water. He sat on a rock and leaned back against the side of the pool.

Hamel dipped under the water to wet his hair. He then laid back again, closed his eyes, calmed his breathing, and took the opportunity to think through his next steps. The city would be on alert, and it would be far more dangerous from that point on.

He hoped to exit the city that night, along with Gollos and Lemmel. To make that happen, he would need a way to get out of the palace with Gollos. He would need three horses, a traveling cloak for Gollos, and food and water for their journey. He would also need to ensure that they would not be summoned by Pulanomos. None of those would be simple problems to solve, but he would need to address each one.

He realized as well that he would need to let go of the matter of getting into the silque laboratory. While it was extremely important, it was not worth their lives. He would have to leave it.

He began to work through the plan when he heard the horses approach. When they came to a halt, he opened his eyes and gave a fake yawn as he looked over the men who had just arrived. There were four, all regular guards.

"Get out of the water!" one of the men screamed. "We have been ordered by the High Chancellor to find you and take you to him immediately. Your slave-girl is already there."

Hamel nodded and slowly stood up, taking the time to show how much he needed the stretch. His back cracked a little, and it added to the effect. He hoped he would appear as though he'd been soaking for a long time.

He stepped out onto the bank of the small pool, and the man hollered, "Hurry! The High Chancellor will not be kept waiting!"

Hamel decided it was best to appease them. He made a point not to dry his hair or his body, but instead threw on his cloak, pulled on his shoes, and followed the men back to the palace. Once there, two of the men dismounted and led him to Pulanomos's apartment.

Hamel entered and took a quick look around. There were six Naromite soldiers—three Lieutenants, the Captain, a Colonel, and an older gentleman, a General, with a star on his chest. The six stood before Pulanomos. The High Chancellor was somewhat disheveled in his appearance. Off to the side of the room stood Gollos. Her head was bowed, and there was a bruise on her cheek.

The six Naromites and the High Chancellor eyed Hamel in suspicion. The Colonel was the first to speak. "Where have you been all morning?"

Hamel turned to Pulanomos. He knew he should not speak.

At first, Pulanomos remained silent, but after a moment, he spoke up. "I will ask the man the questions."

He waved Hamel to follow him, and the two walked to the sitting area. As soon as they passed the curtains, Hamel spoke up, "What's happening, Pulanomos? The entire palace is in an uproar. I was soaking in a pool out in the forest when four soldiers on horseback came and demanded I come with them. When I get here, I find Gollos with a bruise on her cheek and six Naromites trying to interrogate me. Did something terrible happen?"

Hamel looked around for effect. He knew his only chance to get out of the situation was to distract Pulanomos until he no longer suspected Hamel's involvement.

Once he had scanned the room sufficiently, he turned back to Pulanomos and in a panicked voice asked, "Where is Churoi? Is he okay? Has he been injured?"

In asking if the matter was about Churoi, the suspicion faded from his friend's eyes. Pulanomos took a deep breath before answering. "No, no, Churoi is fine; do not worry for him. He is simply not back to the palace yet. It is another matter. There appears to be a security threat in the city, and the Naromites naturally suspected you first."

Hamel nodded his head. He hoped the water dripping from his wet hair, and the way his clothing stuck to his body would allay any remaining suspicion. "Yes, yes," Hamel replied. "That would make sense. I am an unknown to them in every way, and the secrecy surrounding me must add to their suspicion."

"I will admit, I suspected you as well. When I returned, the guards had not seen you at all for most of the day. Finding you in the forest was a relief."

Hamel nodded yet again but decided it was best to continue to distract his friend from the matter at hand. "Gollos... she is standing in the corner, and there is a terrible bruise on her face. Who struck her?"

"Do not fret about such a matter, Hamel," Pulanomos said. "The Colonel was trying to get some information from her. It is of no concern."

"It is of concern to me," Hamel replied. "I have taken the child as my daughter. If a man strikes her, I am obligated to come to her defense. To do otherwise is to declare myself a coward and without honor."

Pulanomos's eyes narrowed on Hamel. "Your traditions certainly do not make matters simple for me." His former friend shook his head before adding, "We are in an emergency situation right now. I cannot accommodate your traditions at the moment as I expect the Colonel will not make it out of the encounter alive. I need him for the next couple of days. If you will let the matter go for a time, I will give him to you in three days."

"I will accept that, Pulanomos," Hamel replied, "unless a situation presents itself at an earlier date."

His friend responded with a slow nod and then led the way back to the Naromites. "I have determined that my friend and his… girl… are not involved in any way in this matter. You may look for the answers elsewhere, but not with these two." Pulanomos then turned to Hamel and said, "We have much to discuss here. Please, leave me now, and this evening we will speak again."

Hamel nodded and retrieved Gollos. He was certain the opportunity to deal with the Colonel would present itself to him soon enough. Not only did the man need to learn that it was not acceptable to strike young girls, but the Colonel also wore the uniform that Hamel planned on using to get out of Olmos.

CHAPTER 44

THE DAY OF INTERROGATION

For the rest of the afternoon, Hamel and Gollos did their best to act as if nothing were out of the ordinary.

At the evening meal, they managed to stuff bread and meat into their shirts. As they left the dining hall, they asked a servant if he would bring some water, tea, and some more bread to their apartment. Hamel had, over the previous days, developed the skill of accumulating waterskins. He found four, one for each of them and one extra—just in case. In Gollos's travels through the palace, she had managed to collect some bags for the journey.

They left the food scattered across a small table in the middle of their apartment. They laid it out in a way that suggested they were slobs. Treating the food in such a way would cause it to go stale, but if their apartment was searched, they would be less likely to be accused of preparing for a journey. The waterskins themselves were left empty for the time being. Water in the palace was easy to come by, and an empty waterskin was far from suspicious.

For the cloak, Gollos had a solution. She slipped down to the laundry rooms and retrieved a small cloak her size. Hamel had to explain to her that it was not only for disguise but also to protect her from the harsh climate of the wilderness outside the city.

The matter of the horses would be a challenge. Hamel expected to leave late that night. He knew the stables in the palace would be a busy place. The challenge would be getting out without another Naromite coming through at that time. It would be a simple matter for Hamel to exit the building through the stables, but to have Gollos with him would draw attention.

Finally, Hamel needed to create a situation in which Pulanomos would not summon them. His former friend had mentioned they would see each other that evening, but if they were on their way out of the palace, it would be detrimental to their escape if the High Chancellor called for them. They had to ensure they would not be summoned during their escape.

Hamel had also added the matter of the Colonel to his list of needs. Gollos did not appear too upset about the assault, but he suspected that was less to do with how hard the man had hit her and more to do with the fact that she had been struck many times as a slave. Being used to such a life, however, did not diminish the need to respond.

Finding the Colonel would be a problem. If he had left the palace, he might be anywhere in the city. Hamel suspected, however, that he was coordinating the search of the city from the palace. If that were the case, it was just a matter of finding him alone.

"Let's go for a walk, Gollos," Hamel said. It was evening, and they had finished spreading the bread across their table. The breeze flowing through the windows felt good on his skin.

The two left the apartment and walked through the palace and out into the estate grounds. Hamel took great care to walk at a casual pace so as not to raise suspicion. The sun had not yet set as they entered the forest, following one of the paths.

Hamel did not think they would be accosted. There was too much tension in the city for such reckless behavior. As they walked, Hamel steered them toward the area where they had stored the soldier's sidearm.

When they reached the area where they had hidden the weapon, Hamel watched for guards or servants out for an evening stroll while Gollos retrieved the sidearm from its hiding place. He quickly emptied it of all the bullets and took a moment to show Gollos how to hold and fire it. He hoped there would be no need, but he wanted her to have the feel of the weapon and be prepared.

Once she had pointed and pulled the trigger a few times, he showed her how to work the safety, load and unload the gun, and then, with the safety on, she secured it discretely in her belt under her shirt. She found it uncomfortable, but she nodded her head to let him know she would manage.

On their way back to the castle, Hamel explained his plan. She would need to act with confidence and a great deal of control if they were to succeed.

They would return to their apartment and pack up their things for the journey to Ridge. They would then store everything in the empty apartment before seeking out the Colonel. Once they found him, they would tell him they wished to speak with him and the High Chancellor alone. Hamel expected the man's ego would cause him to jump at the chance to be part of a secret conversation with the High Chancellor, without the General's presence.

"What will we do when we enter the High Chancellor's apartment?" Gollos asked.

"I will challenge the Colonel," Hamel explained.

"Will the High Chancellor not object?"

"I do not think so. He knows I am upset that the Colonel struck you earlier, and that my honor will not let me ignore such an insult to you."

"I do not think it is necessary to do anything about it. As a slave, I endured many blows."

"You must learn that regardless of your station in life, abuse is unacceptable," Hamel said. "Besides, as a Man of the Ridge, I must act."

Gollos came to a halt and asked, "Then will you also kill the High Chancellor? He captured and imprisoned your son for all these years."

"Yes," Hamel replied, "but not today. I expect he will live for a time yet. He will, however, have to answer for his actions."

The young girl nodded her head and began to walk again along the path. "So, why do you think the High Chancellor will allow you to challenge the Colonel?"

"Because I believe I am more valuable to him than the Colonel. I do not think he sees any value in the Colonel at all. He will allow the challenge to continue right until the end. When it is finished, then I will need you to draw the pistol quickly and point it at the High Chancellor. We will attempt to glean whatever information we can from him, and then we will need to bind him so we can make our escape."

They came to the edge of the forest and moved toward the building. The sun was just about to set as they reached the door and stepped inside.

In their apartment, they packed up as they had intended and put the pistol in a small carrying bag Gollos had found. They then moved all their supplies and traveling gear to the unused apartment.

Just before they stepped out of the empty apartment, Hamel cautioned Gollos. "When we begin to interrogate the High Chancellor, understand that he is not a man who tells the truth. He is adept at deception and will use it to manipulate us. Whatever he tells you, do not react in any way.

If he tells us something you know is a lie, do not correct him. If he tells us something we already know, do not give him any indication we already know. Just be calm and relaxed. If he mentions Lemmel, act as if you have never even heard his name."

Gollos nodded her head, and the two left the apartment. The stairs leading down to the main level led into another hallway which branched off to the dining room, the estate grounds, the main hall, and more.

They took the one to the main hall, hoping to find the Colonel. When they did not find him, they searched some of the smaller hallways and moved past the Naromite barracks in the hopes of seeing him. Eventually, Gollos asked a passing Naromite who informed them that the Colonel was expected to return at any moment.

"Excellent," Hamel whispered to Gollo. "This is perfect. We will head straight to the stable."

At the stable, they found the Colonel just riding in. Upon seeing Hamel and Gollos, he scowled.

The man dismounted and handed his horse off to a stable boy. While the focus of the stable hands and the Colonel was elsewhere, Hamel casually grabbed a length of rope off a nail on the wall and stuffed it in Gollos's bag.

When the Colonel had collected everything from the saddlebags of his horse, he walked toward the doorway leading into the palace. Hamel and Gollos stepped into his way, and both bowed low before him.

"Please, Master," Gollos began. "We must speak alone with you and the High Chancellor. It is of utmost importance that we speak with the two of you immediately. That is, if you would humble yourself to such a level as to hear what we have to say."

Once again, Hamel was impressed with how adept she was at interacting with Olmosites in positions of power.

The Colonel grunted and said, "Follow me."

He led them through the hallways to the stairs leading to Pulanomos's apartment. At the door, the two soldiers bowed low and stepped aside for them to enter, then closed the door behind them. Inside, they found Pulanomos working at his desk. The Colonel announced that the two guests of the High Chancellor had an important message for the two of them.

As soon as they were inside with the door closed, Hamel made a big show of closing all the windows and doors leading out to the balcony. He was confident the Colonel would see this as an indication of how secret the information was.

Pulanomos growled and said, "You could not wait, could you?"

Hamel decided it would not hurt to reveal his Olmosite accent at this point to Pulanomos. The man would just assume he had been practicing it. "No, High Chancellor, I could not wait any longer. There are matters that must be dealt with this evening."

Turning to the Colonel, he said with his Olmosite accent, "This young girl has been taken into my family and is my daughter. You have struck her, and I will not ignore such an attack on her dignity."

"What?" the Colonel hissed. "This is nothing more than some archaic defense of honor? High Chancellor, we do not have time for this idiocy. I know this man is your friend. What are your orders?"

Pulanomos sighed loudly before saying, "Fight him, Colonel. You might find he is more than a match for you."

Hamel knew he had not yet met an Olmosite soldier who was any challenge to him, but he would not assume he could best the Colonel. Overconfidence had claimed the lives of many, and he would not be its next victim. Not only was the man older and far more experienced than the other Naromites he had fought, but he was also a similar height and build to Hamel.

He approached the Colonel cautiously and waited. He knew it would be best to let the man make the first move. It would also reveal the man's patience and discipline.

Hamel did not have to wait long for the man to lunge. He moved slightly to the right, just out of the way of the Colonel and brought his fist up into the Naromite's ribs. The man went down with a thud but sprang to his feet and attacked. The next attack was far more cautious and deadly. The man had not drawn his weapon, but his fists flew faster than Hamel had expected.

Hamel took a blow to the stomach and one to the side of the head within moments of the man's second attack. He had not been bested in hand-to-hand combat in many years, and he felt the fear bring a surge of strength into his arms. His mind cleared, and he fought back in a frenzy.

The man was difficult to overcome, but Hamel managed to break through his defenses and connect squarely with the man's jaw. The Colonel hit the ground hard and did not move.

Hamel examined the man who had nearly defeated him until Pulanomos's voice broke through the silence. "You are probably best to kill him, Hamel, not just knock him out. If you let him live, he'll be angry when he comes to. Oh, and by the way, excellent work on learning the Olmosite accent."

Hamel had no intention of killing the man. He had responded to the insult. To kill the man was not only unnecessary but was also taking matters too far. It was not the Ridge way.

Instead, he turned to Gollos and nodded. She pulled out the sidearm and pointed it at Pulanomos, clicking the safety off.

"What is this, Hamel?" Pulanomos hissed with both anger and panic in his voice. "Your slave comes here with a gun and holds it in my face—after all I've done for you!"

Hamel checked the Colonel again and then heaved the man over his shoulder. The man was heavy, but Hamel carried him to the door behind Pulanomos's desk. On the other side of the door was a large room with doors open to what appeared to be the High Chancellor's bedroom, a lavatory, a small library, and a meeting room.

He tossed the man down on the floor with a complete lack of gentleness and waved Pulanomos to follow them. "Come with me, friend."

Pulanomos stopped in the doorway and smiled, "I could scream for help, and the two Naromites at the door would come to my aid."

Hamel had dealt with many defiant men in his time. It was always a matter of finding what the man loved. Pulanomos loved himself more than anything. "You could, my friend, call them, but you have to ask yourself whether or not you think Gollos here would shoot you. They would certainly come, but I think you would be dead. They might stop me, but it is unlikely. If they do not stop me, they would be dead as well, and you would have no one to carry out your revenge. So, feel free to scream if you like, but it will cost you your life."

Hamel grabbed Pulanomos's shoulder and pulled him into the other room before his former friend could fully consider his options. While Gollos held the High Chancellor at gunpoint, Hamel stripped the Colonel of his armor and tied him to a chair using part of the rope from the stable. He gagged the man in case he awoke, but Hamel was confident the man would not come to for several hours.

After searching Pulanomos for weapons, he tied him to a chair and set him in the center of the room. Hamel did not think he would gain much from the High Chancellor but hoped he could gain at least a little information.

"I treated you with honor, Hamel," Pulanomos began.

Hamel noted the attempt to motivate guilt. That approach had never been effective. When Hamel knew the path he needed to walk, he walked it—confidently.

394

"There are some things I wish to know, Pulanomos. I know you are not my friend. I know this because I pay attention to the details. You know this yourself. Let us skip by the manipulation and jump right to the matters before us. I suspect you may have once been my friend, but you are no longer. I wish to know two things. The first thing I wish to know is how you are poisoning my people, so the Dusk overtakes them."

"I told you already, Hamel," Pulanomos began. His voice cracked and wavered. Tears streamed down his face as he continued. "We do not know why. We have tried so hard to find an answer." As he continued, his voice raised to a shriek. "You are our allies! You are our friends! You are my closest friend, Hamel! You have always been like a brother to me!" He choked out the last words.

If Hamel had not seen his son in the pit, he might have felt some compassion for the man and perhaps even been drawn into his deceptive words. Instead, he pulled up another chair and sat down across from Pulanomos.

"Listen, brother," Hamel began, adding some sarcasm to his voice. He would not torture his former friend. The People of the Ridge would never stoop to such a level. He also did not expect Pualnomos to give him any information that wasn't tainted with deception. He did, however, think that he might be able to piece together some truth amidst the man's lies.

He continued. "I am not without means of gaining information—even here." At that statement, Pulanomos's eyes brightened, and Hamel suspected he was mentally moving through the entire palace staff, evaluating which one he thought might be capable of treason. "I know we are not friends. I know you are not to be trusted. Tell me how you are poisoning my people."

Pulanomos shook his head again and choked back a sob. "We are friends, Hamel; I would never harm you!"

Hamel had to admit, the former Ambassador was an expert manipulator. The tears flowed freely, and if Hamel had not known better, he would have fallen for every word.

"All right, then perhaps you could tell me something else," Hamel said.

"Of course, Hamel," Pulanomos said as he gasped for air. "I will tell you anything. I have no secrets from you."

"Tell me why there is a statue of me outside your palace."

Pulanomos laughed, despite the feigned grief. "The statue? You want to know what the statue is? That is a testimony to our friendship! It is there to declare to all of Olmos that you and I are friends forever and that you were my brother, my comrade, my mentor."

Hamel slammed his fist into the side of Pulanomos's head. He did not wish to knock him unconscious, but he did wish to anger him. He then grabbed a piece of cloth from a table and ripped a gag similar to the one he had used on the Colonel.

As he was about to gag the man, he was stopped by Pulanomos growling out two words, "Your son…"

Hamel stopped and crouched down so his face was level with his former friend. Pulanomos might be an excellent manipulator, but Hamel was just as adept at acting. "What about my son?"

"Lemmel… it's about Lemmel."

"Lemmel?" Hamel asked. "We found his bloody uniform wrapped around a Beastchild at the wall. Lemmel was declared a traitor of the people."

"He is not dead, Hamel," Pulanomos said through tears.

"Not dead?" Hamel asked. He hoped Gollos would not give away that he already knew this information.

"No, he's not dead."

"Do you think I will be this easily manipulated?" Hamel asked, allowing rage to enter his voice.

"No, Hamel, it's true. He's not dead. He was captured by the Naromites some years back. That was before I had control of the Naromite clan. They interrogated him for weeks, despite my resistance. When they were finished, they were going to kill him. I used every last bit of influence I had to keep him alive. He is alive today!" Pulanomos stopped and hung his head, gasping for each breath.

Hamel paused for effect and then asked, "If this is true, why have you not released him now? You certainly have the authority over the Naromites now."

"No," Pulanomos replied, "I cannot. He has been charged with crimes against Olmos, and even I cannot release him. All I could do was keep him alive."

"Where is he?" Hamel hissed as he grabbed Pulanomos by his shirt. He noticed as he shook his former friend, a gleam of victory appeared in Pulanomos's eyes.

"He is in a cell," the High Chancellor explained. "The prison is ten miles to the south of the city. If you take the main southern gate and follow the road, you will find it. I can give you a note, telling them to release him into your custody for interrogation, but that is all I can do. It will be up to you to get him safely back across the border."

Hamel tied the gag securely onto the man's face. He then tied both chairs together and blindfolded each man. He did not think it would hold them forever, but he would not need forever. He would just need a few hours. Before he left the room, he whispered in Pulanomos's ear, "I will tell my people of the poison. They will be... displeased with Olmos."

They stuffed the Naromite's armor and weapons neatly into Gollos's bag. It did not fit well, but she was able to close the bag. She struggled under the weight, but Hamel told her she would only need to carry it until they were out of sight of the two Naromites guarding the door.

When they stepped outside the apartment, Hamel closed the door tight. He addressed the two Naromites in his

Olmosite accent, "The High Chancellor is with the Colonel. Do not disturb them."

The one soldier growled, and the other asked in anger, "Do you think we take orders from you?"

"No, Naromite, I do not. I do, however, think that you would appreciate solid advice when you hear it."

The man paused for a moment and nodded his head before saying, "Off with you. The High Chancellor will not be disturbed again this evening."

Hamel and Gollos made their way back to the empty apartment. Gollos put on her traveling cloak while Hamel put on the Colonel's uniform. The hood was such an effective disguise, he thought the stable boys might even mistake him for the exact same Colonel they had met just an hour before.

They grabbed all their supplies, including their food and filled up all four wineskins with water for their journey. They did not speak during the time in the apartment. Both focused on preparing themselves to leave.

Once they were ready, they rushed to the stable where Hamel demanded three horses. The mounts were prepared, and Hamel and Gollos climbed into their saddles. Hamel took the reins of the third horse.

On horseback, the trip to the Square took only ten or twelve minutes. While they rode, Gollos asked, "Why did you not tell the High Chancellor you knew your son was alive? Why act as though you believed him?"

"Tell me, Gollos, when the High Chancellor is found and released, where will he send his soldiers to find us?"

Gollos laughed and said, "Of course! I did not think of that. What will he do once he finds we did not go south?"

"He will know we did not believe him and will search for us to the west, toward Ridge. We will, however, have a night and half a day's ride on them. We will not be able to move as fast since you are still learning to ride, and it is possible Lemmel will be too weak to maintain a fast pace. We will need every minute of lead we have." Hamel smiled. "It was a convenient time for Pulanomos to tell such a lie."

When they reached the Square, most of the guards were unfamiliar to Hamel, aside from two men he recognized from earlier in the day. They quickly informed the lead guard that the Naromite was there, and the man began to section off the Square. The lead guard from the day shift had obviously passed word along to prepare the night guard.

There were six guards in total. Two men stood sentry by Lemmel's pit, while the other four stood guard at the entrances to the Square. He waved to the four men to indicate they were to meet him at the guardhouse. When the first two arrived, he took them inside and quickly killed them. When the other two guards reached the guardhouse, he did the same.

When he and Gollos reached the pit, Hamel approached the first guard. In a moment, the man was dead. The other guard turned and saw Hamel, dressed as a Naromite Colonel standing over the body and quickly resumed his sentry position. Hamel suspected they would not challenge a Naromite, even if he killed one of their number.

The second guard went down just as easily, and Hamel moved to the side of the pit. In the darkness, he could just make out a shape. "Lemmel?"

"What do you want, Naromite?" Lemmel called up.

Hamel ignored the question and raced back to the guardhouse. Inside, he found a large ladder and carried it out to the pit. Lowering the one end down into the darkness, he felt Lemmel grab the other end and set it securely on the ground. Within seconds, he could feel the vibration on the ladder of someone climbing up.

Lemmel set foot on the ground, and Hamel threw back his hood. The two men stared at one another for a moment before stepping into an embrace. Hamel could not contain himself. The tears flowed, and the two men wept together.

It was Lemmel who first ended the reunion. "I do not know the situation, my Patir, but I suspect we do not have time for many tears."

Hamel laughed, "Of course not! It's time to leave Olmos."

They climbed onto the horses, and as they did, Hamel introduced Lemmel to Gollos. Lemmel said, "Ahh... I see now what caught your eye with this one. Even in the dim light, I can see a similarity to Karotel. Are you grooming another future Honored Matir?"

Hamel did not reply. Instead, he smiled in response to Gollos's look of confusion.

The three rode out of the Square toward the west side of the city. Hamel was pleased. He had certainly not fulfilled his mission to determine what was agitating the Beasts, but what he had learned about the silque was far more valuable. And to know he was riding home with his lost son was far more than he could ever have hoped for.

They were heading for the gate, heading for the wall, heading for home.

CHAPTER 45

THE DAY OF GATES

The three rode west at a trot. The sun had long since set, and there were no people on the streets, aside from soldiers or guards. Hamel hoped a steady trot would help them make good speed, but not attract too much attention.

At one point, they were stopped by a Naromite patrol. In the light of some nearby torches, Hamel's Colonel colors quickly dissuaded the young Lieutenant from too many questions. Within the hour, they reached the city gate.

The gate was closed for the night, and when they reached the guard, Hamel dismounted. He approached the soldiers and demanded the gate be opened.

The soldier bowed low. "Forgive me, Master, but I am under orders direct from the palace not to allow anyone to leave the city this evening."

"We have just come from there, less than 2 hours ago, soldier," Hamel replied. "I will give the order to allow you to open the gate. Open it now, or you will not be returning home in the morning."

The man remained bowed for another moment before saying, "Yes, Master, I will do as you say. I must report to the Captain on duty."

"Do as you must," Hamel said, and slowly walked back to his horse.

A moment later, a Naromite Captain came out of the guardhouse. Hamel had noticed the Naromites did not salute or bow to one another. He suspected it was a matter of pride for them, but also an attempt to hide any weakness or humility.

Hamel decided to speak first. "Captain, why is the gate not open for me? I have given the order."

The Captain studied Hamel for a moment. The hood was well over his face, and Hamel knew the man would only be able to see his chin in the darkness.

"We have been ordered by the General to seal up the gates. I have been posted here to ensure that the order is followed," the Captain said.

Hamel could not help but notice the man's hand resting on his belt near his knife. He did not think the man would attack a Colonel with a Captain sitting on a horse a short distance away. He clasped his hands behind his back in a show of confidence.

"Captain, I am not accustomed to my orders being questioned," Hamel said. "I have grown used to my orders being fulfilled immediately."

Hamel worked through the problem at hand. He knew the man could not defy the order, even to a Colonel. But they needed to get through. He would have to make it appear as though the soldier could make a safe compromise.

"Tell me, Captain," Hamel began, "why you have been commanded to seal the gate?"

"There is, as you undoubtedly know, Colonel, a man pretending to be a Naromite in the city."

Hamel felt confident he had the man where he wanted him. "And tell me, Captain, what do you know of this man?"

"We know nothing, other than he is dangerous."

402

"But that is not true, Captain," Hamel said. He added just a touch of anger into his voice and watched as the Captain shifted on his feet. "We know that this man has a Naromite uniform, correct?"

"Yes, Colonel, that is true."

"And we know something of this uniform, correct?" Hamel asked.

"Yes, Colonel, we know that the uniform he is wearing is an Acolyte's uniform."

"Correct!" Hamel said. "So, we know that it would be foolish to think that I am that man."

The Captain paused for a moment and then barked, "Yes, Colonel."

"And we know as well, Captain," Hamel said quietly, taking a step closer to the Captain, "that a man of your rank would like to continue to be promoted, yet that process might be more difficult with a Colonel as an enemy."

The Captain did not move for a few moments. Hamel feared he had misjudged the man and was not winning the battle of wits, but then the man began to nod. "Yes, Colonel, I suppose that would be true. But it would also be true that it would be even more difficult if I had a General as an enemy."

Hamel nodded. "So, you are at a crossroads, Captain. Consider the risk. If you stand in my way, you know I will be your enemy. If you let me pass, there is a chance the General may hear of this, but you would have to ask yourself who here would tell him."

The Captain paused yet again for another full minute before he smiled. Nodding to Hamel, he said, "Yes, Colonel," before turning back to the gate and yelling, "Open the gate by order of the Colonel."

The gate opened, and, after Hamel remounted his horse, the three rode through at a walk.

Outside the city, it was far too dark to move at a decent speed. If they moved at a trot and a horse lost its footing, Hamel feared one of them might be thrown from the saddle.

Hamel hoped to be at the border town by mid-to-late afternoon the next day, although he suspected it might take longer with the three of them. On the way to Pollos, the journey had taken twelve hours, but he had been able to move at a steady speed since he was strong and by himself. On the return journey, Lemmel would be limited by his years in the pit, and Gollos was still new to riding.

After a few hours, Lemmel and Gollos needed a short rest. Both were sore, and their skin was worn raw.

Hamel took a seat on a large boulder. Both Lemmel and Gollos kept to their feet, and Hamel smiled as he remembered his early days as a soldier. It was common after the first full day of riding to take the new recruits to a banquet in the evening. The banquet would require everyone to sit for hours listening to long, boring speeches. He had, as a young man, felt it was a cruel and terrible way to treat people but had done the same thing himself to new recruits years later. He was tempted to ask each to sit and then to embark on a long, boring story.

He noticed Lemmel's eyes fixed on him with a knowing smile. His son had been a Colonel. He would have given many of those long, boring speeches for no other reason than to torment sore recruits.

After a moment, Lemmel turned to Gollos. "I feel that we have not been properly introduced. My name is Lemmel. I am the adopted son of Hamel."

"Hamel has told me of you," Gollos said. She had taken the submissive posture she regularly took around anyone other than Hamel.

"Why are you standing like that, and why will you not make eye contact with me?" Lemmel asked in a harsh voice.

"Lemmel," Hamel cautioned. He noticed Gollos shrink back in fear.

404

His son hesitated before softening his tone. "I apologize. I have lived a life where no tact was necessary for many years. I did not mean to offend. It is simply that you stand as though you fear me. I am not one to fear."

Hamel examined Gollos's reaction. He was curious to see if she could navigate her way through the situation. She took a deep breath, squared her shoulders, stood tall, and looked Lemmel in the eye. "I apologize, Mas... Lemmel. I have lived a different life than the one I now live and have not yet grown accustomed to speaking to people as though I am their equal."

"Ahh... I see," Lemmel said with a thoughtful expression on his face. "I have long suspected that the people of Olmos kept slaves. Was that the case with you?"

"Yes, Lemmel," Gollos said, this time with more confidence.

"Well, we are returning to the People of the Ridge," Lemmel said proudly. "No one there will tolerate such a barbaric practice so you will have to get used to speaking to people with respect, not fear."

Gollos nodded her head but stepped up next to Hamel. She whispered, "What is the difference between respect and fear?"

Hamel leaned in close and whispered, "One is driven by love, the other by power."

She nodded and turned back to Lemmel. The two continued their conversation while Hamel checked the horses and fed them. They had stopped by a small creek. The horses drank their fill, and Hamel topped up the waterskins. They had a long journey ahead, and they were only just at the beginning. They would need to push hard to reach Ridge Nation without incident.

Hamel had his sights set on Benjelton. If they rode straight through, they would make it there by evening the following day, but he did not think either the horses or his son and daughter would be able to manage the journey.

He was not sure how long before they would be pursued. Pulanomos was not likely to be found by a servant or a soldier until the morning. Once he had been found, the High Chancellor would send soldiers to the south as he would assume that Hamel had believed the story about Lemmel. Hamel hoped the that he, Gollos, and Lemmel would have twelve or thirteen hours of travel time between them and their pursuers.

After another ten minutes, Hamel announced it was time to move. The sun would rise in less than four hours, and he wanted to get farther along the road before they stopped for any length of time.

The three mounted, and Hamel watched both Lemmel and Gollos grimace as they settled into the saddle. They set out at a slow pace, careful not to move too fast in the dark.

When they finally did stop for a few hours rest, they moved into the cover of a small forest. They set up camp, and within moments, all three were asleep.

When Hamel awoke, the sun had just come up and was shining directly in his eyes. He turned away and shook his head to try to push the exhaustion down. He suspected he had only slept for just over an hour, but he hoped it would be enough.

He woke the others, and they set out again along the road. Just after dark, they reached the border town, and Hamel struggled to remember the correct path through the city to the wall. The city was laid out poorly, and many of the buildings looked the same. On his first journey through, the distraction of the injury to his leg along with the shock of seeing people who had lived far longer than he would have thought possible had occupied his mind far more than which street was the proper one to take.

Throughout the day's travel, there had been no sign of pursuit, but Hamel did not think they would be far behind. He pushed them through the streets as quickly as he could.

At the gate, Hamel counted fifteen Olmosite guards within sight, although all were on the top of the wall. He dismounted and banged on the door of the guardhouse, hoping to find the soldier in charge. He did not want to fight his way through; nor did he think all three of them would make it through such an attempt. When a guard opened the door, Hamel stepped inside and left the other two on their horses.

"Master," the guard began. His voice was steady, but his eyes betrayed his fear. "It is good to be visited by a man of such rank. How may I assist you this evening?"

Hamel examined the room, the exits, and the condition of all six guards. They each bowed low before him, and no one moved or spoke aside from the one guard before him.

"I will have you open the gate for me, the Captain, and our companion," Hamel replied, adding a cold, threatening tone to his voice.

"Yes, Master," the man replied, "I can open it for you at dawn. As you are aware, it is against the law to open the gate after sundown."

Hamel had feared that was the case. He despised having to resort to threats at every turn, but Olmosites only recognized power and intimidation. "Captain," Hamel began, allowing his voice to drip with disdain. "I have grown accustomed to men obeying my every word without question. I am not concerned with trivial matters of the law. What I am concerned with is soiling my outfit."

The Captain remained in his deep bow, bent over in silence. Hamel hoped the man would not fully understand at first. "Colonel?" the Captain asked.

"I mean I do not wish to cover my garments with blood before I even leave Olmos," Hamel explained. "Do you think that you will be a challenge for me? Do you think that your fellow soldiers will come to your aid at the risk of offending the Naromites? Even if they were to try to help you, do you think I have not killed six men at one time before?"

The Captain's breathing sped up, and when he spoke, his voice was no longer steady. "Master, I do not wish to offend you or disobey you. I have orders that I must follow."

"Yes. You do have orders, Captain," Hamel said, nearly shouting. Each of the six men cowered in fear, their heads bowed low to the ground. He did not know what the Naromites had done to instill such fear in armed soldiers, but he hoped it would once again work to his advantage. "Your orders, Captain, are to open the gate for a Naromite Colonel, a Captain, and their traveling companion. Do you think I will ask you again? Do you think I will not simply kill you and move on to the Lieutenant who is kneeling behind you? Perhaps he would like to be Captain in your stead?"

Hamel drew his knife, and the man stepped back. He grieved that even the final exit from the country would require bloodshed. He hoped the man would submit. "I will allow you to draw your blade, Captain. I will not kill you, unarmed. I will give you a fighting chance." He then turned to the man behind him. "Lieutenant, I would encourage you to consider your response to me when I promote you to Captain and order you to open the gate."

"Nooo!" the Captain hollered. "Forgive me, Master, I have acted the fool. I will open the gates for you immediately."

The Captain jumped to his feet and turned to the five men behind him. "Go immediately and command the men to open the gate on the Colonel's orders. If they question you, kill them, and open the gate yourselves."

Hamel followed the men out of the guardhouse and climbed back into his saddle. In less than a minute, the gate began to open. Before they were able to move through, the

Captain returned with his men and escorted them through to the other side.

When they were out of earshot of the soldiers, Gollos whispered, "How long of a ride will it be to your people, Hamel?"

"It is a solid six-hour ride to Benjelton, but we will take longer. Benjelton is an abandoned city. We may end up spending some time there before we continue on our way. From Benjelton we have about the same distance again to an oasis followed by a decent day's ride by horseback to the city. But we will not be going directly to the Capital. We must warn someone first."

CHAPTER 46

THE DAY OF THE AMBASSADOR

Hamel turned north, leading Lemmel and Gollos parallel to the wall. There were few people out, aside from soldiers on patrol. Most buildings they passed were warehouses and storage facilities. Hamel assumed they were for import and export. Outsiders were not allowed into Olmos, so all traders from other nations would need to buy and sell in the area outside the gate.

As they moved along, the occasional patrol approached them, but each one bowed and turned away the moment they recognized the Naromite uniforms. After an hour's ride, they found what Hamel was looking for.

"What strange looking buildings," Gollos said.

Lemmel laughed to himself. There were dozens of buildings behind a short wall, and the sight of them lifted his spirits. "The buildings appear strange to you, Gollos," he said, "but to us it is familiar. They are built in the style of Ridge architecture."

Hamel cautioned the other two, "Do not speak while we are here. Both of you must hold your tongues, and

Lemmel, you will need to maintain your disguise. This is the Ridge Embassy building, but we must not let them know who we are until we are alone with the Ambassador. It is difficult to know whom to trust."

Hamel had not been to the Embassy before but was familiar with the layout. It was built just under a mile from the Olmosite wall and appeared undefended.

The Olmosites had insisted the building not have a wall made of anything more solid than wood surrounding the buildings, and Ridge was only permitted to have ten armed soldiers for protection. Ridge had honored the request, to a point. No one had been stationed to the Olmosite Embassy unless they were skilled in all forms of combat. They had also dug below the Embassy and built a hidden safehouse in case of need.

Hamel led them to a small door built into the wall, next to a large gate. Both the door and gate were locked for the night. He banged on the door and waited.

A small hatch opened at chest height to allow a young woman to peer out. "Yes, Olmosite soldier, what may I help you with?"

Hamel suspected he knew the young woman. Her voice was familiar. He thought she might have been a Lieutenant, if she was who he thought she was, but she played her part well as the doorwoman.

"We must speak with the Ambassador. It is of the utmost importance," Hamel said in his Olmosite accent. "We cannot wait until morning."

The young woman nodded. Hamel was already appreciating the Ridge interaction. There was no groveling, nor was there a struggle for power.

"Thank you for coming to us," she said. "May I ask you your name?"

"My name is Wos. Please, I must speak with the Ambassador immediately," Hamel said, adding a level of urgency to his voice.

411

"Yes, Wos," she replied. "Please wait here while I confirm with the Ambassador. I believe he has retired for the evening."

The small hatch clicked shut, and he could hear her footsteps moving away from the wall. He took note that the sound traveled easily through the thin walls. His people could hold out for a time if attacked, but not long. It would be their skill in battle and their courage that carried them through, not their perimeter. He knew as well that the buildings inside the wall were far more solid than they appeared and built with the need for defense in mind.

They waited nearly five minutes before the young woman returned. The hatch opened briefly, presumably for the woman to confirm that the same three were standing outside, and then clicked shut again before the large gate opened. Two men and a woman came out and took the reins of their horses while the three followed the young Lieutenant to a large building in the center of the Embassy grounds.

The building itself was tall, round, and built of solid stone. Hamel smiled to himself as he could see various slits and openings built into the walls. At first glance, they looked like they served no purpose, but Hamel knew weapons could be fired through them. While Olmos had been their ally for years, there was enough about their relationship to suggest a careful approach.

They took the five steps up to the solid door leading into the building and entered a large, open hall. Hamel's and Lemmel's hoods remained drawn low over their faces. There was always a chance their people had been infiltrated.

The woman walked to a large door guarded by two soldiers and knocked. They waited a few moments before the door opened to reveal two more guards.

Hamel recognized the men. Each one was well built, and he had trained them both. He rarely let down his guard, but he knew both men to be honorable. The Ambassador, who stood a short distance behind them, was also a man

Hamel knew well. Sitting with his back to the door was another man, drinking a hot beverage. The steam from the drink floated up toward the ceiling.

"Please, leave us," the Ambassador said to the guards. "I know Wos well, and he is not a threat to our nation."

Hamel wondered at that comment. He had not known the name himself until he had received the identity papers from Mellel in the oasis. He considered the man sitting with his back to him and wondered whom he might be.

After the guards had closed the door behind them, the Ambassador nodded to the three travelers. When he spoke, he addressed Hamel. "It is okay. We are alone. My friend here can be trusted. But I do not know who your traveling companions are."

Hamel pulled back his hood and nodded at Lemmel to do the same. Gollos had not worn her hood as she had no need for disguise.

When Lemmel dropped his hood, his face was beaming. "Mikkel!" he said and rushed to the Ambassador.

Ambassador Mikkel didn't move. His whole body tensed, and his face drained of color. "Lemmel?" he said with a shake in his voice. "Is it you?"

"It's me, my friend," Lemmel replied, and the two men embraced.

Hamel had been looking forward to that moment. Mikkel and Lemmel had been close since they were young. Mikkel had even stood with Lemmel at his wedding as his Union Guard. It had long been a tradition to ask a most trusted companion to stand by your side to guard you against outside threats while you made your marriage vows. It was an honor of deep friendship and trust. Once he had known he would be leaving Olmos with Lemmel, he had longed to lead his son to the Embassy before taking him home to his wife and children.

Sadly, Hamel could not allow the reunion to last. Pulanomos would send soldiers. There was little time for friendship.

"Ambassador Mikkel, I must speak to you immediately. Unfortunately, we cannot stay. We must be off."

The Ambassador nodded his head. He had always been an intelligent, quick thinker. He had probably assumed as much the instant he saw Lemmel. "Yes, Hamel, I do know that you will need to leave, but it is difficult for me to listen to what you have to say. I have heard how you conducted yourself in the Capital. Word of your actions and speech have reached me. I know what you said to the Honored Matir and how you dishonored yourself before Rezin Mariel."

Lemmel took a step back from his friend. Hamel had still not yet told either Lemmel or Gollos the entire story of what had happened. His son would not, however, remain by Mikkel's side while there was a question of trust. It was dishonorable to remain by a friend when your family was challenged. Lemmel moved to Hamel's side.

"Is it true?" Lemmel asked.

"Yes, Lemmel, I challenged and spoke ill of Honored Matir Karotel in the Council Chambers and refused Mariel's wedding without proper cause," Hamel began, "but we do not have time to deal with this matter now."

"But if you have no honor, why would I listen to you?" the Ambassador asked.

Before Hamel could answer, the man who had sat silently with his back to them spoke. Hamel recognized the voice and smiled. He had suspected it was Mellel, although he had no idea how he had come to be in the Ambassador's Chambers on such a night.

Mellel eased to his feet and returned Hamel's smile before turning to the Ambassador, "Mikkel, I do not think we have time to settle matters of honor now. There is a greater urgency to the issue the former Honored Patir speaks of. I

414

give you my word that you can trust Hamel, even though he has been dishonored."

The Ambassador's eyes bored into Hamel's for a few moments before he relaxed his shoulders and nodded. "I will forgo this matter, then, on your word, Mellel. Hamel, tell me what is of such an urgent matter."

Hamel did not want to take the time to explain every detail. He had decided to share only a portion of the situation in the hopes it would be enough. Ridge politicians were people who appreciated brevity, so he laid out the matter quickly. He had decided not to mention that Pulanomos was the High Chancellor as it would raise far too many questions. "Our alliance with Olmos has come to an end. You and the entire staff here will not be safe. It is clear you are well fortified, but if you stay, your defenses will fall. The High Chancellor will be in pursuit of me, and if he does not capture me, he will come for you. There is no kindness in this land anymore. You must leave immediately, and you must not be seen. We are traveling by way of Benjelton and require haste, but you must travel by a less direct route."

Mikkel's mouth hung open. Hamel noticed a sadness in Mellel's eyes, but there was no surprise at the news.

"Does he speak the truth, Mellel?" Mikkel asked.

"He does," Mellel replied in a voice that betrayed disappointment and resignation.

"Put your hoods back up," Mikkel said to Hamel and Lemmel as he rushed to the door.

Once the door was opened, he invited the two guards back into the room. He closed the door behind the men and quickly informed them that the entire staff would need to abandon the Embassy. He then asked, "How long will we need, and what are our security concerns?"

The older of the two guards, a Major, responded. "We will need just over an hour to make all the preparations. We have two security concerns. The first security concern is that we have two Ridge women and one Ridge man whom we

415

suspect are compromised. We have watched them closely but are unaware of their true loyalty. The second security concern is the two guard posts within sight of the Embassy. Both are disguised as Olmosite homes, but the families are watching us and reporting on our actions. We will not get past them without alerting the Olmosites, unless the threat is addressed."

Hamel, with his hood over his face, nodded at the Ambassador. The man considered his offer for a moment and then said, "These two men are loyal to Ridge. They will be able to deal with the guard posts. Give the tall one the information he needs and have your soldiers deal with the preparations to leave. Make sure you also address the first security concern."

"Do you have a preference as to how we should address the matter?" the guard asked.

The Ambassador's face showed sadness and compassion. Hamel understood. It was difficult to think a Son or Daughter of the Ridge would betray the people, but it was good to hope the suspicion was unfounded.

"Bind them, and we will take them with us. We must move fast, Major. I wish my horse to be saddled and ready to go with the entire Embassy staff in exactly one hour from now."

The man saluted and rushed out with the second guard. They were competent soldiers, and Hamel knew they would do their best.

"We cannot keep them, Mikkel," Mellel said, stepping up behind the Ambassador. "They must move quickly. They have wasted precious time by warning us, although they have shown their honor in doing so."

Hamel tried to make sense of Mellel. As an Honored Patir, there was not much in the inner workings of Ridge that he did not understand; yet that man appeared to be exactly where he needed to be when Hamel needed support. Hamel did not believe in coincidences.

"Hamel," Mikkel said in a formal voice, "I pass on to you a blessing on behalf of the People of the Ridge and wish you all speed and safety. I do not understand what is going on here, but I will listen to Mellel." Turning to Lemmel, the Ambassador smiled, but there was sadness in his eyes. "I have grieved your death every day since you were lost to us. If I had known you were alive, I would have come for you."

"I know you would have, my friend," Lemmel replied. "You and my Patir would have fought side-by-side to rescue me if you had known."

Hamel held his face steady. On the one hand, the reminder of his son's suffering brought with it great pain. On the other hand, he was proud that his son knew of the loyalty offered to him and at his son's ability to give honor to a disgraced man in front of the Ambassador.

Mikkel nodded, and his face filled with resolve. "There is much to be done here. Go." With that, he turned away. The audience with the Ambassador was finished.

Hamel led the way out of the room. The calm atmosphere they had found upon entering the Embassy had been replaced with the bustle of dozens of people preparing to leave. The lights were still low, and the staff made little noise, even running in their bare feet. From the outside, Hamel knew there would be no sign the place inside was alive with activity.

He, Lemmel, and Gollos would need to move with the same careful focus in order to remove the immediate security threat to the Embassy. He hoped he had not committed to something that might compromise his mission.

CHAPTER 47

THE DAY OF THE SENTINELS

One of the guards stationed at the door to the Ambassador's office escorted them out. The man would believe that they were Olmosites, but the Major would have informed the guards that they could be trusted.

When they reached the gate, Hamel, Lemmel, and Gollos climbed up on their mounts. The horses had been fed, watered, and brushed down. He felt pride well up in his heart at the hard work and dedication of the People of the Ridge.

Before they could leave, the young Lieutenant rushed up. She quickly described the two Olmosite houses and that there was a man, woman, and child living in each location.

Once outside the gate, Hamel took in the situation. It was easy to identify the houses. They were far from discreet as they were the only two houses within sight of the Embassy.

Without a word, Hamel turned toward the one on the left, and Lemmel turned to the one on the right. Gollos followed close to Hamel, pulling up next to him on her horse.

"Will we need to fight the soldiers inside that house?" the young girl asked with a shake in her voice.

"Yes, I expect so," Hamel replied. "I do not know what we will find in there, but my uniform will give us the

418

time we need to evaluate the situation. Do you feel ready to fight a trained soldier?"

"Yes, Hamel," Gollos replied.

Hamel smiled and replied with a simple, "Good. If we are required to fight, I would prefer not to kill them. Try to merely incapacitate whoever you might face."

He had trained many soldiers in his time and knew Gollos had a long way to go before she would be ready to enter a serious fight, but he did not think the people in the house would pose much of a threat, nor did he think she would be a target for them. Once they realized what was happening, their focus would be on Hamel. He did, however, appreciate her confidence. She had come far in a short time.

They reached the small house and climbed down off their horses without a word. The house was in darkness, but Hamel knew there would be at least one person observing them. He expected when he banged on the door, they would take their time to answer to maintain the illusion that they were a simple family, sound asleep, and not watching the Embassy.

Around the back of the small house was a field with some sickly-looking crops. It would provide enough to feed the family but considering the growing conditions and the obvious lack of care, it would not give much more.

Hamel banged on the door and hollered in his Olmosite accent, "Open up!"

In the darkness, Hamel could not see far enough to make out the second house on the other side of the Embassy. He expected Lemmel was there already and perhaps even inside dealing with the people.

He banged again and hollered, "Open up now, or I will come in and wake you up."

He felt that threat needed a bit of work, but he had not thought ahead to come up with something which could create more fear.

A light came on inside and, through a curtained window, Hamel could see it move toward the door. When the door opened, a man stood in his nightgown, pretending to have been just awoken.

He feigned surprised and said, "Naromite, please forgive me for taking so long to answer. Please, come in."

Hamel and Gollos stepped inside and found a small room with a few chairs and a table on the right-hand wall. Through an open doorway directly ahead, he saw a dark kitchen and off to the left of the room were two closed doors.

Hamel moved into the center of the room and took one of the seats, directing Gollos to sit in a chair to his right against the wall.

When he turned back to the man, he found him bowed low to the ground. The man remained silent.

"You are not alone in this place, are you?" Hamel asked.

"No, Master, I am not. I am joined by my son and my wife."

Hamel considered the man's answer for a moment. It would certainly complicate matters if in each of the homes there were actual families, but he suspected the man was trying to maintain his cover.

"Call everyone who is in the house. I wish to speak with all of you," Hamel replied. He hoped to get a better idea of the situation. He did not have much time, but only a fool attacked without at least a basic understanding of the battlefield when the chance to learn and evaluate was available to him.

The man bowed even lower, dropping to his knees in order to brush his forehead upon the ground before he turned his back to Hamel. He banged on the one door and yelled, "Ronos, get out here!" He then turned to the other door, threw it open and yelled, "Woman, get out of bed and present yourself to the Colonel!"

Within seconds, a young boy rushed out of the one room, and a woman stepped out of the other. Hamel commanded all three to stand up straight so he could evaluate the situation. He was about to consider the woman for a moment, but something about the boy caught his eye. He looked him up and down and realized he was not a boy at all. He was an adult, just short and thin. He then turned to the woman. She was quite young and not the mother of the small man. Her face bore far too many bruises to suggest anything but abuse. He was reminded again of the difference between what was acceptable in Olmos and what was not acceptable in Ridge.

"Is this your family?" Hamel asked.

"Yes, Master," the man replied.

"Listen closely," Hamel began. He spoke in a soft enough voice that the man had to lean forward to hear. "I don't want to argue with you; nor will I bear with anything but the truth. I know you have a story that you must stick to, but this woman is not the mother of this boy, and this boy appears to be nearly as old as you are. Stand up straight and tell me the arrangement and your mission right now."

The man shook as he bowed low once again. Before he spoke, he stood straight and addressed Hamel. "I apologize, Master; I was commanded to maintain the illusion even when questioned. I never dreamed a Naromite would come to our home to question us, and I do not know why you have come. The Embassy guards will have seen you approach, and they will know a Naromite has business here. That will cause them to suspect us."

"What you say is true," Hamel said. "Go on."

"Yes, Master. My name is Quos. My friend and I have been stationed here to watch the Embassy. This girl is not my wife, nor is she the mother of my friend. She was given to us to help us appear as a family while we are stationed here. We watch the Embassy and send daily reports to the Captain of the Guard at the wall."

"Do you have any weapons?" Hamel asked.

"No, Master, we were not given any in case our house was searched by the Ridgers."

"Excellent," Hamel said. He then turned to the woman and said, "Go into the kitchen to prepare me a warm drink."

The woman bowed low and then rushed to the kitchen. In seconds, he could hear pots clanging.

"Quiet, woman!" the small man yelled. "The Naromite does not need to be disturbed."

Hamel stood up and addressed both men. "This is what is going to happen. Quos, I will speak with you right here. Ronos, you will speak with my associate outside."

Both men bowed to Hamel, and Ronos made his way to the door. As he rushed by, Hamel grabbed his arm and said, "Ronos, I know most women around here are treated poorly. I would recommend you not treat my associate with anything less than the same respect offered to me."

Ronos nearly wilted under Hamel's gaze. When Hamel let go, the small man stood straight and rushed out the door. Hamel had not planned to have Gollos fight, but the young man was small, had little to no muscle, and his thin shirt and shorts hid no weapons.

He smiled to himself as he watched Gollos follow the man outside. Her face betrayed terror mixed with confidence. He had never seen such a combination of emotions on a face before.

Once the door was closed, Hamel slammed Quos up against the wall, and the man slumped to the ground unconscious. At the sound of the crash, the woman rushed into the room. She nearly screamed out in fear when she saw Quos's body on the ground, but Hamel silenced her by holding up his index finger. The poor woman had no fight in her eyes. He suspected she had been nothing more than an object for her entire life.

"Sit down in that chair," Hamel said to her in a quiet, but authoritative voice.

He stepped to the window and pulled the curtains aside. Gollos stood over the young man's body. With his years of training, he could tell the small man was not actually unconscious.

He checked Quos, opened the door, and motioned for the woman to follow him outside. Tears flowed down her cheeks as she stepped out of the house. He hated to leave her in fear, but everything had to be dealt with in its time.

When he reached Gollos, he stepped up next to her and placed a hand on her shoulder. He pointed out the rate of the man's breathing, and the way he had fallen, protecting his head from hitting too hard. Hamel waited to see if she could draw the right conclusion.

Gollos reached down, grabbed the man, and put him in a chokehold. He began to struggle, but within seconds, his body went limp.

Hamel picked the man up and ordered the woman back into the house. The young man would not be unconscious for long. Once inside, he ordered the woman to get him some rope, and he tied both men securely.

"Sit down, please," he said to the woman.

She rushed back to her seat, and the tears began to flow once again. She made no noise as she wept, and Hamel suspected she had learned to weep in silence.

He sat opposite her and motioned for Gollos to sit down as well. Turning to Gollos, he asked, "What do you make of this situation?"

"I think this woman is a slave."

Hamel waited for more but then realized there was not much else to say. "What do you think our options are?"

Gollos's face filled with shock and horror, and she cried out with panic in her voice, "You are not thinking of killing her, are you?" The woman's weeping did not change.

She had resigned herself to death. He suspected her weeping pointed more to fear of the pain and a broken spirit.

Gollos fell to her knees before Hamel and begged him. "Please, Master. Please. I beg you. Do not do such a thing. I know you have the power to do it, but please show her mercy."

Hamel felt sick to his stomach. They had come so far, yet she still thought like a slave and saw him as an Olmosite slave-master. He gently lifted her to her feet and put both hands on her cheeks. "Gollos, have you never even met me?"

The fear and despair in her eyes increased for a moment before understanding dawned. "Wait, no. You would never do such a thing. No, that is not why you are asking me. You are thinking of my training. You are asking me because you want me to think through our options." She laughed as relief flooded her face.

"We are very short on time so we must act quickly. Now, what are our options? Ignore the extremes of emotion and evaluate our options based on strategy and compassion."

Gollos returned to her chair. She examined the woman for a moment before she nodded her head. "We have two options and only two. We can either tie her up with the two men and leave her to her fate, or we can offer her a chance to go to Ridge."

At that final comment, the woman stopped weeping. "You are not going to harm me?" she asked.

Gollos put her hand on the woman's shoulder and said, "I am a former slave, but this man has freed me. Would you like to be free? If so, you must go with us to the Ridge Capital."

"You are going to the Ridgers?" the woman asked.

"Yes, I am," Gollos replied with a big smile on her face.

The woman's face turned to disgust, and she leaned in close to Gollos. Hamel could hear her whisper, "But they eat Olmosite women."

Hamel decided to speak up. The little time they had was up. "Young lady, we do not eat Olmosite women. I suspect that was a lie told to you to keep you from straying too far from this house."

The woman's eyes grew large, and she stared at Hamel as though she was seeing him for the first time. Her eyes then dropped to the floor as she considered the possibility. At last, she nodded her head and mouthed the word, "Yes…"

Gollos knelt next to the woman's chair. Hamel could not help but smile at the sight of the child consoling the adult woman. "We do not have much time. We must leave now. You will have to choose. I cannot promise things will be easy, but I can promise that this man will not harm you."

The woman took a look at the two men. The smaller one was beginning to stir, and Hamel assisted his return to an unconscious state. After a moment she said, "I will go with you, as long as you will not eat me."

"I promise I will not eat you," Hamel said. "I do not feel you have enough meat on you to make a decent meal."

The woman's face filled with horror, and Hamel shook his head. "I'm sorry. I have tried to learn how to speak only words of wisdom and maturity, but sometimes I slip. I was making a joke. No one in Ridge will eat you."

The woman's expression turned to resolve, and she rose to her feet. The three left the house, and Hamel quickly ran to the back. He entered the small stable, saddled a solid looking horse, and brought it to the Olmosite woman. Once they were mounted, they made their way back to the Embassy.

The entire compound still appeared silent, but Hamel knew much was going on within the walls. He could hear faint noises of horses and the movement of people.

Lemmel had already arrived back at the Embassy, and he too had a young woman with him. Hamel spoke to the guards at the gate and, within moments, the Major arrived to speak with them. Hamel explained that both guard posts were

425

out of commission and told them the women were promised safe passage to Ridge. The Major shook his head in disapproval but accepted responsibility for the women.

Before they went inside, Hamel spoke to both of the women. He informed them that they might be bound for the journey to Ridge, but that would be the decision of the Major. He let them know they would be bound only until they reached the Capital, but once there, they would be freed.

The two women accepted the idea without question. Hamel hated the thought of binding them, but he knew if he were in charge, he would do exactly that. There was too great a risk on the journey that their loyalties might change, and the Ambassador might be in danger. Once in the Ridge Capital, he expected they would not look back to Olmos.

After handing the women over to the care of the Major, Hamel, Lemmel, and Gollos set out along the road leading toward Benjelton. That road was, by far, the fastest route to the Capital. He assumed if they were to be pursued, that would be the road. The Ambassador would take a slower, less direct route, but have a safer journey.

CHAPTER 48

THE DAY OF FLIGHT

The sun was up by the time the three travelers took their next rest. Hamel's muscles and joints ached in every spot imaginable. He had, out of the three, spent the most time on horseback over the last while and knew if he hurt as much as he did, the other two would be in agony.

Neither Lemmel nor Gollos complained, so Hamel let it be. There was nothing he could do about their pain.

He did, however, have other matters on his mind. There was still no sign of pursuit, but Pulanomos would not let them go. It was only a matter of time.

The imminent pursuit was the immediate threat, but not the only danger. He knew Pulanomos well, and he had spent many years as both a political leader and an officer in the Ridge armies. It was not difficult to piece together Pulanomos's next move.

The High Chancellor would do his best to silence Hamel and, if he suspected any contact with the Ridge Ambassador, the entire Embassy. If Hamel made it back to the People of the Ridge, they would know their alliance was finished and that the Olmosites were poisoning them. Ridge would then face the question of whether or not to attack Olmos or shore up their defenses.

Pulanomos would not want either of those options. The People of the Ridge were feared on the battlefield. If they attacked, Olmos would fall.

If Hamel could not be stopped before he warned his people, Pulanomos's best option would be to attack before Ridge could prepare. War was coming.

Hamel knew his mistake. He had been so focused on getting Lemmel and Gollos back to Ridge, he had not communicated with them any of his plans. Lemmel knew his Patir would never leave himself without a plan, but that was a long ways from knowing what that plan might be. Gollos, on the other hand, would not know either the threat or that Hamel had a plan.

"We need to talk," Hamel began.

"I think it's about time you let your Colonel in on your plan, General," Lemmel said with a big smile on his face.

"You are a General?" Gollos asked. "I did not realize you had such a high rank." She looked embarrassed and about to retreat back into her old shell.

"Gollos," Hamel began, "I have been a General for many years. I was disgraced from my people, and my status among the people was removed, but I am still a General. Nothing, however, has changed from when we spoke earlier today. You do not need to speak to me in a different way."

He addressed Lemmel and Gollos and laid out his plan. "We are likely about two hours from Benjelton at a steady trot. I expect we will be there by noon. We have made no attempt to hide our trail, and there have been a few traders who have seen us pass by this way. I expect the High Chancellor will have sent a group of Naromites to track us down."

Gollos shook her head. "Why have we not made an attempt to hide our trail or hide from the traders?"

428

Hamel kept his eyes firmly on her and waited. She would figure it out.

Her brow furrowed, and she said, "You wanted them to follow us!" The look on her face suggested she wished to slap Hamel.

"Yes, I'm sorry I didn't explain any of this," Hamel began. "I've been preoccupied with getting the three of us out of Olmos. I set up a few traps in one of the buildings on my way to Olmos a couple weeks ago. If we can lead our pursuers into the city, we shouldn't have too much trouble taking care of them."

"You set up traps? You expected to be chased out of Olmos before you even entered the country?" Gollos asked.

At that question, Lemmel broke out in laughter. "Expected? No, Gollos, he is a Soldier of the Ridge. He does not expect something like that. He merely prepares for it. It is the way we are trained. We always prepare for the possibility of retreat."

Hamel smiled at Gollos's shocked expression. He then went on to lay out as best he could what traps he had set up throughout the Council Chamber building.

Once they had talked through a basic idea of how to move through the building without getting killed, Hamel explained that he wanted to keep one of the Naromites alive. He felt the best way to move forward was to allow one to return to Olmos.

"Would it not be better to kill them all and then the High Chancellor would not know what to do?" Gollos asked.

Hamel shook his head. "No. If no one returns, the High Chancellor will wait for a few days and then struggle with how to proceed. It will be difficult to know what he will do or how he will react. If, however, word reaches him that we have escaped his Naromites, he will know we will be free to warn our people, and he will attack right away. If one of his men returns, we will know to expect an attack rather than just

429

suspect it. It is always better to know what your enemy will do."

"Is Ridge prepared for war?" Gollos asked.

"Ridge is always prepared for war," Hamel said, raising his arms above his head and stretching his neck. "It's time to move."

Hamel groaned as he pulled himself into the saddle. His complaint seemed to give the other two freedom, and they each added their own groan. He began to long for his own bed once again. It felt like his last breakfast with Markel had been a lifetime ago.

He smiled at the thought of Markel. The young man had been terrified of Cuttel, but Hamel knew he would be fine. He would work hard, learn fast, and be an officer by the time he was eighteen.

"My Patir!" Lemmel hollered. "They've found us!"

Hamel watched Gollos twist around in fear and fall off her horse. He quickly came to a stop and rushed to her side to find she was bruised and cut, but no bones were broken. He was grateful the horses had been at a walk, not a trot.

"We have to go!" she said as she pulled herself to her feet. He could see tears in her eyes.

"Yes, Gollos," Hamel said. "But we must be careful. We cannot panic. If we panic, we will ride the horses too hard."

He helped her back into the saddle, and the three took a moment to turn their horses toward their pursuers. The ground in that area of the wilderness was flat but rocky, and as such, their view of the Naromites was clear. The road itself wound back and forth around some of the larger rocks and boulders. As best as Hamel could figure, they had about a mile lead.

At that distance, it was too far to tell how many were after them, but Hamel was not concerned. As long as they did not have more than ten or twelve, he felt they would be fine.

430

More than that would prove to be quite the challenge, but if they were careful, he figured they might survive upwards of eighteen.

"All right, let's move. It looks like a larger group and, judging from the dust, they are moving quite fast. If we go to a trot and then to a canter when we can, we should be able to make it to the city in an hour."

He was concerned for the horses but hoped the recent rest and watering would give them an advantage. He expected the Naromites had their eye on the three of them and would not stop to rest their horses anytime soon.

The three rode as hard as they felt they could without pushing the horses too much. At the faster speeds, the pain was worse than it had been, but Hamel knew they would be able to rest once the soldiers were dealt with.

In a short while, the city walls came into sight. The road reached a crossroads, and they turned left into the city. The Naromites had gained on them, which suited Hamel. He did not want to lose them in the streets. It would be hard enough dealing with them if he knew where they all were.

As they entered the open gates, he looked back and counted fourteen Naromites. It was more than he had hoped, but he thought with the three of them, they would be able to manage a larger group.

CHAPTER 49

THE DAY OF LOSS

"Listen closely," Hamel hollered as they rode down the streets of the city. "We will head to the Council building. I have secured the Council Chambers so we could hold out there for a time if necessary. There is a rope on a makeshift hinge on the back of the door leading into the Chambers which will help us quickly drop the beam across the door. Gollos, you will remain in the Council Chambers until the Naromites are dealt with."

Hamel then continued on through his explanations. He explained how they would move from room to room until the Naromites were nearly finished off. Then they would have to defeat the final ones face-to-face before letting one of the men to think he had narrowly escaped.

Hamel slowed their pace enough to allow their pursuers to follow the dust trail. Within a matter of minutes, they had reached the small oasis at the center of the city. Hamel led them to the Council building, and they reined up just outside. Hopping down from his horse, he grabbed the reins and began to lead his horse carefully up the steps.

As much as Hamel wanted to leave the horses outside as a sign to let their pursuers know which building they were in, he knew the Naromites might be just as quick to kill their horses as let them be. He intended to lock the animals inside the Council Chambers to protect them. He was aware if they did not make it through the experience, it would be a cruel death for the horses, but he did not see another way.

"So... you didn't explain this part of the plan, my Patir," Lemmel said as he coaxed his horse up step after step. "What exactly are we doing with the horses?"

"I'm sorry, Lemmel," Hamel said as his own horse struggled with the steps. He kept an eye on Gollos's progress as well. While she was not doing well with leading her own horse, she was doing no worse than the other two. "I've been keeping a lot of plans to myself for a long time. It's turned into a bad habit. We're leaving the horses in the Council Chambers. The door is well secured. Gollos, you and Lemmel will lead the horses into the Chambers and then secure the door behind you. Gollos, you will stay in that room while Lemmel exits through a small door at the back of the room. You should be safe in there while we deal with our pursuers. I'll leave the sidearm with you in case you need it. Naromites do not carry sidearms, as far as I've seen, so it should give you an advantage if you are confronted."

They led their horses through the large doors and into the Council Chambers. Hamel was just about to step out when he noticed Gollos's face. There were streaks of dust clinging to her cheeks where the tears had poured down.

"Lemmel," Hamel commanded, "keep an eye out for the Naromites. They should be here soon. Don't be afraid to let them see what building we are in."

Lemmel rushed out the door, breathing heavily. A Soldier of the Ridge rarely dealt with such exhaustion unless they were in the midst of battle or exercise, but Lemmel had been confined to the pit for so long. It would have been difficult to maintain a decent level of fitness. He had done well, but there were limits.

"Gollos, there is no time. Quickly, tell me what is wrong. Do you wish you could be a part of this fight? Are you angry that I have planned for you to remain here while we face the Naromites?"

Gollos's face bore a look of incredulity. "NO!" she shouted. "I am not prepared to fight a Naromite!"

"Then are you afraid for our safety?" he asked.

"No," she said quietly. "It is because I am alone."

"Alone?" Hamel asked. "What do you mean that you are...."

Hamel turned away from Gollos. Something was wrong. He couldn't put his finger on it, but the sound in the air was different.

He left Gollos's side and ran to the doors to the Council Chambers. He slammed them closed and pushed the beam into place. Before running to the back door, he stopped to check on Gollos. She looked terrified.

He grasped her shoulders and said. "I must leave you now. Be strong."

Before leaving her, he leaned down and kissed her on the forehead. He knew she would not understand a Patir or Matir's kiss of blessing, but he would give it to her anyway. He had given it before, but it would be a good reminder. Once given, his act of adoption was complete in every way. Even if he died, she could claim him as her Patir, and the adoption would be recognized by every court in Ridge.

As he left her side, she wept. "I lo..." she began to say, then closed her mouth.

"I love you too, Gollos," he said as he placed the sidearm in her hand and rushed to the back door. "Follow me and lock the door securely behind me."

Without another word, Hamel stepped out of the room and pulled the door shut behind him. He heard the latch close and rushed down the hall, making his way to the front of the building.

His heart beat fast, and he could feel the adrenaline flowing through his veins. He began to sweat, and the pain from the day-and-a-half ride no longer seemed important. He was confident Lemmel was in danger. The Naromites should have reached the building, although they likely had dismounted and approached on foot. He did not think they would catch Lemmel unaware, but no Ridge soldier could stand alone against fifteen Naromites.

He found his way to the front of the building and came to a stop, just inside the doors. When he peered out, his heart lurched in his chest, and the tears began to flow almost immediately.

The horror of the moment about to take place nearly drove him to charge forward, desperate to see if there was anything he could do, but he knew it was too late. He had always had the ability to think through a situation or strategy in seconds, evaluating danger and threats. It allowed him to determine a wise course of action and execute it, often before others had a chance to even recognize the danger.

The cost of his ability, however, had not been fully realized until that moment as he looked into the courtyard, and his eyes met Lemmel's. The younger man gave a slight shake of his head. There was no way to stop it.

Hamel, in that instant, thought of poor Hethel and the two children who had lived all those years, not knowing their husband and Patir was alive. He saw himself clothed in red, kneeling before her, informing his daughter-in-law that her husband had been rescued, only to die a matter of days before taking her in his arms once again. He thought of the despair, pain, and anger she would feel.

He thought as well of the rage that was about to build inside him. He knew, as angry as he would be, his anger would only hinder his ability to survive and, in turn, Gollos's ability to survive.

He also felt pride as he considered the three Naromites lying motionless at his son's feet. Olmos had paid a high price for Lemmel.

The largest of the Naromites drew a knife. While two men held Lemmel's arms like the cowards they were, the man sunk his dagger into Lemmel's chest.

Hamel could not contain his pain as he watched his son's body slump to the ground. He screamed out in rage, and the remaining Naromites turned in his direction.

They rushed to the stairs, and Hamel's training took over. He pushed out the anger he felt and drew in the discipline he needed for the moment. If he could have faced them one at a time, he would have done so. But they were men without honor. He knew they would not hesitate to act in accord with their desire for power.

He turned and ran down the hall, listening closely for the steps of the men behind him. His first trap was just around the bend. He suspected he might be able to kill at least three before moving on to the second trap.

As he turned the corner, he grabbed a short section of rope, holding a board with six sharpened stakes secured to it. It had been weighted in such a way that a simple pull of the rope would release the tension and swing the stakes toward his pursuers.

When Hamel reached the stairs, he risked a glance and was pleased to see he had killed three men and injured a fourth. The man who was injured was the large one who had killed his son. He took a quick glance at how many still pursued him and counted seven. They would be easy to finish off.

At the top of the stairs, he jumped over the snare he had set on the floor. He couldn't be sure the first one would step on it, but the chances of seven men passing by it without setting it off was unlikely.

In the next room, he stopped at the far side and held the rope. He heard the men reach the top of the stairs and

436

then the sound of the snare released. It was difficult to know for sure, but he suspected their numbers were down to six.

When they entered the room where he was waiting, he pulled the rope, and four heavy sacks of salt came crashing down on two of the men in the lead. If his count was accurate, he was down to four.

In two more rooms, he had killed all but one man with his traps. That last one fell to his own knife.

Hamel made his way carefully back through the rooms. He forced himself to ignore the pain of Lemmel's death as he checked each man in turn to make sure he was dead. He would not have killed an injured man who posed no threat, but he did not want them to suffer either.

When Hamel reached the first trap, the Naromite who had been injured was not in sight. He rushed around the corner, toward the entrance, but there was still no sign of the man.

His mind kicked into gear, and he evaluated the situation. Gollos was secure in her room. He did need to leave at least one man alive to report to Pulanomos, but he needed the man to leave on *his* terms as the man was a threat if Hamel did not know where he was.

There was also a chance there were others present in the area or the building if Hamel had miscounted. That thought reminded him of the three men who had fallen to Lemmel. The memory brought a jolt of pain to his heart, but he pushed down the thought. Grief was best left until the battle was finished.

Hamel moved down the hallway toward the entrance and stopped just inside the door. He carefully peered outside and surveyed the situation. There were four bodies, but no one else in sight. If he moved quickly, he could confirm the three Naromites were dead and make it back to the door before anyone hiding outside could reach him.

He raced down the stairs and drew his knife. He confirmed the first man to be dead and moved around to the second, being careful not to look at his son. He feared if he examined Lemmel's body, the grief would overtake him, and he would not be able to complete his mission. Such a course of action would condemn Gollos to death.

The second man, as well as the third, proved to have fallen to Lemmel's blade, and Hamel quickly made his way back into the Council building. He had one more Naromite with which to deal.

Hamel returned to the trap where the man had been injured and looked for a trail of blood. When he found it, he was surprised at the amount of blood but impressed at the man's ability to disguise his trail. He followed it down the hall toward the stairs, only to find that the blood trail led around behind the Council Chambers. When he reached the small door, he saw that the man had moved the curtain out of the way, but then obviously moved on when he found the door locked. The trail led to an old rotten desk.

Hamel's mind went to a similar desk in the same location in his own Council Chambers. There had been a woman who had worked there for years, coordinating appointments for the Council meetings. She always presented herself as cross, but Hamel had been fond of her. Her husband had served as a night guard along the city limits and had proven himself honorable on many occasions.

He shook his head and brought himself back to the situation. He knew he was growing nostalgic as a result of his son's death. To lose focus at that point could invite disaster.

He glanced around to make sure the man had not found a way to come up behind him, then followed the trail. He wondered if the man was hiding behind the desk, but as he stepped around the side, he found no sign of him.

Hamel crouched down and examined the trail of blood. It had come to an end at that point. There was nowhere to go from there, which meant either the man had stopped bleeding, or he had found another route.

Since the man could not have climbed the wall, nor was there any place to climb to, Hamel considered the idea that the bleeding had stopped. The man would have had to tie up the wound to stop the bleeding, which suggested he had waited until that point to do so. If that were the case, the trail was left to mislead Hamel.

He was about to double back when something about the blood trail and the dust on the floor caught his eye. There was a little blood on the wall, just a short distance up, inside a crack.

He crouched down and examined the crack before he realized the same crack led around several blocks, shaping a door. He gave the blocks a push, and with a groan, they moved inward as one.

The light from the windows shone in through the newly found doorway. Before him lay a dark hallway, leading to a small wooden door. He stepped up to the door, pulled it open, and found a curtain hanging in the way. He had found another passage into the council Chambers.

He stepped through the curtain and came to a halt, drawing in his breath. The injured Naromite stood across from him. The man's knife was drawn and held against Gollos's throat.

The look on the man's face was both defiant and triumphant. He pressed the blade tighter against Gollos's neck and laughed as Gollos winced.

CHAPTER 50

THE DAY FOR THE LIVING

The man standing before him was the Colonel that Hamel had fought in Pulanomos's office just two days before, and the same man who had killed his son. Hamel considered the pool of blood at the man's feet, focusing on strategy to help him ignore the loss of his son.

He had served in enough battles to recognize the danger facing the Colonel. The man could not have long before he grew weary and lost consciousness, but Hamel did not think he would be able to stall long enough for that to take place.

Gollos herself stood rigid in the man's arms. Her face betrayed fear, and tears rolled freely down her cheeks.

"So, I get to face the great Honored Patir Rezin Hamel a second time," the man sneered. The hand that held the knife was covered in blood, and Hamel feared even a slight move would injure Gollos. "I had to pretend for the last week not to recognize you. I was one of the few who knew who you were from the start. The High Chancellor kept me out of sight for fear that you would recognize me, but in the end, you did not seem to. Your memory is failing you, old man."

Hamel examined the man's face. He did look familiar, but Hamel had dismissed the possibility that they might know each other. He rushed through his memory of the Olmosite soldiers he had met while Pulanomos had served as Ambassador to Ridge. Few of their faces stood out in his mind. From his training, he had learned to expand his thinking to consider other possibilities, and he thought through his many roles in life. When he considered his role as Honored Patir of the Council, the man's face seemed to fit.

He thought about the secret door behind the desk leading into the Council Chambers. The Naromite Colonel had checked the door behind the curtain, then gone directly toward the door behind the desk. Hamel himself had not known the second door was there before coming to Benjelton. It seemed unlikely the man had just happened upon a section of the wall that moved. The man was familiar with the layout of the Council Chambers.

He remembered the Colonel. At least ten years prior, the man had served as a guard in the Council Chambers. His face had aged, but he was definitely the same man. Soldiers would only be present in the Council Chambers during a meeting if the Honored Matir or Patir felt there was a threat to the Council or if the military was involved. The man had been a soldier under Hamel's lead, and Hamel himself had appointed him to serve as Council Guard on many occasions.

Not only did that explain how many secrets of state had been funneled to Olmos, but it meant that his people and his nation had been far more infiltrated than he had imagined possible. He made himself another mental note to deal with the matter. Olmos had been working against Ridge for many years.

"If I recall, Captain Hussel was the name we used to refer to you, but that is obviously not your name, nor your rank," Hamel said. He slowly drew his knife and watched as the Naromite Colonel smiled.

"Yes, that was the name I used," he replied. "My actual name is Hallos. My time in your nation earned me a place among the Naromites."

"If I remember right…" Hamel began. He felt it was time to irritate the man. He did not think it to be the wisest move, but an angry man thought with less clarity than a man with a clear head. "…you were never quite up to the caliber of the other soldiers. I did not want to send you out into battle, for fear that you would die. Offering you a ceremonial position in the Council seemed the safest way to keep you alive."

It worked. The man's eyes flashed, and the grip on the knife grew tight. For the time being, Gollos was safe as she was the only thing keeping Hamel away, but their time was short.

"I would be careful, Hamel," the Colonel said through clenched teeth. "I will not hesitate to kill the slave."

At the threat, Gollos's expression changed. Her body relaxed, and the fear left her eyes. Until that point, she had gripped the man's arm. She let go and stood firmly on her two feet.

"No," she said in a quiet, yet confident, voice. "I am not a slave. I am a daughter of Hamel. I am a Child of the Ridge." She then met eyes with Hamel and smiled. When she spoke again, her voice rose in volume and authority, and she addressed Hamel. "I am not alone. I have not been alone since I met you. You are my Patir. If I die right now, I will not die a slave, nor will I die an Olmosite. I am a Woman of the Ridge, and I am free. My name is Rezin Gollos!"

Hamel's eyes blurred with tears of joy and pride. She was a free woman, and he was proud to call her his own family. He knew the People of the Ridge would also be proud to call her their own.

He reached up and wiped the tears from his eyes and set his mind to the situation at hand. He needed to rescue Gollos from danger, but he also needed the Colonel to live.

As much as he wanted the man who had killed his son to die, he had to let him go. Pulanomos needed to be driven to act.

He considered the man's way of thinking. While he was an Olmosite, he had spent many years in Ridge. That would likely have helped him to understand the Ridge way of approaching life, but Hamel did not think the man would have allowed that thinking to influence him much as it would limit his ability to succeed in Olmos. Olmosites valued power and used fear to gain it. By holding Gollos at knifepoint, the man was acting as an Olmosite. It was, however, unclear as to what power he was trying to gain.

"What do you want?" Hamel asked. He had to deal with matters quickly. If the situation were resolved in short order, there would be less opportunity for him to act on his desires.

"What I want is to kill you and your slave girl," the man said as he laughed. "But I don't see that happening. With my injury, I don't think I could stand against you. I do, however, think there's another option."

Hamel nodded his head. He knew he would not like the man's idea, but there was always the chance if the man took too long, he would lose enough blood and collapse. "What is your idea, Colonel?"

"Here is what's going to happen. I'm going to take the slave girl, and you are going to let me walk out of here. Once I'm at my horse, I'll let her go, and she can run back to you so the two of you can play house or whatever this 'You are my Patir' garbage is all about."

Hamel shook his head. "I will never allow that. Olmosites are not men of honor. You will lie just as quickly as you will tell the truth. Your words are worthless. You are just as likely to take her on your horse and ride back to Olmos. I will not allow you to have her."

Gollos stood with confidence, and her smile grew. There was no more fear in her eyes. She no longer imagined herself to be expendable. Ridge children were taught their

443

value from birth. He was pleased to see the recognition in her eyes of her own value.

"Then we might be at an impasse, Hamel. I think you are at a disadvantage, however, because I have something you want. For reasons beyond me, you care for this beast of burden. I, however, do not. So, I don't mind killing her, but you want her alive."

"Yes, you do have something I want, but I also have something you want. You want your freedom, and you will not gain it if I do not grant it. I also have an advantage over you," Hamel said. He hated the back and forth but saw no other way with the man.

"What advantage would that be?" the man asked.

"Time."

"Time?"

"Yes," Hamel replied. "Time. You are bleeding, and I believe in about five minutes, you should have lost enough blood that you will no longer be a threat to anyone."

The man nodded his head. Hamel did not think the matter of time was a surprise to the Colonel, but he would never draw attention to it on his own.

"So, we have four minutes," Hamel said with a smile. "I want the girl handed over to me, unharmed. You want to ride out of here, also unharmed… or no more harmed."

"I don't see a way we can guarantee we will both get what we want," the Colonel replied and firmed his grip on his knife. "But understand this. If I start to lose consciousness, I will cut open her throat. We need to settle this quickly and to my satisfaction, or she dies."

"I agree." Hamel stepped into the middle of the room and tossed his cloak to the side. "It is simple. If you drop your knife, leave the girl unharmed, and make no move to attack, I will allow you to climb on your horse and ride away. I will not harm you if my conditions are met."

"Give me your word, Ridger!" the man screamed. He was losing control. There wasn't much time before he passed out. "I want you to promise on your honor!"

"Colonel," Hamel replied in a calm voice. "You spent many years among us. Do you still not understand the People of the Ridge? We are men and women of honor. We will not dishonor ourselves easily. My word is true."

"But you dishonored yourself in the Council. You have been disgraced," the Colonel declared.

"True. But honor is never truly granted or taken away by the Council. My honor is my own. I have spoken the truth. I will let you live if you drop your knife, leave her unharmed, and do not attack."

The man's eye's shifted, and Hamel feared he would kill Gollos, but he pulled himself back and nodded. "Agreed."

He then let her go and pushed her toward Hamel. He tossed his knife to the side of the room, and it clanged on the ground, slipping under one of the lower Council benches.

Gollos rushed to his side, and he put his arm around her for a moment before letting go. He was a man of honor, but there was no doubt the Naromite was not. He needed to be prepared.

The Naromite took two steps toward the door and stumbled to the ground. On his knees, he wobbled back and forth, and Hamel rushed to the man's side. He could not let the man die. If he did, Pulanomos's next move would be unpredictable.

Hamel grabbed the man before he realized his mistake. The man was anything but unsteady. He felt firm and ready for action, and Hamel saw the flash of steel.

When the knife entered his side, he reacted more on instinct than anything else. He grabbed the Colonel's arm and twisted it until he heard the arm pop out of its socket. He then slammed his fist into the side of the man's head, and the Naromite went down without another sound.

It would not help for Hamel to die before he could warn his people, but the Naromite could not lose too much more blood. Gollos was at his side as he collapsed to his knees, and he told her to grab his cloak. Using his knife, he cut strips of bandages for himself before giving instructions for Gollos to pull out the knife and how to apply the pressure he needed to stop the bleeding.

"Before you pull it out," he said, "where is your sidearm?"

"The Naromite tossed it behind that bench," she said. "I didn't see him coming."

"That's okay, Gollos," Hamel said. "Retrieve the gun."

Once she returned, he instructed her to draw the knife from his side, apply pressure to the wound, and to wrap it. "If I lose consciousness and the Colonel wakes before me, shoot him. Do not hesitate. Shoot him in the heart."

She nodded her head and stepped back. Her head twisted around, and she asked, "Where is Lemmel? Where is my... brother?" The last word came out with a strange smile on her face.

Hamel shook his head. "I'm sorry, Gollos. He fell to the Naromites. He's gone."

Her face betrayed a lack of understanding for a moment before it turned to a look of sheer horror. She collapsed on the floor before him, but he grabbed her arm and said through his own tears, "I'm so sorry, Gollos. I know this is all so painful, but we must hurry. I need you to set aside your hurt and anger and deal with this wound."

She shook her head for a moment. At first, Hamel worried it would be too much for her, but she nodded her head and grabbed the rags.

As much as it had hurt for the knife to go into his side, it hurt far worse coming out. Gollos immediately went to work applying a strip of the cloak, leaning in with her weight to add pressure.

446

While she worked, he did his best to examine the wound. It was difficult to know what might have been damaged from the knife, but he hoped it was not a fatal injury.

After a minute, he raised himself off the floor enough that she could tie a strip around his waist to hold on the bandage. He did not look forward to climbing into the saddle. He knew the pain would be intense.

Once he felt the bleeding had been slowed somewhat by the pressure applied by Gollos and the bandage, he moved to the Naromite. He did a quick search of the man for more hidden weapons and found three more knives. He tossed them to the other side of the room before he examined the man's wounds. He pulled back the armor and shook his head.

"What's wrong?" Gollos asked as she came close, holding the sidearm pointed at the man's chest.

"The blood loss was a deception," Hamel replied.

He pulled back the armor to reveal the injuries. While the man had been genuinely stabbed by the first of his traps, the wound was relatively superficial and was already well bandaged. Inside the cloak, he found a waterskin that had been filled with blood. The Colonel had drained the blood from one of his dying men. He had used it to lead Hamel to the Chambers and give the impression he had lost a great deal of blood. The deception had been planned, and Hamel had fallen for it.

He examined his own wound once more. "Let's hope this does not turn out to be too costly. Help me to my feet."

Gollos came up under his shoulder on his good side and helped him to a standing position. He had been stabbed four times in the course of his life. Not one had resulted in an easy recovery. He thought through each incident in turn and realized the others had felt different than the stab he had received from the Naromite. This time, something was wrong.

On his feet, Hamel found he could walk by himself, albeit slowly. He hobbled toward the door, and he and Gollos managed to move the beam. Hamel's bandage needed to be retied after the movement, but they were able to stop the bleeding.

Once the door was open, Gollos led the first of the three horses out of the building. When she saw Lemmel, she dropped the reins and rushed to his side. Hamel was not sure how to get him into the saddle of his horse. He would not leave his son to the predators in the wilderness.

He approached his daughter and slowly crouched down. The sound of her sobbing was overwhelming, and he fell to his knees, nearly collapsing on her.

"My son," he cried as placed a hand on Lemmel's cheek. He knelt down and, in the tradition of the People of the Ridge, gave the Patir's kiss on Lemmel's forehead, his final blessing to his son. "You have maintained your honor…" he began, choking out the words. He planned on burying him in the oasis, or, if possible, the Capital.

Gollos interrupted his thoughts by jumping to her feet. She screamed loud enough that he had to cover his ears before she stormed away. Her grief was not for a long-time friend or brother. They had only known each other for a matter of days. Her grief was the death of a vision, a vision of a life with family—a life she was only beginning to comprehend.

"I cannot stay here!" she yelled out in rage.

Hamel had seen enough death to know the rage was not a rejection of his son, but a reaction to the loss. He knew as well that his attention should not go at that moment to the dead, but to the living.

"I will not stand here and watch my brother bleed!" she shouted. She came up to Hamel and struck him in the shoulder as he knelt by his son. "We must go! We must leave this place. We must never come back here! Ever!"

She struck him again, then again, before she turned and ran up the stairs, grabbed the reins of the horse still waiting for her and led it awkwardly down the steps. She then ran back into the Council Chambers. He was about to try to rush after her, concerned to leave her alone in case the Colonel awoke, when she appeared again at the door with Hamel's horse.

"We will leave now!" she screamed, her face red and her fists clenched.

"Yes, Gollos," Hamel said in as calm and gentle a voice as he could. He did not think a calm voice would help her at the moment, but he would always start there. "We will leave now. I…"

Hamel stopped and turned back to Lemmel. Gollos's words settled into his mind. He crouched down as best he could and examined Lemmel's side. "He is bleeding."

"Yes!" she screamed again. "I will not stay here and watch my dead brother bleed!"

"No, Gollos," Hamel said. The tears began to flow down his face, and he choked out the next words. "Dead men do not bleed."

The rage on her face turned to confusion and back to rage again. I don't care what happens to someone after they die. I want to leave!"

"No, Gollos, listen to me. A man only bleeds if there is a heart pumping blood. Lemmel is alive!"

Gollos's face scrunched up, and she began to scream again. Hamel so greatly desired to comfort her and help her to understand, but he knew the pain and rage and fear and all she was experiencing would leave her in denial.

He went to work. He used his hands to rip open the shirt and examine the wound. The knife had indeed entered the chest, but as best as he could see, Lemmel had twisted his body enough to redirect the blade from its intended target. Hamel assumed it must have missed the heart and lungs.

With his knife, he cut off strips of Lemmel's cloak and began, as best he could, to bandage the wound. Lemmel's pulse was weak. His son had lost a lot of blood.

Once he felt he had stopped the bleeding, he struggled to his feet. He approached Gollos and put a hand on each shoulder. The experience in Benjelton had been too much for her. It would be a while before she could think or act without clear guidance. He had dealt with countless soldiers over the years who had lost themselves in a crisis. The way to deal with the situation was to fall back on training and discipline.

The moment did not call for compassion but for a General. "Child!" he said with as much authority as he felt he could use with her without breaking her spirit.

Gollos tensed, and her eyes focused. Her hands unclenched, and her face turned pale.

"Listen closely," he said with a gentle, but authoritative tone. "Take the waterskins from your horse and mine and go immediately to the spring in the center of the courtyard and fill them with fresh water. When you are done, come back to me."

She nodded her head and went straight to work. The effort would be good for her. He assumed by the time she had finished filling the skins, she would comprehend what he had told her about Lemmel.

While she ran to the spring, Hamel climbed the steps back into the Council Chambers. He found the Colonel unconscious, or perhaps pretending to be, and he led Lemmel's horse through the door.

Before leaving the building, he pulled the door to the Chambers closed and then also the outside doors. Once the Naromite was up and moving, he wished to slow him down so they would have time to exit the city. He knew the Colonel would not follow them alone and with a broken arm, but he knew if the man was close to them, he would still be a threat.

He pushed a large rock in front of the door. It would not be enough to keep the man inside, but it would scrape loudly if the Colonel tried to open the door. It would serve as an early warning.

Once he had Lemmel's horse down to the bottom of the steps, he met Gollos. She carried three waterskins, two from his own horse and one from hers. She had a dazed look on her face as she handed all three to Hamel.

He secured the waterskins to the backs of the saddles and handed her the one from Lemmel's horse. As he did, he said in a firm, but gentle voice, "Thank you, Gollos. Now go fill up Lemmel's waterskin. He has lost a lot of blood and will need more water."

He watched her go for a moment before turning back to Lemmel. He took the one skin he still had in his hands and tried to give some water to his son. Lemmel did not swallow the water at his mouth so the most Hamel could do was wet his lips and put a few drops in his mouth. He was pleased to see Lemmel move his tongue slightly around the water and added a little more in the hopes of helping his son replenish the blood he had lost.

As he finished, a shadow fell across Lemmel's face. Gollos had returned with Lemmel's waterskin. "He needs water?" she asked.

"Yes, Gollos. He has lost a lot of blood. We need to make sure he has enough fluids."

"Then he is alive?" she asked. Her face held no expression.

"Yes, my daughter, your brother is alive."

At first, she simply nodded and handed the skin to Hamel. After a few moments, comprehension crept back into her eyes, and she began to breathe quickly.

"I thought he was dead," she whispered.

"Yes, Gollos, we both did," Hamel said. "I was wrong. He is alive. Now we need to move. Do you think you can help me secure Lemmel in his saddle?"

Gollos smiled and nodded quickly. She turned and rushed to Lemmel's horse and led it to its master.

Normally, Hamel would have had no difficulty picking up someone of Lemmel's size and putting them on a

451

horse. Lemmel had lost a great deal of his bulk during the years in the pit. Hamel, however, could feel the pain in his abdomen at every move and knew he would not be able to manage on his own. He had Gollos lead the horse next to a broken statue near the steps. It would serve their purpose. He then had her pull out a rope from his own pack.

The process of getting Lemmel in the saddle took nearly fifteen minutes. Hamel kept his eye on the sun, watching its descent. He did not want to travel in the dark as he feared he would not find the oasis, but they would not be able to rush the matter, nor could they stay in the city for the night.

The two struggled to pick up Lemmel and carry him to the statue. They climbed the steps, struggled to the base of the statue, and moved next to the horse. They were about level with the saddle and could slip him into it with difficulty. Hamel tied his son into place and shook his head at the thought of the rough ride ahead.

Once finished, he gave Lemmel some water and was pleased to see him accept it. He even took a small sip.

Hamel struggled to get himself into his own saddle. He wished he had found a way to keep the trader's cart. It would have served them well at such a moment. He had Gollos bring his horse to the statue and used it to climb into the saddle. He wasn't sure he would have been able to mount his horse on his own. Within another few moments, they were on their way.

He had tied the reins of Lemmel's horse to the back of Gollos's saddle, and the three made their way out of the city. They traveled as fast as Hamel felt they could manage with their injuries. Their time in Benjelton had been costly, but they had made it out with their lives.

CHAPTER 51

THE DAY WANES

Every step the horse took felt like the knife was going back into his side, and each jolt made him worry more for Lemmel. He could not believe he had almost lost his son. He had still not quite come to terms with the idea that Lemmel was alive, but to lose him so close to home was agony.

A shot of pain brought him back to his own situation, and he called a halt. His head felt too heavy for his neck, so he drank nearly a quarter of the water in his waterskin. Moving up next to Lemmel, he helped his son drink as well.

"Where is Hethel?" Lemmel asked, looking around. "Is she out in the fields?"

"Perhaps, my son," Hamel said. "But for right now, you need to drink water. You need water if you are to see her."

Lemmel's wife had been raised by farmers and loved to walk among the crops during the growing season. If she was not around, she was often among the fields with the children.

"Then I will drink," he said in a raspy voice.

Hamel helped him drink as much as he could take in. It wasn't nearly enough, but it was far better than nothing.

They resumed their journey. Hamel moved as fast as he felt his and Lemmel's wounds would allow. He did not wish to lose more blood and checked each of their bandages often.

As the sun began to set, he found the area where they would need to leave the path. A short while later, they arrived at the edge of the oasis and began their descent.

At the river, Gollos helped Hamel out of his saddle, and the two worked together to carefully lower Lemmel to the ground. When they were finished, Hamel set to work on the bandages. Both he and Lemmel were bleeding after the dismount, and neither could afford to lose much more blood.

Gollos filled all four waterskins, and they drank their fill. Lemmel was still somewhat confused about where he was but was able to drink well, and the three ate their fill of the charis fruit growing in the oasis.

Hamel had been evaluating their next steps. He wished Mellel was present in the oasis but could not imagine the man had left the Ambassador, nor could he have made it to the oasis before them. He was convinced Lemmel could not make the next leg of the journey on horseback in his condition. He would need a few days before he would be well enough, or they would need a cart to transport him.

As much as he hated the decision, he knew he had to leave both Lemmel and Gollos behind. He had to warn the Honored Matir, and he could not leave Lemmel alone. He would need someone to care for him. He was not sure how Gollos would take the news, but a Daughter of the Ridge must sacrifice to care for others in need.

He turned to explain the next steps to her, but she spoke first. "Hamel?"

"Yes, Gollos?" Hamel asked.

Her eyes were fixed on the flowing water of the river as it quickly moved through the floor of the oasis. "If you are my Patir, should I call you Patir?"

"A Daughter of the Ridge is always to speak the truth," Hamel replied.

"The truth?" she asked. "What does truth have to do with it?" Her faced filled with confusion for a moment before understanding won over. "The truth is that you are my Patir. So, if I speak the truth when I speak to you, I will call you 'Patir.'"

He smiled. He was in terrible agony from his wound and felt overwhelmed with stress for his son, but she brought joy to his heart.

She smiled in return and then asked, "What does 'Patir' mean?"

"It's an old word," he explained. "It means father. A mother is called Matir. We use those terms in our families, but also in our leaders. They are those who love and care for the nation, and they are called Matirs and Patirs as well. The one who leads our nation is then called the Honored Matir or Honored Patir."

"Before you were disgraced, were you a Patir of the nation?" she asked.

"Yes. For many years."

"Were you ever the Honored Patir?"

Hamel laughed and instantly regretted it. Pain shot through his side. "I was, my dear Gollos, an Honored Patir until about three weeks ago. It was a very different situation. There is normally only one Honored Leader at a time, but since I did not die when expected, I remained the Honored Patir, even though a woman named Karotel is the Honored Matir."

"Is she a good leader?" Gollos asked.

"Far better than even she realizes," Hamel said with pride in his heart. "But there are other matters we must discuss."

She nodded her head in reply and turned to face him. "Of course, Patir," she said with an embarrassed look on her face. She appeared to want to call him Patir but felt awkward.

455

He decided to just let her work it out on her own. "But Patir…"

"Yes, Gollos?"

"I notice you change the topic every time we speak of your disgrace."

"Yes, Gollos. I do." Hamel smiled.

"Then you do not wish to talk about it?"

"No, Gollos."

"Then I will not ask again. What is our next step?"

"Thank you, Gollos. We can speak of it at a later time but not now. Our next step is to warn the Honored Matir as soon as possible about the Olmosite threat. There will be some preparations they will need to make, and the earlier they know of the danger, the better." He did not think she would respond well to the idea of being left in the oasis but knew she would act with honor. "Lemmel is not fit to travel by horseback. He will need time to heal."

"Yes, Patir, I know. I will stay with him here in the oasis while you go to our people."

Hamel smiled again. "You impress me, Gollos. I thought you would be angry at the thought."

"I do not want you to leave me, Patir," she said, still looking like the word was hard to get out. "But I believe my sacrifice will be honorable." As she spoke, her face betrayed a formality and maturity far beyond her years.

Hamel's eyes watered as his heart filled with pride yet again. He reached for her and pulled her in so he could give her a kiss on her forehead. "You make me proud, my daughter."

With the compliment, Gollos's attempt at looking formal and mature was lost, and she giggled. He was reminded once again of how young she was and was pleased with how far she had come in such a short time.

"There is a cave in the side of the wall. It has a small entrance, but if we go in there, there is a bed on which we can lay Lemmel. If I recall, there might be some clean clothes in

456

the cave that we can use as bandages. Give me a hand with him."

Lemmel, by this time, was nearly awake. It made it easier to move him and to give him more water, but it meant he was aware of the pain he felt. The three made their way to the hidden entrance of the cave and, with the effort of all three, managed to get Lemmel inside.

Hamel lit a few candles and examined the supplies Mellel had left. He found not only clothes but actual bandages, clean and ready for use as well as salve and alcohol for cleaning wounds. Mellel was well stocked to deal with injuries.

They set to work cleaning and re-bandaging the wounds. While they worked, Hamel explained to Lemmel his plan to leave them and told them that if the Olmosite army moved through the area, they would need to remain in the cave as it was not only quite defensible, but it was nearly impossible to see the entrance if one did not first know the cave was there.

He then began to lay out everything he had learned about the Silque, the Beasts, what he could recall from the maps in the border-town and more. He found some paper and a pencil among Mellel's belongings and drew what he could from memory of the markings on the maps. He hoped he would be able to relay the information himself to the People of the Ridge, but he knew he had been a fool to keep it all to himself for so long.

They settled in for the night. Hamel did not feel he had the time to rest but knew he could not venture out at night. The chances of losing his way, even with the roads, was far too great in that area. He was also far too tired to manage.

The next morning, the pain was intense. Hamel cried out in pain as he opened his eyes but quickly caught himself.

Hamel waved off Gollos's concern as she rushed to his side and asked her to prepare some breakfast while he dressed his and Lemmel's wounds. Lemmel, by that time, was alert, able to drink plenty of water, and looked much stronger, although he was in terrible pain. Hamel did not want to hide his own suffering but knew it would only worry the other two. There was nothing they could do about it. He packed some extra bandages, as well as some of the salve that Mellel seemed to have in plenty.

Hamel and Gollos climbed back out through the cave. He knew his wound was serious and dreaded the thought of the journey ahead. If Gollos had been raised among the People of the Ridge, he would have considered sending her as she would be able to move faster and get word to the people, but as it was, she was unfamiliar with travel, unfamiliar with the area, and he was confident it was far more than he could ask of her.

At the river, they filled the waterskins once again, and he asked, "Will you be okay?"

"Yes, Patir," she replied, this time saying the word comfortably. "Patir… my Patir? What do I call you? Lemmel would say, 'my Patir.' Is that what I should call you?"

"I was a Patir among the people, so everyone called me Patir or Honored Patir. Only my children, their spouses, and my children's children have the right to call me 'my Patir.' That is a privilege given only to family."

She smiled, "Then I will call you my Patir."

"Good. And you will be okay?" he asked again. He hated the thought of leaving either of them behind.

"Yes. I will take good care of Lemmel. I learned a little bit of caring for wounds when I was a slave. When he is sleeping, I will read. There are hundreds of books in that cave."

Hamel smiled. He had been surprised at the books the man had hidden away out there in the oasis. "Good. Then I must leave now."

458

She rushed to his side and wrapped her arms around him. He nearly cried out in pain as her arm squeezed his knife wound, but he managed to keep it in. He did not want to ruin the moment for her.

"I love you," she said into his cloak and then turned and ran back toward the cave. He watched her disappear behind the bushes and heard the rocks and gravel shift as she climbed into the hole.

"I love you too," Hamel said quietly in the direction she had run before adding with a chuckle, "And… I kind of need your help to get into the saddle."

He shook his head and smiled again as he turned and walked toward his horse. He managed to find a large rock that he could step onto and used it to get into his saddle.

CHAPTER 52

THE DAY ENDS

As his horse climbed out of the oasis, he thought ahead to the next leg of the journey. It had been a two-day walk to get to the oasis by foot. On horseback, if he had not been injured, he could have covered that distance in a few hours, but the pain in his side would be too much.

He moved as fast as he could but found himself unable to maintain the speed he had hoped. After about an hour of moving at a walk on horseback and then stopping to take a break, followed by some more walking, followed by yet another rest, he was in agony. The pain was so intense he feared he might lose consciousness. When he checked his bandages, he found he had started to bleed again and had lost a great deal of blood.

He pushed himself, letting the horse continue along the old road leading back to the Capital. As the horse walked, he tried his best to tighten the bandage, but the most he could do was slow the bleeding.

Hamel had served in the army for over twenty years. He had served all the way from a new recruit up through the ranks to his current position of General, a rank which held little true authority for a man without honor. He had been in more battles than he could count and seen more men and women injured than he cared to remember. One thing was certain from all his experience, he was losing blood too fast.

He pushed his horse to move faster. If he did lose consciousness, he would likely fall from the horse. If that happened, he would be food for the birds or the wild dogs. He had to reach his destination, or he would be lost.

His mind drifted back to Pulanomos. It was the first time he had been alone since leaving Olmos, and he felt himself falling into self-pity. The grief at the loss of his friend was overwhelming. Tears flowed freely as he thought back to the years they had known each other. He had never had a closer friend.

He wondered if anything of their friendship had ever been real. He hoped for a moment that it had been, but then the memory of Colonel Hallos came back. The Naromite Colonel had been stationed in Ridge as a spy. He likely had reported to Pulanomos, or at the very least, the information was funneled through the Embassy. The man had served in Pulanomos's final years in Ridge.

Pulanomos had never truly been his friend. Or, at the very least, Pulanomos had never been his ally.

After another hour or so, the path began to look familiar. He had traveled the area around the Capital many times over the decades. He began to recognize familiar looking rocks and trees, many of which held memories for him as he recalled stopping at various places with fellow soldiers. One or two spots along the way he could remember having stopped at with Lemmel over the years.

As he turned his head to look at all the sights, his head spun, and he had to grab the saddle. It took the better part of a minute before he could see clearly again. He added more pressure to the wound, but the bleeding would not stop. He drank more water and pushed on. It would not be far.

The city was directly ahead. At the rate he was traveling, he would be there within two or three hours, but he would not arrive at the Capital that day. It did not matter, however. The one he wanted to see was not in the city.

He pulled out each of the two waterskins he had brought with him but was shocked to see he had already emptied the one and the other one was only half full. His mind was slipping.

Hamel turned the horse off the road, down through a crevice between two hills. If the young man had followed orders, he would be waiting in the fortress.

Hamel placed his hand on his side, adding more pressure. It hurt to touch, but the pain helped to keep him alert. On the path ahead, he could see a small hill. It felt like years since the last time he had been in that area, but it had not been more than a month or so. His mind drifted to the cave. It would be cool, and there was water. The cave would be a welcome rest from the heat of the sun.

After a few minutes, he reached the bottom of the hill and did his best to climb off his horse. His feet were not as solid on the ground as he had hoped, and he collapsed. When he hit the ground, he cried out in pain. In the fall, the bandage ripped right off the wound, sliding up his chest. The blood poured out, and he quickly pulled it down again. He would not make it to the Capital that day. He only hoped he could make the climb.

Hamel pulled himself to his feet and grabbed the waterskin. He drank what he could and dropped the skin on the ground. He did not have the strength to pick it up or to stop the water from pouring out onto the dry earth.

As he began to climb the side of the hill, he longed to be back in the city with his children and with his people. The last month had been costly and painful. He was half-way to the cave before he collapsed again. His lips felt strange, and his hands had begun to shake. He feared he would not make it.

Taking a deep breath, he pulled himself onto his hands and knees and continued his ascent. He was nearly there. He pushed himself. He was at the entrance. He crawled inside and felt the welcome, cool, moist air of the cave. Just inside was a large boulder. After the bright sunlight outside, the darkness of the cave was intense. He could see nothing, but he knew the layout of the cave as well as his own home.

He placed his hands on the boulder and used it to pull himself onto his feet. He took a few steps, holding the walls of the cave for support as his eyes adjusted to the dim light.

Ahead was a small turn in the cave. As he stepped around it, three lanterns were lit, revealing five Ridge soldiers. He nearly laughed out loud with relief when he saw them but did not have the strength.

The man in front stepped forward, holding a rifle pointed directly at Hamel's heart. He was young but stood tall and confident. Hamel immediately recognized Captain Cuttel.

"Olmosite," Cuttel said. "You have wandered a little far from home. You will drop any weapons and surrender immediately."

Hamel steadied himself against the wall with his right hand as he used his left to pull back the hood of his cloak. He did not have much time left. He could feel his strength fade.

When the hood fell back and the light landed on his face, all five soldiers gasped. One of the men who had stood near the back stepped into the light, and Hamel smiled. It was young Markel. He had stayed close to the Captain as Hamel had wished.

Cuttel's face lit up, and he cried, "General!"

Hamel began to slip. The Captain rushed to his side, and Hamel collapsed into his arms.

"Quick," Cuttel hollered at one of the men, "bring some water." He then turned to a young recruit and ordered him to find a medic. "Markel," Cuttel said, "come help me with the General."

Hamel had so much to say but so few words. His loyalty was to the nation, but he could not act on it while he was disgraced. He had to make the effort to regain his honor.

He reached up and placed his hand behind Cuttel's neck and pulled the man down close. When he was near, Hamel said, "This is for you and Mariel," and then gave Cuttel his Patir's kiss on his forehead.

With as much strength as he could, he gave a shortened version of the Patir's blessing on their marriage. "You are mine. I am yours. You will treat me as a Patir, and I will treat you as my son. We are bound together." He then paused before looking Cuttel in the eye and declared, "You are no longer left to face the world alone."

The tears poured down Cuttel's cheeks as he wept. "Thank you, my Patir. You have no idea how much we have longed for your blessing. We have wept together every day since our wedding."

Hamel smiled. "You need not search for it any longer. But there is another matter."

"Yes, my Patir," Cuttel said through tears.

"In the oasis between the Capital and Benjelton, there are two people. The one is a long-lost Son of the Ridge. You must retrieve him immediately. He is injured and staying in a hidden cave belonging to a man named Mellel."

"Yes, my Patir," Cuttel said. "I know Mellel and the cave you speak of. I have been there many times."

Hamel was shocked. "Does everyone know Mellel?"

He turned his eyes to Markel and saw the young boy nod his head. "He's a friend of my uncle's. I thought most people knew Mellel."

Hamel closed his eyes for a moment. He felt he was far less connected than he had thought.

Turning back to Cuttel, he said, "With the man is a young girl. I have taken her as my child. If I do not survive, you and Mariel must take her as your own. She will be yours to raise."

Cuttel bowed his head as a sign of his acceptance. The adoption of a child was a great honor, and everyone knew

464

both the weight of what was asked, as well as what Hamel's request meant about his view of the young Captain.

The medic arrived at that moment and brought in more light. Hamel was sure he recognized the young woman, but he had met so many soldiers over the years. His mind was far from clear. She began to order everyone to back away, but Hamel grabbed Cuttel's hand.

"You must listen," Hamel rasped.

"Yes, my General," Cuttel replied, regaining some of the discipline in his voice. "I am listening."

"How many troops are here in the fortress?" Hamel asked.

"We have twelve thousand, my General," Cuttel replied.

"Excellent. You must move your troops through the Southern Pass to flank the enemy."

"The enemy?" Cuttel asked.

"Olmos."

Cuttel took in a deep breath and leaned back for a moment before coming in close again. "The Honored Matir's suspicions were true?"

"Yes," Hamel replied. "And you and Mariel played your parts well."

"Was your mission successful, General?"

Hamel shook his head slowly. "No, but I learned of an even greater threat." He closed his eyes and forced out the words. "I have been to Olmos. I have met with the High Chancellor. You must tell the Honored Matir... you must tell my daughter... you must tell my Karotel that Olmos is the enemy. Tell her the General says it is time for phase two of her plan."

With that, Hamel's world turned dark. The pain faded, and he felt himself slip away.

EPILOGUE

Six Years Earlier.

"Truth be told, I hate the whole thing," Patir Heppel declared. As the former Honored Patir, he was afforded a seat on the Council until his death. It would not be long. His Dusk was well advanced. It was good to hear from him while he was still able to speak. "But whether I hate the idea or love it, it does not matter. We all agree that you are correct. There is something sinister happening in our midst. We must find out what it is."

"I hate it too, my friend," Honored Matir Karotel replied in a quiet voice.

Hamel was impressed with his daughter. She had stepped into the role less than a month before, but she carried herself well. It was no surprise. She was well suited for her position, and no one became the Honored Leader without a great amount of training and mentoring.

She turned her gaze to Hamel and said, "This plan will be costly to you, my Patir." By dropping the formality and bringing in the intimate familial title, she implied that the cost would be great to her as well. No Patir could be dishonored without his children bearing some of the pain.

"I don't see why we must dishonor Patir Hamel!" Matir Thortel declared. "He has honored himself and brought more honor to the nation than perhaps any other member of the Council in a century. Could it not be anyone else?"

Karotel shook her head. "I wish it could be. But the fact that his honor is so great is an asset. His fall will be noticed more than perhaps anyone else in this room. If the enemy proves to be in the lower sections of the city, then they will be pleased to have someone such as Patir Hamel among their number. If it is Olmos that is the enemy, then Patir Hamel's friendship with the late Ambassador Pulanomos will hopefully help him gain a hearing with the High Chancellor, and his disgrace will make his defection that much more appealing."

"Then he must spend the next five years resisting your leadership and undermining your authority?" Matir Thortel asked. "Is it necessary to go that far?"

It was time for Hamel to speak into the matter. "Yes, my friend," Hamel said. He and Thortel had been close for many years. He had mentored her prior to her joining the Council. "It will take that long to make it seem believable. At the end of that time, we will need to find a singular event through which I will dishonor myself before all—a catalyst to bring about my disgrace."

"How long exactly?" Thortel asked.

"It is difficult to know," Karotel replied. "We will adjust the timeline as needed."

Hamel wanted to ask a question that he had asked twice before. It continued to weigh heavily on his heart. "If my investigation takes me to Olmos, do you wish me to push it out into the open?"

"If there is deception, we must bring it out for all to see," she replied. "Someone is agitating the Beasts. Many have died, and many have dishonored themselves by going over the

467

wall. If the attacks continue to increase in frequency and severity, we will eventually fall to the Beasts. Whatever it is that is going on must be found out and stopped. Perhaps there is far more happening than we realize."

"Should I push matters even to the point of war?" he asked.

Karotel closed her eyes before replying. When she spoke, she spoke in a whisper. "Even to the point of war."

CONTINUED IN

RIDGE: DAY TWO

CHECK OUT THESE BOOKS BY
Shawn P. B. Robinson

Adult Fiction (Sci-fi & Fantasy)

The Ridge Series (3 books)
ADA: An Anthology of Short Stories

YA Fiction (Fantasy)

The Sevordine Chronicles (5 Books)

Books for Younger Readers

Annalynn the Canadian Spy Series (6 Books)
Jerry the Squirrel (4 Books)
Arestana Series (3 Books)
Activity Books (2 Books)

www.shawnpbrobinson.com/books

Manufactured by Amazon.ca
Bolton, ON

36386204R00282